"A SUPER, BUBBLING, AMAZING NOVEL, ONE TO BEG, BORROW, OR STEAL."

—Peter Giddy, *The Bookseller*

When two women's lives go topsy-turvy, the reason is love, sex, and that unspoken desire of every woman to try out a different life . . . and a very different man.

Swapping

Shirley Lowe and Angela Ince

"*SWAPPING* is the story of two women who unintentionally swapped husbands and lives. It intrigued this bachelor from start to finish."

—Cleveland Amory, author of *The Cat Who Came for Christmas*

"PLEASING . . . THE MEN GET THEIR COMEUP-PANCE."

—*Kirkus Reviews*

"A VERY FUNNY TALE OF INFIDELITY. . . . LOWE AND INCE CREATE SCENE AFTER SCENE THAT BOTH TOUCH AND WICKEDLY AMUSE."

—*Publishers Weekly*

Swapping

Shirley Lowe
and
Angela Ince

A DELL BOOK

Published by
Dell Publishing
a division of
Bantam Doubleday Dell Publishing Group, Inc.
666 Fifth Avenue
New York, New York 10103

ISBN: 0-440-20443-7

Reprinted by arrangement with Little, Brown and Company

Printed in the United States of America

August 1989

10 9 8 7 6 5 4 3 2 1

KRI

1983

Ann

The 15:20 Tisbury to Waterloo is just beginning to pull out of the station as I wrench open the nearest carriage door and hurl my suitcase at a man in a gray flannel suit. Adroitly fielding the case and pulling me in after it, the man says: "Hey, steady on!" in a jokey tone and then, more gently, "Steady on, now," as he notices my tear-stained face.

Between Salisbury and Andover he tells me that his name is Philip Gilham, that he is a London solicitor and has been visiting a client in the country who's in a spot of bother. I tell him that I'm Ann Forester-Jones and I'm on my way up to London to stay with my mother. I don't mention my spot of bother, which is that my husband has just announced his intention of marrying an attractive actress called Felicia Harman, thus making my position as lover, housekeeper and wife redundant. Mr. Gilham goes in for a lot of eye contact during this conversation and then jumps to his feet and says he thinks we could both do with a drink. "Gin and tonic? Whiskey? Brandy?"

"Oh, just a glass of white wine if they have it, please."

I am unable to get on a train without having Orient Express fantasies about meeting a tall, dark, handsome stranger and being drawn, irresistibly, into pulse-thundering passion on British Rail; and am rather shocked to realize that I am gazing speculatively at Mr. Gilham, even though I have just left my husband and three children and my life is in pieces.

The truth is that none of this seems real, to be happening to me at all. Ever since Antony arrived home unexpectedly early this afternoon, I feel as though I've been living in a soap opera, acting the part of the wronged wife, delivering all the cliché lines of a familiar script.

Antony had gone over to the drinks cupboard and started fiddling around with bottles and glasses so that he didn't have to look at me and then he'd said: "You know I'm very fond of you, Ann?"

"Well, yes, I suppose . . ." What I did know was that after sixteen years of marriage my husband had not driven all the way from London to say how fond of me he was.

Fond? That's a sneaky word which usually means "I don't love you and I'm about to say something unpleasant."

"Fond?" I said, "what do you mean by that?"

Antony handed me a drink, slumped onto the sofa and peered earnestly into his tumbler. He looked awful. Rumpled, haggard, as though he hadn't slept or changed his suit for a week. He took a large gulp of whiskey and said what I knew by then he was going to say.

"I've met somebody else, Ann. I love . . . well . . . we both love each other very much."

It's the kind of drama I would have made a point of watching on television. But this wasn't something to tick in the *Radio Times* as worth seeing. It was my life.

I felt nothing but rage at that moment. How could Antony chuck away sixteen years for a casual affair? What about the children, Sarah, Mark and Emmy? The dogs, Larkspur, Ladysmith and dear old Sadie? And Rocket? My God, who's going to look after the pony? And how about my seeds? All those hopeful little shoots, sprouting away on the kitchen windowsill, affirmation of the future, of the seasons revolving in their customary, comforting way? How could he do it? Sacrifice all that for a . . . for a quick screw?

Antony misinterpreted my tears and gave my left shoulder an awkward paternal pat. I wanted to shake him off, to hit him, but I was too tense to move.

"Oh Ann, Ann," he said, "I didn't mean to hurt you. I didn't want this to happen, I swear it."

"Who is she?" I snapped.

"She's . . . it's Felicia," said Antony and a very silly expression flashed across his face as he mentioned her name. "You remember her? Felicia Harman. Married to Donald Harman, that American banker who took me to the Kissinger thing at the American Chamber of Commerce. And then we invited them to the box at Ascot. You remember? We met them at the Morrisons about . . . oh, about eighteen months ago, I think."

It was pathetic watching him pretending to pinpoint a date which was obviously printed in block capitals on his heart.

Remember Felicia Harman? Of course I did. She's pretty, witty and a size 10, damn her. On that dreadful day at Ascot she'd looked poised and perfect in elegant khaki and had glided along to the paddock in sensible pumps and her hat stayed on in the wind and she did not appear to get wet when the rain poured down. My high heels sank in the turf, the dress which had looked so suitable in Yolande's window, as I darted past on the school run, clung damply to my thighs and my picture hat blew off the moment I stuck my head out of the box.

"That bitch!" I said. "That silly, vulgar actress. Surely you could have done better than that?"

"Better than Felicia?" said Antony. "Oh no. I'm not good enough for her, Ann. Not good enough for you either," he added quickly and went on to tell me far more than I wished to hear about what a wonderful actress she is— "A true performer, Ann. A natural . . ."—and the growing attraction which neither of them had been able to withstand.

He spoke lingeringly of their stolen moments together and subsequent worthy heart searchings. "We didn't mean this to happen, Ann. Honestly. We didn't want it to go this far."

Apparently we'd all been catapulted into this crisis by Tom Harman, Donald's twenty-five-year-old son by his previous marriage, who had chanced to spot his stepmother and Antony lunching at some obscure trattoria— "Our restaurant," as Antony put it —and after watching Antony adoringly kissing each of the fingers on Felicia's left hand, he'd reported back to his father.

When Felicia arrived home Donald had demanded an explanation, Felicia had broken down and confessed her love for Antony— "She's not the kind of person who could lie," he said proudly—and Donald had thrown her out.

"He hit her, Ann. I'd never have believed it of him. He seemed such a decent sort of chap. But there were bruises on her arms, a red mark on her face . . ." Antony shook his head, dispelling the image. "He threw her out, Ann . . . with nothing. She didn't know where to go, what to do, so she came straight to me, to the flat, and we talked all last night and . . . God . . . I don't know how to put this, Ann, but I think we both realized that we can't live without each other; we must be together." He forced himself to look at me. "I want a divorce, Ann, I want to marry Felicia."

"She came to the *flat?*" I didn't want to think about the divorce and remarrying bit. "To the company flat? That must have been an eye-opener for Mrs. Haskin." Mrs. Haskin caretakes the penthouse above Antony's agency, looks after any of the out-of-town directors staying in London during the week and has a habit of springing into bedrooms at an early hour with cups of tea.

"Felicia hid in the bathroom when Mrs. Haskin came in," said Antony, "and then, when the coast was clear, we made a dash for it."

"And where did you dash?"

"Well, I had to go to the office. You know I had that big presentation to the wholefood people this morning, Ann, the muesli commercial"—he always assumed that I knew, by some instinctive thought transference, the day-to-day doings in his diary— "and Felicia went to Harrods."

"To Harrods?"

"Yes, of course. She had to get some things. I mean, she only had what she was wearing when she left home last night and I wasn't going to let her go back to St. John's Wood, to that swine . . ."

"And where is she now?"

"She's on her way here." I jumped to my feet and Antony added hastily: "Oh, please be reasonable, Ann. The three of us have to sit down and talk things out. You know we haven't been . . . well . . . exactly *happy* together recently, not really, and I thought that if we could just sit down and talk this thing out like . . . well . . . like civilized human beings . . ."

And that was when I shouted a great many unforgivable things which somehow made me feel a bit better, and rushed up to my room and flung a few essentials into a suitcase.

"But you can't leave, Ann, just like that." Antony was standing in the hall as I opened the front door, the glass of whiskey still in his hand, a doll's pram just behind his right ankle. I hoped he'd trip over it.

"You can't walk out just like that. What about the children?"

"The children? You weren't thinking of them, presumably, when you were carrying on with that slut."

"But there are the meals to get? The school? Who's going to take them to school? And collect them?"

"Jenny Balfour's doing the run today," I said, "and Mrs. Simmons can take care of everything. She's done it before when you dragged me off to play the dutiful wife at one of your boring conferences. You'll find her in the card index under *H* for *Help*." And I left.

It will only be for a couple of days, I thought. I'll phone Sarah the minute I get to London.

"I hope this will do. It's very unpretentious indeed, I'm afraid."

Philip Gilham gives me a sharp look. "I say, are you sure you're all right? You don't want anything stronger? You do look rather shattered."

"No, really. I'm fine. Just a bit tired, that's all."

The odd thing is that I'm not angry or sad anymore. I just feel disembodied. The last few hours have blurred into unreality and I can't seem to focus on the future. I'm not even wondering how my unexpected arrival is going to mess up my mother's meticulously arranged timetable. Mum hates surprises.

"Good gracious, Ann, what on earth are you doing here?"

When we arrived at Waterloo, Philip Gilham had put me into a taxi, and although I'd been suitably enigmatic when he suggested meeting for lunch, we both knew I'd given him the opportunity to track me down when I gave the taxi driver my mother's address.

Squinting through a four-inch opening in her front door, Mother spots my suitcase. "Where are you going, dear? Are you on your way somewhere? And where's Antony?" She looks behind me, down the mews. "Is he with you?"

"I've left Antony."

"Left Antony?"

"If you let me in I could explain," I say coldly.

"Yes, yes, of course." My mother unlatches the chain on her front door. "I was just finishing the new Jilly Cooper. It's awfully amusing, Ann. You'll love it but . . . oh, never mind . . . I can get back to it later."

She sits me down on the cretonne-covered sofa and immediately disappears to make a cup of tea. "You look as though you could do with one," she says, but what she really means is that she needs the ritual of tea making to come to terms with this disruption in her routine.

"Now darling." She puts down the tray, apparently adjusted to the turn of events. "Now tell me what's happened."

As I tell her, I'm not acting a part anymore. It is all painfully real.

"My poor darling. Oh Ann, dear, how dreadful . . ." My tears flow with the sympathy. "But what are you going to do, dear? What are you going to do now?"

"I'm going to phone Sarah." I dump my things in the hall and make for the phone.

The following morning, after a sleepless night in my mother's spare room, ironing board rampant in the corner to repel guests from settling in, I still have no idea.

Divorce Antony? I don't think I love him anymore. But I'm not going to give up my children.

Felicia

I have never been so cold. Look at that ridiculous excuse for a fire.

Oh God, what am I doing here?

I haul an uncomfortable chair a few inches nearer the fire. It makes no appreciable difference. I take my shoes off and sit on my feet.

The door slams open and a flood of dogs pours into the room. As it happens, I am very fond of dogs, though I haven't actually had much to do with them. What I really like is little dogs that you can pick up and put somewhere else when they are in the way.

There are two Labradors. One is black and one is yellow, and they are both eyeing me suspiciously. The yellow one's hackles are up. Why aren't there any people in this house? Where is Antony, for heaven's sake?

I clear my throat and whisper placatingly: "Hullo. Good dogs."

The black Labrador heaves a sigh and lies down. The yellow one, its worst suspicions evidently confirmed, growls.

At least they are keeping their distance. A venomously headed stocky little dog that weighs about a ton has leapt onto the chair beside me and is making vigorous (and eventually successful) efforts to sit on my knee. Its paws, I can't help noticing, are exceedingly muddy.

"Larkspur! How dare you!"

What a beautiful child. Almost certainly Antony's thirteen-year-old, Sarah. The one, I seem to remember him saying, who was most likely to make trouble.

"Get down off there at *once.*"

It is clear that the child is not worried about the state of my skirt; her tone suggests that Larkspur has been caught rootling about on the top of some particularly disreputable midden.

"You must be Sarah . . . ?"

"Must I? If you say so," she says indifferently. "Come here. *Bad* dog."

Larkspur slides off my lap, leaving behind enough earth to plant sunflower seeds in, and crawls apologetically towards Sarah.

"He's very obedient, isn't he?" I say, despising myself for talking to this child in a way that would suggest, to an outside observer, that I am about to beg her to lend me large sums of money.

Sarah flings me a contemptuous look; almost certainly the first of hundreds.

"She," she says. "They're all bitches in this house."

The words "and a new one arrived today," though not spoken aloud, hang so palpably in the air between us that I would quite like to slap her lovely little face.

Another dog has wandered in; is there no end to it? This one is very old and white, jerking along on arthritic legs, with sightless alabaster eyes. It makes unerringly for the fireplace, cannons into the leg of my chair, screams, and falls back on legs which collapse under it.

"My poor old darling," says Sarah, swooping over and picking it up. It snarls ungratefully at her, and attempts to bite her wrist with teeth that even I can see are long past doing any damage.

"Ladysmith is very old and totally blind," says Sarah, addressing the painting over the fireplace. "She knows her way around by memory, and none of the furniture on the ground floor must be moved *at all.*"

She looks accusingly at me, and I obediently shove my chair back again. Anyone would think Larkspur and I went to the same school.

"Come along, dog-bogs."

As Sarah leaves the room she murmurs to Ladysmith (using the exact degree of decibel so perfected by thirteen-year-old girls all over the world to ensure that the offending grown-up hears clearly what is said, but in enough of a mumble to make viable an attitude of wide-eyed innocence if challenged), "Did the nasty, adulterous lady move her chair so that poor old Ladysmith bumped her nose, then? Never mind, my angel. She won't be here long."

Once outside the room, Sarah speaks in a clear, carrying voice; reporting, I presume, to her brother and sister. "Ghastly. Absolutely *frightful*. Doesn't know anything about dogs. She was terrified of Larkspur, who was only trying to make friends. I only hope she didn't catch anything. Dyed hair . . . dripping with makeup . . . hideous London clothes . . ."

I look down resentfully at my irreproachable Jaeger tweed skirt (bought especially for the occasion and costing a bomb and a half), my flat brown shoes, my ribbed stockings, my dark green cashmere sweater and single row of pearls. If these aren't country, then what on earth is? I am, as a matter of fact, wearing almost exactly what I wore when I played Lady Somebody in a Home Counties comedy of manners, and nobody told me I looked wrong then.

The two younger children appear in the doorway, as if to confirm for themselves the full horror of Sarah's report.

Mark, who I happen to know is ten, and looks dreadfully physically active to me (the kind of boy who goes round asking people if they want a hard shoulder, then giving them one), throws himself backwards onto a sofa, which causes it to slide several inches towards the window.

"I thought all the furniture has to stay exactly in place?" I say coldly.

Nobody bothers to answer this admittedly quite dull remark.

Emily (eight, and the highly strung one, Antony had proudly told me during one of those long, intimate Italian suppers; God, how long ago *those* seem) drags her way over to the piano and lies down under it with—I might have known—a bloody dog. She is crying, and the dog sympathetically licks her face in a way I privately consider rather unhygienic, though do not have any intention of saying so.

"Oh, isn't this nice?" Antony, at last, has bustled his way through the door, followed by Sarah.

He is going to say something silly.

"Making friends already. You've met the children, darling? Wonderful. That fire needs seeing to, doesn't it? Mark, would you . . . ? Be an angel, Sarah, and put the kettle on. Emmy-Wemmy," (no wonder the child's highly strung if that's what they call her) "what are you doing under the piano, my darling?"

"Crying," says Sarah, leaving the room. "Something to do with being part of a broken home, no doubt."

Antony raises a wry, ironical eyebrow at me. I find it minimally less attractive than I did when he raised it in those Italian restaurants. He is, in my view, being incredibly crass. Right now I actually prefer Sarah, who appears to get her exit lines from Tom Stoppard.

I ask myself again what I am doing here. This isn't my world at all. Icy cold inside and nothing to look at outside except wet trees and a black-and-white horse who is irritably snatching at grass with his ears back.

How did it happen? I have torn my life in two, walked out on a husband who never did me any harm (well, until that last scene) and deserted Laura and Harry, the two most important people in my life. And (I do love my comforts) I have left my lovely warm elegant house in St. John's Wood for this vast, well-bred icehouse.

I bet there's only one bathroom, and I bet it's at the end of some corridor, and I bet its lock doesn't work so you have to shout "Sorry, I'm in here," every time you hear someone outside.

We'd known the Forester-Joneses, on and off, for several years. Donald met Antony at some business function and rather liked him. I can't think why, they couldn't be more different. "I'm having lunch with that Forester-Jones guy," Donald would announce every so often, "he's very shrewd, you know." "Shrewd" is Donald's highest accolade for men, just as "vivacious" is what he says about women he approves of. I suppose I'm vivacious; what a depressing thought.

I didn't meet Ann until Antony invited us to share his customer facilities box at Ascot. Well, he didn't put it quite like that.

"Antony Forester-Jones has asked us to spend Gold Cup Day with him," said Donald, rather impressed. "I'd better get on to Moss Brothers right away."

It took Ann and me less than fifteen seconds to discover that we had nothing in common. She was wearing one of those vague silk things that nobody could possibly object to, or even notice, while I was in khaki counterpointed with a sharp pink. Her hair had been nicely washed and set by someone who was pushing it if he charged more than three quid. Mine had been blow-dried by brilliant Robert. Her hands—I can remember thinking, How can any woman have so little self-respect?—had shapeless short nails that she had rather foolishly put dark red varnish on, and I couldn't help seeing that her fingertips were actually ingrained.

Conversationally we weren't exactly soul mates, either.

"Aren't the horses beautiful?" said Ann. I hadn't actually got round to looking at a horse yet.

"I say, do look at that woman's hat," I said. "She's either mad or blind."

Ann nervously fiddled with her own hat, a navy straw with upturned brim that would have made Marilyn Monroe look repressed.

"It is rather loud, isn't it?" she said. "Antony says your house is lovely. Has it got a garden?"

"Well," I said, "a sort of patio, with tubs and things. You're keen on gardening, are you?"

A safe remark—with those hands her hobby had to be either gardening or rummaging through manure for buried treasure.

"Oh, yes, I love it," and she was off, roaming on about cuttings and germination temperatures and daffodils under the apple trees.

I certainly wasn't looking for a man at that time. I was perfectly happy with Donald and my two marvelous children. But even if I had been, Ann would have put me right off Antony. I could never be attracted to a man who had actually chosen to live with that dim dump.

We occasionally had dinner with the Forester-Joneses in Antony's pied-à-terre above his office, and they once or twice came to us. It was all very amiable and dull, and I wouldn't have cared if I never saw them again.

Until that day I turned up at the TV studios to shoot a commercial, and discovered that Antony's agency had commissioned it, and Antony was there to make sure, as he said cynically, that the product was in focus throughout. On the second day he asked me out to lunch. I wanted to say yes so much that I cautiously said no. That night Donald got home tired. He wanted to tell me the terrible things the yen had done to him that day and how the new man in Tokyo wasn't working out. He wasn't all that enthralled with my chat about the bright young director, his cunning camera angles, the way Antony had effortlessly held the whole thing together. It was one of those evenings when marital communication leaves the room with its tail between its legs.

So I was just in the mood next day to accept Antony's renewed invitation, this time for dinner. And by the time we'd reached coffee and brandy, the damage was done.

Ann

When we first met, Antony was an account executive in one of those advertising agencies which keep rearranging their name as directors come and go. Five years ago, when he became chairman and managing director, it expanded into Forester-Jones, Friend, Lock, Baker; but eighteen years ago, when I was Antony's secretary, it was just Friend & Lock.

I hadn't planned to be a secretary. I'd always wanted to be a journalist, English was the only thing I'd been any good at at school; but my father, a cautious accountant who died seven years ago with his affairs prudently in order, considered journalism a risky business.

"Take a secretarial course," he said, "and then you'll always have something to fall back on." Parents often said that to their daughters in the early sixties.

The secretarial college sent me to Friend & Lock. I wore blue all the time in those days because a man I doted on had once told me that it went with my eyes.

"I wonder if you realize," Antony had said, gazing at me appreciatively over his desk, "that your dress brings out the color of your eyes in the most extraordinary way?"

Antony was nine years older than me, and desirably sophisticated. He wore his hair long and curly to the collar at a time when "proper" men still got scalped at the barber. And he shared his flat in Chelsea with a young barrister who drank Chartreuse the way other men downed pints of bitter.

For more than a year we worked together, ate together, listened to Buddy Holly together, even went on holiday together; but we didn't sleep together. I had been brought up to believe that nice girls didn't.

"No, no," I'd cry, pushing Antony back across car seats and sofas. "No, no. You won't respect me if I do." God, what a little prig I was. And Antony was eventually pushed into a proposal. Then, the current code allowed me to sleep with him.

"Was it good for you? Did the earth move?" Antony had asked in a humorous way. I didn't like to tell him that the earth had remained disappointingly stable. By the time I'd messed about with evil-smelling contraceptive gel and the elusive Dutch cap, proper sex was rather less exciting than our gymnastics in the car.

After we married I moved over to the accounts department because the managing director didn't think it suitable for a husband and wife to work together. For more than two years I typed invoices and cleaned and washed and ironed and gave candlelit dinner parties with Provençale daubes and cheap Algerian wine.

I'd given up any idea of being a journalist or even a copywriter. I was far too busy to bother about a career. My career was Antony.

When I told him I was pregnant, he said straightaway that London was no place to bring up children. And so we bought White Walls, an eighteenth-century pile outside Tisbury, a pleasant little country town in Wiltshire. Though it was only a stone's throw from Stonehenge, Antony could get up to London in less than two hours.

He saw himself as the country gentleman, doing a little fishing and shooting and riding to hounds, perhaps. What he actually did was dig out the dry rot in the cellar, put new slates on the roof, lay a terrace in the back and plaster eight bedrooms. It was a grand old house, demanding a team of skilled craftsmen and a wing full of servants to keep it that way. What it got was Antony crossly doing it himself, with me in the role of plumber's or plasterer's mate, getting shouted at if I didn't hold the ladder steady and why wasn't there anything in the fridge for supper?

By the time Mark came along, three years after Sarah, Antony was worn out with the manual labor and the hassle of a daily commute, and never going anywhere without a carrycot and Paddi-Pads.

"Why don't we move back into town?" I said.

"Nonsense," said Antony, "I love the country."

So I stayed in Wiltshire and Antony moved into the company penthouse during the week.

Arriving home every Friday evening in his city suit, he was an adult intrusion into my nursery world of Yogi Bear, strained spinach, and cozy chats with the other mothers outside the kindergarten about toilet training and when did you put your youngest on solids, then?

At first I made an effort to keep up standards.

I found Mrs. Simmons and left her in charge while I dashed up to London to shop and get my hair done. I'd stay with Antony in the company flat, and we'd take in a show or go out to dinner, and it was almost like old times.

After Emmy it was harder. I seemed to be tired all the time. When Antony came home at weekends there were no longer fresh country flowers in the living room and the children weren't always neatly tucked into bed.

"Can't you keep those children quiet?" he'd say, fretfully tripping over Dinky toys in the sitting room and plastic boats in the bathroom. The house never seemed to look tidy no matter how hard I worked, the laundry pile loomed large in the kitchen and why was Em still wetting her bed every night? I cried a lot and I think I might have had a nervous breakdown if there'd been time for it.

"Why don't you get away for a few days, stay with Antony in London? I'll look after your lot with mine," said Jenny Balfour, my next-door neighbor. Jenny is skilled at unsettling the village with a subtle innuendo here, and a backhanded compliment there. I was just about to thank her for this uncharacteristically thoughtful gesture when she added: "I saw Antony in town yesterday, lunching at San Frediano with a very attractive woman. Oh, don't worry, dear, I expect she was a colleague. They're all so glamorous in advertising, aren't they? Still, you mustn't let yourself go or that handsome man of yours will start looking elsewhere."

Of course I did let myself go. My waistline thickened with the solitary bacon sandwiches and my hands roughened with housework and gardening. But there were compensations in the close community of village life. I grew quite competitive about my flower arrangements at the Women's Institute show, baked for garden parties, and when I delivered Sadie's puppies, I felt as proud as if I'd had them myself.

I don't think Antony enjoyed coming home to sofas shedding dog hairs and me clad in comfortable old corduroy trousers, but he did enjoy passing on the chores.

"How about slapping another coat of paint on the nursery?" he'd say, as he climbed into his Rover on Sunday evenings, and drove away from the children and me.

I suppose I ought to give Antony a divorce, if that's what he really wants. But what about me? What do I want? I think I'd like my own life. I'm thirty-nine. That's not too late to start again, is it? There must be something I can do. But what would bring in enough money for me, the children and somebody to look after them while I'm working?

Felicia

It is six hours since that depressing scene in the library, and I am lying in bed in this aggressively Laura Ashley bedroom. It is flounced and gathered to smothering point. It actually looks like the way Ann dresses, I might have expected it, and the soap in the bathroom is Crabtree & Evelyn in well-bred country odors. To be fair, it is very pretty and comfortable, but I am not in a mood to admire Ann's taste at the moment. I REALLY LOATHE HER CHILDREN, ROT THEM. I keep on saying to myself, Look at it from their point of view. Almost overnight their mother rushes up to London in a state, and is replaced by, there's really no other honest way to put it, Dad's new mistress. But it wasn't *like* that, I keep on wanting to say. We meant to give each other up, we didn't want to break up our families, and then my wretched interfering stepson, Tom, over from New York on some ludicrous fact-finding mission, happens to catch us gazing at each other in some trat and rushes off to tell Donald what I'm up to. The lasagne was overcooked, too. It was a rotten meal, one way and another.

And then, Donald in his boring, banking way tells me never to darken his elaborately alarmed front door again, after a scene which I really prefer not to think about, and I am left with nowhere to go but here. I am missing Laura and Harry terribly, the whole situation is the most dreadful mess, and I'd forgotten how ghastly the country is. Even now out there some animal is shouting at the top of its voice, there's something scrabbling in the wall, and Antony's lovemaking, agreeable though it is, can't possibly be worth the waves of unhappiness that are washing over this house.

On the other hand, let it be said, I have been trying to make some contact since I arrived here. I have been trying to make the best of a bad job and blow-all have I had in return. Emily sobbed throughout, Mark paid me rather less attention than he gave to the Flintstones, and Sarah is actually malignant. If I were her mother I'd worry about her.

It started with supper. There was virtually nothing in the fridge, of course, and to be fair, why should there be? You'd have to be some kind of a saint, and a silly one at that, to leave lamb chops for five and the makings of a green salad for a woman who has ruined your life. There were some tomatoes, though, and a chunk of Cheddar.

"I know," I said to Sarah, hoping that the minutiae of domestic life might in some remote female way draw us together, "I'll make macaroni cheese. I like it with slices of tomato in it, don't you?"

"Lovely," said Sarah, brightening, "that sounds really delicious."

Thank God the child's hungry, I said to myself. She's looking much more friendly and helpful.

So I made the macaroni cheese (I had to ask Sarah where the salt was, nothing labeled, of course; I thought Ann was supposed to be such a great little homemaker?) and put it triumphantly on the table. I'd even nipped out and picked bunches of wildflowers—they brought on Mark's asthma, it goes without saying—and it all looked so pretty.

"Macaroni!" yelped Emily, her eyes filling with yet more of her inexhaustible supply of tears. "I don't eat macaroni. It looks like white worms crawling out of dead men's stomachs."

"Then I will make you a boiled egg," I said with admirable control.

"Oh darling, I should have told you," said Antony, "I'm afraid Mark is allergic to cheese, so could he have a boiled egg too? But Sarah and I love pasta, don't we? Oh"—his voice went tiresomely peevish as he plunged the spoon in— "tomatoes. The acid in them is terribly bad for my gallbladder." He never mentioned his silly gallbladder in all those trats and everything there was *riddled* with tomatoes.

Sarah helped herself to an insolently small helping and ate it in tiny mouthfuls, with the interested look on her face of one who is eating bird's nest soup for the first time.

I gave myself a defiantly large amount, and eagerly picked up my fork. I was actually starving. My first mouthful explained Sarah's air of interest. Macaroni cheese flavored with sugar rather than salt is not easy to force down. But I made myself eat every scrap on my plate, occasionally murmuring "mmm" and "aah" in order to demonstrate how delicious it was. Why I didn't simply say, "Oh heavens, there's sugar in this instead of salt," I still don't know; but I think it was because of the look on Sarah's face.

After supper, when they'd all moped off back to that dreadful cold library, I washed up (not exactly snowed under with offers of help) and gave the remains of the macaroni cheese to Sadie, the black Labrador. She wolfed it down in a curiously furtive fashion. I watched approvingly. At least someone in Nightmare Abbey likes my cooking, I thought with a stir of affection.

And now I am waiting, in someone else's spare bedroom, for someone else's not so spare husband. Antony, in a quite astonishingly thick way, suggested I move into his and Ann's bedroom right away. I simply couldn't, and I can't think what made him suggest it. I can't say I care for his children, very much, but one has to see it through their eyes. What seems to us one of the world's great passions is going to look to them rather more like Sadie wolfing down the macaroni, and on sheets last slept on by their mother, too. Actually I don't honestly feel very like it tonight.

I happen to know that Antony's lovemaking is ardent, cheerful and affectionate, exactly what I like; but right now I'm awfully tired, everyone hates me, and sweet macaroni cheese will never take the place of powdered rhino horn.

I can hear Antony slinking surreptitiously along the corridor. I should imagine Donald in St. John's Wood could too, if he pricked up his ears. The door creaks open—excellent late-night horror-movie sound effects—and Antony slides in beside me.

"Darling, oh darling . . . at last," he murmurs, his hand moving down my body in quite a pleasing way if only I could keep my eyes open. "You and I together in my own house." My tummy rumbles venomously. Antony elects to ignore it.

"What is that funny noise?" I ask, rather unfortunately.

But what I'm referring to is not vengeful gastric juices; it's a thin wailing sound coming from somewhere inside the house.

"Just one of the dogs, I expect," says Antony, lifting himself on one elbow and displaying an attractive pair of naked shoulders in the process. "No, hang on—I think it's one of the children . . . I'll just go and—"

"You're not supposed to be in this room," I hiss, "I'll go and see what's happening."

The wailing has got noticeably louder; when I open my door I see that it is Emily, complete with regulation tears. She is kneeling and swaying in front of one of those mahogany chests that everyone puts in their hall in the country to keep a Monopoly set and some old Christmas cards in. On it she has put a large photograph of Ann, a cardboard cross imperfectly covered with silver foil, and some drooping bunches of wildflowers purloined, no doubt, from my supper table.

"Please, God," she is chanting, "please let Mummy and Daddy live together again. Please let Felicia get mumps and have to go away. Please make Daddy think she is too thin. If you do all that, God, I will . . ."—here she pauses, obviously to think of some promise amazing enough to cause God to sort things out— "I will give up smoking." She falls into a dreary version of my least favorite hymn.

"Emily," I say, "I'm sorry you're so unhappy. I'm unhappy too, and I didn't mean any of this to happen. Grown-ups don't always get things right, you know. Go to bed now, and we'll try and sort things out in the morning. Shall I come and tuck you up?"

She shakes a bedraggled little head and shuffles off with her shoulders slumped. I go back to Antony, feeling like Herod.

"Does Emily smoke?" I ask, trying not to sound disapproving.

"At eight? Of course not. She is violently against Ann smoking, on about it all the time. Why do you ask?"

"Oh, never mind." God hasn't got much of a bargain there, I hope He realizes. With any luck I'll get away without the mumps. Antony is warmly gathering me to him again.

"Antony—I'm sorry, but really not. How you can even think about sex while your child is crying her heart out is beyond me. The coast is clear out there. Go back to bed, for heaven's sake, and let me get some sleep. You really are quite selfish, you know, and I'm about to lose my temper, so just go away now."

He shuffles out in much the same style as Emily—this family does a fine line in slumped shoulders—and I am about to fall gratefully asleep when I am swept by pangs of guilt. The child was dreadfully upset . . . I get up and creep along the corridor towards the sound of murmuring voices.

Laying my eye to a crack in the door, I see Emily, her eyes miraculously clear of tears and glowing with the knowledge of a difficult mission carried out to perfection, perched on the end of Sarah's bed.

"Did I cry enough? I sang 'All Things Bright and Beautiful,' too, to make it sound as though I was in church."

"I know, I heard you. Perfect. I do wish I could turn on floods, it's so useful. Now tomorrow, phase two. I'll ring up Mum and tell her we're starving. It's true, anyway; that woman has obviously never been near a saucepan in her life. And you must get Dad alone somehow and tell him his little Emmy-Wemmy has wet her bed because Mummy isn't here."

"But I always do wet my bed, Sarah, you know I can't help it. Anyway," she adds sanctimoniously, "Mummy says I'm not to be worried about it."

"Well, just wet it some more. Go to bed now, and don't forget to have a couple of glasses of water on the way."

Ann

"Time's up now, Mrs. Forester-Jones." The senior interviewer at the South Molton Street Secretarial Services Bureau stops telling her friend about what Gary said to her during the film at the Odeon last night—a more diverting dialogue than the one I'm typing between EEC member countries about container lorries—and rips the paper out of my typewriter. "Now, let's see how we've got on."

We have not got on very well; the senior interviewer scans my typed-up notes of the shorthand she'd dictated half an hour ago with the critical eye of a senior monitor. Goodness knows she looks young enough to be in the sixth form. She laughs, patronizingly, at the typing errors.

"Something's a bit rusty, Mrs. Forester-Jones. Is it the shorthand or the typing?"

"It's probably me." I stand up, straighten my sensible tweed skirt and reach for my good leather bag. I should have put something more dashing into that going-away suitcase; even jeans would have been better than facing this dauntingly fashionable girl in my middle-aged, middle-class country uniform.

I'd started the day, positively enough, by combing through the crème de la crème classifieds in the *Times,* but soon realized they were just a lot of boring old secretarial jobs concealed behind enticing descriptions.

"Assistant to the managing director of a busy West End PR agency" gave the game away in the small print with "some shorthand and typing essential." "Girl Friday needed for small group of architects. Must have sense of humor" meant that Girl Friday would be expected to keep a merry grin playing about her lips as she made the tea.

My mother spotted the South Molton Street Secretarial Services Bureau in her paper. "Thinking of going back to work? Start a second career with us," their ad urged, and went on to list the dazzling jobs on their books.

"That sounds like you, dear." She propelled me out of the door, adding that as it was her bridge night would I mind bringing in something for my supper? And now, here I was, failing the simplest shorthand-typing test and longing to be home in Wiltshire where I belonged and wasn't considered an idiot if I couldn't locate QWERTYUIOP on an electric typewriter.

"Well, thank you, anyway." I make for the door.

"Oh, don't rush away," says the senior interviewer. "It's not as bad as that, you know. Just a little rusty, as I said. You could soon get your speeds back. Why not do a crash course—evening classes, perhaps—and then come back and see us again?"

"I will. Thank you. Thank you very much." I can't get out fast enough. I can't wait to collapse over coffee in the nearest café. I must phone Antony, I must see the children.

I must go home to security, to a world where I am in charge. Surely Antony will realize soon what a frightful mistake it was to bring that woman into our house. An actress! She'll know nothing about the country and I bet she's never seen a solid-fuel cooker in her life. I spend a few pleasing moments imagining Felicia Harman loading buckets of anthracite in the rain and my loyal old Aga spitting fretfully at the damp fuel and spluttering out. That'll show her. I don't suppose she'll even stick out the morning. A phone box. I'll phone the bastard now.

Felicia

My first morning in Heartbreak House begins badly. I get up and make for the bathroom and almost instantly cannon off the wardrobe. Half-asleep I have, of course, made for the bathroom in St. John's Wood. The bathroom here is not half-left, through a door and first right. It is straight ahead and mind that silly little table with a skirt on. No doubt I'll get used to it.

I listen sadly to the familiar sounds of children rising to a new day, and wonder what Laura and Harry are doing. I told them before I left, as calmly as possible, that Dad and I were going through a rocky patch, but that nothing would change as far as they were concerned. Lies, of course, told to comfort them temporarily. Everything has changed, I'm not there.

Oh well, better get on with it. Thank God it's the half-term holiday and I don't have to drive anyone to their stupid schools. *Must try* not to be irritable, I do wish I were better in the morning.

Arrive in the kitchen to enthusiastic greetings from the dogs. They surge round the door, and I let them out. I shortsightedly bend down to pick a dead leaf from the floor, and realize just in time that it is not a dead leaf.

Heaving slightly, I grab handfuls of paper towel and clean it up. You would think, with five dogs, Ann would have got them housetrained.

Mark watches me, tossing a tennis ball from hand to hand. Harry would have helped. Laura would have said, "Oh poor Momma, how horrid—I'll make you a cup of tea." Mark just tosses a tennis ball from hand to hand. You would think, with those great big hips, Ann would have made a better job of motherhood.

The dogs tumble back into the kitchen and look at me expectantly. Am I supposed to feed them, or what?

"Which of you did that?" I growl, pointing accusingly at the floor. Four of them retire hastily to their beanbags, avoiding my glance and clipping their tails between their legs. Old Ladysmith makes decisively for the door; on her way, with any luck, to a fatal fall down the cellar steps.

"It was Ladysmith," says Mark. I think those are the first words he has addressed directly to me, and on what a fascinating subject.

"She is very old, you know, and not reliably continent. It's not her fault—she mustn't be punished."

"Wouldn't dream of it," I say shortly, and with a certain disregard for the truth.

Sarah walks in and screams at once.

"Look! Look!" she cries, pointing to—oh what fun—several little yellow piles of sick next to the refrigerator. "Sadie's had one of her attacks!"

We all—Antony and Emily have turned up in time for the high point of the morning—look at Sadie, who is trying to pretend she isn't here.

"She must have eaten something," says Sarah. I wish I could forget the furtive look on Sadie's face as she was polishing off that wretched macaroni cheese.

"Felicia doesn't know about Sadie's liver," says Antony. "You didn't give her anything last night, did you? She's on a special low-fat diet."

"I may have let her lick a plate or two," I say evasively, "how was I to know?"

"Sarah, where does Mum keep Sadie's pills?"

"Probably quite near the salt," I interject. There is only one person in the room who has the faintest idea what I'm talking about; she looks out of the window in a prim way.

Sadie's pills having been successfully administered while I make toast and coffee, we sit down to breakfast.

"Isn't there any orange juice?" says Antony plaintively.

"In the fridge," I say briskly. I hope he doesn't think I'm going to run round after him.

After a pause which I am expected to register, Antony goes over to the fridge, opens the door and says, "There isn't any."

"Oh, for *heaven's sake.*" I march over to the fridge, get out the carton of juice and plank it down in front of him.

"Foolish of the manufacturers, really, to label it orange juice in orange letters next to an orange picture of an orange. No wonder you were misled."

He frowns and says, "Where is my glass?"

"I thought it might be rather amusing, for a change, to keep the glasses in the airing cupboard. Where do you think your glass is? On the shelf behind you with all the other glasses."

Emily officiously leaps up and brings him a glass. Sarah says, "My mother always sets the table for breakfast the night before."

"How very provident of her . . . what kind of dog is Larkspur? Some kind of mongrel?"

I am trying to be friendly, but they all, to the last Forester-Jones, draw back affronted.

"Larkspur is a Staffordshire Bull Terrier," says Sarah in capital letters. "Of course," she adds. She has added "of course" to her answer to every query I have so far made, from "Where is the bathroom?" to "Do you think it will rain tomorrow?" The effect, to a disinterested listener, is that I am a congenital idiot.

"She has an amazing pedigree," Sarah continues, and adds (putting on that silly voice they all seem to use to the dogs) "and she's going to have puppies very soon, isn't she, the clever baby."

"Oh, is she pregnant? She doesn't look particularly large."

"Well, she can hardly be pregnant yet. Of course. She hasn't come into season yet. But when she does," (silly voice) "she's going to visit a very handsome young man, isn't she?"

Doesn't this family ever talk about books or music or even shopping? So far it's all been waste products and sex. This time last week I was discussing *Northanger Abbey* with Laura. Oh Laura, I am so sorry.

Later in the morning I am tidying upstairs (I rather gather the mother figure round here is expected to make the beds; there'll be some changes made, I'll tell you) and discovering, with absolutely no surprise at all, that Emily's sheets are dripping wet. Sarah is using the phone in her parents' bedroom. She is using it with admirable clarity.

"Would you believe, Mum, macaroni cheese with sugar in it? Of course Mark couldn't eat it and Emily wouldn't . . . tomatoes, well you can imagine what Dad said . . . yes, that's exactly what I thought . . . know anything about how the Aga works? Don't make me laugh . . . called Larkypoos a *mongrel* . . . of course I've done my best to help, if only for Dad's sake . . . Sadie's had a bilious attack . . . knocked one of your boxes of seedlings off the work top . . . I dunno, I think it was *Cobea* something . . ."

The litany of smug complaint continues endlessly. I go downstairs with my arms full of wet sheets. Nothing like being Passion's Plaything, I always say. My way to the washing machine is blocked by a strange woman pottering round the kitchen. I am just about to ask her who she is and what she is doing here, but she gets in first with the same question. Of course—she must be Mrs. Simmons, Ann's daily help.

"Well, er," I say, "I'm staying here for a little while."

Mrs. Simmons's kind face creases into a happy smile.

"Oh," she says cheerfully, "how nice for Mrs. Forester-Jones. I always think she's a bit lonely, between you and me. You'll be an old friend, then, madam?"

"Um . . . well, actually Mrs. Forester-Jones is having a few days in London—"

"And you've come down to help out. There's nothing like a friend in need, I always say."

Enter Antony, who doesn't notice little Mrs. Simmons tucked away behind the fridge.

"I really cannot make up my mind," he says merrily, "whether your left breast is more beautiful than your right, or vice, ho ho, versa. Let's quickly go upstairs and—Mrs. Simmons. I'd forgotten it was your day. How lovely to see you . . . how are you? . . . terrible weather we're having, aren't we?"

The three of us gaze out of the window. The garden is bathed in faultless sunshine.

Ann

"Mr. Forester-Jones's office"—it is the familiar voice of Sally, my husband's secretary. "May I say who's calling, please?"

Oh come on, Sally. We've only been exchanging pleasantries and inanities with each other for the last ten years.

"It's Mrs. Forester-Jones, Sally."

"Oh, Mrs. Forester-Jones. I'm so sorry. I didn't recognize you for a moment. I'll just see if Mr. Forester-Jones is available."

Available? Normally, Sally offers to put me straight through, but already I'm an outsider, somebody to be tactfully sidetracked if the boss doesn't want to speak to me. The boss is, however, available.

"Ann?" At the sound of his voice, nervous and uncertain, my palms start sweating, my heart beating and thumping in my chest; all the symptoms I exhibited when I heard that voice eighteen years ago, only this time there's no joy in it.

"Antony?"

"Yes, yes, of course. What is it? I'm on my way to a meeting."

"It's just . . . just . . . how are you? And the children?"

"I'm fine, Ann. The children are fine. Or they were when I left home this morning. Was there something you wanted to say? Because, unless it's important, I think it would be better after what you said yesterday—you made your feelings all too clear—if we didn't see or speak to each other for a while."

"But . . . the children?"

"The children are perfectly all right with Felicia," says Antony, the firm chairman bringing our meeting to a swift end. And while I'm thinking, Oh God, she's still there, the bitch! he adds: "She's very good with children, you know. Our lot seem to have taken to her instinctively."

Even Antony realizes that this is too much for a rejected wife to take, and adds quickly: "Please don't think I'm trying to take the children away from you, Ann. Just give them a few weeks to settle down and then we'll have a talk about the best way to handle this.

"If you can make a home for them, and naturally I'll be happy to give you an appropriate allowance, then they can live with you and I'll see them at weekends, holidays and so on. Otherwise, they can remain with Felicia and me and I shall not, of course, deny you access."

Access? He's been talking to his solicitor already.

"And meanwhile, Ann, where can I contact you? At your mother's?"

"Yes." I put the phone down. "At my mother's."

"Mum?" The phone is ringing as I let myself into Mother's cottage.

It's Sarah. Thank goodness it's Sarah.

"Darling . . ."

"Oh Mum," she says, "oh Mum, *why* did you go off like that and leave us with this beastly woman?"

Sarah is right. I should have stayed and fought my home ground for the children's sake, if not for my own. My feelings of guilt are almost instantly overwhelmed by pure pleasure at the description of Felicia.

"What's so beastly about her?" I eagerly enquire and Sarah describes a series of happenings which would be over the top in a farce.

"*Sugar* in the macaroni?" She put *sugar* in the macaroni, and I think, Oh, clever little Sarah! as she adds smugly: "Of course, I've done my best to help, if only for Dad's sake."

"Of course, darling. And you just carry on like that. I'll soon be home."

". . . and Sadie's had one of her really bad attacks, she's been frightfully sick," Sarah is saying.

So, not content with preparing a meal which produced either nausea or an allergy in every member of my family, the stupid woman has also, quite obviously, thoughtlessly fed the remains to poor old Sadie.

"Well, I expect Mrs. Harman gave her the leftovers from your dinner . . ." and I'm just going on to explain that Mrs. Harman knows nothing about dogs or cooking or running a home properly, when I pick up the awful fact that Felicia Harman has not only poisoned my husband, my children and my dogs, but finished off my *Cobea Scandens* as well.

"The bitch . . . the bloody, bloody bitch!" I can feel the tears coming now and it's only Sarah saying cheerfully, "I didn't hear that, Mum!" (my God, I do believe the child is enjoying this in a curious way) that stops me breaking down completely.

"And how's Emmy?" The conscientious mother takes over from the conniving adult and although I'm sorry for my youngest child —it can't be easy to present an elegant stranger with a soaked sheet —I once again experience an unworthy glow at the notion of Felicia Harman taking over the most unglamorous task in my daily routine.

"She's wet her bed, of course," says Sarah, "and I've told her that she's got to give Mrs. Harman the sheets . . . and the blankets . . ."

I make sympathetic-to-Em noises and promise to see them all soon.

"Sooner than soon, Mum," says Sarah. "Leave it to me."

Why does that conversation leave me feeling a little more cheerful and hopeful? It can only be because I am not, as I had always supposed, a nice woman but someone capable of venom, deceit and a deep desire to see Felicia Harman terrorized by my dogs, despised by my children and, as I feel sure will ultimately occur, turned out of the house and by my husband. I decide to write her a useful list of do's and don'ts to help her on her way, and am interrupted by Mother.

"Must you use my desk, dear? Can't you do that in your own room?"

"On what? The ironing board?" This childish exchange fuels my misery so effectively that I come up with the perfect ending; the insulting suggestion that Felicia may find the easy-to-follow recipes in my Penguin Cordon Bleu cookbook particularly useful. I seem to remember that the last time we had dinner with the Harmans the food was delicious.

Or did she have someone preparing it for her in the kitchen? Or buy it in from Marks & Spencer? I wouldn't put anything past that woman.

Felicia

Antony has gone up to London. For a meeting, he says, unexpectedly called because some American has advanced his trip dates by a week.

I have absolutely no doubt that the real reasons are (a) he needs time to work out exactly how to look Mrs. Simmons in the face, and (b) the Aga has gone out.

I think he is a rat of the first water. Looking back, I am amazed at the folly of my overturning my perfectly acceptable life on the basis of a few shared plates of fettucine, a whimsically raised eyebrow, and the fact that Antony listened to what I said more often than Donald did. And, of course, the fact that I love him; though on the basis of the last twenty-four hours, I cannot recall exactly why.

"The Aga has gone out." The dread message spreads through the house like wildfire. Everyone I met told me the Aga had gone out, and to all of them I replied: "Well, we'd better light it again, hadn't we?" They all reacted as though I'd suggested going out in the garden and finding a cure for cancer before lunch.

"You don't just relight *Agas,* darling," said Antony. "They're very temperamental, these old ones. Ann always has someone in."

"You need an expert," says Sarah. "Of course."

"It takes about a week," says Mark.

"The poor dogs will be terribly cold tonight," says Emily, the tears flocking about on her cheeks.

This, of course, is all rubbish. I am temperamental too and I'm damned if I'm going to be worsted by a lump of metal which is, after all, designed to burn solid fuel and must surely do so if approached scientifically.

"Everyone out of the kitchen except Mark," I order.

"Why me?" says Mark resentfully.

"You look to me like the only person around here with the vestiges of practical common sense. First of all, I imagine, we have to get rid of all these embers and things."

The embers, though nominally "out," prove to be very hot.

Mark has the bright idea of bringing in a zinc bucket of cold water, which sizzles and smokes in an exciting way when the embers hit it. In his enthusiasm he unfortunately overloads the bucket and water overflows onto the floor. He gives me a worried look.

"Never mind about *that,*" I say bracingly, "you've done a super job so far. Who cares about a bit of water?" (Ann almost certainly does, by his expression.)

Six hours later the tiny diffident flame that flickered among firelighters, newspapers, twigs and anything else that Mark and I considered faintly combustible has caught on to the solid fuel and is beginning to crackle and glow. It is our seventh attempt. Our faces are filthy, my skirt is dripping wet from kneeling on the wet floor and Mark has scalded his wrist. We are terribly pleased with ourselves. "They always had to get someone in before," Mark keeps on saying.

It was during our second attempt, I think, that Antony came in with his rigmarole about an unexpected meeting in London.

"I do honestly think you're wasting your time," he said. "Shall I look up the number for you? The floor's a bit mucky, isn't it? You coming outside to wave good-bye to me, Mark, old chap? Emmy and Sarah are out there already."

Apparently the entire family cluster round the gate when Antony leaves for London, waving excitedly until his car is out of sight. No doubt it's some ploy dreamed up by Ann to demonstrate what a really united little family unit they are. Catch me standing out there in the rain as though royalty has just left the premises. It started raining shortly after the Aga went out. That's another thing about the country. The weather's always there. In London it sort of comes and goes when you need it.

Sarah wanders into the kitchen. She is plainly rather put out by our success with the Aga.

"It'll probably go out in the night," she says. "Has anyone fed the dogs?"

"You're the one who's supposed to be so potty about them," says Mark astringently, good old Mark. "Anyway, it might have escaped your attention, but Felicia and I have been rather busy."

"I suppose I'll have to do it, then" says Sarah, bringing a complex variety of tins out of the larder.

"You'd better tell me what they all eat, for when you're at school."

Sarah explains, with many *of course*'s and heavy sighs. I am strongly reminded of the time some nice young man tried to explain computers to me.

I go in search of Mrs. Simmons. As Antony has eased himself so guilelessly off the premises, I suppose I've got to try and smooth things out. I find her upstairs putting clean sheets on Emily's bed.

"Do let me help, Mrs. Simmons." I grab the other side of a sheet and start tucking it in.

"Thank you, madam, I can manage *quite* well on my own." Mrs. Simmons's already small mouth has practically disappeared. She flicks the sheet adroitly out of my hands.

"Mrs. Simmons, I do feel I owe you some sort of explanation. The thing is . . . well . . . Mr. Forester-Jones and I . . ."

"I am paid to do the cleaning in this house, madam, and if Mrs. Forester-Jones is coming back soon, then I will be happy to oblige. Of course, if there is going to be a change in the circumstances, madam . . ."

She pauses, leaving ample time for the threatening words to swoop about over the sheets. Great. I am about to be left to organize this large house with no help.

"Mrs. Simmons, let's be frank. No doubt you disapprove of me, and I can't say I blame you. But I can't run this house without any help. And I do think the children need a familiar face they can rely on. Mr. Forester-Jones has had to go up to London . . ."

Mrs. Simmons sniffs. "He was never one to face the music," she says. "That time all the lights went out in a thunderstorm and the cistern in the green bathroom leaked, he had to go to London then, too. What's his excuse this time? An important meeting, I suppose?" This last sentence is spoken in tones of quite venomous sarcasm. "Poor Mrs. Forester-Jones is always left holding the baby. The way that woman works. Nothing too good for her family, out gardening all hours, all those dogs, a lovely cook she is, and all so that *he* can bring his smart friends down at the weekend and play *quite* the country gentleman. And now look what it's got her. Another woman taking her place."

I suppose I should lengthen my neck at this point and say firmly that I will not be spoken to in this way. But Antony's hideously embarrassing faux pas is still ringing in my ears (as I have no doubt it is in Mrs. Simmons's) and I simply do not feel up to it.

"Obviously you must do what you think best, Mrs. Simmons. But please don't make up your mind without thinking how your leaving would affect the children."

She sniffs again, mutters, "Poor little innocents," and leaves the room. There is no doubt where her sympathies lie; even before I arrived on the scene she obviously didn't think much of Antony. Odd; all the people who work for him in London seem to worship him.

Mrs. Simmons leaves at four, telling me she will be back on Tuesday. For the Moment, she adds enigmatically. Until We See How Things Go.

About an hour later I am pottering about in an outhouse (there's nothing much else to do) when I discover a vast deep freeze, loaded with neat foil-wrapped packages. There's no good old Bejam or Findus, though. I take out one labeled "Shepherd's Pie Oct. '82 Bake 20 mins. after defrosting." It will do nicely for tonight. I really must get some shopping organized and think up some proper menus.

On my way back to the kitchen, I am accosted by a jolly-faced youngish woman with boring hair.

"You don't know me," she says, "but I thought I'd just pop in. I'm Dorothy Maxwell—my husband's the vicar here. How are the children taking everything?"

"Oh . . . then you know . . . ?"

"Met Mrs. Simmons outside the post office. The Town Crier, Gerry and I always call her." She laughs immoderately at this witty and innovative description. "Now you mustn't think I am here to criticize. Gerry, my husband, you know, always says, and I do agree with him, that it is not for us to Question. The One Above guides our actions, and wrong as they may seem to us mortals, it is all part of the Divine Plan. And anyway, look at Mary Magdalene."

(Would very much prefer not to, under the circumstances.) "Now, what can I do to help? Things will seem a *little* strange to

the children at first; they'll miss their mum's cooking, won't they?"
(I'll say.) "But things will soon settle down, you'll find, Mrs., er
Miss . . . I'm afraid I don't know your name."

"I'm Felicia Harman, Mrs., actually."

"Kiddies of your own?"

"Yes, two . . . in London with my husband. It's all a dreadful
muddle, I'm afraid."

"There's always light at the end of the tunnel," says Dorothy
Maxwell (cannot see that this has any relevance whatsoever), "and
if ever you feel really down, Gerry's door is always open. Just drop
in and get it off your chest." (Have absolutely no intention of doing
any such thing, but smile gratefully and shift my weight onto my
other foot.)

Actually, I find all this highly unsatisfactory. I do not think a
parson's wife should talk to a woman taken, as it were, in adultery
as though she had merely dropped knitting in favor of needlepoint
or made some other trivial change in her life. I wouldn't exactly
relish receiving a brimstone-and-hellfire lecture while standing here
holding a deep-frozen shepherd's pie (for one thing, it is beginning
to stick to my hand) but I reckon she is carrying Not Questioning
to absurd lengths. Any minute now she will be asking me to help
out with her Mums and Toddlers group.

"Must be off now," says Dorothy Maxwell, "or I'll be late for
my Mums and Toddlers. I am going to ask a big favor, and you
must be Perfectly Frank."

I nod earnestly in order to demonstrate how Perfectly Frank I
am capable of being.

"Our church fete is in three weeks' time. This year the proceeds
are going to the new Sappho Sisterhood Center they are starting in
Swindon. *Such* a good cause, don't you think?" No I do not, but
since it would be churlish to speak my mind on why I think lesbi-
ans should shut up and get on with it like everyone else, I confine
myself to raising my eyebrows in an admiring way.

"Well, in past years, dear Ann always did the Snacks and Scraps
stall, and I rather wondered if you . . . ?"

I certainly hadn't anticipated that taking over Ann's husband
would result in taking over her Snacks and Scraps stall, too.

"What exactly is involved?" I ask cautiously.

"Well, everyone always feels so peckish at fetes, don't they? So
we run a stall of little bits and pieces—ham rolls, cheese and onion
on sticks—you know the sort of thing, and charge twenty-five p a

portion. Last year we made nearly twenty pounds. Think about it, dear, and let me know, and you must call me Dotty, everyone does. Dotty by name and Dotty by nature," she adds inevitably.

"I'd love to help if you really think . . ." I must be out of my mind; but this woman, to be fair, is full of goodwill, and I've got to find something to do round here.

"Marvelous, marvelous," cries Dotty, and gets into her Metro, which is full of long twigs. Perhaps she is going to give them to the Mums to hit the Toddlers with. "Basket weaving today," explains Dotty, "flower arranging every other Thursday. Which reminds me, I must talk to you about the church flower rota. I'll give you a ring."

The phone rings as I go back into the house. Surely not Dotty already? No, it is Antony, who is clearly feeling guilty.

"Sorry I had to go off in such a rush," he says, "but I ought to be back early tomorrow morning. Luckily this Yank is due in Madrid for lunch. How are things there? Have you had a talk with Mrs. Simmons?"

"Well, up to a point . . . in fact she's threatened to leave."

"She can't leave. It's out of the question. You'll have to talk her round."

"Why don't you talk her round? If you hadn't rushed into the kitchen without looking. . . ."

"Let's not go into that right now," says Antony hastily, "all right, I'll see what I can do tomorrow. How's the Aga?"

"Oh, that," I say airily, "Mark and I lit it hours ago. I can't think what all the fuss is about. Mark was brilliant, I must say."

"Right. What? Be right with you. Sorry darling, got to go, see you early tomorrow. I love you, love you, love you. No, not you, you fool, I'm talking to my girl. 'Bye, darling. Kiss Kiss."

My girl, indeed. Kiss Kiss indeed. And he didn't even say "well done" about the Aga.

I would never actually have described myself as a woman who lurks and lies low; shouts and arguments and let's get it all out into the open has always been my way. But I have discovered, quite by chance, that if you stand in the walk-in linen cupboard, you can hear every word of what's going on in the playroom.

I am in there, getting some clean towels, and vaguely listening to Sarah and Mark playing an evil-minded and argumentative game of Monopoly, when I hear the playroom door bang open.

"Dad's coming down tomorrow," announces Emily, "and Mrs. Simmons has threatened to leave."

"How do you know?" says Sarah.

"Heard Dad talking to Mrs. Horribly-Thynne" (I suppose, grimly, that this witty name is clever Sarah's idea) "on the telephone. I picked up the extension," says Emily with some pride, "at exactly the right moment so they didn't hear the click."

"Nice work. What else did they say?"

"Mrs. Horribly-Thynne said Mark was brilliant about the Aga. Then Dad said he loved her three times, yuk, and called her 'my girl,' double yuk, and said 'kiss-kiss,' mega yuk."

"Disgusting," says Sarah. "At his age, too."

"Why does he like her so much, anyway?" says Emily. "She answered him back at breakfast, and hadn't even laid the table . . ."

There was a pause.

"It's my bet," says Sarah, "that that's what he rather likes about her. Men like tempestuous women, you know," she adds loftily.

Irritated as I am at hearing my private life dissected by a thirteen-year-old, I can't help grinning slightly; a whole shelf of Sarah's bookcase is devoted to Georgette Heyer, I noticed yesterday.

"Then why did he marry Mum? She isn't temp- . . . what you said."

"She might have been, when she was young."

"Felicia said I was brilliant, did she?" says Mark.

"Whatever she said, she's still the enemy. Your turn, do get on. Ha! a hotel on Leicester Square . . ."

My second morning at White Walls (cannot imagine why they called it that, as I haven't seen a white wall yet) is something of an improvement on the first, as I succeed in making it to the bathroom without first contacting the wardrobe. Even better, when I get down to the kitchen, I find the floor is clean. The dogs bounce about excitedly when they see me, and I let them out. I must admit it's rather nice, the way they welcome one. I shout "Stop that!" at Larkspur, who is teasing poor old Ladysmith. To my amazement, she stops it at once. I am conscious of a heady feeling of power, which fades instantly the moment the children walk in.

Emily has the air of one who is searching confidently for something to cry about. Mark has got that ruddy tennis ball with him, and succeeds in lobbing it into a pan of milk I am warming on the

Aga. I don't think he actually did it on purpose (though you never know, with this lot), which doesn't prevent me thinking fondly of thumbscrews and dear little slivers of matchstick. Sarah looks hopefully at the kitchen floor, and frowns slightly when she sees it bears no evidence of chronic alimentary disturbance.

I grimly pour some more milk into the pan, stand over it protectively while it heats, and pour it over Emily's bowl of cereal. It is one of those health cereals that looks, to my jaundiced eye, like the sweepings off a granary floor studded with rat's droppings and bits of old tooth, but if that's what they want, let them have it, I say.

With immaculate timing, Emily says primly, "I don't like warm milk on my cereal, Mrs. Hor- . . . Harman."

"You said you did, last night."

"Yes, I like it warm at night. But in the morning, I like it cold."

"Then for heaven's sake get yourself a clean bowl, some more cereal, and some nice . . . cold . . . milk."

I must have spoken rather sharply. Emily has now found something to cry about.

"Your father will be here soon," I say bracingly.

"Oh, Dad's coming down, is he?" says Sarah.

"Oh, Sarah, you *know* he is, I *told* . . ."

Emily stops suddenly as Mark kicks her quite viciously on the shin. The tears turn into a noisy waterfall, and naturally this is the moment Antony chooses to walk in.

"Emmy-Wemmy . . . darling . . . what's happened to my little girl?"

"She put warm milk all over my cereal," sobs Emily into his shoulder.

"And Mark kicked her," I add. Well, I know he helped me with the Aga, but one's got to think of oneself in a combat situation.

"I've brought the mail up from the box," says Antony, urbanely disregarding all this (I am sharply reminded of Mrs. Simmons's diatribe) and tactlessly, as it turns out, dropping a long envelope on the kitchen table. "This one's for you, darling."

"That's Mum's writing," Emily says, "why is Mum writing to you?"

"Perhaps she's sent you some recipes," Sarah says guilelessly.

I tear open the envelope and unfold what turns out to be a vividly offensive document. Patronizing, confusing; and, I realize, a direct result of Sarah's phone call yesterday. Antony reads it over my shoulder:

Dogs to be fed once a day, half a tin of Waitrose PLEASE and two handfuls Winalot. Sadie on special diet because of her liver; only Whiskas Rabbit cat food because low fat content. DO NOT LET her touch anything else.

Ladysmith only eats Mr. Dog because of her teeth.

Seedlings require mist spraying every morning and again in the evening if it's hot. Take special care with the Cobea scandens.

Emily will not eat pasta. Mark is allergic to cheese. Do not let Sarah diet. I enclose list of their after-school activities. Make them exercise Rocket every day, if they don't you will have to. He is about due for new shoes, the blacksmith's number is in the card index under P for Pony.

Don't let the Aga go out. Riddle twice a day. ["What is 'riddle'?" I moan, but Antony reads faster than me and is snarling "Over my dead body—we've got far too many dogs already."] Solid fuel is in shed with tumble-dryer and deep freeze.

Watch Larkspur carefully; as soon as she comes into season ring Mr. Barrow (number in card index under B) and arrange to take her over to his dog in Norfolk on the ninth or tenth day. Keep me informed; the puppies will be worth £250 each. I have promised Sarah she can keep one of them.

DO NOT say ANYTHING to Emily about her bed-wetting. Just change the sheets every day. The doctor says she must not be made to feel guilty.

The sloe gin should be bottled this month. Make Higgins take that mulch off the asparagus.

Please try to do as little damage as possible. The Penguin Cordon Bleu cookbook (on shelf next to Aga) has excellent and easy-to-follow recipes, you evil little bitch.

After reading all this, I raise my head and look coldly across at Sarah.

"The *Cobea scandens,* I take it, are the ones I knocked off the work top?"

"Yes, I believe they were," says Sarah cheerfully.

"Bloody silly place to keep them, if you ask me."

At night, after Antony has left me (grumbling irritably that it's quite ridiculous . . . the children know perfectly well . . . after all, it is his house . . .), I retrieve Ann's instructions and read them again. This morning I took them at face value; malevolent outpourings designed to cause me as much trouble as possible, and make me feel hopelessly inadequate into the bargain.

Now, after making love to her husband, I see them as a deep cry of grief. I have taken Antony from her, which is bad enough. But I've also taken her children, her dogs, her whole way of life. Even her wretched little seedlings.

I have a sudden uncomfortable vision of Ann and the children sitting round the fire and planning Larkspur's puppies.

Emily would certainly have said, "Can I watch her having them, Mum?" And Ann would have said, "I expect so, darling, as long as she doesn't mind. We'll see."

Emily: "It won't hurt her, will it?" Ann: "I'm sure it won't. And even if it did, it'll be worth it to her because of the puppies."

She probably stroked Emily's hair then, and Emmy stretched out her toes cosily to the fire, knowing that what Mum really meant was that she would have gone through anything to bring Emmy into the world.

I've ripped that small circle of warmth away from her. Fortunate Felicia has got what she wants, and Ann is stuck in her mother's flat in London, without a child, a dog, or even a garden.

Ann planted those seeds in the first hopeful weeks of spring. She made secure, cheerful plans for where she would plant them out when they were strong enough. And some clumsy Londoner knocks them off a work top because, if I'm honest, I was tired and irritable and didn't care very much about a box of earth with some green things in it.

I get up and put on my dressing gown (must get something more serviceable—Janet Reger, divine for the warmed corridors of St. John's Wood, lets in draughts in this chilly house) and go downstairs and into the kitchen. The dogs open bleary eyes at me and flatten their ears, pleased by a change of routine.

Sadie's tail beats like a drum on a cupboard door.

"Shut up, Sadie. You'll have everyone up." I open the back door; I had crammed earth and seedlings back into the box after it fell (hissing crossly about the silliness of turning a kitchen into a greenhouse) and shoved it outside. Some of them might still be alive.

I put the box on the kitchen table, a pathetic tangle of roots and leaves and dried-out earth. They are wilting. I wish I knew more about plants. In London I just went to the Clifton Nursery and bought trays of blue-and-white-striped petunias for the window boxes. I try to disentangle the roots, which are matted together.

When Sarah walks in, tears of frustration and guilt and sadness are running down my face.

"What on earth? Oh, it's you. I thought we had burglars."

She watches me for a moment, ineffectually trying to put some remnant of her mother's life back together again.

"Mum usually uses an old fork," she says. "I'll get some more compost, shall I?" She brings the compost, and some empty Gold margarine boxes with little holes jagged in the bottom and watches me while I clumsily separate the seedlings and plant them out.

"They need some water," she says, taking the boxes from me. After she has gently trickled water over the seedlings, she puts the boxes back on the work top and says she is going to bed. At the door she turns and looks at me.

"Would you like me to show you how to riddle the Aga in the morning? It's really quite easy."

My third morning here, and it's a beautiful one. I make my way effortlessly to the bathroom, the sun is shining gently outside, and above all, Sarah last night. She really gave the impression of beginning to see, not my point of view perhaps, but that I might be something more complex than a coldhearted woman coldbloodedly destroying her family. When she shows me how to riddle the Aga, I shall tread very carefully, and try to throw a few bridges across.

The kitchen floor is not quite so satisfactory as it was yesterday. Sadie's liver, I am grateful to see, appears to be functioning well. The same cannot be said for Ladysmith's arrangements. I clear up and scatter disinfectant lavishly.

The children come out of the vast walk-in larder carrying boxes of cereal, jars of homemade jam and marmalade, and a packet of sliced wholemeal bread which I bought in the village shop yesterday. Very conscious, incidentally, of the interested glances of fellow shoppers.

Emily tells me that this is the Wrong Bread.

"Then write down the name of the Right Bread," I say obligingly (nothing is going to spoil this morning) "and I will buy it. I think the seedlings are going to make it," I add to Sarah. "Thank you for your help last night."

"Are they? I'm afraid I haven't bothered to look." She gives me a tough little smile, glittering like diamond chippings.

"Oh. Er, well . . . you're going to show me how to riddle the Aga, aren't you?"

"Surely Mark's the Aga expert round here, isn't he?" She flashes more diamond chippings, and adds that she thinks she will have breakfast in the gar.

Mingled with disappointment about Sarah's change of attitude is my irritation over this family's way of shortening perfectly ordinary words to the point of extinction. Why can't they say "garden" like anyone else? They have a frightful tendency to go and read in the libe, to eat rats instead of ratatouille, and to play, if the weather is fine enough, tenny.

I detect Ann's hand in all this. I suppose she thinks it's lovable.

Antony comes in while Mark is showing me how to riddle; not a particularly testing task, as it turns out, merely a rather dusty one.

"Good morning, good morning," he says cheerfully. It's being in advertising, no doubt, that makes him think that if a thing's worth saying, it's worth saying twice.

"Morning," I answer. "Good, you're just in time to fetch the solid fuel." I hand him the hod. He pauses, looks at his hands, which are, as always, beautifully groomed, and reluctantly takes it from me.

"For you, my darling, anything," he says roguishly.

"I don't want *anything*; just some perfectly ordinary solid fuel."

He comes back a few minutes later with the hod only half-filled, and puts it down in front of me with the generous air of an oil sheikh tipping a commissionaire with a Rolex.

"It goes in the top of the stove. Here," I say, lifting off the little lid. "I shouldn't think that will be enough."

"I'll go and get some more, shall I, Dad?" says Emily, jumping off her chair.

"Oh, Emmy-Wemmy, that would be kind. Thank you, my darling."

"Nonsense," I say briskly. "She's far too young to go lugging solid fuel about. Just go and get it, Antony, and stop making such a performance."

He decides to make a joke of it and goes out moaning: "Bullied, bullied. But," he adds, rolling his eyes at me in the kind of leer you see at Annabel's, "I'll get my own back." I do wish he wouldn't talk like that in front of the children.

Sarah has come back from the garden, and is looking at me in a way I find difficult to interpret. I suppose she disapproves of the

way I am bossing her father; and yet, for a flicker of time, I feel
. . . I don't know . . . I feel as if I'd been admitted to some club.
It doesn't last, though.

Antony elects to drive them to school, and they go off without
any of them saying good-bye to me. I gather I am expected to
collect them at the end of the day. Antony has given me the keys of
Ann's old Renault, and I decide to drive it into Salisbury to pass
the morning and do a bit of routine shopping. Driving Ann's car, I
discover disconcertingly, seems more invasive than sleeping with
her husband. Cars are very personal things; scattered about in this
one are bits and pieces of Ann's life. Old shopping lists, a half-
empty bag of Extra Strong mints, a packet of King-Size Silk Cut
and a matching lighter, a collection of cassettes. Mozart, Brahms,
songs from the Auvergne; not what I would have expected. I suppose, in a rather patronizing way, I would have assumed Ann
would go for light Muzak, if I'd bothered to wonder about her
musical taste at all.

The car is a beast to drive. Its clutch badly needs seeing to and
the brakes are so soft I nearly bump into the back of a lorry at
some traffic lights. I must instantly get it serviced.

Salisbury's shopping center has masses of parking and is full of
the good old familiar names. Wandering from Boots to W. H.
Smith, looking in at Benetton (oh God, I do wish Laura were with
me) and buying the right brown bread at Sainsbury's, I feel at
home for the first time since I left London. Something to think
about: Am I a totally superficial person, to be so easily cheered up
by spending a little money?

On an impulse, passing Marks & Spencer (one really cannot
continue to riddle in cashmere and pearls), I go in and buy a pair
of their men's corduroy trousers—so much better cut than the
women's—and two of their Viyella-type shirts in rather good tat-
tersall checks. Also men's, of course. One look at their "blouses" is
more than enough.

I change into my purchases when I get home, and go down to
Antony, who is smoking a cigar and enjoying a pre-lunch sherry
outside the library French windows. He eyes me narrowly.

"Darling, do you think it's a good idea to borrow Ann's clothes?
You're always going on about being tactful in front of the children . . ."

"These are mine, actually. I bought them this morning in Salisbury."

"Not exactly you, are they?"

"I really cannot continue to riddle in cashmere and pearls."

"Oh. Well . . . but you'll change for dinner into something sexy, won't you?"

"If I'm not too tired," I say sulkily. Talk about wanting the best of both worlds.

It has started to rain when it's time to collect the children, so I snatch an old, muddy blue jacket with a pretty checked lining from the hooks in the kitchen passage.

The two older children scowl when they see me, and Emily's eyes brim over.

"That's Mum's Barbour," she says accusingly.

So this is a Barbour. I always thought those distinctive waterproof jackets were something preppies wore outside Harrods to show they were spending the weekend in Gloucestershire. It is actually very practical. I rather like it.

"And aren't those Mum's trousers you've got on?" says Sarah.

"For about the millionth time, they are mine, mine, mine. I'm sorry about the Barbour. Do you think your mother would mind?"

Sarah gets into the car and winds down her window. "Why stop at a simple jacket? I am sure you could think of something to steal that would really upset her."

We drive home in silence.

Ann

I've been waiting and waiting for Antony to phone and say what a terrible mistake he's made and will I please come home? I don't seem to have the energy to do anything except bicker listlessly with Mother.

"Why don't you phone up one of your friends?" she keeps saying. But I don't want to see any friends. I've lost touch with all the people I used to know in London and everyone Antony and I met in the country knows me as part of a double-turn, Ann-and-Antony, an attractively acceptable couple to slot neatly around their dinner tables. I wonder if it's Felicia-and-Antony now?

Each morning, Mother gazes hopefully over the teapot and asks if I've followed up this or that job or been in touch with a solicitor yet. She exhausted her maternal resources that first night, and now she's obviously longing to get me back on the other end of a telephone and out of her spare room.

"Why don't you put your pride in your pocket and phone Antony?" she'd said this morning, making it clear that she was as anxious as I was for Antony to come dashing along with a bouquet and carry me back to Wiltshire.

Well, of course I'd phoned Antony. And each time, Sally was terribly sorry but Mr. Forester-Jones was in a meeting or had just popped out for a moment. "I'll tell him you rang, Mrs. Forester-Jones."

And then, yesterday, her smug secretary's voice informed me that Mr. Forester-Jones had asked her to say that he'd be in touch with me tomorrow.

The letter flops onto the mat with the second post. Mum has gone shopping. "I suppose you'll want some of those Bath buns from Nathans again and I see you've finished the chocolate biscuits."

She gazed critically at my plump upper arms, swelling out the delicate silk of the dressing gown she'd lent me. "I don't think you should, you know. You're putting on an awful lot of weight."

This was another fact I preferred not to face. Some people can't eat when they are unhappy. Misery brings them the bonus of a fashionably slim figure and the sudden sighting of interesting cheekbones. It's not like that for me. I eat constant consoling snacks; childhood treats like buns and biscuits and toast and honey. I see from Mother's bathroom scales that I have gained seven pounds.

Reaching out, automatically, for a piece of cake and another cup of instant coffee, I open the letter. It is not from Antony, but from Piggott, Smiley & Garratt, Solicitors at Law & Commissioners for Oaths, announcing that they are acting for Mr. Antony Forester-Jones and will I be good enough to furnish them with the name of my solicitor at my earliest convenience.

Of course, I haven't got a solicitor. The only time I needed one was when Rocket escaped from his field and hoofed up a neighbor's meticulously maintained lawn. And then I'd fired back from my side of the fence through Piggott, Smiley & Garratt, who are now, I gather, no longer on my side of the fence.

This cold official prose is the beginning of the end of my marriage. How could Antony do it like this? Why didn't he phone me himself? It's that bitch. She won't let him speak to me. She's scared. She knows she's got nothing to offer Antony except the novelty of a new body. A new body? Looking down gloomily at the soft rolls of fat where my twenty-four-inch waist used to be, I mutter: "The bitch . . . the bitch . . ." but it's just a ritual incantation. I know Antony too well to believe that he could be manipulated by anyone, especially a woman.

He is either very angry or hurt. It must have been something I said when I let fly at him that awful evening. What did I say? I can't remember exactly . . .

I do recall taking a satisfying sideswipe at his blue-rinsed, battleax of a mother: "And what has she got to be so grand about, with all those empty gin bottles stashed about all over the house?" And there was a long list of neglected parental duties: "Where were you when Mark was rushed off to hospital . . . when Sarah won the Trasker Memorial Prize for Natural History? . . . when the doctor thought it might be a good idea for us all to get together and have a talk about Emily's little problem?" But these were familiar reproaches, used in previous marital skirmishes without bringing on a solicitor's letter or even a stony silence. Could it have been . . . ? Oh God, I remember now. I'd reached out, instinctively, for the most potent verbal weapon to strike Antony and I'd brought up the Kuwait incident. There was an unspoken agreement between us that we would never mention it, and I had.

Ten years ago, Antony was over there, clinching a deal with an oil company and, as he confessed later, holding me close and weeping and agonizingly explaining why he couldn't make love to me, he'd had too much to drink and accepted the entertainment kindly provided by his host: a call girl who'd called at his hotel and given him VD. He was so ashamed, so sure I wouldn't forgive him (perhaps I haven't or I wouldn't have let the word "Kuwait" pass my lips so easily), so grateful that I didn't want to talk it out together as the agony aunts would, no doubt, recommend.

I had paid a discreet visit to an anonymous doctor in Harley Street (I had no wish to meet up with a knowing smile from our local GP over the gin and tonics at one of Jenny's cocktail parties) who assured me that I was "clean as a whistle," and advised me to refrain from sexual relations with my husband until he was passed similarly fit.

What had I said, just before I left White Walls? It was something

about his squalid promiscuous sexual habits and . . . yes . . .
practically the last words I'd said before I flung out of the house
were: "And do you honestly imagine that I've enjoyed our lovemaking even once after you brought home that filthy disease?
Don't you realize how I feel? That I can't bear you to touch me?"

I go to bed after that. I tear the solicitor's letter into little bits,
throw them in Mum's rosebud-trimmed wastepaper basket and
huddle under the bedclothes. I find a bottle of sleeping pills in the
medicine chest and take a couple to blot out the world for a while.

Mother, arriving home with the shopping, goes into the bathroom, notices that the medicine cupboard is open, the pills gone,
and comes rushing into the room, trying to drag me out of bed.

"Get up, get up," she cries. "You've got to get up and walk, keep
walking, that's what they always say. Ann, for goodness' sake, help
yourself. Get out of bed. I'll make some black coffee . . . I'll
phone the hospital . . . Oh, my God, which hospital? I'll dial
999 . . ."

"Mum, what on earth's the matter? Have you gone out of your
mind?" I'm a confirmed non-pill-taker who is knocked out by one
aspirin, let alone two Mogadon, so I come slowly awake, fighting
her off, pulling the bedclothes back around me into a womblike
nest.

"Are you all right, Mum?" I regard her anxiously as she slumps
down heavily on the end of my bed.

"Of course I'm all right. It's you I'm worried about. Oh Ann,
Ann, I thought you'd done it . . ."

"Done what?"

"Taken the pills, the sleeping pills; the bottle's not in the medicine chest."

"Oh Mum, really." I'm still too sleepily confused, too self-ab-
sorbed, probably, to see that she's trembling.

"You didn't honestly imagine I'd taken the lot? Did you think I
was trying to end it all or was it just a cry for help?" I wished I
hadn't been facetious when Mum puts her head in her hands and
begins sobbing quietly. I can't remember seeing her cry before. I
reach out and touch her shoulder. "Don't cry, darling. It's all
right. I'm all right. I just took two sleeping pills to help me forget,
that's all."

Mother shrugs my hand away. She's cross, the way she was

when I was five and ran out into the road in front of a car and she'd pulled me back and slapped me.

"I'm so worried about you, Ann, can't you see that? What are you going to do with your life? What are you going to do about the children? You can't just abandon them, you know. And where are you going to live?" The tears are drying on her cheeks and there is a crisper note in her voice: "There isn't room for us both in this tiny house and besides . . . you can't stay here forever . . ."

I don't want to think about what I ought to be doing or make any decisions. I want to sleep, opt out of living for at least a week. I explain this to Mum, who says: "Are you ill, then?" My mother is the kind of puritan who wouldn't pick up a novel before midday, or relax in an armchair, if there was washing-up in the sink. "There's a lot of flu about," she says, seeking a rational reason for my being in bed in broad daylight.

It's difficult to convince her that unhappiness can make you feel sicker than flu and I produce a number of symptoms, all of them genuine, to make it easier for her.

"I feel so tired all the time, and my heart is sort of thudding in a weird way and I just long for sweet things . . ."

"Oh, don't be absurd, Ann," she says. "You've always been greedy." But she draws the curtain to shut out the light and tucks in the bedclothes with a gesture which manages to be both fond and brisk.

"Antony's on the phone."

I pull the covers over my head again and turn to face the wall. "I don't want to speak to him."

Mother tugs them back, equally firmly. "Oh, for heaven's sake, pull yourself together, Ann."

She's been longing to say that for over a week. Every time she tiptoes into the room with a dainty invalid meal on a tray and a bracing "Well, how are you feeling now, then?" I know she's swallowing that phrase and almost choking on it.

"He wants to know if you've received the letter. What letter? I haven't seen a letter."

I gesture towards the solicitor's letter lying, in tiny ripped pieces, in her wastepaper basket and she "tsk-tsks" irritably and goes out.

Returning a few minutes later, she says: "I told him you weren't well enough to speak to him, I told him you had the flu, that's what I tell the children every time they phone. Really, Ann, you're being most inconsiderate. You're not the only wife whose husband has been unfaithful, you know."

"It's more than that," I murmur, "she's living there, in my house with my children . . ."

Mother looks exasperated. "Well, of course she is. You're not there. Somebody's got to look after them. If you hadn't rushed out into the night in that hysterical manner, she'd probably be back with her husband in St. John's Wood or wherever it is she lives. You're just going to have to face up to things, Ann. You can't just lie there, hoping it'll all go away."

But I do go on lying there and when the trays stop appearing I wait until Mother goes out and then drag myself into the kitchen for bread and cheese and other easy-to-prepare snacks.

A few days later my favorite fruitcake, the one Mum used to make as a special treat when I was a child, appears in the cake tin. So she knows I'm raiding her cupboard. I eat the cake at one go and then I throw up. I feel a little better, as though I've cleared more than a rich fruitcake out of my system.

The following morning I receive two letters. The first is from Antony, very short and to the point. He is sorry to hear I've not been well and hopes I am now better. He is also sorry about the official solicitor's letter but would be grateful if I could find the time to answer it. Both he and Felicia—damn her for interfering—think it would be wiser to keep things unemotional and business-like and later, he hopes, we'll be able to discuss the children's future, like civilized human beings. Pity he hadn't been a bit more civilized and kept his mistress out of our home.

The second letter is from Philip Gilham asking if I would like to have dinner with him on Thursday evening. I decide that I would. Philip Gilham is not part of my past. He knows nothing of Antony or my children or me. Best of all, he has never heard of Felicia Harman. It would be nice to have dinner with Mr. Gilham. I could do with a decent meal, for a start.

I have two days to pull myself together, as Mother would put it. I try on the black dress. Tight but wearable. Mother is surprised to see me out of bed and dressed. She's pleased to see I'm pulling myself together, she says.

Philip Gilham is even better-looking than I remember, and I wonder why this desirable man should have the slightest interest in me.

"Ann," he says, "I hope you don't mind me calling you that? How very nice this is. And what can I get you to drink?"

"A glass of white wine would be lovely, thanks." We seem to be doing an encore of our last meeting.

I sit down with my back to the wall. There is a gap at the back of my dress where the zip wouldn't meet, which I have attempted to camouflage with a wide cummerbund I unearthed from my mother's wardrobe. I'd planned to dash out this afternoon and buy something more suitable (something bigger is what I really mean) and, just as I'd located my checkbook, Donald Harman had rung and asked if I'd meet him for lunch tomorrow.

"This is a highly unsatisfactory situation, and you and I ought to discuss what we're going to do about it."

At first I couldn't think who Donald Harman was, and then I remembered that he was the husband of the woman who's sleeping with my husband. I agreed to meet him for lunch.

I seem to be having a lot of hot meals these days, I reflect, as I put on my going-away outfit again (I *must* get to Jaeger or somewhere and replace this dreary skirt and jacket with something more fashionable) and prepare to meet Donald. It's unlikely, though, that any more meals will be forthcoming from Philip Gilham.

Just thinking about last night brings on a hot flush of embarrassment. The dinner was all right, and the wine—rather a lot of it—was delicious. Philip was flatteringly attentive. He admired the black dress extravagantly and rather went down in my estimation for doing so, since a glance round the room revealed that what is appropriate for a Tisbury cocktail party is wildly inappropriate for a London restaurant.

He gazed into my eyes a great deal. "Do you know that they are the most extraordinary color of blue?" he said.

Drawing me out, in courtroom fashion, he fell back in his chair in a pantomime of amazement when I got to Felicia.

"He must be mad. How could any man look at another woman if he has you?"

Even with all that wine, I knew that this was a dumb question. I'd been thinking along these lines myself and had come to the conclusion, early on, that if I were a man who had to choose between an overweight, familiar, dogsbody wife and a pretty, slim actress, with a sparkle to her eyes and conversation, I'd dump the fat one.

I said as much to Philip and he said that all abandoned wives felt like that, at least all the ones he dealt with did. I told him my Piggott, Smiley & Garratt dilemma and he offered, as I'd hoped he might, to act for me in *Forester-Jones* v. *Forester-Jones.*

"We'll give them a run for their money," he said, and I had the uneasy feeling that it was no longer a matter between Antony and me, but had already become my solicitor divorcing his solicitor.

"Trust me, Ann," said Philip in the taxi going home. Going to his home, I realized. The address he had given the taxi driver had not sounded like Caldecott Mews.

I wasn't sure whether he was speaking personally or professionally, because I could feel his hand moving gently under my cummerbund, locating the zip gap, and insinuating itself around my body and up towards my left breast. My first thought was Goodness, he's got long arms, and my second was that I couldn't believe this was happening to me.

I'm thirty-nine, married, well . . . sort of married, and I gave up being groped in taxis nineteen years ago. I was astonished it still went on. I thought women had been liberated in some way, so that it was possible to go home after dining with a man without having to pay for the meal with a sexual favor. Perhaps I should have offered to pay for my share of the dinner? I didn't know the new rules, that was the trouble.

It appeared there weren't any new rules. It was the same routine I remembered from my teenage days, except that there was a difference.

I was no longer a timid virgin, and I found Philip Gilham arousing. As he drew me towards him, my body sent up clear signals of acceptance.

It was when he murmured that he'd wanted to make love to me from that very first moment I'd lobbed my suitcase at him— "You looked so adorably helpless"—and how he longed to peel off the black dress that my brain took over from my body. I wanted Philip Gilham, there was no question about that, but I was not going in for any dress peeling until I'd lost at least fifteen pounds.

I went rigid in Philip's arms as I imagined myself naked, with heavy breasts, a thick waist and dimpled thighs. I was vulnerable enough without letting myself in for *that.*

"I'm sorry, Philip." I'd regressed to pushing men across taxis again. "I'm sorry, but I can't come home with you tonight . . ."

He protested, but I made him give the driver my mother's address.

"Forgive me, Ann," he said. "It's Antony, isn't it? It's too soon. How insensitive of me."

But it wasn't Antony at all, sod him. I wonder how many other women have refused to take off their clothes only because they are ashamed of their bodies?

It is clear from the moment Donald grips my hand—painfully hard —saying: "Whatever made you walk out like that, Ann? It was legal suicide . . ." that this is to be a businesslike meeting about future strategies rather than a mutually consoling sob about the past.

"How do women usually react when your wife moves in with their husbands?" I reply nastily.

Donald is wearing a pin-striped navy suit, a crisp white shirt, a boring navy blue tie, with a tasteful motif, center front, signaling that he belongs to the right American fraternity. He looks more English than anyone else in Throgmorton Street; and now that I inspect him closely, I can see that he also looks an unhappy man.

"I'm sorry." I put my hand briefly on his. "That wasn't a very clever remark, but I'm feeling a bit raw just now. I expect you are, too."

Donald withdraws his hand swiftly, as though I'd pounced on it and covered it with kisses, and sidesteps any emotional revelations by hiding behind a vast tasseled menu. Each dish has a prose poem to itself about being freshly picked on a dew-fresh morning and, over the watery prawn cocktail and dry lamb cutlets, I wonder why the quality of food now seems to deteriorate in direct ratio to the size of the menu. I also wonder why I am coining such a trivial Great Truth at such an important moment.

Donald tells me that he didn't know that Felicia and Antony were having an affair, didn't even realize she was unhappy. "She had the house, the children, and we do . . . did . . . a fair amount of business entertaining—she was good at that—and she was always in demand for commercials." I feel an involuntary twitch of sympathy for Felicia as he says this, since I seem to remember Antony telling me that she was a successful actress before she married her American banker.

Neatly switching the conversation from his wife to my husband,

Donald says: "How about Antony? Does he do this kind of thing often?"

"Not so far as I know. Does Felicia?"

"I don't think so. But how do we know, Ann? It came as a bolt from the blue to me. And you, too, I guess?"

I admit to being equally thunderstruck, and am even more so when Donald suggests that we "play it cool and wait for them to get over this ridiculous infatuation."

"But, would you take Felicia back? After all, it was you throwing her out which started all this."

He looks ashamed. "Yes, yes I would. Sure."

He is not, I suspect, a regular wife beater but a man who keeps his emotions so firmly in check that they are liable to erupt all over the place when unexpectedly released.

"I don't know why, Ann, but it was Tom telling me that made it so much worse. He seemed . . . well, I thought he seemed kind of pleased about it."

"I don't expect he likes her much," I say. "You did leave Tom's mother for Felicia, I suppose?" Donald nods.

"Well, that's it. He probably thinks you sacrificed his childhood and his mother's happiness for a worthless bitch. Felicia has just confirmed that he was right and you were wrong. No wonder you're angry."

Donald seems as impressed by this amateur psychiatry as I am myself. "Yeah," he says, "you're probably right. But Felicia isn't a worthless bitch, Ann. She's highly strung, that's all. I'm afraid she may just have gone off the rails again, for some reason."

I'm thinking, Highly strung? Off the rails? So there's a madwoman in charge of my children, as Donald says, worriedly, that Laura and Harry can't stand the woman he's got in from a nursery nurses' bureau.

"You've got two, haven't you," he says, "a boy and a girl? Who's looking after them?"

I tell him that I have three children who are still in Wiltshire being looked after by his neurotic wife. Oh, in *that* case, Donald assures me, Felicia will soon be back in St. John's Wood: "She doesn't like children much, not other people's, anyway, so stay calm, Ann, stop talking this divorce nonsense and all this will soon blow over."

I am less sanguine. I've seen Antony's solicitor's letter and it doesn't read like nonsense that will soon blow over. I tell Donald all this and add that meanwhile, while we're staying calm and doing nothing, what's to become of my children? I see my son's face, pale and withdrawn, the way he looks when he is unhappy and doesn't know how to tell me what's wrong, and I push away the beastly cutlets and burst into tears.

"Ann, steady on now." Donald looks uneasily around the restaurant, where the other pin-striped diners have stopped discussing the Monopolies Commission's reaction to the latest takeover bid to concentrate on our table. "Come on . . . I know it isn't easy for you. I'm having a tricky time myself. Harry keeps asking for his mother and I've had to tell Laura that Felicia's just gone away for a bit of a rest . . . it's damn difficult trying to cope with all this as well as the Nigerian finance minister."

"But, what can we *do*, Donald?"

"Like I said, Ann. Nothing. It would be crazy to disrupt our kids' lives. Would you believe I've had a hysterical letter from Felicia, demanding that she has Laura and Harry down in Wiltshire with her? Those children are going to college in America, and there's no way I'm going to confuse them by putting them through the English educational system. We'll leave the children where they are, in familiar surroundings, in the schools they know, with their friends around them and then, when that irresponsible couple come to their senses, there'll have been the minimum of upheaval."

"But, what if they don't? What if they don't come to their senses?"

"They will," says Donald confidently. "And, meanwhile, Ann, I've had a great idea. Why don't you move in with me?" He sees the flush spread tiresomely upwards from my neck to my eyebrows and says quickly: "No, no. I don't mean *that*. No, no. Don't misunderstand me here . . ." The flush settles into a mottled throbbing red as Donald says reassuringly: "You're a very good-looking woman, Ann, make no mistake about that, but what I'm offering here is a platonic proposition. You've got nowhere to live and you need a job and I've got no one to look after my two kids. They're too old for a nanny, temporary help is unreliable, and besides, Laura and Harry can't stand that woman I got in from the domestic agency. If only one of my sisters lived over here . . . I'd hazard a guess that you're pretty good with children and I expect you could cope with the occasional formal dinner, if I have to invite people over?"

"Well, I'm not sure . . ." I'm not sure I can cope with anything, anymore, even this forceful American who is obviously trying to help me.

"It's decided then." Donald relaxes, gives me an encouraging smile. "You'll come and work for me, I'll pay you the going rate, plus a bit over the top, and it goes without saying that you'll have a daily woman and your own bed-sitting-room." He grins suddenly, and for the first time I catch a glimpse of the charmer Felicia fell for. "I assure you, Ann, that it will all be very *proper*."

I am so anxious to convince him that I haven't mistaken his job offer for a subtle seduction that I find myself nodding my head; agreeing to become my husband's mistress's husband's house-keeper.

Felicia

I have now spent nearly three weeks in this house, and I am missing my children dreadfully. I have been up to London to see them, and of course I telephone them every day, but I feel worse every time I put the phone down. Harry talks a lot about food, which I have no difficulty in interpreting as a cry of insecurity. Laura keeps on apologizing and saying she's so sorry she's taken me for granted. And that makes me feel very nearly suicidal, except it would be letting them down even more.

Ann and I made a complicated, cold-voiced arrangement, which involved me dropping her children at her mother's mews house. It turned out to be in a rather dreary part of London I never seem to have been to before. As I drove away, I looked at myself in the rearview mirror and thought, You don't look all that bad. You look quite a nice woman, actually. Ann never did you any harm; so, she was dull, but did you have to muck up her life in quite such a comprehensive way?

The house had really upset me. It was sort of genteel grotty; clean net curtains at all the windows, but somebody hadn't bothered to sweep up a broken milk bottle. And I was going back tonight to a man and elegance. Freezing cold elegance, admittedly, but large rooms and an ancient garden and not a broken milk bottle to be seen.

I still had the front-door key so I let myself into our house.

Donald's house. He was there, waiting to hand the children over to me with icy propriety.

"I will be back at five," he said.

"Donald," I said, "I do wish we could talk . . . ?"

"Good-bye, Laura honey," he said, " 'bye Harry. Be a good boy now. See you later." And he was gone.

"So what shall we do?" I said, sitting on the sofa with Laura as close to me as she could get, and Harry on my knee. "Oh, babies, it's lovely to see you. And how are you? You've had your hair cut, Laura. It looks amazing."

Harry felt a lot heavier than he had the last time he'd sat on my knee. And he looked positively podgy.

I took them out shopping. Laura said one of her friends had bought some really great things from Monsoon, so could we go and have a look? And Harry talked a lot about an electronic robot that was programmed not to fall off the edge of tables. So I spent quite a lot of money, one way and another, and then we went to McDonald's. I felt a qualm as I watched Harry munch his way avidly through a quarter pounder with cheese, large fries and a milkshake, followed by apple pie. Laura contented herself with the smallest hamburger on offer.

I found, to my dismay, that I was Making Conversation, and asking them boring things like "How's school?" I was so terrified of saying the wrong thing that everything I said sounded stilted.

When we got home, Harry slipped off to the kitchen. I could hear the fridge door opening. I was just going to put a stop to *that* when Laura said: "Mom, when are you coming home?"

"Laura," I said, "darling . . . this is still my home as far as you and Harry are concerned. But my home isn't with your father anymore. He is a very good and kind man, but we weren't making each other happy . . ."

Was that true? It sounded like an old end-of-marriage cliché to me, but there was some truth in it. Looking back, I realized that while we weren't exactly making each other sad, we didn't laugh when we met. We didn't hand out quick hugs if we passed on the stairs. I didn't long to tell him all my news. Half the time he wasn't listening, anyway.

Antony and I, with all our arguments and shouting, only seem to come alive when we're together. I was the product of a famed theatrical couple, and was reared on fireworks. As far back as I can remember, my adoring parents had screamed insults at each other.

Breakfast was always fun. My mother, wearing clouds of pale blue, with white lace falling away from dangerously fragile wrists, would cast vast blue eyes dotingly at Father.

"Harry," she would murmur, "that dressing gown—too divine and Noëlish. Coffee, my angel? You certainly buggered up my entrance last night."

"Felicia," my father would respond, "did you know your mother was the most beautiful woman in London? I was only trying to help, my precious. After fifteen minutes' deathly hush I was seriously contemplating firing that Little Miss Prompt-person."

"Are you implying? I have *never* dried. When a woman walks into a room and hears her husband making love to her best friend over the telephone, naturally she pauses. I could feel the audience . . . where is the honey? Thank you, my heart . . . I could feel the audience grieving with me."

"Really? I could feel them looking at their watches."

"Yes, but then you never have been one for interpreting audience reaction, have you, pet? That Lear performance in Edinburgh . . . God, how I suffered for you . . ."

And they'd be at it, hammer and tongs, with me gurgling merrily between them, and learning early that when people love each other, they shout a lot. Is it any wonder that I found Donald's equable refusal to argue rather disquieting?

As I drove home, with Ann's children sitting glumly in the back, I thought sadly that I might as well have stayed in Wiltshire. I had spent a lot of money, made Laura even more unhappy, and done very little for Harry, except fill him with unsuitable food.

Ann

"Ann?"

It's Felicia. I hope she's not going to suggest bringing the children here again. I'd so looked forward to seeing them and it had all been such a disaster. This poky little house seems even less welcoming to children than it is to lodgers. Every small occasional table is poised to tip over, smashing precious ornaments and treasures, and Mother had spent the whole afternoon slipping flowered plate mats under mugs, brushing imaginary crumbs off chairs whenever a child got up to go to the lavatory, and saying: "Must you make that awful noise, dear?" every time Mark did his Miss Piggy impersonation. He did it a lot. Mark is very into funny voices at the moment.

It was painfully obvious that my children were surviving all too well without me. I was pleased, of course I was, when Emmy said she'd been dry for a night, but it hurt that Felicia had achieved something for my child that I'd been unable to do in years.

They looked so well, still a family. Piling up dishes in the sink, my mother said: "Well, they don't seem to be coming to any harm, do they? Mark's his same old self and the girls look better than ever."

I wasn't sure whether this was meant to be comforting or a criticism of me. I suspected the latter, but this was not a moment to have a set-to with Mother. "Yes, they do seem well," I agreed.

And then, Mark came in with a dirty mug and started thoughtlessly referring to Felicia and Antony in tandem. Fel and Dad had come to watch him play cricket last Saturday; Fel and Dad had been up to London to see a play and said it was really good, Fel and Dad, he pronounced, seem to be getting on okay.

I was sorry to hear that. I wanted Fel and Dad to be as miserable as I was, because, looking at the children, I could see that there was no way I could take them away from their secure background and bring them to London; even if there were somewhere for us all to live.

I'm not proud of the way I behaved that afternoon, but Sarah had gone on and on about Larkspur having puppies, and eventually I'd said: "Just because a dog is mated, it doesn't necessarily mean she'll have puppies. It doesn't always work, you know."

Sarah's face had fallen. I wonder if I said that because it's true, or because I sensed that Sarah was more worried about the dog and her wretched puppies than she was about me?

Perhaps they found the visit as upsetting as I did and that's why Felicia is phoning . . .

"I just thought I ought to tell you," she says, straightaway, in the cool, clipped voice she uses when she speaks to me, "that Larkspur has now been mated . . ."

"You phoned to tell me *that?*" I can't believe what I'm hearing. Here I am, frantic with worry about my children, my husband, my *life*, and this woman is babbling about dogs.

"The children told me," I say firmly. I certainly don't want to have any more discussions about dogs. And I can't resist adding: "Perhaps *you* ought to know that I am moving in with Donald."

"With *Donald?*" I can tell from her tone that she finds my news item rather more intriguing than hers. "What do you mean, you're moving in with Donald?"

I explain that Donald needs a housekeeper, I need a job, and Laura and Harry need someone to look after them until she and Antony come to their senses. "I should have thought you'd be glad to hear that someone is looking after your children."

She makes protesting noises about speaking to them every day on the telephone and how much she's missing them.

"We are on the defensive, aren't we?" I say, putting down the phone.

"Let's get this straight, Mrs. Forester-Jones." Mr. Dwyer eyes me prayerfully over tipped fingers. "You are intending to cohabit with Mr. Harman, and his wife, Mrs. Harman, is presently cohabiting with your husband, Mr. Forester-Jones?"

"Put like that it does sound rather odd," I say, "but we're not actually cohabiting. I am taking up employment with Mr. Harman but my accommodation will be entirely separate from Mr. Harman's accommodation. In other words," I lapse into basic English, "I'm not sleeping with him and we're not wife swapping." Mr. Dwyer blanches at this frank departure from legalese and scrabbles among his papers.

"Oh, dear me, Mrs. Forester-Jones, I hope you don't imagine that I'm suggesting anything of that sort, but putting on my solicitor's hat here, I can't help wondering if it's . . . well, *suitable* for you and Mr. Harman to be in such close proximity. It does give the other party grounds for questioning whether adultery is taking place and, since you left the marital home and, in effect, deserted your children we must ask ourselves if it is . . . well, *prudent* for you to be taking up residence with Mr. Harman at all?"

I'd been put on to Mr. Dwyer by Philip Gilham, who phoned up the day after the taxi grapple to apologize again for his behavior. He didn't know what had come over him, he said, except that he found me disturbingly attractive and would very much like to see me again if I could forgive him. I said of course I forgave him and it was probably just as much my fault as his, for being so disturbing.

He laughed politely and said that under the circumstances he was sure I'd understand that it would be impossible for him to act for me in my divorce; which was bad news since I needed a lawyer more than a lover.

I understand from Mr. Dwyer that I would be entitled to half the value of White Walls and probably some sort of settlement in recognition of sixteen years' loyal service; but would be unlikely to be awarded alimony since it was now felt that a woman of thirty-nine can earn her own living.

"We will of course fight that, on the basis that you have been engaged in child rearing and keeping a home for Mr. Forester-Jones and his children and were, therefore, unable to maintain your skills . . . Your husband will, of course, pay maintenance for the children."

"But suppose they live with him?"

Mr. Dwyer purses his lips disapprovingly. "I had presumed that you would wish to have your children with you, Mrs. Forester-Jones. If, in the future, that should become the case, we can always go back to the court and ask for maintenance."

He struggles with conflicting emotions when I tell him that I've come for advice rather than action, since I'm hoping there won't be a divorce. He's obviously pleased to hear I've the right motherly instincts but he's spoiling for a fight.

"I'll do nothing until I receive your instructions," Mr. Dwyer says gloomily.

Felicia

The girls have taken to calling me Fellow. Antony buoyantly interprets this as an affectionate shortening of my name. From the naughty way they look at my chest while saying it, I have no doubt that (Sarah-inspired) they are implying that above the waist I am shaped like a chap. This is sufficiently near the truth to be rather mortifying.

On the other hand, Emily and I share a secret. About two weeks ago, when I was crossly changing her sheets and muttering rather, I looked up to see her standing at the door; I had forgotten she was home from school with a cold.

"Is it an awful nuisance, Mrs. Harman?"

I contemplated saying waspishly that no, no, it had always been my life's ambition . . . but one look at her woebegone face stopped me.

"Of course it isn't a nuisance, Emily. I just wish I could help, that's all—it must be an awful bore for you."

"When I'm asked to stay with a friend I have to say no . . . and we pretended I had flu for the Pony Club camp last year."

"Why don't we do something about it?"

"The doctor said I'll grow out of it and I mustn't be worried."

"Would it worry you if I woke you up an hour after you go to bed? Then you could nip off to the loo, and maybe last through the night."

"Do you think it would work?"

"It did with me, when I was about your age," I said nobly. "I had a horrid nanny who looked after me when my parents were acting. She said it was because I was wicked, and my mother wouldn't love me if she found out."

"Did she find out?"

"Yes, when Nanny Brigshaw left. My mother was furious with her."

"What did she say?"

"I couldn't repeat it, really." ("The flatulent old *bugger,*" my mother had shouted. "Darling, you must always tell me everything. Nothing could ever stop me loving you, you know that." From then on, one of my parents had woken me when they came home from the theater. And in a few weeks my shaming problem had turned into something unimportant that had happened when I was younger.)

"Anyway, why don't we give it a try?"

Emily hesitated, and looked at me nervously.

"You're afraid Sarah won't approve," I said.

"I think she'd think . . . if it was a good idea Mum would have done it."

"Yes, but your mother doesn't know about it like I do. Why don't we keep it a secret?"

Emily's face lit up. "I know," she said, "it could be a sort of game. I'll be the prisoner in Gestapo headquarters, and you can be someone from the Resistance creeping in to rescue me."

These children watch far too much television; but as mine do too, I am hardly in a position to criticize.

"Anysing you say, Mamselle."

Emily giggled, and looked guiltily over her shoulder. I was well aware that we had only been able to have this conversation because Sarah was out of the house.

Since then, every night at around ten o'clock I have left the *Hauptmann* and her father watching television, and slipped upstairs. "Cherie," I have hissed into Emily's ear, "now's your chance."

After a couple of nights we got tired of Cherie and her boring Gestapo friends, and have tried several variations. "I come to free White Squaw from Black Eagle" went down very well. Right now I am Gene Hackman telling his colleague where the drug drop is going to be. It's all go round here, I can tell you. But she has had several dry nights, and we're now in the position of if she has three in a row, I will take her into Salisbury and buy her the most amazing nightdress we can lay our hands on. Sarah knows something is going on, but is not sure what.

As of this week Mrs. Simmons has agreed to come in every day, instead of just Tuesdays and Fridays. To think that only three weeks ago, I was wondering what to do with the day; Ann must have been mad, not to say exhausted. Mrs. Simmons has very nearly Come Round. She has found out what I am doing for Emily, and unbent to the extent of saying, "I did say to Mrs. Forester-Jones that these things don't go away by themselves."

I have taught Antony how to open the dishwasher and put plates into it. He is coming along nicely, but needs to work on his habit of putting the cutlery in the wrong way up.

I have conscientiously worked my way through nearly all of Ann's memo. The sloe gin, as far as I am concerned, is on its own. I can't find it, and if I could I wouldn't know what to do with it. Surely it must be bottled already, otherwise it would just be a puddle somewhere? I have told Higgins (the jobbing gardener who comes here twice a week in order to find a quiet place to smoke his pipe) about the asparagus mulch. He counters with a bold suggestion of planting more brussels sprouts nearer the house. I veto this ghastly plan on Ann's behalf. Rocket has got some nice new shoes, but the idea of even being alone in a field with him, let alone getting on his back, makes terrible waves of panic swim about in my stomach. However, Sarah seems to potter about on him quite a lot, so that's all right.

Larkspur came into season yesterday. The less said about that the better. I have rung Mr. Barrow, who called me Missis, and arranged to arrive with Larkspur at his house on the outskirts of Thetford at nine A.M. next Wednesday. "It's always better in the morning, Missis," said Mr. Barrow. I feared he was about to tell me why, so I diverted him by asking for directions. It wasn't until I put the phone down that I realized that in order to get to Norfolk by nine, Larkspur and I will have to get up right after *Hill Street Blues.*

I have done a massive amount of cooking. Partly because, stung by my first night's failure, I have been forcing rich, dinner-party food into the family as though they were Strasbourg geese. Baby lamb, salmon, pâtés, mousses, you name the exotic vegetable, I've tried it. They stagger bloated away from the table as though they were holidaying in the Dordogne.

And, of course, I have been preparing for the Snacks and Scraps stall; the fete is tomorrow. Have no intention of messing about with dull ham rolls and bits of onion, so have produced several quiches, some *jambon persillé,* and two cheese-and-avocado roulades. Also some rather fetching stuffed mushrooms.

Sarah watches my preparations with a sardonic eye. "They'll never eat that sort of stuff," she says, "of course."

Church fete day. Enlivened by panic, I leap from my bed at ten past six. Down in the kitchen (clean floor; I tell the dogs what clever girls they are. This is not the first time I've caught myself talking to animals as though they were people. It must be something in the atmosphere here), I lay out my wares for the Snacks and Scraps stall. It doesn't look enough to me. If they made twenty pounds last year at twenty-five p a throw, how many portions . . . ? I have to get a pencil and paper to work it out. Eighty portions . . . have I got eighty portions here? Surely it's got to be enough. On the other hand . . .

When Antony comes down, "Good morning, good morning," I am making kipper pâté.

"Oh, lovely—kippers for breakfast," says Antony.

"Don't touch them—they're for this bloody stall I've got myself embroiled in."

"Darling, you'll never sell all this stuff, enough for a regiment. Anyway, isn't it a bit high-flown for the yokels?"

"If there's any left over we can have it for supper tonight."

Antony looks at the food dubiously, and I know he's thinking that jambon persillé that has spent a warm afternoon on a trestle table is going to be unattractive, if not downright dangerous.

Emily breezes in and gives me a quick thumbs-up while nobody is looking. I evidently owe her the most amazing nightdress in Salisbury.

"Oh Felicia, that looks yummy. Will there be enough? I could eat most of that myself."

Sarah enters in time to hear Emily's comforting reaction, and gives her a look which should have had her groveling. But Emmy is too pleased with herself, bless her, to notice.

It is only halfway through the afternoon, and my stall is practically empty. Sarah and Antony (I think complacently) rather underestimated the degree of sophistication country people have these days. What with television, travel, and the vast range of exotic foods that supermarkets stock, your average farmer's wife seems to take avocado roulade in her stride. In fact, so many people have asked for recipes that shrewd Dotty has suggested I sell them for ten p each.

I have met a fairly frightful woman called Jenny something. Dotty and Gerry might well call Mrs. Simmons the Town Crier, but she at least is frank about her interest in local goings-on. This Jenny smiles all the time, so you smile back; but when you take her sentences home and think about them, you wish you'd hit her.

"Hullo," she says, "I'm Jenny." She hands over twenty-five p, takes a slice of courgette quiche and nibbles at it. "Delicious—so you can cook as well, can you?"

"As well as what?"

"As well as whatever it is you do well enough to make Antony leave Ann."

It is actually rather a relief that someone has at last brought the subject up. All my previous customers, though eager to eat my food, have been slightly ill at ease. No doubt kind Dotty has been going round saying "It is not for us to criticize," in her Christian way. But if I were in their boots I'd be criticizing like mad.

"I suppose . . . are a lot of people talking about it?"

"We speak of little else at the Women's Institute meetings. And I bet your ears were burning yesterday morning. The kneeler needlepoint bee at Mrs. Grainger's. Poor old Dotty had a hard time putting across her 'we must all pray for a sister who has fallen' bit. Though I must say Mrs. Simmons surprised me rather, muttering about everyone has something good about them. Ghastly vulgar kneeler she's embroidering—hope I never get to pray on it."

"Look, I really didn't intend—"

"Nobody ever does, do they? How many women get up in the morning thinking 'Today's the day I shall ruin another woman's life and destroy her children's security?' Though I must admit Ann did rather buy it."

"What do you mean?"

"Well, we all know that Antony's a bit of a rover; made a pass at me on New Year's Eve, but I wasn't interested, thank you very much. And look at the way she let herself go. I told her myself, months ago, to go on a diet and get her hair decently done." Jenny complacently tosses her own excellent hair and visibly sucks in her already flat stomach. "Antony! Darling, what excellent quiche your new lady makes."

I turn to find Antony has appeared behind me. He is looking shifty, which to be fair is about all he can look under the circumstances. Jenny drifts off to laugh merrily at an elderly farmer, who blenches in return and looks round nervously.

"God, how I loathe that woman," Antony hisses.

"Really? She says you made a pass at her on New Year's Eve."

"Rubbish. She was reeling about and draping herself across any man who was unwise enough to sit down. Don't take any notice of anything she says—Ann never did."

"Anyway, shut up while I count my takings."

Counting the orders for recipes I have taken, I have made nearly seventy-nine pounds. Nearly four times as much as Ann did last year. How gratifying. I can't remember feeling so pleased since the television critic in the *Observer* said I was both luminous and disciplined.

Sitting round the kitchen table after supper (scrambled eggs is all I can rise to) we sound, for the first time, like a family: "Did you see Mrs. Grainger's hat? Looked like one of her kneelers . . ." "Percy Grainger cheated in the egg-and-spoon race . . ." "You're not seriously telling me that Mrs. Grainger christened one of her sons Percy? . . ." "Yes, why not?"

Mark swears he heard old Mr. Barker ask Higgins what a Sappho Sisterhood Center was for. To which Higgins answered, after some thought, that it was probably the new kabob takeaway in the

High Street. We all laugh like fools, until Sarah suddenly realizes she is laughing in the same room as me, snaps her jaw shut, and exits. Still, it's a start.

Ann

"Ann. What a surprise."

It is Jenny Balfour, the woman you least want to meet when your life is in ruins.

"May I join you?" She looks around at all the other women up from the shires for a day's shopping and adds archly, "You're not meeting anyone?"

I wish to God I was. I'd gone to ground in Harrods' Dress Circle restaurant after a dispiriting morning dragging from shop to shop, getting lost in department stores and finding nothing to wear unless I wanted to look as though I were auditioning for *Dynasty* or enlisting as a guerrilla. I was due to move to Donald's in two days' time and I desperately needed the kind of clothes that would, at least, make me *look* like a woman who could, at a pinch, take over Felicia Harman's household. I was uncomfortably aware that everything I'd brought from Wiltshire was either too tight or too boring.

Unloading her tray, Jenny settles chummily close. "You're looking very well, I must say."

"Thank you." I have no intention of giving anything away.

"Now I'm dying to know what you've been up to . . ." Jenny shoots me an avid look. "I can tell you the village is agog with the goings-on at White Walls. Of course, everyone is totally on your side after the appalling way Antony's behaved; but then, she is rather attractive, isn't she, the actress . . . ? Felicia Whatsisname?"

"Harman."

"Yes, that's right. Felicia Harman. Madly glamorous, but rather out of place in our little village."

I murmur something noncommittal about people not being what they seem, and Jenny pounces on this enthusiastically. *"Exactly.* Well, the first time I saw the woman and *that* was a bit of a shock, love, I can tell you, but we all knew that Antony must have done something unforgivable for you to walk out like that, leaving the children . . ." She pauses for me to describe the vile behavior which drove me from my young, and when I continue gazing enigmatically into my coffee cup, goes on: "Well, the first time I saw her I thought, That flashy actress won't last more than five minutes in the country, but there she was, dear, as large as life at the village fete and doing *quite* a brisk trade in an exotic quiche and an avocado thing. . . . Of course, Antony is obviously potty about her, but then he was always one for a pretty face . . ." She gives a self-congratulatory smirk. "I can tell you now, Ann, that I've had trouble from that quarter more than once . . ."

She is still talking relentlessly on—". . . of course, one can understand *Dotty*, she's always so determinedly liberal about everybody, but poor Mrs. Simmons has been totally taken in. 'Mrs. Harman is doing her best,' she says in that surly tone of hers . . . well, dear, if stealing somebody's husband is the best she can do . . ."—when I make my excuses and leave.

I'd been agog as the village to know what was going on at White Walls and, safely locked in the loo behind Childrenswear, I brood on the news I've gleaned from Jenny's gossip.

My children, it seems, have never looked better and dear Em had "positively sparkled" in something that sounded like a new dress at Jenny's daughter's birthday party. My husband is evidently so besotted that he has cleared the bramble out of the shrubbery, mended the porch light and bought a new sports jacket; three things I've been trying to persuade him to do for years. Felicia, in spite of her flashiness, has been sighted gardening, walking the dogs and, damn her, damn her, she made seventy-nine pounds at the church fete. That's nearly four times as much as I made on the Snacks and Scraps stall last year.

I've never felt so useless or lonely in my life. I wish Sarah was with me to protect me from garments like that Linda Evans number ("God, Mum, you can't wear *that*,") and urge me towards something youthful but suitable in shops like Way In or Hennes, where I feel diffident about venturing without a teen escort. Sarah would say: "Hey, Mum, it would look great if you put this skirt with the silk T-shirt and the stripy jacket," and then I'd buy her an outfit and a new pair of espadrilles and it would be lovely, all the fun of having a daughter. But Sarah isn't here. She's at home with Mark and Em and Antony—and that gaunt clothes peg, but I'll try not to think of her—and I just don't know what will happen to us all if I give Antony a divorce. I don't really know how I feel about anything, except that Harrods' loo is not the ideal place to make vital decisions. I'll make some trivial ones instead, play safe and get a good suit from Country Casuals, some pretty dresses from Laura Ashley, and a few necessities from M & S. *That* should see me through at Acacia Road.

The house is cream and white, a setting for Felicia. I can picture her making an entrance down those stairs with the bleached antique pine banisters, walking delicately across the thick cream carpet, lounging on the pale gold sofa. And I can see me spilling nail polish on the carpet or walking dog mess into it.

It's hard to believe that this house contains children. Mine would have turned it into a ramshackle home within a week.

The drawing room is on the ground floor, next to a dining room flagged with white tiles and filled with white flowers. On the next floor are two large double bedrooms with bathrooms en suite and on the second floor, two more bedrooms and bathrooms, one set of them mine. The bedroom has been made into a pretty sitting room with a bed piled high with cushions, a chaise longue, a television set, two armchairs. As Donald puts down my cases, a loud and insistent rhythm thumps through the ceiling.

"The children's floor," Donald explains unnecessarily. "Why don't you come up and meet them?"

The top floor has been turned into a whitewashed studio with a skylight window. At one end there are two cubicle bedrooms and a small kitchenette; at the other two exquisitely dressed children are playing a complicated board game with a mousy-looking woman wearing virulent shades of polyester. She looks as out of place in this house as I do in my navy suit and classic courts. "You can never go wrong with good shoes and a good handbag," my mother used to say, but I'm doing it now. As we come in, all three spring to their feet, Miss Mouse in nervous haste to turn off the loud sound.

"Hi kids," says Donald, as the two children rush across to hug him. "This is Laura." He puts his arm around a tall, slim, blonde girl, wearing jeans and a checked shirt. She is only eleven but looks as though she's escaped from the cast of a high-class American western. "And this is Harry." He pulls Harry in close to his side and ruffles his hair. The buttons on his shirt are under pressure, the seat of his Bermudas taut.

"And this is Miss Jamieson, who has been kind enough to look after these monsters." Donald looks at his children with pure besotted love.

"Say hullo to Ann, children."

"How do you do, Ann." Harry shakes my hand politely. The poor child has spots, too.

"How do you do, Ann." Laura graciously extends a limp hand. She seems disturbingly grown-up and, as she looks straight into my eyes—calculating the strength of the opposition?—I think, Here comes another Felicia.

"You are reprieved, Miss Jamieson," says Donald. "Mrs. Forester-Jones has kindly agreed to take us all on and lick us into shape."

It is a curiously emotive choice of words and I look nervously at Donald. He is busy helping Miss Jamieson on with her coat and pressing wads of notes into her hand.

"Well, I'll be off then," she says. And do I sense a quiver of sympathy coming my way as she scuttles out of the room?

"You don't have to worry about us, Ann," says Laura at breakfast next morning. "We can take care of ourselves."

The kitchen is a sunny white room, running the complete length of the lower ground floor, with French windows onto a patio massed with flowers. White flowers. Heavens, even the flowers are color-coordinated. There are machines banked around the walls, it's a chic Cape Canaveral. I feel a deep longing for the untidy mess of White Walls. I long to trip over a dog or two, but instead, bump into Laura, neatly stacking half a dozen brightly packaged breakfast cereals onto the table and whipping croissants out of the deep freeze and putting them in a microwave.

"I'm sorry."

"You're welcome. Do you want Oat Toasties or Cheerios?"

"Well, I'm not quite sure . . ."

"Apple turnovers or spiced cinnamon layers?"

"Well, just a piece of toast . . . ?"

She disappears into the biggest fridge I've ever seen and puts a packet of white sliced bread and a selection of garish jams on the table.

It is all too clear that the Harman children—well, Laura, anyway—do not need looking after.

I'd discovered that already. The previous evening, as Donald relaxed with a whiskey in the drawing room, and I unpacked my cases, Laura and Harry had disappeared into the kitchen, put a selection of boxes into the microwave and turned out a—not very nice, but naturally I didn't say so—meal for four. They were courteously distant at dinner.

"Do you live in the country, Ann?" "How many children have you got, Ann?" "What are your children called, Ann?"

Wishing they wouldn't keep tacking my name on the end of every sentence, I answered their questions and asked a few of my own.

Laura, I learned, was in the sixth grade of middle school and it was okay. Harry told me he'd moved up to the second grade in lower school when he was seven, and that his teacher's name was Mary Anne Colby and his counselor was called Suzanne.

"Counselor?"

"Sure," said Laura. "We each have a guidance counselor to deal with anything that comes up outside of our academic studies. You know, behavioral problems and so on . . ."

"Ah yes." I guessed that if this self-contained child had any of those she'd keep them well concealed.

As the children cleared away and loaded the dishwasher—they seemed remarkably well trained—Donald and I sat across the fireplace from each other in the drawing room like an old married couple. Except that somebody like Donald, rangy and relaxed in a designer tracksuit, would never be married to somebody like me, uptight traditional in a navy pleated skirt, a neatly buttoned-up blouse and flesh-colored tights.

Donald asked me if I'd take the children around the corner to school in the morning so that I'd know where to pick up Harry in the afternoon. "Although Laura's meant to leave at three, she's usually got some extracurricular music or drama and I don't like Harry coming home by himself."

"Of course I will." I'm pleased to be of some use in this self-sufficient household.

The American School seems more like a university than an English school. Laura is quickly absorbed into a crowd of friends, who all look so much older than my Sarah. Perhaps it's the campus kit, or maybe it's their urban, international backgrounds. Donald says that a lot of the children's friends have lived in at least three different countries and have had the same number of switcharound parents.

As they clatter up the stairs, I hear one of them say: "Hey Laura, who's she? Is she your new stepmother?" and Laura reply: "Oh no. She's just the housekeeper."

"Ask Mrs. Parsons anything you want to know," Donald had said as he left for the bank this morning. "She's been with us ever since Felicia and I moved here and she knows more about the running of the house than I do."

"More than Laura?" I said.

"Oh sure, a lot more than Laura." Donald looked at me shrewdly. "Don't mind Laura, Ann. She's been . . . I guess devastated is the only word for it, since Felicia left. It seems like the only way she can cope is to kind of take over Felicia's role; it's almost as if she's keeping her mother's job open for her."

"I thought that was what I was supposed to be doing?"

"Sure that's what you'll be doing and I'm grateful." Donald put on his coat and gave my shoulder a reassuring pat. "The kid's only eleven, Ann. Give her a break. This is a hell of a time for all of us."

"I know," I said. "I'm sorry."

"Okay. Take care now, and don't worry if there's nothing in the freezer for dinner. I can always fetch in a takeaway."

What an odd statement. I've never met a man before who gives a thought as to how his food reaches his plate. "I say, Ann, haven't you been a bit heavy-handed with the ginger?" Antony might remark, but it would never occur to him to wonder whether I'd bought his dinner at the delicatessen, dug it out of the deep freeze, or spent the whole day blending and marinating to get that exact piquant flavor he so dislikes.

And why the freezer or the takeaway? Didn't Felicia ever do any cooking? Looking around the kitchen I see that nothing much goes on here except a bit of button pushing. The food cupboards contain unopened packets of mixes to which you add an egg, to show what a great homemaker you are, and lots of jars full of fattening biscuits and jams. There are butter, milk, eggs and fruit juice in the fridge, and something so disgusting that I slam the door on it while I think what it can be. It is a minute piece of blood-stained bone with a tiny piece of flesh hanging off it. A child's tooth, put there, no doubt, by Harry Harman to keep it fresh for the tooth fairy. Remembering all the many times I've gazed fondly at my own children's discarded milk teeth, I feel another comradely twinge of sympathy for Felicia. I'm not sure if I like other people's children much either.

A leggy blonde is draping a satin bomber jacket on the kitchen chair. She looks like an actress . . . the chorus line. Sitting down at the table and lighting a cigarette, the blonde says that she's Su Parsons. Aha, the cleaner. This is not the lovable cockney char I had expected.

"I'm Ann Forester-Jones," I say, "and I've come to look after the house and Laura and Harry." Unnerved by her steady stare, I add foolishly: "Felicia . . . that is . . . Mrs. Harman, is in Wiltshire with my husband and three children."

Mrs. Parsons smiles. "Yeah? I've read about that kind of thing in the papers."

I launch, yet again, into my explanation of why I'm here and Felicia's there. "I'm just acting as a temporary housekeeper until Mrs. Harman comes back."

"Oh really?" Mrs. Parsons blows a sophisticated smoke ring or two to show she's not impressed by this unlikely tale. "I wouldn't have thought you were his type. I'd have expected someone a bit more . . . no offense meant, mind . . . sexy, if you know what I mean."

I know exactly what she means and don't care for it.

"Take Fel now," she says, as I wonder how to stop her, "she's got something about her, hasn't she?"

I'd do almost anything to avoid a scene. I'm the one who apologizes if somebody bumps into me with a wire trolley in the supermarket and am, therefore, as surprised as Mrs. Parsons seems to be when I hear myself making authoritative noises: ". . . and until Mrs. Harman returns I'm in charge here and you'll do as I say or look for a job elsewhere . . ."

Mrs. Parsons shrugs her shoulders, puts on a frilly apron and offers to Do the Usual. As she's wiping the odd stray crumb off a gleaming work surface, she tells me that the local grocer, laundry and dry cleaners deliver once a week, the Wine Society once a month and Town Flowers pop in every few days to keep the flowers nice. I hope they don't all bump into each other on the doorstep.

Going over to the French windows and studying the plants intently, I see that they are in pots. "Isn't there anything actually growing out there, in the ground?"

"Felicia thinks potted plants are easier to manage," says Mrs. Parsons.

Felicia also seems to have found it easier to give up eating. "Where does Mrs. Harman keep her provisions?"

"Doesn't have any, to speak of," says Mrs. Parsons. "You know how these Americans are. They don't do much cooking, not the everyday kind. They buy it in, don't they? Fel, she started off cooking the English way, when I first worked here. She'd make dinners and that but Mr. Harman didn't expect it. So she goes to the Freezer Center once a week and stocks up with their gourmet dinners and gets pizzas, hamburgers, ice cream and that for the kids. They just help themselves, when they get back from school."

"You mean she doesn't cook?"

"Of course she does. She's a lovely cook," says Mrs. Parsons defensively. "You should see the special dinners she does for Mr. Harman's business friends. That table looks like something out of a magazine by the time she's finished."

So . . . Felicia Harman's meals are just for show, like everything else about her. I ask for the names of the best shops in the area and make out a list. I may not appear to have much about me, but at least I can see to it that those children are given decent, nourishing food.

Harry takes my hand as we walk home from school. He's a pleasant child really, in spite of his tooth.

"I've got your tea ready."

"Oh great. What is it?"

"It's fish. Smoked haddock. It's very nice."

Harry sniffs it suspiciously, as though I'm slipping him a dish of poison. "I don't like fish."

"It's good for you," I say encouragingly.

"Momma never makes us eat fish . . ."

The child's lips are beginning to tremble, and I speak bracingly of proteins and vitamins and how, if he eats up his fish, he will grow up to be tall and strong and handsome.

Harry says he doesn't want to be tall and strong and handsome. He wants a pizza, preferably a tuna and tomato pizza and chocolate ice cream for dessert.

"But that kind of food is fattening . . ." I begin, and wish I hadn't as Harry gets up and bolts out of the kitchen. "I'm *not* fat,"

I can hear him sobbing as he scrambles up the stairs. "My momma doesn't think I'm fat . . ."

"Harry . . ."

"Go away, go *away* . . ." and as he reaches the top floor, there's a mutinous sob followed by a muffled "Anyway, *you* can't talk. You're fat and . . . ugly."

I clear away the haddock. There isn't even a cat in this soulless house to eat up the fish.

Laura comes in an hour later. "Hi, Ann. Where's Harry?"

"He's in his room." I fetch another plate for Laura. "He wouldn't eat his tea. It's smoked haddock, cooked in milk."

Laura takes the plate from me, and I'm just thinking, Thank goodness she isn't going to be difficult, when she walks across the kitchen, tips the haddock in the sink and switches on the waste disposal. That's the second hot meal it's had this afternoon.

"We don't eat fish," she says, "and we like to get our own tea, thank you, Ann. I'd better go upstairs and see to Harry."

"Hi there." Donald sheds his coat, tie and briefcase as he comes in. "How did it go today?" He looks round. "Where are the kids?"

It would be sensible to say that everything went a treat and the children are upstairs happily watching television, but I feel the need of an adult ally.

"I've had a bloody day, thank you, and both the children refused to eat the meal I cooked for them."

"Well, that was nice of you, Ann." Donald, a practiced chairman, is picking up the positive and disregarding the negative. "Felicia doesn't usually bother. She says life is too short to waste time preparing food that nobody wants."

"Oh, does she? Perhaps that's why Harry is overweight," I say unwisely.

"She said he was fat." Laura appears in the doorway, Harry close behind, anticipating a lively scene.

Descending to child level, I tell Donald that Harry wouldn't eat his fish and then Laura was extremely rude and threw hers down the waste disposal, and see at once that Donald is not an ally but a father.

Putting an affectionate arm around each child, he says: "We'll talk about that later, if we may, Ann. Now come along, you two. That's quite enough. Tell Ann you're sorry and we'll go upstairs and you can tell me what happened in school today."

"Sorry," says Harry automatically.

"I'm not." Laura looks at me defiantly. "She shouldn't have said that about Harry."

"Would you like to eat now or shall I just chuck your dinner straight down the sink?" I ask Donald later.

"I'm sure it will be very good, Ann." He is not smiling and, as he forks the fish fastidiously around his plate, gives me a lecture about the psychological dangers of making Harry self-conscious about his weight problem.

I don't bother to argue and, for the next few days, continue serving the children fresh vegetables, salads and fruit and making tempting low-calorie meals. God knows, there's nothing else to do in this house. I can't think how Felicia managed to fill in her days. Lounging in bed with other people's husbands, I suppose.

Laura and Harry greet even an ungarnished lamb chop with pursed lips and, when Donald comes home, whine and complain, and manage to convey the message that I'm starving them.

Eventually, Donald says: "Let them eat what they like, Ann. They're healthy enough and I can't face this sort of atmosphere every evening."

Having won the food battle, the children embark enthusiastically on the "why should I go to bed when you say so?" campaign and swiftly follow that with the "I'm not going to tidy my room, so there" tactic. It's easier to give in, and Donald says he's pleased we're all getting on so well.

The trouble with looking after other people's children is that you can't lash out at them.

"Do you have any dirty clothes for the washing machine, Laura?"

An insolent shrug: "I dunno."

If it had been Sarah I'd have yelled, "Well, bloody go and look," and it wouldn't have mattered because she knows I love her. I can't risk a row with these children. At the merest glint of discipline they're on the phone to Felicia (". . . she's always picking on me, Momma . . .") or lobbying Donald.

"Why don't you show a bit of understanding, Ann? You've got children of your own. You know how difficult they can be at this age."

Mr. Dwyer would approve the situation. So far as Donald Harman is concerned I am, as his daughter remarked, just a housekeeper. We are not thrashing about in bed together, reveling in the delights of adultery; we hardly see each other. Donald leaves at seven-thirty most mornings for breakfast meetings or "to get some work done before that damn phone starts ringing" and is rarely home before nine in the evening. "With New York five hours behind us I can't get hold of anyone before midafternoon." If his sexual needs are being satisfied it certainly isn't at Acacia Road. There's a woman called Marcia who occasionally phones and asks for him in a proprietorial manner. I suppose that she's entertaining him on the evenings he doesn't return to the uneventful suppers he shares with me over the shiny white table in Felicia's kitchen.

Felicia

"Do you realize it is our three months' anniversary," Antony murmurs from behind me, as I gaze critically at myself in the looking glass.

"Have I been here three months already? It can't be that long."

"Three months to the day, and what a way to celebrate."

"Oh God, I hope it goes off all right. The food will be smashing, that's no problem. Mrs. Simmons is a brick—she's coming in to do the vegetables and serve so I can concentrate on Mr. Kapperman. Do you think he'll like me? Such a marvelous part, darling, you're brilliant."

"If he doesn't love you he'll be made of stone."

"Oh, that's nice, darling, but I must get *dressed*. Off you go and let me concentrate. What about the wine?"

Mr. Kapperman is an American tycoon whose firm is sponsoring one of those TV extended series. He is over here with the director in search of a patrician-type Englishwoman, beautiful yet steely, intelligent and sensual with it. I have read one of the scripts, and I know everybody laughs at soaps, but she's a really complicated, interesting character, and I ache to play her. And the money sounds astronomical to me. A lot of it will be filmed in England, so I wouldn't have to be away too much. It would be simply too perfect, if it came off. And it will, I know it will.

And it's all due to Antony, the old clever. He met this Kapperman at some do in London, and succeeded in selling him the idea that Felicia Harman is the one woman in England who embodies Flame Carraway. (That's something I'll have to learn to live with, but nothing's perfect. "Flame, Flame, you bewitching devil," I murmur to the looking glass. "It's not funny," I add severely.)

Antony has inveigled Kapperman, Mrs. Kapperman, and the director, Sol Venture, down to spend a night. I really do not believe these show biz names, they must make them up as they go along.

The setting, of course, is perfect. White Walls is a classic example of eighteenth-century architecture, with the original privy thirty yards from the house. The children keep their bicycles in it. The grounds are beautiful; old walled orchards, ancient recumbent mulberry trees, sudden surprising views of herbaceous borders through arches. If I can't look patrician yet sensual here, I don't deserve the part.

"Oh Felly, you look like a *princess.*" Emmy looks pretty good too. She is wearing her best dress, and comes and stands in front of the looking glass with me. I really do love Emmy; she is so good-natured and affectionate.

But it ought to be Laura admiring my Joseph Tricot with me.

Sarah wanders in. She is wearing old jeans and a rather awful Sex Pistols T-shirt, and still succeeds in looking rangily elegant.

"What a lot of fuss for some crummy Americans," she says. "I hope they won't worry Larkspur—she's due to whelp any day now."

"I should keep her in the kitchen—nice and peaceful there."

Nine weeks ago, Larkspur and I got up at four in the morning. I was in a terrible mood, it was pitch-black outside, and I wondered how Larkspur would react to being put in the car in the middle of the night. In fact she greeted me with extravagant joy, stood reasonably still while I put on her collar and lead, and trotted eagerly out through the kitchen door.

Sarah had got up to say good-bye (not to me, of course). I overheard her whisper "Oh baby, I do hope you like him," which made me feel tearful, for some silly reason.

I drove for hours up the M4, round the North Circular, onto the A10, Newmarket and northeast. As the dawn started to come up I had that disconcerting feeling of driving in a foreign country, that if I stopped to ask for directions they'd answer me in a language I didn't understand. I hadn't got round to having the clutch repaired, my knee was agony by the time I got to Thetford and started following Mr. Barrow's instructions. We achieved 14 Apple-tree Close at eight forty-five and waited in the car with Larkspur on my good knee looking cheerfully out of the window. At nine, I said, "Oh well, better get on with it," and got out and rang the front-door bell. Larkspur stood on her hind legs affectionately pawing my knee, her eyes shining with trusting goodwill. I felt like a traitor.

It was about eight hours later that I finally rounded the last corner and saw, through fatigue-blurred eyelids, the gates of home. My knee juddered every time I changed gear, my hands were shaking, and I had a headache. Larkspur, on the other hand, was contentedly asleep on the passenger seat. She was dreaming; her eyes rolled and she whimpered occasionally, no doubt reliving her triumph of this morning.

"The first thing I must do when I get home," I thought, "is ring up the Barrows and find out how that poor dog is."

The Forester-Joneses en masse were watching out for us and poured out of the front door as I pulled up and put on the brake.

"Larky, darling, how are you, baby? . . . Did she get married, Felly? Did she fall in love at first sight? . . . Poor Larkspur, I expect you're exhausted, aren't you?"

"Never mind about Larkspur," I snarled, "I need an exceptionally large drink and a lot of quiet. Antony, that bloody car. If it's not serviced tomorrow I shall set fire to it. I've never been so tired . . ."

I staggered into the library and Antony poured me an extravagant whiskey.

"Bad as that, was it?"

I looked round cautiously, but the children had accompanied Larkspur to the kitchen.

"The moment they opened their front door and she saw their dog, she went berserk. Snarling and raving and snapping. So Mr. Barrow said we should take them for a walk so they could get to know each other. Antony, people crossed the road when they saw us coming. She bit my leg once, when I got in the way. It wasn't all that amusing at the time." He could stop that grinning for a start, I thought, I'll have a terrible bruise tomorrow.

"Please don't laugh, darling, it was awful. I suppose I thought we'd let them loose in the garden and they would sort of recognize each other. I thought it would be beautiful and natural." I took a hefty gulp of whiskey.

"My poor angel. Sarah and I have arranged supper, so . . ."

"He kept on talking about his dog's private parts all the time. He kept on saying, 'We don't want Teddy ruptured, do we?' Honestly, and after it was all over she slipped her collar and went for him. I must ring them up, he was covered in blood . . ."

When I rang next day Mrs. Barrow was surprisingly good-natured.

"Oh, that's all right, Mrs. Harman. He's still limping a bit but his eyelid's stopped bleeding. Got a lot of spirit, your little bitch. Let us know when the pups are born and George will come over and choose one."

Every day since then Sarah and Emily (and, to a certain extent, Mark) have peered searchingly at Larkspur. "She looks a bit fatter to me, what do you think? Have you noticed she isn't moving so quickly? That means she's instinctively taking care . . . Would you say her teats are distended, Felly?"

"I wouldn't know," I said shortly, "I didn't study them all that closely before."

I had dutifully reported to Ann by telephone. Considering all the instructions she'd issued, she had the nerve to snap my head off. She'd obviously lost interest in the dog, and when she told me her news, I could see why. She'd told me she was moving in with Donald; "He simply can't cope by himself. I should have thought you'd be glad to hear that someone is looking after your children."

"I speak to the children every day, and I've been up to see them—"

"We are on the defensive, aren't we?"

On the defensive? Of course I was on the defensive. Some arbitrary organization of hormones had caused me unnaturally to desert my young before they were naturally ready to desert me. It was bad enough talking to Harry on the phone. "It's so boring without you, Momma," he said, "Pop's so grumpy every night. He's got this lady to cook and look after us. I don't like her, she smells funny and all we ever get to eat is stew. She doesn't let me watch *St. Elsewhere* . . ." Worse talking to Laura. "Don't worry, Momma, everything's going to be all right. I know you wouldn't have gone if you hadn't had to. It's our fault really, we all took you for granted. I'm sorry, Momma, I didn't know you were unhappy. Please can I come and live with you soon?"

"Laura darling, don't talk like that. Of course it's not your fault. I'm going to sort things out very soon. You'd love it here . . ."

But how can I sort things out? If it ever came to court, who would get custody? Kind solid Donald, the innocent party . . . or the adulterous wife whose four-year-old son once spent days in hospital because of her negligence?

I took Larkspur in to see the vet five weeks after the mating. To my eyes she looked ominously slim. The thought of having puppies messing up the kitchen floor doesn't appeal much; but after all that effort I shall be quite cross if it doesn't work. The vet was very brisk and irritating.

"Nothing here, Mrs. er, oh, Harman."

"Are you sure?"

"Which day did you mate her? Ninth? . . . too early. Ten to fourteen, I always advise. No, you're not pregnant, are you, lass?"

Larkspur and I went and collected the children.

"What did the vet say?"

"Sarah, I'm sorry. He doesn't think she's pregnant." Emily cried and Sarah looked out of the window.

"Perhaps she's on the pill," said Mark. Nobody laughed.

Sucks to that vet, I think now, while I am applying judicious amounts of well-bred English eyeliner. Right after he'd seen Larkspur, Mrs. Simmons went on holiday. She came back a week later.

"Sarah, you've grown an inch. Got some chocolate from the duty-free for you. And you, Emmy, don't eat it all at once, now. Mark . . . my goodness, look at Larkspur. Where were you when the lights went out, you naughty girl?"

"Oh, Mrs. Simmons—do you think she's going to have puppies?"

"She's the size of a house, look at her."

"But the vet said . . ."

"Vets," said Mrs. Simmons. "They're no better than doctors, when you get down to it."

The Kapperman car is coming up the drive. The Kapperman chauffeur—oh Lord, where is he going to sleep?—has leapt out, opened doors, and is unloading great bales of luggage. However long do they think they're staying for?

Antony and I float out of the front door, radiating gracious-living bonhomie from every pore.

"Mr. Kapperman! How wonderful to see you again . . . and

what beautiful weather you've brought with you . . . May I introduce—" Antony pauses, in order to get the right note of reverence
into his voice, "Felicia Harman."

There is not much you can do with "How do you do? I've been
looking forward so much to meeting you." But I think I manage to
get across banked fires of sensuality with a steely shaft of intellect.
And of course I'm as gracious as all get-out.

"Mr. Kapperman . . . Mr. Venture, how lovely, do come in
. . . I'll get someone" (who?) "to help your driver with your luggage."

"Now wait a minute, honey," says Mrs. Kapperman, "not all
this needs to go up to our room, though I wouldn't like to leave it
in the car overnight. After we visit with you we are going to stay
with some very dear friends in Edinburgh. That's what these cases
are for. All we need here is this and this. Our chauffeur is staying
in that dear little public house in the village," she adds, to my
relief.

"In that case," says Antony, "my daughter Sarah will show you
up to your room, and then we'll all have drinks on the lawn."

"Be still my beating heart," mutters Sarah rudely. Fortunately
neither the Kappermans nor her father overhears her; though judging by the quick flick of a glance Sol Venture gives her, he has both
heard and approved. I have only spent a few seconds with Mr.
Kapperman, but I have gained the impression that he could be a
testy traveling companion. Larkspur erupts into the hall. Mr. Venture gets behind Mr. Kapperman quite quickly.

"That is a pit bull," he says, "they are dangerous."

"Actually," Sarah says, "she's a perfectly safe Staff—"

"Better in the kitchen anyway, Sarah," I say. "Take her, would
you, and I'll take everyone upstairs."

By the time the Kapperman party have reached their rooms,
exclaimed at the antiquity of it all, exclaimed even more enthusiastically at the modernity of the bathrooms, and come downstairs
again, we are Antony and Felicia; they are Morris and Lady and
Sol.

"Her real name is Patricia," says Morris, "but I call her Lady
because that is what she is. A real lady."

"What a very beautiful thought, Morris," I say, to my undying
shame. But it goes down very well with everyone except Sol, who is
gazing sardonically into the distance, and Sarah, who is standing

out of view of everyone except me, and is doing her celebrated imitation of throwing up.

We fall into quite a long conversation about English trees. Antony swears the one we are sitting under was planted in 1800, though I don't see how he could possibly know that.

Sol looks up apprehensively; he is almost certainly calculating how long that branch has to go before it falls down on him.

"And what have you been doing since we met?" says Antony. "Have you seen some good shows?"

While Antony leads them to the dining room, I nip off to check the kitchen; Emmy and Mark are sitting at the table having their supper while good Mrs. Simmons bustles round them. They have observed the Kapperman arrival from the playroom window.

"Haven't they brought a lot of luggage, Felly?" Emmy says.

"It's all right. Most of it isn't for here. They're going on somewhere else after us. Where did I put the spoon for the smoked salmon mousse? Oh, here it is. Emmy, could you take the toast in?"

"Who's the bum-chum?" asks Mark.

"What a vile expression. I suppose you mean Mr. Venture. He is a very important TV director in America, so . . ."

"So no jokes about gays, I get it."

"I should hope no jokes about gays anyway. Ready, Em?"

It is all going terribly well. The Kappermans love our dining room (well, Lady loves it at some length, and Morris nods agreeably as she burbles), love the view from it—"Just look at that horse standing there under that tree . . . a perfect Stubbs" (even Rocket is on my side tonight)—and I shall be very surprised if they don't love my food.

My excellent mousse, wrapped in slices of more smoked salmon, is very warmly greeted indeed. Morris takes a large mouthful and says: "My heavens, Lady, would you just taste this? Felicia, I raise my glass to you." Antony beams approval, they all raise their glasses to me, and Morris and Sol exchange a tiny look. I know quite certainly that they are going to offer me the part.

Here is Emmy. I wonder what she wants. She is extraordinarily pretty with the evening light falling on her, and she waits composedly until we are all looking at her. I think, and not for the first time, that that child will be wasted if she doesn't go into the theater.

"Felly, Sarah says Larkspur's waters broke ages ago and nothing's happened yet. Should she send for the vet? Would you come and have a look?"

Bloody Sarah. Are there no lengths she won't go to in order to mess me up?

"One of our dogs is expecting puppies," I explain, with a charming little shrug that says "you know children."

"Emmy, I can't possibly come now. I'm sure she's all right. It's a perfectly natural process."

"But Felly . . ."

"Run along, darling," says Antony pleasantly.

But Emmy can't run along, because Lady, enchanted by this further evidence of the quaintness of English country life, is questioning her closely. "Where is the little dog having her puppies? In the butler's pantry? My, do you have a butler?"

Emmy explains that people had butlers in the Old Days, but we don't and the butler's pantry is nice and quiet away from the other dogs. And adds that if only Felly would come and have a very quick look, Sarah and she wouldn't worry anymore. Morris opts to take a humorous stance: "I guess you're needed in the labor ward, Felicia, but don't be long. This room needs a beautiful woman"—Lady's eyes narrow slightly—"so you hurry back, now."

I hesitate; I know Antony thinks I should stay. But something in the rigid way Emmy is standing makes me feel I ought to have a look. After all, I'll only be a minute.

Ann

"Giving a party, are you?" Su Parsons sees me poring over cookbooks, like a child trying to wrest the secrets of trigonometry from a school textbook. "Fel did some lovely dinners. She did a lobster Thermidor once and chicken in a pineapple shell. It looked a picture."

"I'm sure it did."

This morning Donald announced that he had to give a formal dinner party on Friday.

"Can you manage it, Ann? There'll be ten of us. Our vice president is over here with his wife. I'll be taking them out to dinner and the theater and so on, but I really should have them home to meet one or two of our most important clients."

"I expect I can." I'd rather got out of the habit of dinner parties. With Antony only home for a couple of nights a week, it had seemed so much simpler to pay off social debts with a big barbecue party in the summer and a champagne buffet around Christmastime, but I had had a certain success with my dinners when I'd lived in London. "Yes, of course I can."

"That's great, Ann. And it goes without saying that I'd appreciate it if you would act as hostess and join us for the theater."

I've been trying since then to decide what to panic about first, my appearance or the food.

Donald had suggested I get Su Parsons in to serve and clear up and this aspect of the evening also fills me with gloomy foreboding. Looking at her skin-tight yellow satin trousers and purple leg warmers, I venture: "And what are you planning to wear on Friday?"

She bridles. "Oh, you don't have to worry about me. Fel gave me a really nice black dress, low at the front, and a big white apron and I've got some black tights; those new ones with the seams down the back, and a lovely pair of high-heeled sandals, kind of strappy, from Saxone."

She gazes disparagingly at my tweed skirt and brogues. "What are *you* going to wear is more to the point," and snaps on the vacuum cleaner with a rebellious click.

"Why, hot grapefruit. What a cute idea." When I'd given Donald the dinner party menu for him to choose the appropriate wines, I'd forgotten to mention that the grapefruit would be grilled. I hope it goes with his chilled Pouilly Fuissé, but suspect it doesn't by the way he's shifting the grapefruit segments around his mouth, like Antony about to inquire if there's a hint of ginger in it. There is, as a matter of fact.

To follow, I'd made a *boeuf bourguignon*. Su, tripping in on pinhigh heels and revealing more cleavage fallout than a Playboy bunny, serves it with small new potatoes and fresh broccoli. The veg is okay but the bourguignon tastes like school stew. It is a complicated recipe and I have been marinating it in wine and herbs for several days.

"How delicious, dear. Is this one of your wonderful English stews?" politely asks Nancy Schulberg, the vice president's wife.

"No, it's boeuf bourguignon," I smile back, mentally making a note that next time Julia Child can come round and marinate her own wretched recipe.

The ladies all leave neat piles of meat and gravy at the side of their plates. The men, either mesmerized by Su's splendid breasts or unused to such simple schoolboy fare, scoff the lot.

"It is a long time since I have eaten such an excellent stew," compliments the Nigerian finance minister. "At Charterhouse we were given stew every Thursday, but not to touch yours, Mrs. Harman."

"Mrs. Forester-Jones . . . boeuf bourguignon," I murmur defensively.

The Important Client on my left is called Bob McMahon, and he and his wife, Maddie, run an international chain of hotels and conference centers. I'd already decided that I liked Mr. McMahon.

"Don't you worry," he says encouragingly. "It's delicious, whatever it is. And the waitress is sensational. Where did you find her?"

"In the kitchen, when I arrived," I reply curtly. If there are any compliments going around here I'd prefer to collect them for myself, not by proxy for Su. "She's Mrs. Harman's daily woman."

By the way Bob McMahon grins, I know he's decided against making the obvious retort that she could be his woman any day.

"I'm glad you didn't say it."

He grins again. "So am I. And it wouldn't have been true either. A bit over the top for my taste." He raises a hand in instant apology. "Sorry, sorry. There's almost nothing you can say about that young woman which doesn't produce a double entendre."

Over the top Su Parsons may be, but I'm aware that Felicia's daringly low-cut, sleek black dress is more suitable for this dinner party than my Laura Ashley. Not only am I the only woman in the room sprigged like a wallpaper, I am also the only one with her skirt twirling around the ankles.

"Are you ready for the dessert, madam?" Su is back with a dish of succulent early strawberries and my hard-worked crème brûlée.

"Thank you, Su. Perhaps you could serve it for us?"

Bob McMahon is in the middle of describing one of his conference centers—"and, of course, we've got all the latest audio-visual equipment from the States"—when the gentle tapping noise behind my chair changes into an insistent banging, followed by the noise an indiscreet burglar might make cracking a particularly tricky bank vault.

"Excuse me a minute . . . forgive me . . ." At the serving table I find Su hammering ineffectually at the caramel topping of the crème brûlée with the handle of the bread knife.

"I can't get the bloody thing to crack," she hisses. Dodging Donald's raised eyebrow of inquiry, I flash the guests my loveliest smile. "Mrs. Parsons will help you to the strawberries. I'll be back in a minute."

In the kitchen I find that Su is absolutely right. The bloody thing won't crack, not even with forceful stabs from the freezer knife. Sweat dots the Laura Ashley, a combination of sheer physical effort and anxiety. If I do manage to crack the pudding, what appalling injuries might I inflict on the vice president, the Important Clients and their Ladies as they chew politely on fragments of glass-sharp caramel?

Dipping the freezer knife into boiling water, I carefully insert it under the caramel top and lift it like a manhole cover. Now it looks like the semolina pudding Sarah brought home to us so proudly after her first cookery lesson. There is no concealing cream in the fridge, so I slosh two pots of strawberry yogurt over the top.

Su looks surprised as I hand her the plate and ask her to pass it round.

"What on earth's all this muck on top of it?" she whispers loudly. I hope that Donald will find Crème Strawberry Yogurt every bit as cute as hot grapefruit and turn my attention to the man on my right.

"We were just discussing the influence of Béjart on Maguy Marin's current work," he says, drawing me politely into the conversation.

Oh, how I long to be back at White Walls watching *Miami Vice,* but say cleverly: "And what was your conclusion?"

For the rest of dinner the conversation roams from the ballet (Béjart and Marin turn out to be choreographers) through everyone's reaction to Cox's South Indian sculpture at the Tate ("A powerful metaphor," pronounces the Nigerian finance minister's wife. I wish I'd thought of that) to the role of the critic in contemporary cinema. I have little to say on that subject, either, since the last film I'd seen was *E.T.* and I'd missed most of that because Emmy kept bursting into tears.

And when Nancy Schulberg compliments me on the decor of my

lovely home ("White is so restful in a world where there is too much sensory input . . ."), I suggest that coffee might be a nice idea.

Upstairs, we move on to politics and I, emboldened by brandy, say that I find it hard to take Neil Kinnock seriously because of the way this Socialist politician combs his hair sideways over the bald bit.

Maddie McMahon acts as though I'd thrown her a lifeline; perhaps she also thought Béjart and Marin sounded like a couple of French revolutionaries. *"Exactly,"* she says, "it's such a very public display of vanity, isn't it?" We are both about to dive enthusiastically into the psychological aspects of this fascinating topic, when we notice, simultaneously, the dozen or so sandy strands of hair trained hopefully across the bald head of Vice President Charles Schulberg.

"What a lovely dress," says Maddie. "Laura Ashley, isn't it?"

"I'm sorry, Donald," I murmur, piling glasses onto a tray, "I'm sorry."

"What for?" He seems genuinely surprised.

"Well, the dinner . . . and everything . . ."

Donald pours us both another brandy. "The dinner was okay. That grapefruit was a surprise, but I was crazy about the iced yogurt dessert. I don't recall having that before."

"I don't suppose you'll have it again." I explain about the impenetrable pudding and, laughing, Donald sits down on the sofa, patting the cushion beside him.

"Come here." He puts a companionable arm around my shoulders. "Stop *worrying,* Ann. You worry too much about everything . . . all of us." Putting down his brandy, he kisses me and I find myself kissing him back, grateful that the ordeal is over.

Drawing away slightly, Donald says: "I'd always wondered who it was Charles Schulberg reminded me of. I always thought it was Robert Robinson, but of course you're right . . . Neil Kinnock."

We fall, laughing, into each other's arms. It all seems so easy and right, and as we go upstairs Donald says: "The master bedroom, I think . . . further from the children."

The Laura Ashley lies on the floor, a pool of country colors disturbing Felicia's pristine white decor. Donald is in bed, waiting for me. He looks younger and thinner without his city outfit.

"Oh, Donald." I move very close to him, to stop him looking too long and lingeringly at my body. "Oh Donald, I'm sorry . . ."

He takes his hand away from my thigh and falls back on his pillow. "And what are you sorry about now, for heaven's sake?"

"I'm not slim . . . like Felicia . . ."

"Oh Ann"—Donald's hand is curved appreciatively around my breast—"what's so wonderful about you is that you are absolutely nothing at all like Felicia."

Donald is still sleeping as I creep back to my own room and lie there, brooding about how we'll manage to adjust our expressions for breakfast. Difficult to look like a respectable city banker and his equally correct housekeeper over the frozen orange juice, when you've spent half the night enjoying each other's bodies in a warm, tumbled bed.

I feel glowingly alive for the first time in years. Sex with Antony had become a comfortable habit. With Donald it's as physically invigorating as a plunge in the surf after a workout at the gym. Another plus of Donald's lovemaking is that he doesn't wear pajamas. I'd always found Marks & Spencer's Poly-Cotton inhibiting; I wonder if Antony wears them when he's in bed with Felicia?

"Morning Ann, morning Laura. Good, Harry, glad to see you're up for once."

There isn't a hint of delicious debauchery about Donald. He's almost aggressively brisk. Oh dear, I do hope he isn't regretting last night, or worse still, was too drunk to remember.

"Now, you two . . . I'm taking Ann to the theater tonight so you, Laura, can bring Harry back from school and Ann will arrange for Miss Jamieson to come in and keep an eye on you."

"Oh no, Poppa, not her . . . must we, Ann?"

I am ridiculously pleased that at least Laura likes me better than poor Miss Mouse.

Donald and I both arrive early at the theater. He takes my hand and draws me to his side. "I loved loving you, Ann. May we do it again?"

We're soon joined by Nancy and Charles Schulberg and, to my delight, Maddie and Bob McMahon, and take our seats: center front stalls.

I am totally astonished that such explicit sadistic porn is allowed in the all too live theater and would quite welcome Mrs.

Whitehouse standing up and having a firm word about it. "I'm missing *Cagney & Lacey* for this rubbish," I think resentfully.

"Isn't it darling? So stimulating. And don't you love these young people's honesty?" enthuses Nancy Schulberg over the interval champagne. I manage an embarrassed nod and Maddie murmurs: "Load of filth, isn't it?" We both giggle.

Later, in the restaurant's ladies' room, which is done up in pink and green taffeta like a turn-of-the-century bordello, Maddie hands me a packet. "They're the brochures and publicity handouts we had done for our last conference center," she says. "I don't think they work. Would you mind having a look at them, and let me know what you think?"

"Oh, but I couldn't . . ."

"Come on, Ann," she says, "you used to be in advertising, you told me so last night. And you're looking for something to do. Why don't you give it a try. Read through these and see if you can spot where we've gone wrong."

"Oh, but I haven't . . ."

"For heaven's sake, Ann. Just read it, that's all . . . and if you come up with any new ideas call me."

I take the packet. But only because it would be rude not to.

1985

Felicia

A very tempting thought has occurred to me. It involves the new potatoes left over from last night, and great dollops of Sainsbury's French mayonnaise. Not that there's much I can do about it for the moment, though; I am rather pinned down.

I am lying on the library sofa tucked up in a traveling rug. Larkspur is in her usual place, notched between me and the back of the sofa. Her head is on my shoulder and she is snoring. Her beautiful daughter is draped across my stomach, and I shift her gently. I am only four months pregnant, but Kitten does weigh twenty-eight pounds, a bit much for a fetus to put up with. Kitten's official Kennel Club name is Meadow Dancer. (Thought up, I add hastily, by Sarah and Emmy—though I must admit that when she runs through long grass she does leap up to see where she's going in the most beguiling way. I am quite besotted by her, and have been since I first saw her.)

"What a commotion you caused the night you were born," I say fondly.

They flap their tails lazily at the sound of my voice, and I go back to pretending to do the *Times* crossword. I shall be asleep quite soon. One of the really lovely things about being pregnant is that people keep on sternly telling you to rest after lunch. I'm so warm and so comfortable and so terribly happy, now that I'm married to Antony. His baby twitches slightly, that marvelous early movement that everybody tells you is wind or a nerve or something, but you know it isn't because you know your baby better than they do.

I was not only irritated when I left the Kappermans in the dining room to go and look at Larkspur, I was also rather apprehensive. As it happened, I had never actually seen anything being born. My own babies were Cesarean ("I wouldn't count on getting an orange through your pelvic girdle," my obstetrician said, flatteringly implying that I was both small and fragile).

Of course I had seen birth on television; protracted labor with a lot of noise in plays, tidy labor with a lot of efficiency in documentaries. I had even, as a young actress, played the part of a nurse telling the heroine of a costume drama Not to Bear Down Yet, Baby's Head Hasn't Presented. None of this was of any practical use, though; I didn't know much, but I knew Larkspur wouldn't be on her back moaning.

I found when I went into the butler's pantry that Larkspur was sitting about looking bored. Sarah and Emmy were the ones suffering birth pangs. Sarah was so worried she talked to me like a person for the first time since we'd met.

"Oh, Felicia, it says in the book that if nothing's happened after two hours' straining, expert help should be summoned."

We both looked at Larkspur, who yawned and lay down.

"Darling, she's not straining. Look at her . . . nothing's going to happen for hours." And I've just called you "darling" for the first time and you haven't reacted, I thought. "Look, I must get back, it's too rude, leaving them. Call me if anything . . . oh, here's Mark. Mark, be an angel and come and get me if . . ."

Larkspur got to her feet, looking surprised. She panted and hunched and pushed, and a little black packet fell on to the floor. It was shiny as though wrapped in cling-film, and I'd never seen such a professional performance in my life.

But it didn't move. Oh God, I thought, what rotten luck. I must get the children out of here.

"Sarah, would you take Mark and Emmy to see if everything's all right in the kitchen?" I said, making an urgent, one-grown-up-to-another face.

Sarah didn't see my signal. She was watching Larkspur ripping the cling-film off the puppy and licking it briskly. Poor thing, I thought, she hasn't realized . . .

The puppy sneezed and mewed and lifted a wavering head. And I stood there like a fool with tears in my eyes. But it didn't matter, because Sarah's eyes were shining too. Mark looked at us, surprised.

"But that was nice—why should happy things make people cry?"

"We know, don't we, Felly?" said Sarah, and I wondered what she would do if I hugged her. I didn't take the risk.

"What is it?" I said practically.

Sarah lifted a floppy hind leg and said, "Bother, it's a dog."

Emmy said, "Supposing all her puppies are boys? Dogs, I mean. We won't be able to keep one."

"Larkspur's far too intelligent to produce only male offspring."

"Hey, watch it," Mark said.

"Tennis balls to you," I said, and he grinned.

Mrs. Simmons put her head round the door.

"I've taken the lamb in, Mrs. Harman, and Mr. Forester-Jones is looking . . ."—she lowered her voice—"a bit short, if you know what I mean. Oh, isn't he sweet, what a clever girl."

"Sarah, come and get me for the next one. I must get back, what a nuisance."

When I went back to the dining room, I realized I was no longer Mrs. Wonderful. I had turned into Miss Could Be All Right If She Pulls Her Socks Up.

Lady's smile was very faintly glassy, Sol was eyeing Morris apprehensively, and Antony was telling an amusing story that revealed how well he knew several members of the royal family.

Morris gave me a heavy look. "You were longer than I expected, Felicia."

"Oh, Morris, I am so sorry. Bit of an emergency, actually, I was rather worried. But she's had a lovely little—"

"Sol and I were discussing the possibility of shooting part of the action here, darling," said Antony. "He feels, and I am sure he is right, that an authentic old house would be so much better than—"

"How marvelous," I said, "what fun. Those would be the scenes where she backflashes to her previous incarnation as a confidante of Beau Brummell?"

How trivial it all sounded, after what I'd just watched.

The Welsh lamb, spiked with garlic and rosemary, was going down well; so were our own new potatoes and Bejam's frozen minted peas, which I shamelessly declared I'd picked that morning. Antony was circulating apparently endless supplies of excellent wine; Morris was smiling again. He patted my knee under the table. He'd forgiven me, and I was supposed to be grateful.

Larkspur had pricked her ears and looked at her puppy as though she couldn't believe it. I had exactly the same feeling when

I first saw Laura and Harry. Would I really enjoy working with this pompous piece of self-importance? He plainly intended to interfere a lot; I felt a pang for poor Sol.

"As I see it, Felicia," Morris was saying, "the inward motivation of those scenes is going to have to be strong. Very strong indeed. This girl, seeking her identity through the centuries, and yet very much a woman of today, we mustn't forget that, has to speak to us with the authentic voice of the England of Cromwell . . ." (Sol looked uneasy) ". . . the England of the Industrial Revolution, of Dickens, of—"

Sarah put her head round the door.

"Quick, Felly, or you'll miss it."

"Right, just coming. Back in a sec, do help yourselves."

The second one was taking longer than the first. Its paws had appeared, but Larkspur seemed to have lost interest in the proceedings. Sarah picked up *Breeding Your First Litter,* which instantly fell open at "Possible Problems During Whelping." "It says here that it may be necessary to . . ."

"No, look, here we go."

It was a bitch, and it had a white patch on its chest to match its paws.

"Can we keep this one, Felly?"

"I should think so, if Sarah agrees . . . isn't it beautiful?"

Sarah stood up and hugged me. I very nearly cried again. "I'm so glad you were here, I was so frightened it might go wrong. I'm sorry about those Americans."

"I can't tell you how boring they are."

"Are you going to work for them?"

Was I? Probably not. I doubted that Morris would even consider hiring an actress who found puppies more fascinating than Morris J. Kapperman, noted wit and raconteur. I picked up *Breeding Your First Litter,* and riffled through it.

"I suppose I'd better go back . . . good heavens, how interesting, I didn't know they did that."

Antony was looking frankly thunderous. Sol and Lady exchanged worried looks. Morris was sulking.

"Morris . . . you're not going to be cross with me, are you? The miracle of birth, you know, so *immediate.* Do have some more lamb." Morris greedily picked up the serving fork.

"Do you know they actually eat the afterbirth? So practical, nature; full of vitamins to keep them going until they can hunt."

Morris put the fork down again and said he didn't believe he would have any more, thank you. I avoided catching Antony's eye.

The children helped me clear the table and bring in the summer pudding. Perhaps it would soften Morris's heart, I thought vaguely, but I wasn't all that bothered.

"I say," said Sarah, "the atmosphere in there . . . the look on Dad's face. He's furious with you, isn't he, and it's my fault."

"Nonsense, of course it isn't your fault."

The summer pudding didn't get a chance to work its magic. Morris was called to the phone just as Lady helped herself, gallantly pretending that we were all having a perfectly lovely evening and her husband wasn't looking like it was time someone got fired.

"That was my chauffeur," said Morris when he came back, "relaying a call from London. Unfortunately I am needed urgently for a meeting. I am very much afraid," he added, not bothering to look afraid at all, "that we are going to have to leave you good folks. Another time, maybe . . ."

"Oh, but Morris," Antony stood up, "we've hardly started to discuss—"

Don't waste your time, darling, I thought, the ship's sinking and the band is playing "Abide with Me." Morris left the dining room with Antony and Sol dodging about at his heels. I stayed with Lady, who calmly poured a lavish helping of cream on her pudding.

"Is this a Queen Anne creamer? . . . beautiful . . . you certainly blew that one, honey."

"Oh, Lady, I'm so sorry. I must have seemed very rude. But . . ."

Lady gave me a shrewd New York look.

"In my experience, people do what they want to do. I think you made a decision tonight, and something tells me you made the right one. Next time I'm over here I'll call you, let's have lunch."

"I'm afraid Morris is awfully cross."

"I can deal with him. I just pretend I'm frightened of him. He likes frightening women, then he feels guilty because he likes it . . . then he goes to Cartier's. You'll have problems with yours, after we've gone."

"I can deal with Antony. I quite like shouting."

Lady polished off her summer pudding, stood up and gave me an affectionate kiss.

"I'd better go and help him pack. Runs a multimillion conglomerate, and doesn't know you put shoes at the bottom. Hang in there, sister."

She went upstairs and, considerably cheered by this exchange, I wandered into the hall. Sol was forlornly sitting in a porter's chair that was far too big for him, with his suitcase at his feet.

"Sol, can I get you anything?"

"I would give a lot for a very large whiskey. That's going to be one hell of a drive back to London."

I poured out two very large whiskeys.

"Sol, I do owe you, at least, an apology. Is there anything I can do?"

He hesitated, and looked at me shyly.

"Do you think I could possibly take a look at the puppies? My mother breeds Pekinese in Iowa, you know . . ."

We tiptoed into the butler's pantry, and banged into Sarah, who was rushing out.

"Oh, Felly, thank heavens. Another one's been born, but she's not taking any notice of it. It's still wrapped up . . ."

Sol handed me his glass, knelt down, and skillfully disentangled the puppy from its cling-film.

"Here you are, old lady." He put the puppy in front of Larkspur, who began to lick it. "Is this her first litter? Sometimes they get confused."

Sarah gave him a look of real veneration.

"Sol, how did you know what to do? That was brilliant."

"I've done it dozens of times. My mother breeds Pekes." He washed his hands, took his whiskey back and drank about half of it. "If you want my frank opinion, Felicia, you're well out of it. Morris thinks he's bought the right to act as cultural adviser . . ."

"I was going to ask . . . how are you going to get Beau Brummell, Dickens and Oliver Cromwell into the same scene?"

"Simple. Dickens will be writing about Cromwell and Brummell, and thinking about them in flashback."

"God, you're a craftsman."

We both giggled and drank some more whiskey.

"Seriously, Felicia, I've seen you act, and I would really like to direct you. But not on this one, darling, it's going to be a killer-diller from way back. Here comes another puppy."

Larkspur dealt with this one with professional ease, and lay down so the four of them could suckle.

"I've seen it so many times," said Sol, "and it still knocks me out."

Ann

Poor Antony, I used to think, as he drove off to work, muttering irritably about the boring lunch he was about to endure at Boulestin that day. How fortunate I am, I'd reflect gratefully, as I cleaned, cooked, weeded, laundered, decorated, chauffeured and humored my dear ones, that I am able to stay at home in this lovely village, doing nothing.

What a fool. Why had nobody ever told me about the buzz of excitement, the rush of adrenaline to the ego, when you are being paid to do the work you love? It's even more satisfying than sex, only I wouldn't be mean enough to say that to Donald.

My first reaction, when I looked through the Delphic Hotels and Conference Centers Inc. brochures, was how could they have missed something so obvious? It wasn't the publicity material that was wrong but the whole concept. They'd taken turreted castles and beamed mansions, and modernized the character out of them. The leaflets showed designer-bland bleached wood tables and matching chairs, Teasmaids in the bedrooms and staff dressed up in perky navy and red uniforms, as though they were serving snacks on British Airways.

"But aren't you running a unique asset?" I said to Maddie and Bob, rather diffidently. "Shouldn't you be cashing in on those acres of parkland, the box-hedge herb gardens, clock towers and cobbled courtyards? Selling traditional English hospitality in a historic setting . . . that kind of thing?"

Now, of course, I'd call on market research to back up my ideas, or let the client believe he'd dreamed them up himself, but then I just burbled on enthusiastically about filling the rooms with antiques ("You can pick up the big, baronial stuff quite cheaply at auctions—try Lots Road on a Monday"), about dressing up the staff as footmen and butlers and mob-capped maids and never throwing a dinner if you can call it a banquet.

I hadn't spent fifteen years furnishing and refurbishing White Walls without learning a thing or two about how to modernize an old house without sacrificing its charm. I even reeled off a list of garden centers specializing in Old English roses and helibores. ("Go and see John Coke in Hampshire; but he's only open between March and September.")

The McMahons were impressed. They had been thinking along those lines, too, they said. "Get all that down on paper and then we'll edit it and put it to the rest of the board," said Bob.

Donald was delighted for me when I told him. "It's big money, Ann. I've seen their balance sheets and forward budgeting plans. It'll be a great stepping-off point for you if you get in with Delphic." He took me out to dinner to celebrate. "Wear the black cashmere," he said. "Sexy but sophisticated. It's the right image."

He had taken a firm line over my clothes early on. "That flowered thing, the dress you wore at our first dinner party . . . it doesn't do anything for you. Take this, Ann . . ." He pressed a large check into my hand and when I protested that I couldn't take it, I'd feel like a kept woman, he said firmly (and rather insultingly, I thought later) that if I was going to act as his hostess he wanted me to look as well dressed as the company wives.

I told him how I hated shopping, and about my glum shopping experiences before I came to live at Acacia Road, and he recommended an elegant shop in Beauchamp Place and another in the Brompton Road. "And while you're about it, hon, why don't you get a really good haircut?"

"But, I don't know . . . where?"

"Robert." Donald seemed surprisingly knowledgeable. "Robert in Grafton Street is one of the best cutters in London."

Silly of me, of course, not to have realized that since Donald is more likely to be found browsing through the *Financial Times* than *Vogue,* he was simply passing on the names of Felicia's favorite hairdresser and shops.

Trust Felicia to pick the best. The salesgirl in the Brompton Road shop took me firmly in hand and refused to allow me to ruin the line of her subtly draped garment by pulling it in at the waist with a wide belt. She showed me how to sling a narrow leather double belt (fifty-five pounds for a *belt?*) around my hips. I looked in the mirror and saw that I had instantly lost weight. It was a snip. I bought three different outfits, and a bag and a pair of flat pumps. And the belt. I'd never spent so much money on myself in my life.

I'd taken Robert a photograph I'd cut out of *Harpers & Queen* which, I noticed, had "Hair by Robert" written underneath. He looked doubtfully at the picture and said yes, he remembered doing that session but did I think it was really me? I said I realized it wasn't me at the moment, but it was how I'd always wanted to look. Robert said he hoped I didn't mind if he was frank, but even an expensive haircut by an internationally famous master crimper (himself), a perm, and a complete color change could not be guaranteed to turn an attractive, mature woman into an eighteen-year-old model.

"Thanks for the attractive, anyway," I said and told him to do what he liked. The bill was thirty-five pounds and Sandra at Hair Flair in Salisbury had never charged me more than ten. But then, I'd never come out of Hair Flair looking ten years younger. I just came out looking as though I'd had my hair done.

"Hey, you look great."

"Thank you, Donald." It was like one of those films where the dowdy heroine takes off her spectacles and is instantly transformed into Audrey Hepburn.

He studied me, perplexed, as I served up the casserole I'd put into the Slo-Cooker that morning. "You look different. Younger somehow." He must have seen the same film.

"I've had my hair done, bought a few things." I told him about the sales assistant in Plantation and about Robert and Donald said that Felicia was just crazy about him. "She even tried to persuade me to go there for a trim."

"But I thought you didn't want me to look like Felicia?"

"How could you?" said Donald quickly, recognizing a tactical error. "Felicia's fair and slight and . . ."

"Okay. Say it. I'm fat."

"I wasn't going to say that, sweetheart. I was going to say that she's kind of boyish and nobody could *ever* mistake *you* for a boy." He slowly unbuttoned my shirt and kissed my breasts, and we slipped down onto the tiled floor. I wondered if the therapists who urge us to make sex more exciting by taking it out of the bedroom have ever encountered the chilly thrill of a high-tech kitchen. The casserole congealed on the plates while we were down there, and so we took a shower together, which was much more fun, made love again and then called on Miss Jamieson to babysit while we went out to dinner.

"Str-ee-ee-tch those leg muscles; they get shorter as you get older, you know." Mine were stretched to agony point, following the instructions of a lithe young woman who was persuading a class of not so lithe older women to bend their limbs into painful positions.

I went to a Lotte Berk class because I suspected that dance studios and aerobic classes would be full of youthful sylphs moving rhythmically to pop music. I'd never been able to move rhythmically to anything. "Is it a waltz?" I used to ask my partner at school dances. "No, it's Elvis," my partner would reply and go and ask someone else to dance.

"On your knees. Now . . . pelvis forward, keep a very tight bottom and move your pelvis forward . . . back . . . forward . . . back. Good."

I was reminded of my recent workout on the kitchen floor and was not surprised when the lithe young woman assured us that this exercise was excellent for our sex lives. It was very bad for mine. I could hardly walk as I left the exercise class, let alone attempt anything more strenuous.

Donald's doctor recommended a high-energy, biogenic diet, and after a couple of months I'd slimmed down so satisfactorily that I could get into the Jasper Conran black cashmere dress I'd coveted in Beauchamp Place.

Laura had been most impressed.

"Hey, Ann, you look fantastic. You've lost pounds. Can I go on the diet, too? And Harry?"

I stopped buying them pizzas and hamburgers, and we chopped up raw vegetables, simmered pulses, and grew bean sprouts on the window ledge. I liked the bean sprouts. They humanized that kitchen and reminded me of my seedlings at home.

The dramatic change in the children's eating habits was actually much more to do with Suzanne Girshon, an educational therapist at their school, than my new slim figure.

A couple of months after I arrived at St. John's Wood, I'd had a call from Mary Anne Colby, Harry's teacher, saying that she was worried that he "no longer seemed to be achieving his full potential in class." She hinted that he was "currently having difficulties socializing," and wondered if there were any problems at home which Mr. Harman or I might care to share with herself and Su-

zanne Girshon? Thursday, she suggested, would be the best time
for Suzanne, who had a heavy workload.

Donald also had a heavy workload.

"I'd really appreciate if you could handle this for me, hon. Although I must admit, I've been more worried about Laura."

It seemed a good moment for plain speaking and I told Donald
that if Harry had any problems they were being caused by Laura
treating him like a baby and stuffing him full of junk foods.

"She even lets him win at Junior Scrabble and it's not fair to
him. Other people aren't going to let him win . . ."

Donald looked impatient: "Oh come on, Ann. Not that again?"
There would probably never be a good moment to speak plainly to
him about his children. He saw them as he wished to see them and
not as they were, and I guessed Felicia had played along with his
vision of the all-American happy family. But perhaps they were
happy before she went away?

Suzanne Girshon, Mary Anne Colby and I sat around a jolly,
bright red table in the Commons, "the socializing center of the
school," and I asked them if Harry was having trouble making
friends.

"Right now he is experiencing a lot of difficulty relating to his
peer group," Suzanne corrected. "I've talked it out with him and
what I'm getting back is a picture of a child whose motivation is
being hampered by a lack of self-worth."

We agreed that this might have been caused by the breakup of
his parents' marriage, that the current decline of the nuclear family
put considerable pressure on the schools and the caring professions
and that divorce caused a great deal of mental and physical alien-
ation.

We spoke at length about Laura's maternal transference fixation,
and Suzanne promised to talk with Laura's counselor. "I think she
may be able to help Laura understand that her overprotective attitude is, in fact, destructive."

Eventually, we got around to the fact that Harry was overweight
and this might be the root of his problem. "I've noticed it bothers
him when he's changing for gym," said Mary Anne.

"Overweight children eat to compensate if they are unhappy,"
said Suzanne.

They suggested I give Harry a packed lunch, and promised to

try to keep him away from sloppy joes, the favorite school lunch-time dish.

A couple of weeks later, Suzanne came up to me, as I was wait-ing for Harry, and said that he seemed to be integrating better now with his group and Mary Anne reported that he was verbalizing more in class. I couldn't imagine any of my children's teachers taking so much time and trouble to delve into their pupils' psyches and was impressed. Both Suzanne and Mary Anne had put Harry's improvement down to the useful dialogue Laura had had with her counselor. Laura hadn't mentioned any dialogue to me, but she had become much nicer to live with and seemed to have opted out of her Little Mother role.

I wondered if she was beginning to realize that Felicia might not be coming home.

She spoke to her mother often on the phone at that time and, one evening, she'd come into the kitchen and said: "I'm bored with looking after Harry. He's old enough to look after himself."

"Quite."

She opened the fridge, took out the salad, began slicing tomatoes and, looking at me over her shoulder, said: "We took her for granted, you know."

"Took who for granted, love?"

"Momma." She concentrated determinedly on the tomatoes. "We let her do everything for us, and we did nothing. She wouldn't have left us otherwise, would she?"

I thought of the freezer food and the unmade beds and Su Par-sons and the fleet of delivery vans, and then I looked more closely at Laura and saw that she had been crying.

"Of course it had nothing to do with you and Harry," I assured her, and forced myself to add, "I expect Momma enjoyed doing things for you because she loves you."

Felicia

My memories of the Kapperman evening debacle are interrupted by Sarah and Emily returning from school. They now get them-selves to and from St. Berengaria's by a system of linked lifts so complicated that it makes the arrangements for the royal wedding look like a simple stroll down Pall Mall.

"That woman's such a bitch," says Sarah, "God, I hate her."

"Who, darling?"

"Bloody Miss Davenport and her bloody future imperfects. Fel, do I have to take French? It's so boring."

"Another language is so useful, darling. Dad would be awfully upset if you dropped French."

"Who ever heard of a vet needing French?"

"I bet French vets do," says Emmy.

"Funny, funny . . . seriously, Fel, why can't I concentrate on the subjects that really matter?"

"Darling, suppose you were called in for consultation at that racecourse outside Paris whose name I can't remember? Wouldn't it be frightfully useful to know the French for sprained fetlock?"

"Longchamps, you mean. Miss Davenport isn't teaching us the French for sprained fetlock, nothing so sensible. *Il y a quelques jolies fleurs dans la jardin,*" mimics Sarah savagely. "One of these days I'll tell her where to put her *jolies fleurs.*"

"Don't laugh at her, Emmy, you're only encouraging her . . . isn't it *le jardin?*"

"Who gives a toot? Hey, should Kitten by lying on your bump? Isn't she squashing the dreaded sibling?"

"We'll be all right, don't worry."

I have a feeling of deep security about this pregnancy that I never had with Laura and Harry. With them I worried endlessly; and looking back I realize that Donald was largely responsible for the fact that for nine months I thought of myself as a cupboard inside which, on a rickety shelf, was precariously balanced a vase of the Ming dynasty.

As soon as my first pregnancy was confirmed, he went out and bought every book on the subject he could lay his hands on. I was irresistibly drawn to read them, just as a woman alone in a house on a windy night is irresistibly drawn to reading *Salem's Lot.* Thumbing obsessively through these books, I began to wonder if what I was going through really was a natural process. The way these experts wrote, I was left with the impression that childbirth had only just been invented and they hadn't got round to perfecting the process yet.

Was I eating too much spinach, enough protein? Excessive amounts of alcohol could be deleterious, I read, and pondered guiltily about the glass of wine I had with dinner every night. I refused aspirin when I had a headache, and worried when I caught a cold in case what I really had was German measles.

Donald worried along with me. He watched me anxiously at dinner parties ("I don't think Felicia should eat shrimp in her condition"). He asked the gynecologist if he could listen to the baby's heartbeat with his stethoscope, then told him he thought it sounded kinda fast to him. Towards the end I couldn't so much as turn over in my sleep without him switching on the light and springing into his trousers.

It was a great relief to us both when first Laura, then Harry, were born and revealed to be perfect; though it was a disappointment to Donald that they had to be Cesareans. He was looking forward to panting with me and ordering the nurses around.

"I was just thinking," I say to Sarah, "about the night Kitten was born. No wonder Larkspur had such an easy time—she hadn't spent her pregnancy reading about 'Possible Problems During Whelping.' "

"You're a lot less twitchy now than you were then."

"Perhaps it's being pregnant . . . this lovely placid feeling."

But it's far more than being pregnant; I am a totally different person from the defensive, brittle woman who arrived here two years ago. I've stopped worrying about things that don't matter. Mrs. Simmons and I do our best, but I am not prepared to sacrifice my looks and my peace of mind on the house the way Ann did.

I have gone so far as to write down a list of jobs that need doing: I really must get the yellow room curtains cleaned, and there's a faulty banister rail at the turn of the stairs which isn't dangerous because we all know about it. The paint is flaking off the outside of the drawing room windows, and the old herb garden needs a good weed. Nothing, I think lazily, that can't wait. We'll get it done after the baby.

My cooking has calmed down, too. I look with amazement, and some shame, to my patchy culinary efforts in London: convenience foods in the micro for the children, punctuated by weekly dinner parties of startling virtuosity.

Our garden produce figures largely in all my menus. Higgins has, thank heavens, retired to smoke his pipe somewhere else. He has been replaced by Chris, a young horticultural graduate who shares her time between us, Jenny, and the manor. She gets through an amazing amount of work, largely because she enjoys it so much. Her only problem is overenthusiasm.

"You know that boring bit between the privy and the gate to the kitchen garden?" she says. "Don't you think a laburnum walk would be wonderful there?"

"What a lovely idea. How long would it take?"

"Oh . . . about twenty years before it really looked something, I should think."

"I'll never see it. The way I feel now I might not see next year's asparagus."

"Oh, Felicia, you are a scream . . . it would cost hardly anything if we grow them from seed, and we could put in an old brick path . . ."

Last week she wanted a knot garden; next week, no doubt, she will produce elaborate and expensive plans for a marsh garden in that damp bit near the stream. It is one of the great pleasures of my day, making plans with Chris over a mug of coffee. No wonder gardeners always seem to live so long; they can't bear to die and miss seeing how the hostas will look near the pear-leafed willow.

Sarah and Emily go off to do their homework, Emily complaining loudly how boring it all is, and Sarah saying in the insufferable way of older sisters that she should just wait till she starts working for her O's, *then* she'll know what work is.

Sarah, that resentful child who regarded me with stony enmity, has become one of my closest friends. Fifteen-year-old girls these days seem so much more grown-up than we were; there is nothing I feel I can't say to her, and nothing, I hope, that she couldn't confide in me. And it all goes back to the night I chucked the chance of being a soap opera star. . . .

When Antony came back from waving good-bye to the Kappermans and Sol, we were all in the kitchen.

Mrs. Simmons had bustled off, saying, "Now don't you do any more, Mrs. Harman—you must be exhausted. I can get all this tidied up in a twink in the morning."

The girls and Mark and I had cleared the dining room, and the kitchen looked like a battlefield.

"Off you go to bed, children—it's past ten and you've got school tomorrow."

"What are you going to do, Felly?" said Emily.

"I really can't leave all this for Mrs. Simmons . . . it won't take me long."

"We'll help," said Sarah, "I'm much too excited to go to bed anyway—oh, hullo, Dad. You're just in time to help, lucky you."

"Daddy, Daddy," yelped Emily, "come and look at the puppies. Come and see the one we've chosen. She's got a sweet white—"

"For the tenth time, Emily, we are not going to keep one of the bloody puppies. Go to bed now, please, I want to speak to Felicia."

"We can't go to bed yet, Dad," Sarah said reasonably, "we promised to help Felly clear up. And Mum did promise us a puppy, ages ago."

"I never want to hear the word 'puppy' again, is that absolutely clear? For two pins I'd go out and bucket the lot of them. Don't make that silly noise, Emmy, you know I didn't mean it. But really . . . I invite, I *lure,* the best up-and-coming American TV director to the house, along with Mr. Moneybags himself, and what do you see fit to say to him?" Antony puts on a fretful, high-pitched voice. He evidently thinks he is imitating me: "Do have another slice of placenta, you boring old American."

"Oh, rubbish. I never said anything like that, I merely—"

"As good as. I was heaving, for one. I suppose you realize Sol Venture will see to it you never work again. Those gays can be pretty vindictive, you know."

"That's right, trot out the boring old clichés. As a matter of fact he loved the puppies . . . he said—"

"Christ, you didn't take him *in* there, did you? He must have thought you were demented. And he's right. Can't you do anything properly, you silly bitch? Nothing's ever really serious with you, is it? You play at being a wife, you play at being a mistress, you're no bloody use as a mother, and now you can't even land a part when it's handed to you tied up in pink bloody ribbons."

Mark left the room and Emmy crept, crying, into one of the dog baskets. Sarah carefully hung up the dishcloth she had been using, and came and leaned against the Welsh dresser next to me with her arms folded. She didn't touch me by so much as an elbow, but for the third time that night I felt tears coming.

"Actually, you've got it a bit wrong, Dad," she said.

"Don't interrupt, Sarah, it's none of your business. Go to bed."

"It is my business. Shut up, *shut up* for once and listen. *You* brought Felicia down here, *you* made Mum go away. And now, tonight, when Felly really tried to help . . . it was my fault she

left that silly dinner party. I was frightened Larkspur would die"—
she was beginning to lose control of her voice—"I was terrified
something would go wrong. I needed a grown-up, can't you see
that? And Felly was wonderful." She burst into tears, and I put an
arm carefully round her, and handed her a piece of paper towel.
She turned and cried into my collarbone. Part of me noted ab-
stractedly that she had to bend her knees quite a bit.

"It's all right, darling," I said, "we're all very tired. He didn't
really mean what he said, did you, Antony?"

Antony muttered something that could be taken, if charitably
interpreted, as the minor beginnings of a backdown.

"And I'll tell you something else," said Sarah, blowing her nose,
"Sol's mother breeds Pekinese, and he actually helped Larky with
one of the puppies, and he said he'd love to work with Felly one
day."

"Just being polite, I expect."

"Actually, darling, he said I was well out of the Kapperman
series. He said Morris was going to interfere like mad and it would
end up as a disaster."

"I have to admit that a little of Morris goes a long way," said
Antony grudgingly.

"And he tells terrible lies," said Emmy's sniffly voice.

"Do come out of the dog basket, Emmy . . . what do you
mean?"

"I happened to pick up the extension when he got that call from
his chauffeur. I was going to phone Sandra about homework," she
added quickly (Sarah grinned slightly), "and his chauffeur said,
'Very sorry indeed to bother you, sir, but I don't believe we settled
exactly when I am to collect you tomorrow morning.' And Morris
said, 'Never mind about tomorrow morning, you come and get me
out of this goddam house right now.' That's what they said,"
ended Emmy triumphantly, "nothing about a phone call from
London at all."

"Well, I can't say I blame him," said Antony.

"Oh, be fair, darling. Someone with less self-importance would
have found it all rather amusing. Lady was terrific about it."

Emmy, encouraged by the fact that we were no longer shouting
at each other, took hold of Antony's hand.

"Do come and look at the puppies, Daddy. Larkspur's feelings
might be hurt if you don't."

"All right, Emmy. But no talk about keeping one. That is my last word."

Later, Antony and I lay in each other's arms after the best love we'd ever made.

"What you said in the kitchen . . ." I said.

"Darling, you know what I'm like when I lose my temper—"

"But some of it was true," I said sadly, "I never really cooked proper meals for my children like Ann does. And the house always looked beautiful, but it wasn't really a home. I used to wonder why Ann's hands were so grubby . . . but at least her children love her," I wailed.

"Darling, darling, what's all this? Laura and Harry love you, you know that. And look how marvelously you're getting on with my lot. I thought Sarah would never come round."

"Antony," I said, "I suppose you wouldn't reconsider about the puppy? We've messed up their lives so terribly getting what we want; a puppy doesn't really seem much in comparison."

"So I've got to climb down, have I?"

"When that little thing was born Sarah hugged me. I reckon I owe it a good home."

Much later, about three o'clock, I got up and crept downstairs to where the new life was. Somebody really ought to see if Larkspur's comfortable, I said to myself; but I really wanted to have another look at our little bitch. As I might have known, Sarah was in the butler's pantry.

"Oh Sarah—you'll be a wreck tomorrow."

"I just wanted to see they're all right. Isn't it lovely in here?" She looked at me shyly. "Would you like some cocoa?"

"Brain wave. And let's put great globs of cream on top. There's plenty left over from my amazingly successful dinner party."

We both laughed, and Sarah went to make the cocoa. I let Larkspur out, and when one of the puppies whimpered in its sleep, she raced anxiously back. Better instincts than me, I thought dolefully.

We sipped our cocoa in a rather nervous silence. There was a lot I wanted to say, but I didn't know how to start. No doubt Sarah felt the same. She picked up one of the puppies, and said to it, "I've decided I'm going to be a vet when I grow up. Wasn't Sol marvelous? I want to be able to do that." She put the puppy down, and Larkspur inspected it carefully and went back to sleep.

"It's very hard work, you know . . . not all watching puppies being born . . ."

"I know all that. But I'm strong on the science and biology side; Miss Harmsworth said I ought to think about being a doctor, but I prefer animals to people."

"Animals don't let you down, you mean?"

She looked at me carefully.

"Felly—you remember the fuss Dad made when Mark dropped that bottle of milk? You'd have thought it was a petrol bomb, the way he went on. But when Mum left us and you arrived, Dad behaved almost as if nothing had happened . . . 'making friends already' . . . and all that stuff. Did anyone stop and wonder how we felt?"

"Oh, darling, endlessly. How do you imagine I felt about my own children? And I tried so hard to get on with you. Do you remember when you helped me with those wretched seedlings? I was so happy when I got up next morning . . ."

"I hated you that morning. I thought how disloyal I'd been to Mum, feeling sorry for you. The trouble was, Felly," Sarah put down her mug and looked out of the window, "I kept on *liking* you. I kept on thinking, Why didn't Mum ever shout back at Dad like that? and then I thought of poor Mum in London and I hated you even more."

"What you don't realize is that your father and I never meant this to happen. We did fall in love, which perhaps wasn't very bright of us; but neither of us wanted to leave our children. We were sort of catapulted into it by my stepson. Donald and I had the most dreadful scene and after that . . . there was really nowhere I could go but here."

"What's going to happen?"

I wondered how frankly I could talk to an intelligent girl who was only thirteen. I risked it.

"One day your father and I would like to be married, Sarah. Which means, I'm afraid, two divorces."

Sarah picked up another puppy, and when Larkspur got up and looked worried she buried her face in the dog's neck. "Oh Larky," she said, "I can't bear it." The tears were running down her face. "Felly, couldn't you and Dad just go on being friends? I could still see a lot of you, couldn't I? There's nothing for Mum in London, you know, nothing at all. What would she do if she got . . . if she and Dad split up?"

"It might actually be rather good for her in the long run."

"How could it be good for her?" She looked at me shrewdly. "You're saying that because it would be more comfortable for you if it were true."

"Perhaps. But it's perfectly obvious to me after only three months in this house that Ann never had a minute to herself. From what Antony says, she was ambitious and very good at her job when they got married. She gave all that up; and if you want my honest opinion, your mother was being run into the ground and not getting anything like enough appreciation."

She looked at me doubtfully. "We appreciated her."

"I'm sure you told her how wonderful she was now and then, when you thought of it. But it would have been more to the point to make your own beds, don't you think? And did anyone ever say 'You look tired, Mum, I'll get supper'?"

"You're making me feel rotten."

"Well, don't; children always take their mothers for granted, that's what we're for."

Sarah grinned suddenly. "Nobody's going to take you for granted, are they?"

"No, because I shout a lot and get bloody-minded, as you may have noticed. Look, the holidays start next week, don't they? You'll be able to spend the whole time up in London with your mother."

"Oh, but—I couldn't leave the puppies . . . couldn't Mum come down here?"

"She wouldn't want to, Sarah. Think about it, it would be horrid for her. And I promise I'll look after the puppies while you're away. Come on—bedtime."

"Perhaps I'll just go up for a few days." She knelt down by the puppies. "Oh, I do wish Dad would let us keep one, it's so unfair."

A few days ago I would have said, "It's all right, I've fixed it," eager to grab any kudos I could. But I was confident enough, that night, to think that Antony deserved the glory of his generosity all to himself.

As we got to the top of the stairs, Sarah said abruptly, "I expect you heard me describing you the day you arrived—I meant you to."

"Dripping with makeup and horrible London clothes, you mean?"

"The thing was, Felly . . . I walked into the library and

thought, Crumbs, doesn't she look great? Why doesn't Mum ever wear clothes like that?"

"I do understand, Sarah, honestly. Good night, love."

Next morning when we were all in the kitchen, Antony said, "Last night I said some things to Felicia that were untrue and unkind. But she has been kind enough to forgive me, and to celebrate," he paused dramatically, "I think this house needs another dog."

"Oh *Dad.*" Sarah flung herself at him, Mark hit him on the back, and Emmy jumped up and down squeaking. I sat there beaming at the four of them.

"I only wish," Antony said to me, "that my clients received my presentations with such acclaim. Now come and show me which one you want to keep, Sarah."

They talked about the puppies all the way to school. Emmy asked why human ladies had to lie on their backs to have babies.

"So that men doctors can tell them what to do," said Sarah.

"I'm not going to have a man doctor," said Emmy, "I'm going to have a lady doctor, and I shall crouch like Larkspur did."

"You'll look very silly," said Mark.

"You won't be there, bumface," said Emmy, neatly rounding off the conversation as I braked in front of Mark's school.

"You'll be interested to hear," I said to Antony when I got back, "that your younger daughter intends to crouch when she has her babies."

"Sounds perfectly reasonable to me. There's nothing in London that needs me, I can stay here all day." He reached out his hand, and I took it. "Darling, we're going to be all right, aren't we? I want it to work so much . . ."

"Oh, darling, it will. I'm so happy about Sarah. Antony, I don't know if I did the right thing, but last night—"

"I know, you told her we want to get married. She told me when we were looking at the puppies. I think you were absolutely right, it was obviously a good moment. God knows when it will happen, though; it looks as though Ann and Donald are going to be difficult."

"The trouble is, Sarah doesn't much want to go to Ann for the holidays, that won't help. She doesn't want to leave the puppies, and she's such a country person."

"Takes after her mother."

"Ann made herself into the kind of wife that suited you at the time. I rather suspect she's going to surprise you."

"I suppose she'll get some little job for the time being. Best thing for her would be to meet some nice chap and get married again. Make it easier for us, too."

"What an arrogant assumption, darling. She wasn't all that happy being married to you, slaving away down here with a husband up in London who wished she'd take more care of her hands. Do you remember the first time you took me out to dinner? . . . don't, darling, Mrs. Simmons will be here soon . . . you said how lovely it was to eat with somebody who hadn't got seed compost under her nails? And then you suddenly asked me if I made my own jam, and when I said I just went out and bought it—"

"I thought, God, how sexy. Buying jam instead of standing there for hours earnestly stirring and potting and labeling. I never want to see another jar of Blackberry and Apple 1982 in my life."

This was hardly the time to tell him I'd just bought a book about hedgerow cookery; thumbing through it I'd found a recipe for elderflower cordial that sounded delicious and obviously cost nothing.

Ann

"Ann, Ann, I've done three whole lengths." Harry flops down next to me at the side of the pool, wiping rivulets of water from his face with a striped towel. He has gained confidence and lost weight; a different and much happier child.

We've been coming here for about a year now. At first my swimming was as uncoordinated as my dancing and Harry spent a lot of the time shivering on the edge wrapped up in his towel. He said he was scared of the water, but I think he was more frightened of revealing himself in bathing trunks.

"Did you hear me, Ann? I've done *three* lengths."

"Okay, no need to boast." I've only achieved two so far but do not intend to be beaten by a nine-year-old. "Just wait until Wednesday and then you'll see something. I have just discovered how to do the crawl and breathe at the same time. I shouldn't be surprised if I don't whizz up and down at least half a dozen lengths."

"*Now* who's boasting? Ann, can I bring Jack home after school tomorrow? Laura's going over to Sally Anne's and Jack's got hold of the new Raiders video."

"Of course you can. Only promise to do your homework and leave me in peace."

My pretty bedroom in Acacia Road is now an office and I've got more work than I can handle. Maddie and Bob and I have transformed the Delphic hotels into period pieces of Old World charm and a couple of months ago they put me in charge of their publicity. It was much easier than I expected. Journalists, I discovered, do not want to be bought expensive lunches or handed prose poems about my client. I pleased them with exclusive stories about the doings of Delphic's celebrity guests and, in return, they introduced me to a couple of other small companies needing PR.

I couldn't have done any of it without Su, who turns out to be a whirlwind of efficiency under the trendy gear and sharp manner. She has taken over the day-to-day running of the house, even masterminding Donald's frequent dinner parties.

About two months ago, she had spotted me trying to write a press release with one hand while whipping up a fish mousse with the other, and had asked, in her succinct manner, why I was wasting my time with all that crap. "Why don't you buy it in, Ann? Fel always used the Bute Catering people when she was pushed for time."

"Well, I don't know." Donald was obsessive about those dinners. They were part of his job, a necessary slab in his career path, and the silver and crystal had to be shining, the menu well and imaginatively planned. "That hot grapefruit idea, Ann . . . ," he'd said. "Don't do it again, hon."

"Just leave it all to me," said Su.

The other evening, when the last guest had left, Donald had kissed me warmly and told me what a wonder I was. "I know it's a lot of work for you, but these guys are always in and out of expense account restaurants, they really appreciate home cooking."

It had seemed neither necessary nor wise to mention the Bute Catering Company. They were expensive and so was Su, but I could afford it now. Last month I made over a thousand pounds.

Both children seemed to be thriving on what I would once have considered neglect. As I grew busier, they became more helpful. Harry even makes his own bed, in a flung-together sort of way.

On the day the printers delivered the Tadworth Castle Conference Center brochure—my first solo effort—Laura knocked on my door.

"Thought you might like a cup of tea. Hey, Ann, what's this?"

"A brochure. I've just done it for Maddie and Bob McMahon, those friends of Poppa's who own a lot of hotels."

"*You've* done it?" Laura flicked the pages admiringly. Starting at the back, I noticed irritably. Why do people always read things from back to front when they are designed to be read from front to back? "How do you mean, you've done it?"

"I wrote it and organized the photographs. Somebody else designed it."

"Wow," said Laura. "I'm going to be a designer when I leave school. A graphic artist. Maybe I can come and work for you?"

"That would be nice," I said, and meant it. These days, I have an easier relationship with Laura and Harry than I do with my own three children. They come here often, of course, but it's so false, not like being at home together. Every visit involves such intricate planning and they always manage to leave behind some vital item which they've *absolutely got* to have for school on Thursday.

Felicia and I have devised a complicated exchange system of fetching and carrying, and it had been odd going back to White Walls to collect the children that first time. I thought she would have tarted it up, given it the Acacia Road treatment, but, if anything, the house looked shabbier. It looked as though it could do with a good clean, actually.

Sometimes we meet at a hotel midway to swap the children and, on one occasion, Em electrified the other residents in the lounge by saying whimsically: "Mum, when you marry Donald, can I be your bridesmaid?" Felicia gave me a sharp look as I said firmly: "I'm not marrying Donald, darling."

Em says a lot of whimsical things these days. I suppose it's because I'm not with her all the time that her cuteness sometimes seems to me rather calculating. Poor little Em. I hope it isn't a symptom of insecurity . . . the broken home syndrome. More likely it's just her age or the fact that Felicia tends to treat Sarah like another adult, leaving Emily to play the part of the baby in the family.

Laura and Harry were fiercely proprietorial about their belongings at the beginning. "Don't let Mark touch my airplanes," Harry would say, driving away in his mother's car, and Laura once complained: "They've been using my *toothpaste.*"

Donald isn't much better. Just as he can see no wrong in his own children, he can see very little right about mine. Wouldn't it be a good idea if that girl (Sarah) washed her hair? It looks a mess. What's wrong with that child (Emily) that she won't touch pasta? *All* children love pasta. Why is that boy (Mark) so hyperactive, has no one ever taught him to sit down and read a book?

He quite approves of them, I notice, when all the children are here together and my lot provide entertainment for his young. The girls spend all their time trying on each other's clothes and Mark is teaching Harry how to kick a football. Even though Donald hasn't the slightest desire to romp about in Regent's Park with Harry, he contrives to look pathetically excluded when the two boys go off together: "Mark's got his father's nose," he says, an indication of how unpleasant he finds it to have a small boy running around his house reminding him of his wife's lover.

As I feared, the white decor in Acacia Road is a hazardous backdrop for my free-ranging children. I spent one entire evening lounging, concealingly, on one of the white sofas where Mark had spilled some cocoa.

"Stupid bastard," said Su, next day, scrubbing loyally at the stain. I thought she meant Mark, but she had Donald in mind. "Doesn't he realize they're only kids?"

I plan treats and outings when they are here but refuse to go in for the serious shopping with which Felicia bribes Laura and Harry when she comes to London. "You can't buy children's love," I say smugly to Donald, but really I'm all too aware that I can't give the children what they really want, the ordinary family life they once had with me at White Walls.

That first Christmas was the worst. I'd had so much planned. Midnight mass at St. Paul's, seats for the Palladium pantomime, a Christmas Eve viewing of the candle-lit windows in Campden Hill Square. And then Sarah had said diffidently: "Mum, would you mind very much . . . ?" She muttered something about not wanting to leave Kitten—what a ridiculous name for a puppy—and about Em looking forward to seeing the cows.

"The cows?"

"*You* know, Mum. The *cows.*"

When we first met, Antony had read me a Thomas Hardy poem

about the Wessex tradition of going to look at the oxen on Christmas Eve to see if they were kneeling to celebrate the birth of Christ. I thought it was a lovely idea, and when the children were old enough, it became our tradition, too.

I remembered Em, three years ago, clutching my hand and breathing: "Ooh, Mum, it's doing it . . . look . . . it's kneeling . . ." as one of Mr. Parker's cows gradually stood up and regarded us steadily across the barn, no doubt wondering what all the commotion was about.

Even when I'm an old man, Hardy had written, I'll go back and look at the oxen, hoping it's true. My little Em obviously felt the same, and there were no cows in St. John's Wood. I pictured myself sharing a Safeway turkey roll with my mother in front of a vintage oldie on television. "Of course I don't mind," I told Sarah. "I'll be able to spend Christmas with Granny."

I did mind, though. I minded like hell. And I knew whose fault it was.

I did the journey in under two hours, rehearsing in my mind all the sensible things I would say to Felicia and the absurd/thoughtless/bitchy things she would reply. I was hot with rage by the time I arrived.

And then, of course, she wasn't there. I was looking around for the bell pull, it seemed to have snapped off, when Mrs. Simmons appeared.

"Why, Mrs. Forester-Jones, love. It's never you, is it?"

Her kind voice, on top of all the exhausting rage, was too much. I sniffed and fiddled about with a handkerchief, but couldn't conceal the tears. Mrs. Simmons pretended not to notice.

"I'm just going to make myself a cup of tea, so why don't you join me? Mrs. Harman's down the kitchen garden. It's her you've come to see, I suppose, because the children are all in school and Mr. Forester-Jones is at his office?"

I nodded and followed her into the familiar kitchen. Even through the tears I could see it looked a mess. Surely I never had all those boxes of bulbs littering every available surface and dog bowls and cushions all over the floor?

There was rather a sweet puppy, running about making little pools of excitement. "Kitten," said Mrs. Simmons. "How Sarah dotes on that puppy."

This made me cry some more and Mrs. Simmons tactfully bustled about with the kettle and mugs and said she hoped I was looking after myself, I'd lost ever such a lot of weight, but I looked smart, so smart she hardly recognized me.

"Mrs. Simmons . . ."

"Yes, dear."

"Are the children all right?" I hadn't meant to say that, hadn't realized until I said it that it was what I'd really come to find out.

"Oh, right as rain, dear. I was ever so worried when you . . . well, when you went and that . . . and then Mrs. Harman, she seemed such a Londoner, if you know what I mean, I couldn't see her settling down here. I was ready to walk out that first week, and then I thought, Thelma, somebody's got to keep an eye on those children . . ."

All those years and I didn't know Mrs. Simmons was a Thelma. How nice of Thelma Simmons to stay put, in what she must have found an embarrassing situation, for the sake of my children.

"How kind of you, Mrs. Simmons."

She brushed this aside. "Oh, never mind about that, Mrs. Forester-Jones. Anyway, I needn't have worried. Mrs. Harman couldn't have done more for them . . . not if they were her own."

She looked at me nervously, not certain if this was what I wanted to hear. Of course I wanted my children to be happy and well looked after, but I was having difficulty readjusting my image of Felicia, the tough bitch who had stolen my husband, alienated my children, and messed up my life.

At that moment Felicia walked in.

"Mrs. Simmons, is that you? I thought I heard voices . . . ah, Ann. Ann?" She took off her gardening gloves, laid a pair of secateurs down on the dresser and turned to face me. She was different from the way she looked when we met on the child-swapping runs. She was wearing a pair of rather grubby brown cords and one of Antony's sweaters, the old camel hair I had always found so warm and comfortable.

"Ann . . . is anything the matter? The children? Nothing's happened?"

"No, no, they're fine. At school. No, I . . . well, I wanted to talk to you, Felicia."

"I'll be getting on, then," said Mrs. Simmons. "The top floor today, Mrs. Harman?"

"Thank you, Mrs. Simmons." Felicia poured herself a mug of

tea. "Why don't you bring that with you, Ann. Let's go and sit somewhere more comfortable."

She led the way into the library, sat down in one of the big leather armchairs and I took the other. My God, it was cold in that room. I was just about to edge the chair towards the fire when Felicia shouted: "Don't move the chair" at the same moment as I cried: "Oh, I nearly forgot." We both laughed uneasily, and Lady-smith rose slowly from the hearthrug, waddled over and laid her head on my foot in friendly recognition.

"Poor old dog, poor old Lady," I murmured.

"What did you want to talk to me about, Ann?"

I lit a cigarette. I needed time to think, to remember all those powerful phrases I'd rehearsed in the car. But looking at the decent, homely woman sitting across from me in my sitting room, they no longer seemed appropriate.

"I really came here to tell you that I hated you . . ."

Felicia studied the contents of her mug carefully. "Yes. I can understand that."

"But," I continued carefully, "I don't. Not anymore."

I told her how lonely I felt in London without Sarah, Emmy and Mark, that I felt she was deliberately taking Sarah away from me and about the pointless plans I'd made for Christmas.

Felicia said: "Oh Ann, I'm sorry," adding quickly that she knew "sorry" was a silly, inadequate word, but she understood exactly what I meant because she felt the same about *her* children.

"Laura's always talking about you, how efficient you are, what a good cook, the places you go together. And then, there's Harry . . . why didn't I see his problem? That he needed a special diet?"

"And why didn't I manage to sort out Em?"

This honest dialogue wasn't at all the scenario I'd imagined, and I found myself agreeing that it's sometimes easier to cope with other people's children than your own, agreeing about a surprising number of things, including Antony's maddening habit of sensing an oncoming domestic drama and being halfway down the M3 to London before it happens.

She asked if I'd like lunch, and when I said I couldn't even face a lettuce leaf, produced a rather good bottle of wine and two glasses. About three quarters of the way through the bottle, she asked why I wouldn't give Antony a divorce and I explained that I didn't want to formalize anything because I hoped . . . Donald and I both hoped . . . that she and Antony would change their minds.

Giving me a wary look over the top of her glass, Felicia said: "Oh no, Ann. There's no question of that. I know Antony's a bit of an old chauvinist. I know all his faults. But I do love him, you know. We suit each other very well."

I wondered why I found this so hard to believe and saw, in a moment of perfect clarity, that it was because I no longer wanted to live in that chilly house, with nosy Jenny Balfour next door and a weekly boarder for a husband. What's more, I couldn't understand why this package suited an intelligent woman like Felicia Harman.

"But Donald?" I said. "Donald wants you back."

Felicia shook her head. "Oh no, he doesn't. What Donald wants is a decorative accessory for his expensive house, a desirable hostess at the head of his dinner table, confirming his good taste." She looked at the Armani suit I'd put on that morning to do battle in. "I should think you'd fit the bill admirably, Ann . . ."

I knew she was waiting for me to reveal my relationship with Donald, but when I said nothing, she continued awkwardly: "We hardly ever slept with each other . . . Donald found it difficult . . . you know . . . after that awful Harry business."

To ask "What awful Harry business?" would have seemed intrusive; besides, I was busy taking on board the riveting fact that Donald Harman had difficulty making love to Felicia and absolutely no trouble making it with me.

I gazed pensively into my wineglass and waited for Felicia to say more, but she was engrossed in fondling Ladysmith's ear. I saw she was crying and said: "Oh God, what a mess it all is."

Felicia sniffed a bit. "You could come to us for Christmas, Ann. You know that."

I thanked her but said I didn't think it would be Antony's idea of seasonal good cheer. As I left, I noticed my old battered Barbour hanging in the porch. Felicia looked contrite.

"Oh Ann, I do hope you don't mind?"

"Mind what?"

"The Barbour. I borrowed it. It's so useful."

"You're welcome. I was just going to suggest you chuck it out." I pictured myself turning up at Delphic or going to the theater with Donald in the disreputable garment. "It certainly isn't any use to me."

Felicia seemed absurdly pleased. "Oh really? How wonderful.

I'd been going to buy one, but they're so much nicer when they're kind of worn in, aren't they?"

"I suppose so." I was gazing at the Barbour doubtfully as she said: "How can I pay you back? I know. My Joseph knitted thing, black with midnight blue stripes. You'd look marvelous in it, Ann."

"You've been to see *Felicia?*" Donald looked incredulous. "In God's name, Ann, what for?" He and Antony seemed to take it as a criticism of their manhood if their women weren't jealously tearing out each other's hair and clawing at each other's eyes.

I explained how sad I'd felt about Christmas. "It's all right for you, Donald, you'll be in New York with Tom, but this is my first Christmas without the children."

I also told him that Felicia and Antony were determined to marry, and I didn't see any point in continuing to hold out over a divorce.

"My, Felicia's been clever. She's certainly won you over."

"No, no, it wasn't Felicia." I described how, in the car coming back to London, I'd decided that whatever happened, I would never go back to Antony and my old life at White Walls. There was, however, a niggling suspicion at the back of my mind that Donald might be right. I'd given Felicia everything she'd wanted— the promise of a trouble-free Christmas *and* a divorce—in exchange for a nice knitted two-piece.

I assured Donald that I'd never been happier.

"I'm glad, hon." He thought that he was the reason for my newfound happiness and so he was, in a way. It felt good to be wanted when you've been treated like a piece of furniture for years.

But what I was really loving was my job.

Felicia

"Mulberry Jelly 1985" I print carefully on the small label. I had nothing much to do this morning, so I got out some mulberries we froze last autumn and made four pounds of beautiful dark red jelly. I gaze proudly at the larder shelf, where the mulberry looks particularly pretty next to the golden apricot jam.

When my friends come down from London, they hiss enviously, "All those lovely preserves . . . your own raspberry vinegar . . . how do you make it?"

"You put some raspberries in a bottle of vinegar," I answer briskly, "it's no big deal." "And you *look* so marvelous, darling," they all say.

I do look good. The country Felicia is a distinct improvement on the old London model.

For one thing, I've put on weight. Well, of course I have, I'm five months pregnant. But even before I was pregnant I weighed 130 pounds. Three years ago I nearly had hysterics when the scales hit 112 after a holiday in Italy. I actually can't remember why being thin was so important. Something to do with clothes hanging better, I suppose, what a bore.

I hardly wear any makeup these days except in the evenings, my skin's so much better. I've given up all those expensive American jars of goo I used to think my face would die without; now nothing goes on that doesn't come from the Body Shop or Beauty Without Cruelty. Just as good, much cheaper, and some wretched animal hasn't had its eyes stung in the process. I still get my hair cut by Robert in London, of course, which reminds me. I must make an appointment for next Wednesday morning before I lunch with Ann.

I'm not going to turn up looking tacky in front of *that* lady. For starters, she's lost about twice as much weight as I've put on, revealing excellent bones in the process. She also goes to Robert for her hair; it's very short now, very "I know my way around, so no messing." Her neck looks about two inches longer (partly because she's stopped tucking it apologetically into her collarbones) and heaven knows what she spends on clothes. Well I know, actually; very much what I used to spend.

And another thing. I will go upstairs now and put cuticle cream on what is left of my nails after all that bricklaying. Last time I saw Ann her hands looked as if the most strenuous thing she did with them was run them down some man's back.

I think perhaps I'll leave my nails until tomorrow. The baby is moving again, quite decisively. I think I'll just lie here and smile.

Ann

Bob and Maddie have asked me if I can make a meeting tomorrow at three o'clock.

"Sorry about the short notice," said Maddie, "but we're anxious to sort this out as soon as possible."

Before I had time to ask her what they were anxiously wanting to sort out, she'd rung off.

Maddie and Bob, and a couple of directors I'd met before, are in the boardroom when I arrive, looking alarmingly serious.

Had I made an error in the Tadworth brochures or overpriced on the mailing list for the Fairland Hall complex? Hardly a reason, surely, for a board meeting? Perhaps they were going to veto the slogan I'd had printed, expensively, on all their literature? I'd be prepared to fight my corner on that. I knew it was good.

"We're here to discuss advertising," says Bob. (Well, that's me finished, then. Advertising agencies all have their own PR people . . .) But Bob is saying that the company is doing so well that it can afford to plough back some of the profits and expand. They're going into the quality newspapers and magazines, even considering a series of up-market commercials, and they want me to be in charge of it all.

"It's a natural extension of the excellent work you've been doing for us on our publicity and corporate image . . ." He gives me an encouraging smile. "What do you say, Ann?"

If I said what I really felt I'd sound like a child at Christmastime, so I just murmur something about being grateful for the opportunity and their touching faith.

I'm in no state to take in the subsequent in-depth discussions about above- and below-the-line expenditure, but pick up the fact that I'll be able to call on any professional help I may need. Someone to tell me what "above- and below-the-line expenditure" is, for a start.

Over lunch the next day, Maddie says: "We know you've been approached by several other companies, Ann, and one of the reasons we're offering you this job is because we're anxious to keep you with Delphic."

I assure her that my loyalty is to Delphic first, always.

"Good," Maddie says. "Bob and I were wondering . . ."

She's obviously going to ask a favor. I'd do anything. They've done so much for me. "What? What is it?"

Maddie prongs a prawn with her fork and gives me a shrewd glance. "Bob and I were wondering if you'd ever thought of starting your own company one day?"

"Hang on, Maddie," I say, not believing what I'm hearing, "a couple of hours ago I hadn't even thought of running a national advertising campaign."

Maddie smiles. "I know. It's early days yet, but you're gaining experience all the time, building up contacts, and you've got a flair for the job. If this campaign is a success, Bob and I might very well be interested in putting up the initial funding for the Ann Browning Company."

At 1 A.M. I'm lying in bed, gazing with fixed desperation at a spider's web in the corner. I can't do it. I don't even understand the jargon. At 2 A.M. I know that the only sensible thing to do is ring Maddie in the morning and tell her I'm awfully sorry but . . . At 3 A.M. I get up, make a cup of coffee and talk sharply to myself. "If they think you can . . . it's their money after all." At 4 A.M., wishing I hadn't smoked three cigarettes, I get back into bed and, just as I'm falling asleep, remember Sol Venture, Felicia's friend. I wonder if he's too grand for commercials? What luck I'm lunching with Felicia tomorrow (oh God, today). I can pick her brains as well as asking her if she can look after the children over Easter.

Felicia

Ann suggested we meet at the Caprice for lunch. As I go in I find myself thinking how jerky everyone looks, how quickly they move. I suppose two years ago my eyes would have been darting about in the quest for faces I ought to remember, or who ought to remember me. I don't suppose I'll know a soul.

Sol Venture and I see each other at the same moment.

"Sol! You treacherous swine . . . why didn't you tell me you were over?"

"Didn't know myself, darling, until yesterday. Or was it this morning? Time differences, so muddly. Was going to call you tonight. Say, aren't we big and beautiful? Oh Felly, you look so happy."

"I am, I can't tell you how much. Can you spare a night to come down and stay?"

"Going back tomorrow, there's such a lot going on. You heard about *That Search Eternal*, I suppose?" Sol smiles wolfishly.

That Search Eternal was the fearful name Morris Kapperman had insisted on for the long-running series they had so briefly considered me for. Sol had walked out on it very shortly after my disastrous dinner party. He'd rung me up to Tell All:

"That fiend of a Morris, Felly. He doesn't see why Beau Brummell can't cut Lillie Langtry at Cowes. . . . keeps on talking about artistic license, darling, has no idea of history at all. So when he said wouldn't it be great drama if Charles Dickens went down with the *Titanic* . . . well, you can imagine, I said bye-bye Morris, it's been great knowing you. How are the dogs?"

"Very well, thank you. So who's going to be mad enough to take it on?"

"Oh, the buzz is they're lining up around the block, so much money, you see. He'll pick the worst, you take my word for it."

I had later heard, with some glee, that *That Search Eternal* had been taken off after two showings, to the mocking jeers of critics and no ratings at all. I had pointed all this out to Antony, with a prim smile.

I am just about to fall into a pleasing gossip about the horrors of Morris when I see Ann come in. Nearly everyone else sees her come in, too.

She is, as it happens, wearing the old Joseph Tricot number. Dateless, divine, skimming yet curvy, it looks marvelous on her. I couldn't begin to get into it now, I think comfortably.

"Ann, how are you? This is an old friend of mine, Sol Venture, over from the States for about ten minutes, as far as I can gather. Sol, this is Ann Browning, my husband's ex-wife."

"Hi, Ann. How extraordinary—you're wearing almost exactly what Felicia wore when I first met her two years ago."

We both laugh, and I say, "Exactly, as it happens—it looks so much better on her that I swapped it for her Barbour. We were just bitching up *That Search Eternal*, Ann. You know, that thing I might possibly have been in."

Ann's face turns instantly professional. "Of course, as soon as I heard David Sarkie was going to direct . . . is it true, Sol, that the sound man went for him with a knife?"

"Not exactly, what I heard was . . ."

And they are off into the kind of chat I used to indulge in regularly. I listen to them with great pleasure, and almost no interest at all. Eventually Sol says, "I didn't realize you were in TV, Ann? Felicia never said . . ."

"Actually, I'm not. I started with conference brochures, that sort of thing, now I'm moving into PR. Frankly, so much of it is so badly done . . ."

"You can say that again."

Ann eyes Sol speculatively. "As a matter of fact, it's interesting bumping into you, something's coming up that . . . how long are you over for? Could we set up a meeting?"

She takes out her Filofax. Sol takes out his. They look, I think fondly, as though they're enacting some ritual.

"Going back tomorrow, alas. When are you next in the States?"

"New York just before Easter. Nothing to stop me nipping over to the West Coast."

"Except," I point out prosaically, "that you'll have your children with you at Easter."

"Well, actually, Fel, that was one of the reasons I wanted to have lunch with you."

"I see. I'd love to have them, you know that."

"There's my lunch date," says Sol, "I'll call you tonight, Felly. Get in touch when you've got some dates, Ann, and we'll meet in L.A. I'll look forward to that . . . I couldn't ask you a favor, could I?" Ann looks obliging. "I need another Filofax, and the prices on the West Coast are horrendous. I don't have time to get it today, but if you could . . . my black one is great for the office, but I thought a burgundy one for home."

"No problem," says Ann, "I'd love an excuse to go to that shop, it's my idea of heaven."

As soon as we're sitting at our table (Ann merely has to look round with a slight air of impatience, and a waiter is there at her elbow—she's certainly got it taped), I say, "New York today, Los Angeles tomorrow . . . I knew you were doing well, Ann, but it's all getting very high-powered, isn't it? And what's all this about something coming up . . . and where does Sol come in?"

"Oh Fel," Ann looks round cautiously and lowers her voice,

"it's so exciting . . . but you mustn't tell a soul, it's still in the talking stage. Guide's Honor, you promise?"

It is one of the touching things about this new Ann, the Ann that can sear a headwaiter with one eyebrow, that she still uses schoolgirl expressions. I can easily imagine her saying, "Golly, what smashing artwork, Gianni, full marks."

"Cross my heart and hope to die," I say, falling easily into the patois.

"So amazing meeting Sol Venture here. I was going to ask you to put me in touch with him. You remember I told you about Maddie? Oh *Felicia,* " she says as I look vague, "you know, that terribly nice woman I met at Donald's. She and her husband head up the Delphic chain of hotels. Their motto is 'We know what you want before you do.' I thought that up, great, isn't it? Delphic, you see, prophetic and all that. Anyway . . . ," she lowers her voice and her head still further. I companionably lower my head too. My nose is now not more than four inches away from my tomato and mozzarella salad. We'd look quite peculiar if everyone else in the room wasn't muttering at each other in the same furtive way.

"Anyway, Fel, they're planning" (I am now seriously considering lip-reading) "a series of really, really quality TV ads. They've approached one or two people, but Maddie says they have hopelessly pedestrian ideas. If I told you who they were, Fel, you wouldn't believe me." (Wouldn't hear you, either, but let it pass.) "So they've asked me to rough out some ideas and suggest a director. I thought of Sol at once, of course. He's far and away . . . the only thing is, would he consider commercials beneath him? Money's no object, and we're looking for something really top class."

"He might be interested. Our ads are so much better than theirs," I say in a normal speaking voice. A man at the next table jumps nervously, and Ann hisses, "For God's *sake* keep your voice down."

"Sorry. He said he'd ring me up tonight. Do you want me to sound him out?"

"Jolly kind of you, but better not. I don't want this to get off on the wrong foot," says Ann, rather tactlessly, I consider. "Now are you absolutely sure about Easter, Fel? The five of them won't be too much for you?"

"No problem. Sarah and Laura are so sensible, and it's lovely when the house is full of children."

We fall into a discussion of times and dates. I try to tell her about the new herb garden I am constructing, but her mind is obviously miles away.

I am absolutely exhausted when I get back to White Walls. I feel grubby all over—horrid London. I am asleep when Sol calls. Sarah has to come and shout at me, and I yawn my way to the telephone.

"Felly, I didn't know whether you'd want me to talk in front of Ann—though I took rather a shine to her; do you think she'll remember about the Filofax?—but in about two months' time I'm shooting a piece that needs a beautiful and heavily pregnant woman. And who came immediately to mind? What do you think? Is there any chance?"

"Oh Sol, what fun. How kind of you to think of me. I'll be about seven months by then, is that large enough?"

"Sounds enormous to me. It's the way you pregnant ladies move, sort of slightly tilted back. You simply can't get the effect with padding."

"Only, where are you shooting? I don't think they like one to fly that late, and I'm not sure I'd want—"

"France. A week in the châteaux country and quite a nice fistful of dollars. Are you on?"

"Sounds wonderful. May one ask what you came over here for?"

"Strictly between us, I was asked to consider some commercials."

"You don't despise them, then?"

"Some of your commercials are better than some of our drama. In principle I'm very interested. But not in automobile tires, which was what I was offered today. Maybe something more interesting will come along someday."

Round about Easter, I thought, and was rather tempted to put an oar in. But I didn't. I had promised Ann not to mention it, and anyway I was frightfully sleepy.

Ann

As I walk into the restaurant I spot Felicia gossiping happily with a young man, and life being the series of coincidences it is, the young man is, of course, Sol Venture. We talk about the dread

Kapperman epic—good thing Felicia didn't get involved in *that* one—and Sol and I get on so well together that he gives me his telephone number, asks me to call him and agrees to meet me in L.A. when I go over there at the end of March for the Delphic promotional tour.

Felicia rather irritatingly interrupts by bossily reminding me that I'll have the children with me at Easter. But I only have to half suggest how grateful I'd be if she could keep them at White Walls and her face lights up with every appearance of genuine pleasure.

She's turned into something of an earth mother. When Sarah— or was it Laura?—told me, a couple of months ago, that Fel was going to have a baby, my first thought was Thank goodness it isn't me and my second was that maybe this was one of the reasons Antony had strayed. I'd had the tubes tied after Em—three small children seemed more than enough—and Antony was always fond of babies. Fatherhood suits him, so long as he doesn't have to do anything fatherly like changing a nappy or getting up at two in the morning to look in a cot. And he always seemed fonder of me when I was pregnant.

Felicia is looking marvelous, but what she's wearing looks as ghastly as my old cotton smocks. It is one of my old cotton smocks.

"So comfortable," says Felicia, enthusiastically ordering a tomato and mozzarella salad, mixed grill "and sauté potatoes, if I may?

"I knew you wouldn't mind, Ann. I can't bear wasting good money on boring clothes I'll only be wearing for nine months. I need every penny I can save for my new herb garden . . ."

And she's off, droning on about salad burnet and rocket and God knows what other obscure plant, and I can hardly get a word in edgeways, to tell her about Delphic and ask about Sol.

Whenever I do manage to drag her away from bedding plants, or whatever, her voice is so loud that everyone in the place—and I recognize quite a few of them—will know about the Delphic campaign before I've had time to spell it out to Maddie and Bob. I suppose it's living in a house full of children that does it.

Poor Felicia, I think, as she prattles happily on about her garden. She'll soon have another demanding voice to shout over.

Felicia

It's the day of the Easter Egg Hunt, what fun. Last night Antony and I sat up concocting clues, which was really difficult. Antony insisted they had to rhyme, and we also had to vary the hardness to suit all the children. We sat at the kitchen table, sharing a bottle of wine, and by midnight had got quite childish ourselves.

"Listen to this," said Antony, "it's brilliant. 'I fear you'll find this clue quite trivial, but a look behind the privy'll . . .'"

"Not half as good as mine. 'A walk past mint and chives and sage, will take you to Mrs. Tiggywinkle's cage.'"

"Far too easy. How about 'Go to the pond and stand and look. The answer will be an open book'?"

"Oh, Antony, you are a fool. I do love you."

"Try to remember you're talking to one of the best brains in advertising. You really ought to get to bed. How's our baby?"

"Bouncing rather. I think he likes wine."

"She."

"Do you absolutely insist on a girl?"

"I absolutely insist on whatever makes you happy. It's getting quite difficult to get my arms round both of you . . . oh, darling . . ."

Right now I am having my afternoon rest. The turkey has been defrosting since yesterday, I scrubbed the potatoes for baking this morning, and the girls have laid the table. Everything's organized.

How long have they known each other, Antony's children and mine? About eighteen months, I suppose.

Laura and Sarah, rather to my surprise, took an instant liking to each other. They disappeared upstairs for two hours and came down dressed in each other's clothes—the female adolescent equivalent of blood brotherhood. I worried how Emmy would fit in, but they seemed to work it very neatly. She trotted around behind them, admiring them both indiscriminately, and darling Laura, right from the start, treated her like a younger sister.

The boys weren't so easy. Mark despised poor Harry, he was so overweight. I wanted to blame Ann; but reading between the lines, I knew that Laura had been compensating for my absence by stuffing him with food like an overanxious mother. No problems now, though; Harry has slimmed down and revealed a talent for cricket, of all things. I wonder how Donald feels about that. There is no other game but baseball as far as he is concerned. Mark and Harry spent this morning hammering stumps into the croquet lawn and bowling at each other. At the moment they are in the playroom with Kitten, and what sounds like about a dozen cricket balls.

Antony has taken the girls and the other dogs out for a walk. As soon as they are back we will send them all out on the Great Egg Hunt. How easy life is to organize in the country. How lucky I am.

I wrap my hands happily round my stomach. It won't be long now, baby.

Ann

"Do something for me, hon," Donald had said, before I left for the States, "call up Tom and make sure he's all right. I haven't heard from him since he started with those real estate people in Newark."

Looking at Tom, sleeping beside me under the peach satin cover of the Helmsley Palace Hotel bedspread, I decide that he is very much all right. I kiss the nape of his neck tenderly. It looks soft and vulnerable. I'm reminded of Mark, five years old, playing in his bath, and instantly banish the incestuous thought.

Tom looks so like his father, but with none of Donald's toughness. Donald can manipulate a room full of people to suit himself, flattering the men, flirting with the women, leaving everyone with a warm glow of satisfaction that reflects in more business for Donald.

But Tom is only twenty-seven. "Do you realize I'm almost old enough to be your mother?" I'd said to him, tiresomely angling for a compliment as we held hands under the table at lunch.

"Not unless you were an unusually promiscuous fourteen-year-old," said Tom.

Now I'm turning into a promiscuous forty-one-year-old. I didn't mean to go to bed with Tom, but then, I didn't mean to go to bed with his father, either. I seem to be making a habit of behaving badly by default . . . making up for all those years of stagnation in Wiltshire, perhaps . . .

I'd phoned Tom yesterday in between giving a talk to a group of

American travel writers and lunching with the food editor of the *New York Times,* who had stipulated Arizona 206.

"But I was thinking of taking you to Sandro's. Everyone says it's the best restaurant in town."

"That was last week," said the food editor. Clearly he'd rather be seen snacking at a hot dog stand than at last week's "in" place.

I recognized Tom the moment he walked into the hotel foyer. It was Donald as he must have looked twenty years ago; shy and pleasingly unaware of his rangy good looks. There was a hint of Dustin Hoffman and *The Graduate* as he asked the desk clerk to ring my room, and I hoped I looked as good as Anne Bancroft as I walked over and tapped him on the shoulder.

"Tom?"

He jumped, muttered: "Okay, never mind . . ." turned and politely put out his hand. "Ann?"

"That's right. Ann Browning," and surprised myself, as well as Tom, by kissing him warmly. I think it was because he reminded me of Donald. We were both embarrassed by my effusiveness.

I smiled, in what I hoped was a motherly way: "It's all right. I'm practically your stepmother."

There was nothing motherly about the way I felt when he put both hands tentatively on my shoulders and kissed me back.

I don't remember where we had lunch. Tom chose the restaurant, and I'm sure the food editor of the *New York Times* wouldn't have wanted to be seen eating there, either. We ate a lot of spicy Vietnamese food and talked about Donald and about Phyllis, Tom's mother, who he thought was still carrying a torch for Donald.

"I'll never forgive her, you know . . . Felicia. She stole my father."

"Oh come on, Tom. Nobody steals anyone unless they want to be stolen."

"Well, she stole your husband, didn't she?"

"He was there for the taking." I hadn't even thought it before, but I knew it was true. My life had been the children, my home, the village; Antony's was his agency and the friends and colleagues he saw during the week in London. We met up on Friday evenings like friends who had once, long ago, shared a common experience.

"And is my father a good lover?"

"I'm sorry?" Surely Tom hadn't said what I thought he'd said? He ran his fingers through his hair a couple of times in a disarmingly boyish manner. "Okay, okay, I shouldn't have said that. But my father isn't exactly famed for his monkish habits and you're so pretty . . . I just sort of presumed . . . forget it, please. It was impertinent of me to ask."

"True." I tried to look censorious and smiled instead. "How do I know, Tom? I haven't been consumer testing around the Home Counties. I've only ever slept with two men in my life—Antony and your father."

"I suppose you wouldn't care to make it three?" He was blushing and his hand, as he took mine, was shaking; symptoms suggesting anxiety rather than a man playing a practiced line.

It would have been unkind to say no, I told myself, as we went up in the lift.

I kissed him once more on the nape of his neck, and then, slipping slowly down the bed, moved my lips gently along his body.

"Hey Ann. What are you doing?"

How do you judge whether a man is a good lover or not? One woman's heart-stopping ecstasy is another woman's turnoff. I only know that Tom Harman excites me because he doesn't call all the shots—"Do this, do that, now turn over"—or run through a routine as though he's programming a washing machine—"Press here, caress there, *now.*"

Hugging me tightly, thigh to thigh, he says: "Wow Ann, that was the best alarm call I ever had," instead of "How was it for you?" which, I've always suspected, means "Wasn't I the greatest?"

He kisses me again. "Oh Ann, you're very beautiful. Do you know that?" During the next fifteen hours with Tom Harman in Room 1158 of the Helmsley Palace I feel myself growing more beautiful by the minute. Love, I reflect, is a more effective rejuvenator than Lotte Berk or Elizabeth Arden.

"You won't sleep with my father again, will you, Ann? Not now."

Tom is unhappily watching me pack. I snap shut the second of my perfectly matched black suitcases. Ever since I was a small child I'd longed for a set of international jet set matched cases.

I'm about to reassure him, when it occurs to me that this is a one-sided deal. Tom is not, presumably, intending to wait chastely for our next transatlantic meeting.

Smiling enigmatically as I put on my lipstick—a difficult feat—I murmur something about that being rather an unreasonable request.

Tom looks even gloomier. "But I will see you again?" He brightens. "I tell you what . . . a crowd of us are going to Gstaad for Christmas. Why don't you come too, Ann? Say you will. Please."

Christmas. The children will want to be in the country with those bloody oxen again, I suppose.

"Yes. I'll come to Gstaad."

I loved New York but Los Angeles is even better. Some people might find the vistas of brash billboards and cheap motels tacky, but they lead to Beverly Hills . . . Hollywood. Never mind if the Twentieth Century Fox lot is now an exclusive residential estate and most of the other studios are churning out low-budget television soaps; if you've been reared on American films, as I have, it's all magic. I'd have taken the tour of the stars' mansions and peered down Doris Day's driveway with the rest of the fans if I'd had the time.

As the lift to Sol's office swoops me upwards, I think back to that Ann Forester-Jones who sniveled her way onto the London train two years ago. Complacently regarding myself in the mirror thoughtfully provided at the back of the lift—sorry, elevator—I say to myself, No man is ever going to make *you* cry again, Ann Browning.

Sol's secretary seems curiously subdued. I feel a flicker of unease. Surely he's not going to rat on the deal? We've sorted everything out on the telephone. I'm only here to make personal contact and get his signature on the dotted line, before flying home tomorrow. Bloody Americans, I think unfairly and illogically, if he's changed his mind . . .

"Mr. Venture is expecting you, Miss Browning. Do go straight in."

Sol is staring out of the window. When he turns and looks at me blankly across his desk, I see his eyes are red.

"Sol? Are you all right? You look awful. What's. . . . ?"

"Sarah called me half an hour ago, Ann. You weren't at your hotel so she called me."

Oh my God. It's one of the children.

"Felly's lost her baby."

Oh Felicia. How I hated you once, but even then I'd never have wished . . . "No, Sol, no. She can't have . . . how?"

"Sarah wasn't making a lot of sense. Something about an accident." He hesitates and looks at me sadly. "She kept on saying it wasn't Mark's fault."

Felicia

Rosie, who is a determinedly breezy woman in for a hysterectomy, stops by my bed.

"Feeling a bit more cheerful now, love?" she says kindly. It's kind of her to be kind, but I wish she'd go away. "Pity you weren't in here last week . . . there was ever such a nice lady with a prolapse who led us in community singing after tea."

Well, thank God for something. I doubt whether I could deal with ever such nice women urging me to sing "She'll Be Coming Round the Mountain." At least I am in the gynie ward, they've had the tact not to put me in with the mothers and babies. Every so often I hear the wail of a baby being carried down the corridor towards its feed; it actually hurts me, that noise, as though my womb were contracting.

It needn't have happened. If I could go back just three days, all I'd have to do is get up from my rest a minute later, and the baby would still be . . .

"No tears, dear," says Rosie bossily, "we've got to try and look on the bright side."

"Please get back to bed, Mrs. Thompson. Other patients need their rest even if you don't. Off you go, now."

I have only been two days in her ward, but I already know that Sister is one of those people who can be counted on to be in the right place at any given moment. She looks more like an accountant than a nurse; precise, unemotional, with a face that gives nothing away. Until you look at her eyes, which have seen it all.

After Rosie has got back into bed, dropping glad tidings on every patient she passes like some kind of blight, Sister says, "Nothing worse than being told to look on the bright side when there isn't one, is there? But you will come through it, my dear, I promise you. I've had women in here who thought they'd never be happy again . . . and two years later, they've come back and walked out with beautiful healthy babies."

"But I'm thirty-five."

Sister smiles. "You're an infant. There's a woman in the next ward who's forty-one. She had a perfect little girl last night. You've got plenty of time for another one, if that's what you want. Now I really came to ask a favor. There's a poor little thing in a side ward —only twenty and she miscarried last night and doesn't begin to know how to cope. It's often the young ones who can't manage— first time life's really hit them, I suppose. When you feel like it, could you go and have a chat? It's such a comfort to talk to someone who knows what it's like . . ."

I don't really want to, but Sister is the kind of person whose approval one instinctively wants to gain.

When I hesitantly put my head round the door of the side ward, I see that one of the beds is empty. The occupant of the other one, whose face is blotched with crying, turns her head listlessly on the pillow and says, "I've already told them I don't want to see the effing chaplain, if that's what you've come for. I hate God."

"I'm nothing to do with the hospital, I'm a patient. I lost mine too, and Sister thought . . ."

She looks at me properly and says, "I'm sorry. I can't bear it, can you? They keep on saying, 'Never mind, you'll have another one' as though you'd lost an earring or something. I don't want another one. I wanted this one." She cries again.

"I know. There's a ghastly woman in my ward who keeps on telling me to look on the bright side. I only wish I had enough strength to push her face in."

She smiles. It's not much of a smile, but it'll do. "Wait till tomorrow and I'll come and help you. How many months were you? I was only two, and some bloody doctor told me it was probably nature's way of rejecting something that wasn't quite right. Great line of bedside chat *he* has."

"Just over five months," I say, and I look out of the window and I'm crying again.

"Christ." She bends awkwardly over her locker and fishes out her handbag. "Let's have a cigarette."

"I'm not sure we're allowed—"

"Sod the rules, I say." She passes me the packet, and we both light up.

"He was already moving quite a lot," I say.

"He? It was a boy, was it? My name's Suzie, what's yours?"

"Felicia."

"Pretty name. Bloody men, they've got no idea, have they? It was too soon to tell what mine was. Had you done all your shopping for the baby?" She hauls herself up on her pillows and flinches. "Holy cow, someone seems to have tied a hedgehog between my legs. It's a laugh a minute peeing, isn't it?"

"I know. I say—my husband brought me in a bottle of sherry last night. Shall I?"

"Great. And bring a tooth mug, there's only one in here."

Twenty minutes later we are both laughing, though sometimes an outsider might think we were crying. The side ward smells like a working men's club, and we both smile nervously at Sister when she pops her head round the door.

"We'll have to get some fresh air in here before Mr. Amberton does his rounds, and for heaven's sake put that sherry out of sight. I wondered, Mrs. Holbrook, whether you'd care to move into the main ward? The bed next to Mrs. Forester-Jones is vacant, and—"

"Who's Mrs. Forester-Jones? Some toffee-nosed old bat?"

"That's me, actually," I say apologetically.

"Sorry, love. Yeah, that'd be great. I've had it up to here with this room."

"You'll have to watch your language, Mrs. Holbrook," Sister says, "the patient in the bed opposite Mrs. Forester-Jones is very easily shocked."

"What, me? Language?"

"You should have heard yourself last night."

"Well, it was hurting, wasn't it?"

Sister smiles and leaves the room. Cunning old bird.

"So how did it happen, yours?" says Suzie abruptly. "I thought by five months everything was pretty plain sailing."

I pour us both some more sherry. There's hardly any left.

"I fell down the stairs," I say. "It was so silly, Suzie—it needn't have happened."

I was humming "Happy Days Are Here Again" when I got up from my rest. I used to sing it to Laura and Harry while I was bathing them. I stopped at the top of the stairs, thinking that it wouldn't be long, only about four months, before I'd be singing it to another laughing baby.

The boys had come out of the playroom and were playing a decorous kind of indoor French cricket on the landing.

"That's going to ruin the paintwork, Mark," I said.

"It's all right, Felly, house rules, we're only rolling it. If the ball leaves the ground, you're out."

"Much better outside, really. There's Dad and the girls back from their walk. Honestly, Mark, he'll be livid."

"Okay. Just one more go."

Mark carefully rolled the ball towards Harry. Kitten shot out of the playroom and pounced. Her jaws weren't quite big enough and Mark managed to grab it.

"Quick, Harry," he shrieked, chucking it in my direction. It cannoned off the chest of drawers that Emmy had long ago prayed in front of, and bounced down the stairs. Kitten, mad with joy and the excitement of chasing, roared along the corridor, frantically tried to change direction as she saw where the ball had gone, and thumped into the back of my legs.

Whoops, watch it, I thought, as I grabbed for the banister.

It's funny how time seems to hang about sometimes.

As I bumped and rolled and slithered down the stairs I had plenty of time to think, Antony's been promising to mend that banister for weeks. And I had plenty of time to hear Antony, his face a dreadful mask of rage and fright, shout, "You bloody stupid little boy. Get out of my sight before I kill you."

As I landed in the hall Mark ran past me and out of the front door. He was accompanied by Kitten, who had the appearance of a dog who knows something bad has happened and is pretty sure she'll be blamed for it.

They gathered round me. "Don't worry," I said, "I'm fine. Just give me a moment . . . wow, my back."

My three wonderful girls, who had suddenly got much older, exchanged glances.

Then Emmy said, "I'd better go after Mark. Harry, why don't you come with me and help cheer him up?"

Laura knelt down beside me and gently shifted my head onto her lap. She stroked my hair. "There's my clever girl," she said, "it's all going to be all right. Don't you worry about a thing . . . there's a good girl."

She sounded like my mother. That's why I was crying, because Laura sounded like my mother.

Antony said, "We'd better call the doctor."

Sarah was already on the phone. "My stepmother . . . down the stairs, yes . . . I think about five months." She raised querying eyebrows at Antony, who nodded, and added anxiously, "Five months and twelve days exactly."

"Yes," said Sarah, "I'll ask her . . . Felly, he says is there any pain?"

I was hurting all over. I'd scraped an elbow and my knee didn't feel as though it would be reliable to walk on. But the only pain that mattered was the greedy, groping ache at the center of my existence.

I turned my face into Laura's lap and sobbed.

"Yes, there is some pain," Sarah said, "an ambulance, right. Shall I ring or . . . oh, thank you." And then her voice went right back to childhood. "Please, could you ask them to be quick?"

She put down the phone, and came and knelt next to Laura. "They don't want you to move, Felly; we'll just make you comfortable."

"Antony," Laura said, "could you fetch the rug and a cushion from the library?"

Larkspur crept up to me, her hackles up. "Isn't that interesting," I said conversationally, "they put their hackles up when they're worried as well as when they're angry?"

Antony came back. "Here's the rug," he said, "and I brought two cushions. Put Larkspur in the kitchen, someone."

"No," I said, "I want her here." She lay against me, shivering and giving me enormous comfort. "Sarah," I said, "whatever happens, tell Mark it wasn't his fault."

"Nothing's going to happen, Felly. Just a few days in bed, that's all you need."

"Yes," I said, "I'll be fine, don't worry." But the ache was getting more confident, it was beginning to take charge. Anyway, I could feel the blood trickling.

When the ambulance men came, they started to lift me onto a stretcher, and paused and looked at each other unhappily.

"I wonder, sir," said the older one to Antony, "if you have any spare newspapers . . . just to put on the stretcher."

Antony looked round frenziedly. "Will the *Times* do?" he said.

How frightfully amusing. I did think that was awfully funny. "Top people bleed into the *Times*," I said.

"Don't worry, sir," said the younger one, "it's a bit of shock . . . it takes them like that sometimes."

This wasn't at all good for the girls. "Sarah and Laura," I said, "it's high time you were in bed. You can watch television for a bit if you like. Have you had supper yet? Someone ought to put the turkey on. I've done the potatoes . . ." The look on Antony's face made me feel unhappy. "It's all right, darling," I said, holding his hand, "the potatoes are all ready."

"I'll stay here, Dad," said Sarah, "and look after Emmy and the boys. Laura, you'll go with Felly, won't you?"

"Perhaps you could follow us in your car, sir? Then you could bring the young lady back."

"And Larkspur," I said, "Larkspur's coming too."

"I'm very sorry, love," said the young one, "but regulations do not permit . . ." He caught a look from the older one. "Oh well," he said miserably, "I suppose rules were made to be broken."

Laura and Larkspur and I were in the back of an ambulance with a middle-aged man I'd never met before. I was very fond of him.

"You're not ringing the siren," I said, "why isn't the siren ringing?"

"Not a lot of traffic about now, love; but he's going through all the red lights."

"Will the baby be all right?"

He gave me a look of great affection and then peered intently out of the window, as though the driver had asked him to keep a lookout.

"Don't you worry about a thing," he said, "we're nearly there now."

So that's that, one half of my mind thought. The other half pretended it didn't understand.

Ann

I collect my car at Heathrow and drive straight down to Wiltshire. Antony is there, wandering about the house, twitching at an un-made bed, washing a cup, feeding Kit-E-Kat to the dogs. It feels strange to see him at White Walls in the middle of the week; even stranger to be there with him. I can't believe that we were ever married, that we expended so much passion and hatred and misery on each other. Now he is just an old friend in trouble.

"I'm sorry, Antony."

"I know . . . thank you . . . thank you for coming. The children are about somewhere . . ." He looks helplessly around. He is incapable of seeing anything except, I imagine, Fel as she was carried away from him. "We wanted the baby so much, you know."

Exhausted after the fifteen-hour flight, I nearly make an insensitive remark about always being able to have another, but stop just in time and mutter something about getting the children organized.

They are upstairs, silently packing their cases.

Emmy rushes to hug me: "It was Mark's fault, with that stupid cricket ball. Felly *told* him not to play with it in the house."

"Of course it wasn't Mark's fault," says Harry loyally. "How could Mark know that the banister's broken?"

"It wasn't *anybody's* fault," I say. Mark is sitting on the edge of the bed, his head in his hands. *"It wasn't anybody's fault* . . . Did you hear that, precious? And now we're all going back to London, and I don't want to hear any more bickering. Sarah . . . Laura . . . bring the cases and we'll be off."

I hadn't phoned Donald. I presumed someone else had.

"Hi, Ann." He kisses me perfunctorily. "How did it go?"

"Okay. But I had to rush down to . . ."

He is pointing towards the staircase, like a dog who's scented something unpleasant. "What's that hellish din?"

"The children. I was trying to tell you . . ."

"But what are they doing here, Ann? I've got people coming in for drinks in half an hour, and you surely haven't forgotten that we're having dinner with the Kaamaundus this evening?"

"You'll have to drink and dine without me, Donald."

I explain about the cricket ball, the broken banister, the baby, but too much has happened in the last forty-eight hours. I reach for a Kleenex to wipe away the tears.

Taking the Kleenex from me, Donald rubs at my cheeks, hoping to erase the drama. "Felicia's all right, she's going to be okay?" I nod. "Right then. I'll keep an eye on the kids. Go and have a hot bath, a bit of a rest, and you'll be fine for this evening." He gives my shoulder a persuasive pat. "Come on now, it'll do you good. I'll send Fel some flowers tomorrow."

Lying in bed later, I tell myself that even if Donald Harman isn't the warmest human being I've ever met, we've been good for each other. He transformed me into what he needed, a mirror image of Felicia, an efficient homemaker and glamorous consort for his business social life, and in return he's given me a gloss of sophistication and an address book full of useful contacts. Ann Forester-Jones couldn't get a job as a shorthand typist but all the right doors open for Ann Browning. Luckily, I've enough sense to take advantage of the opportunities that come my way, and a keen desire to win, forged by eight competitive years in boarding school.

The children are with me for just over a week. The accident has upset them badly, and I've just had to let the work pile up.

Yesterday, I'd found Em sitting by herself in the kitchen, crying and twisting a handkerchief into tight knots.

"What is it, love?"

Em sniffed. "Isn't this a beastly kitchen, Mum?"

"Yes it is. But it's nothing to cry about. What's the matter? Felly? The baby?"

"Oh, everything, Mum. Everything's so beastly. After you and Dad . . . and all that . . . White Walls seemed sort of safe, like nothing bad could ever happen there again . . ."

Emily has grown up so fast these last few years. I'm sure I wasn't as articulate as that when I was ten.

"And it will be again, love. You do want to go back there, don't you?"

I'm watching as well as listening as she says: "Oh yes, please, Mum . . . if you don't mind . . . ?"

I wonder if I have inherited my own mother's unmaternal streak —her heart is certainly fonder when I'm absent—or am I rationalizing because I can't have my children with me all the time? No, it hurts like hell to see them going back so cheerfully to another woman who can give them the life I can't.

And Felicia needs the children. She phoned up and asked, in a muffled, subdued voice, if I'd mind putting them all on the train. "I'll meet them at Tisbury."

"All? Are you sure, Fel? Can you cope?"

"Can't cope without them, that's the problem. Sarah and Laura are so good together, so helpful, and I do want to see Mark and tell him everything's all right. He wasn't to blame, Ann. The doctor says there was a chance I'd lose the baby anyway."

Sol is doing wonders with the commercial. He's concentrating on Tadworth, photographing it through early morning mists, golden sunsets. The stills are great and I've managed to sell one, of the box-hedged herb garden, to the *Sunday Times Magazine* for a cooking feature. Thousands of pounds' worth of free publicity. Maddie is delighted.

This morning we're setting up a shot in the stable courtyard and I've got Su Parsons, dressed in riding gear, sitting warily on Conker, a docile chestnut.

"Christ, Ann! The thing moved!"

"Well, it will if you shift around on it like that. Just sit tall and relax."

Sol is charmed by the scene and impressed by Su. "Just the right Sloane image, Ann. Which agency is she with?"

Su's haughty country look is actually bad temper at having got up at six to get to Tadworth by seven forty-five, in order to spend two and a half hours having her face made up and her hair tonged, brushed out, sprayed, blow-dried and finally confined in a snood under her bowler.

When I'd suggested the modeling job she had been thrilled. "Twenty quid an hour for sitting on a horse? I'm on."

But thirty-five minutes with Kevin the hairdresser and Martin the visagiste *("The what??"* said Su. "The makeup artist," I said) and she was ready to pack it in and get back to the Hoover.

"What do you use on your face, darling?" said Martin.

"Oh, anything that's lying around," said Su and Martin winced.

"Who does your hair, darling?" said Kevin.

"I do," said Su, "and my husband does the highlights."

"How *cozy,"* said Kevin.

She leaves, in a chauffeur-driven limo: "Bloody boring job, isn't it, Ann? Having people messing about with your hair all day; it'd drive me crazy."

Sitting in the Garden House sitting room over a self-congratulatory bottle of champagne, Sol says: "Guess who I saw kissing the tips of whose fingers in the Groucho Club yesterday?"

"It's got to be Antony. That's his line."

"Right." Sol is suddenly serious. "Actually Ann, it isn't funny. I'm worried for Fel. She couldn't take another knock right now, and it looked like kind of a heavy scene."

"The woman? What was she like?"

"Young. Earnest. Gazing into his eyes like a puppy yearning to be stroked."

"Oh dear."

"Exactly . . . I think I recognized her. His assistant or secretary, someone like that . . ."

It can't be the redoubtable Sally, who knows Antony far too well to go in for any adoring gazing. "What does she look like?"

"Sensible tweedy skirt, passable pale blue sweater, pearls, nice open face, unmemorable shiny dark hair, and a *very* large bust, dear. I've never met a school prefect, but I guess she'd look like this one."

I recognized that girl. "She sounds like me, twenty years ago."

Sol shakes his head. "Ann baby, she is *nothing,* I repeat, *nothing* like you."

Fel and I met up a couple of times that summer. And we were always on the phone to each other, checking doctor and dentist appointments, reporting strange rashes or curious changes of mood, fixing times and dates. When experts warn about the stress of divorce, I'm surprised they don't mention the tension generated by arrangements. "Ann? It's Fel. This weekend?"

"Yes?"

"The thing is, Sarah and Mark come out of school at four, but Em has a rehearsal and won't be free until five-thirty, and Antony has made an appointment for the car to go in for servicing, so I won't be able to get them to the station by six-thirty, but Jenny is going to a cocktail party on the other side of Salisbury at about seven, so she could take them in and put them on the six-forty-five coach if you can meet them at Victoria. I'll check what time it gets in and let you know. And, by the way, Sarah's Open Day has been changed from the fourth to the fifth, but, as Mark's Sports Day has been altered from the fifth to the fourth, they kind of cancel each other out. Are you still there, Ann? Ann. . . . ?"

During the holidays, I managed to get tickets for *Starlight Express,* and Felicia brought the children up to London to see it. It was very noisy and Fel and I enjoyed it enormously.

"Rock and roll. It's a bit passé, isn't it?" said Mark, and Em said: "I don't see how trains can have faces and roller-skate."

"Why are children so literal?" I asked Felicia, in the Spaghetti House after the show. "I thought they were supposed to be naturally imaginative."

"Not our Em," said Felicia.

Felicia was looking better. Less strain around the eyes. But she seemed to be putting on a great deal of weight. I advised against the Black Forest gateau after the spaghetti carbonara, but Fel told me cheerfully to shut up and mind my own business.

There have been further sightings of Antony and the prefect in the Groucho Club from Sol, and others, and I was thinking of having a stern word with Antony when he phoned me and suggested lunch.

Felicia

There's something very cheering about looking through seed catalogues. Last year, of course, I grew hardly anything, just some basil. I remember saying to Antony, "Did you know you can actually grow your own basil? I thought you had to buy it in little pots from Justin de Blank." And Antony hugged me and said, "You are so beautifully impractical, darling—promise me you'll never change."

That's all very well, but buying bedding plants like I did last year is frightfully expensive, and we seem to need so many. And it's not half so satisfying; I clearly remember that day in May of 1984 when I gave my little margarine box of damp compost its routine, not very optimistic glance. It seemed so unlikely that those dry little specks of dust could turn into green plants. The compost had shifted in places, and when I investigated . . .

"Look," I said to them all when they came down to breakfast, "do look—my basil's coming up."

"Aren't they sweet?" said Emmy obligingly.

"Oh Felly," Sarah said, "you are funny. If you put seeds in the right medium and give them moisture and warmth, they do tend to germinate, you know. They're programmed to."

"I've never germinated anything before," I said. "Antony, do look—tiny little basil plants."

"Lovely, darling," he said, picking up the *Times*. He reminded me, disconcertingly, of Donald.

The basil grew and thrived and I don't ever remember eating anything so delicious as tomato salad liberally sprinkled with *my* basil that I grew. Early this year I sowed lots more seeds: marjoram and French parsley (so much more flavorful, the catalogues told me, than the curly variety), chives and sage. Aubretia and Sweet William, convolvulos, petunias and phlox. The kitchen was littered with little furry green boxes.

When I came back empty from the hospital, they had all withered. Nobody had remembered to water them.

I tidied them all away, and we had macaroni cheese cooked by Sarah and Laura for supper.

"Not half as good as yours, Felly," said Sarah, grinning, "oh, it is lovely to have you back."

Now, over breakfast coffee, I am laying plans for next year. Chris has already supplied me with a list, running to two pages, of seeds for the vegetable garden. Twenty-eight pounds' worth, my calculator tells me. But great value in the long run, and now I'm adding my suggestions. The trouble is it's all so tempting; whoever does the photography for these catalogues should command a fee of thousands. A new kind of geranium, in ravishing shades of palest pink . . . delphiniums as tall as the Brigade of Guards . . . lovely shady foxgloves that would look marvelous in the shrubbery . . .

By the time I have finished ticking all those little boxes I've spent £42.20. And that's only Suttons. I reach eagerly for the Thompson & Morgan.

I shall have to leave the catalogues until this evening, because here is Dotty Maxwell. I'd completely forgotten she was going to drop in this morning for our Harvest Festival contributions.

"I know we've got lots of marrows," I say hopefully; the wretched things keep on coming, the children won't eat any more, and Chris has point-blank refused to take any home.

Dotty's face drops slightly. "So has everyone else," she says; "if I accepted all the marrows I've been offered we wouldn't be able to see the pulpit."

Chris fortuitously comes in for her coffee, and on our behalf generously offers tomatoes, runner beans, and two ears of corn.

"*And* a marrow," I say firmly. I actually wanted all our runner beans for the deep freeze, but can think of no way of saying so without sounding both irreligious and mean. Must make sure Chris doesn't give her too many.

After Dotty has left, I go upstairs and put on my jodhpurs. I can see they could look rather dashing, but not until I've got rid of this tummy. That's why I started having riding lessons; Jenny told me there was nothing like it for tightening up the muscles. The way she ran her eyes over me as she said it made me want to pour my coffee over her head; but I didn't think the ladies at the kneeler needlepoint morning would appreciate such a forthright gesture, so I smiled sweetly and said, "What a good idea."

I can't remember what I used to do in the evenings in St. John's Wood; Go Out, I suppose, or Stay In and have people to dinner. How much nicer it is to sit in front of *St. Elsewhere* (which I really couldn't bear to miss, it's so good) and stitch away at my needlepoint.

I'm currently working on my second kneeler; I have learned so many new stitches, I can't wait to work them in.

Wary as I am of Jenny, I have to be grateful to her for dragging me along to a needlepoint morning all those months ago.

"You've got to do something," she said in her managerial way, "there's more to life than crying about the baby."

This impersonal briskness was oddly consoling; everyone else had tiptoed round me, thinking before they spoke in case they said something tactless. Her let's-get-on-with-it attitude was as bracing as a facecloth full of cold water.

I turned up at my first needlepoint morning at Dotty Maxwell's feeling rather diffident.

I knew (Jenny herself had told me) that Antony and I had been the subject of gossip for weeks when I first moved in. And I also knew that country people were slow to accept strangers and I'd probably still be that New Lady at White Walls when I was having my grandchildren to stay. I was accepted instantly, and with a kindly social grace that would have done credit to an experienced ambassador's wife.

"Come and sit next to me," Mrs. Grainger said, "budge up, Ethel, there's room for a little one. And how are you feeling after your mishap? We saw the ambulance, you know, and I said to Perce I don't like the look of that, that'll be one of the children."

"You can never be sure with children," said Ethel, "always getting into something."

"And when I heard," said Mrs. Grainger, treating Ethel's contribution as mere punctuation, "I thought, poor Mrs. Forester-Jones, she'll be feeling a bit low for a month or two, but she'll get over it, you always do."

The other women began a conversation mainly composed of the kind of clichés I would once have laughed at. "I lost my second right after I heard Reg had been wounded. . . . men don't know what it's like, do they? . . . that doctor said I'd never carry our

George to full term . . . Never mind what it is, nurse, I said, just tell me it's all right . . ."

But I didn't laugh then; it seemed to me they were swaddling me protectively in the old truths. It has happened before and it will happen again. Mustn't let it get you down.

I've been riding twice a week for a month now, and yesterday the scales dropped below 130 pounds. My tummy muscles are beginning to flatten, and it's certainly done a lot for my thighs. It's a pity Antony hasn't had a chance to see them—he's working so hard on this new account that he has only been able to get down twice in the last month, and then he was so tired all he wanted to do was sleep.

My first riding lesson was rather a surprise—I'd expected a strapping person of indeterminate sex who would shout loud, worrying commands at me. Julie wasn't a bit like that; slight, slim and fair, she approached me with a friendly smile as I got out of my car.

"You must be Mrs. Forester-Jones. Isn't it a lovely day? Come and help me get your pony out of his box . . . you said on the phone you've never ridden before?"

"Well, I did once sit on a horse. I am, I used to be an actress, and there was this scene—I had to sit sidesaddle while someone proposed to me. There was a man out of camera who was holding the horse's head. And even then," I added honestly, "I hated it."

"So why are you here?"

"I'm not very fit and I want to lose weight."

"You might even end up enjoying it," said Julie, leading out a pony who looked, to my relief, distinctly on the sleepy side. "Come on, Jester, you idle old man, time for a bit of work."

Getting on was easier than I expected. Apparently you had to stand with your back to his head and put your left foot, no, Mrs. Forester-Jones, *left* foot, in the stirrup. And then with a leap and a lurch and pull, there you were, up there.

Jester heaved a sigh and flicked an ear at a sparrow who was foraging in some dung.

"He won't do anything, will he?" I said, clutching at the reins.

"I promise you he'll just stand there. Don't bother with the reins for the moment, just get comfortable. Relax, Mrs. Forester-Jones."

"Do call me Felicia, it'll be quicker." Relax? Get comfortable? Of my own free will—nobody had made me—I was sitting on half a ton of muscle and sharp feet and large teeth. The saddle, evolved by generations of dedicated craftsmen-sadists, was sticking bits of itself into my knees.

Julie leaned against a hay bale and lit a cigarette. She was standing just to the left of a large notice saying "Smoking is not permitted under any circumstances on these premises." Marvelous, I thought, when that hay bale goes up Jester will panic . . . I've paid for half an hour, so I suppose I'll have to stick it out.

After a while Julie dropped her cigarette and vaguely trod on it.

"Right," she said, "let's walk around a bit."

Julie and Jester and I walked round the school.

"Don't try and cling with your knees," she said, "concentrate on feeling him move beneath you."

I could concentrate on little else. He could flick me off as easily as Julie had flicked her cigarette away. When I hit the ground he'd probably tread on me. And why did he keep on twitching his ears back?

"Talk to him," said Julie. "The voice is a very important aid, you know."

"Hello, Jester," I whispered. He heaved another sigh. I took a surreptitious look at my watch. Only another ten minutes and I need never get on a horse again. Typical Jenny Balfour, of course; I might have known she wouldn't suggest anything that didn't lead to humiliation and fear.

"We'll just have a little jog before you stop."

"What is a little jog?"

"The next pace up from a walk. Relax as much as possible."

She clucked at Jester, who instantly started throwing me around in the saddle. I wobbled and clutched and thought that my knees, if I could spare the time to look, would probably be bleeding.

"How do you stop him?" I asked.

"Feel the reins gently."

Jester stopped.

"Did you do that?" I asked.

"No, you did."

"Could we try it again?"

We tried it again, and Jester stopped again, and Julie looked at her watch. "You've had about enough for the first time. Make much of him."

"What does that mean?"

"Slap him on the neck and tell him he's lovely."

After I'd got off—following Julie's instructions with as much nervous attention as if she were telling me how to defuse a bomb—Jester rubbed his ear against my shoulder.

"Can I come again on Friday?" I said.

When I came down to breakfast next morning, I found to my great joy that Antony had driven down the night before, thoughtfully sleeping in the yellow room so as not to disturb me.

"Darling. How lovely . . . how long are you down for?"

"Got to go back this afternoon, I fear. Why are you walking like that?"

"I'm frightfully stiff. My back, the agony, and these muscles up the inside of my thighs. I had a riding lesson yesterday, I just sat there for half an hour, and I cannot tell you what pain I'm in."

"Well, now you know you don't like it—"

"I love it, I'm going again on Friday. It's all communication, you know. You send these little messages to the horse, and he does what you tell him. It's true, isn't it, Sarah?"

"Up to a point," said Sarah; "quite often you send him little messages and he doesn't take a blind bit of notice."

"Not Jester," I said loyally. "He's a dark bay from the New Forest, Antony, and Julie says he's got a perfect mouth."

"Good God," said Antony.

"What?"

"Patterson Warbeck are making a bid for United Grip. Listen to this." He read out a long bit from the *Financial Times*. I didn't understand a word.

"What's so interesting about that?"

"United Grip is one of the really big accounts everyone's after. I told you that, Felicia, ages ago. I do think you might take some interest."

"I do, darling, I'm very interested. It's just that I don't understand all that about takeovers and things."

"You used to."

"Donald was always droning on about them, so I had to pick up a bit of the jargon in self-defense. Come and look at where I'm going to plant the daffodil bulbs."

"I think I'll phone Donald. He's bound to know what's going on. I'll come and look later."

But after he phoned Donald, he decided he'd better get back to town. He's working far too hard, I thought, I do wish he'd relax more.

"I'm off," he said to Sarah, "coming to wave me good-bye, darling?"

"No, I'm bloody not," she said.

What on earth was the matter with her?

Ann

"Connaught. One o'clock?"

"Goodness, that's grand, Antony."

"Doing a presentation in Berkeley Square. I'll put you down as client expenses."

I guessed Antony would want to discuss the children—there'd been talk of Sarah wanting to be a vet, Mark needing spectacles, Em going to a new school—but he deals with that agenda before we finish the oysters, and we're on to the Brie and strawberries before he reveals what's on his mind.

"I hear you've got a little job?"

This is so irritating that I can think of nothing to reply except yes.

"To do with advertising, Sarah tells me . . . ?"

"That's right."

I'd fantasized boasting of my success to Antony but this isn't the right script. "Delphic have asked me to handle their publicity *and* advertising. I'm working on the first commercials now . . ."

"Ah, well done, well done." He's drumming his fingers on the table; he's about to say something he knows I won't like. "The thing is, Ann, I don't mind you using the name as an initial leg up, but it's a bit embarrassing having *two* Forester-Joneses turning up in the pages of *Campaign.*"

I'd chuck my wine at him if we weren't at the Connaught. "Antony, my job has nothing whatsoever to do with you. I met Maddie and Bob McMahon, the Delphic directors, at Donald's . . ."

"*Aha*, friends of Donald's, are they?"

It's no good. Antony will always see me as the girl who took his dictation or the woman who cooked him dinner. "That's right. Friends of Donald's, and they know me as Ann Browning, which is the name I use at work."

"Oh, that's all right then. Sensible girl. Hope you didn't mind me mentioning it." Relieved, he orders another bottle of wine. "I must say, Ann, it seems to be suiting you. You're looking great, absolutely great."

Relaxing more comfortably into the tapestry chair, he gives a lopsided grin which is obviously intended to be beguiling. "It's fun, this, isn't it? You and I, here together, like old times?"

"Not exactly like old times, Antony. I don't seem to recall you wining and dining me at the Connaught very often."

"Perhaps I should have done." He takes a long reflective sip of the Mouton Cadet. "Perhaps that's where I went wrong. I didn't appreciate you, Ann, that's the trouble. Didn't realize how lucky I was."

"Possibly not." I can hear my voice becoming crisper by the minute. "And how is Felicia?"

"Fel? Oh, she's all right. Pottering about in the garden, knee-deep in compost and our four-footed friends; you know the kind of thing . . ."

"But, that's what you want, isn't it, Antony?"

"Is it?" He is surprised. "I don't think so. What drew me to Felicia . . . I hope you don't mind me saying this, Ann . . . ?" It's a bit late for such delicacy, I should have thought, but I give him an encouraging nod. "What I loved about Felicia was her gaiety and wit; she was such *fun.*"

"And so you took her down to White Walls and turned her into a country housewife?"

"Ann, what an extraordinary thing to say."

He's looking at me as if I've just told him, confidentially, that the world is, after all, flat. Does he really not realize that he has this habit of falling in love with one woman and then turning her into somebody else?

I'm just going to say this, when the thought occurs that he wouldn't be able to go in for any Pygmalion nonsense if women like Felicia and me weren't prepared to put up with it. "I wonder why we do it?"

"Sorry?"

"I was just wondering why we let you do it."

I can tell by the satisfied way he's smiling that he thinks it's something to do with his heart-stopping charm. He is also picking up my right hand and fiddling with the fingers in a tiresome way. Guessing that it's the run up to the kissing routine, I withdraw my hand and start fiddling with cigarettes and lighter. He is murmuring all the things I longed to hear two years ago.

"Can't believe how you've changed . . . look so fantastic . . . sweet of you to come down that time, darling . . . dreadful mistake . . . you and I . . . the children . . . not too late . . . why don't we have dinner?"

"Antony, stop it, please." Surely he wasn't like this when I first knew him and through all those years of marriage? I want to leave now, but he *is* the children's father, and for their sakes I must stay cool and keep the lines of communication open, as Mr. Dwyer put it when he was handling the divorce.

Repressing the disagreeable things I'd like to say, I advise him, as agreeably as possible, to think of Felicia and to stop making passes at every woman he meets across a lunch table, including me and the girl in the Groucho Club.

"What girl?" says Antony.

"You know perfectly well who I mean. The one whose fingers everyone keeps seeing you kissing. The one who looks like a school prefect; not unlike me, I suspect, when we first met."

He's smiling again. "She *is* a bit like you, Ann. I expect that's what I like about her."

"Well, thank you." I pick up my handbag decisively. "But try to remember what a mistake it was, you and I."

Felicia

I can now rise to the trot.

"Don't try and push yourself up," says Julie; "relax into him and let him throw you up."

Jester and I have a very adequate working relationship. He plainly thinks I am laughably ignorant, but is amiably prepared to put up with me. After I've got off—I can now do it without staggering as I hit the ground—I give him a couple of Polo mints, which he is very partial to.

"You did awfully well today," Julie says. "You've got a real feeling for it, Felicia."

"Oh, come on . . ."

"No, seriously. That first day, I thought, We'll never see her again, but now you're beginning to look really good. Jester enjoyed himself today."

I suddenly have an absurd vision of myself saying earnestly to Sol Venture: "Jester enjoyed himself today." I really ought to ring Sol, he's been so kind. He came down to see me last week, looking a bit worried. He didn't seem his old self at all, something's obviously gone wrong in his life. I didn't like to ask too many questions, so I burbled on about the dogs and showed him my new needlepoint design and walked him round the garden.

"Felly," he said, as he got into his car, "is everything all right?"

"Have I got over the baby, do you mean? Oh, well, of course I still feel sad, but I'm much better now and one's simply got to get on with life."

"You ought to come up to London more. Let's have lunch next time you go to Robert."

"Oh, I've stopped going to Robert. There's not much point in spending thirty quid on a hairdo just to squash it under a sweaty hard hat. I always have to wash it after I've been riding, and Dotty Maxwell's put me on to a very good hairdresser in Salisbury. Only eight pounds, and just as good, really. Sol, you're looking rather tired . . . not working too hard, are you?"

It was all go that day. No sooner had Sol left than Antony arrived.

"Darling. What a treat. You haven't been down for ages. I've got so much to show you."

"I was down last month," he said defensively. "I tried to tell you . . . I haven't got a moment to spare, with the United Grip presentation on top of everything else. The moment I come in the door, you're getting at me."

"I'm sorry, darling, I do know you're busy. Come and have a cup of coffee."

We settled cosily at the kitchen table and I was just explaining my new design for another kneeler to him, when he sniffed peevishly.

"What is that frightful smell . . . one of the dogs?"

"Certainly not, they're all beautifully house-trained, aren't you, my angels?"

"The place is reeking of manure. I think I'll have my coffee outside."

We both got up, and his eye fell vengefully on my nice new rubber riding boots.

"Great lump of dung on your boot, Felicia, look at it . . . can't you take them off when you come indoors?"

I wandered over to the bootjack, hiked them off, and chucked them casually into the corridor.

"Don't you ever wear anything but jodhpurs, these days?"

"Well, I am riding a lot, and look how much weight I've lost. Have you finished your coffee? Antony, do come and look at my kneeler, the first one I made; it's actually in the church now."

"Well, I didn't really come down . . . oh, all right, if it means so much to you."

I love being in an empty church, especially with Antony. I found, somewhat to my annoyance, that my kneeler had been moved to a dark little side pew. I wondered who was on the church cleaning rota that week—Jenny, I bet. I moved it firmly up to the front; it's easily the nicest anyway.

Antony had gone into the churchyard and was looking moodily at gravestones. I wondered why he was so gloomy. I tried to think of something to cheer him up.

"Darling, I've had a lovely idea, come and help me pick the quinces."

Ann

There's an excitable, last-day-of-term feeling in the Delphic boardroom.

"Hullo, Ann, don't turn on the light," says Maddie, "just look at this shot, it's so perfect."

She and Sol are looking at the first rushes of the Tadworth commercial and there is Su Parsons, regally riding out of a cobbled courtyard into the misty golden morning.

"And this is where we have the voice-over, 'We know what you want before you do,' " says Sol, "and that's it."

"Excellent." Maddie turns on the light and pours us each a glass of wine. "Well done, both."

"Good lunch?" I'd told Sol that I was meeting Antony.

"So-so."

"And Felicia?"

"Happily unaware of what's happening to her, or Antony, so far as I can see . . ."

I tell them some of the things Antony had said and Maddie asks: "And what is Felicia doing, while this ex-husband of yours is wooing other women over lunch?"

"She's down in the country . . ."

"I went down to see her the other day." Sol shakes his head. "She looked as though she was auditioning for a backwoods domestic drama. I did try a few tactful nudges, but whenever I felt I was getting somewhere she showed me a seed catalogue. Ann, do you remember Felicia in *Vogue,* in one of those best-dressed-women features? And now she's reading *seed* catalogues."

"I begin to feel a certain sympathy for Mr. Forester-Jones," says Maddie.

Sol is looking at me speculatively. "Somebody has got to do *something,* to put her wise, and I think it ought to be you, Ann. You could do it."

"Me?" If I were losing control of my face, my figure and my husband, the last person I'd want telling me frankly about it would be my husband's ex-wife. But I have a picture in my mind of Emmy, crying in the kitchen at Acacia Road. "White Walls seemed sort of safe, like nothing bad could ever happen there again . . ." It's not only Felicia who will suffer if things go wrong.

"Okay. I'll do it. I'll give Fel a ring tomorrow."

Felicia

When I get back from riding, the phone is ringing. "It's all right, Mrs. Simmons. I'm back. I'll get it," I shriek.

"Felly—it's Ann. How are you?"

"Marvelous, thank you. And you? I meant to ask you, how are those ads you're doing with Sol going? I saw him the other day, and I thought he looked a bit depressed."

"He's doing a wonderful job, he's so *nice,* Fel. Listen . . . I've got a spare day today, and I'd love a bit of fresh air. Any chance of my coming down and bumming a late lunch off you?"

"I couldn't think of anything nicer."

"Just an omelette or something, don't go to any trouble, Fel."

I shall make her a sorrel omelette, how delicious.

When she arrives, I give her a glass of white wine, and drag her out to show her my new herb garden. It's right near the kitchen door, and I have personally built four brick raised beds. I started it ages ago, in the spring, but for one reason or another, I've only just finished it. I can't wait to stock it next year.

I show Ann diagrams of where I'm going to put the different herbs.

"Have you seen this year's Thompson & Morgan catalogue, Ann? I could spend pounds . . ."

"Do you know who you sound like, Felly? Me, two years ago."

"Two years ago I'd have been quite cross if you said that. Now I take it as rather a compliment."

"I had let myself go, though." Ann stretches one elegant leg and fondly regards a brown leather shoe that couldn't possibly have cost less than seventy pounds.

"You needn't worry about *me,* if that's what you mean. I'm far too vain to let myself go. Though I really must do something about my hands."

"Felly . . ." Ann stops looking at her shoe and looks out of the window instead. "Do you remember that time I came roaring down here in a temper?"

"Could I forget? . . . We polished off a bottle of Antony's best Le Corton."

"That was the first time I stopped thinking of you as a conniving bitch, Fel. You'd stolen my husband, but if I'm honest he was up for grabs anyway. It was the children I missed. I still do, but it's no good pretending I could have earned a living and been a full-time mother as well. I've never said this before, but if you hadn't pushed me out of this house, I wouldn't be where I am now. Absolutely between us"—she looks round, but we're alone except for four dogs and a cat—"I've been approached by Patterson Warbeck. They've practically finalized their takeover of United Grip, and they've asked for some ideas from me."

"United Grip? That sounds vaguely familiar."

"Well, of course it does; they're only the biggest . . . anyway, what I'm trying to say is, I'm very fond of you, Felicia. Sol's very fond of you too. Love, we're a bit worried."

I beat the eggs and chop some sorrel. Nothing too bad can happen while you're cooking. Some butter sizzles in the frying pan.

"Oh, do stop cooking that bloody omelette, I'm not hungry anyway. Fel, someone's got to tell you . . ."

Ann

If I'm going off to the Palace Hotel in Gstaad to rub shoulders with the rich and famous, as the travel brochure promised, why am I at Gatwick at five o'clock in the morning, surrounded by Indian cleaners, and left-over-from-the-sixties hippies sleeping on their backpacks?

There's something incongruous about setting off in this down-market manner when I've spent nearly three thousand pounds on the holiday, not to mention all the pre-, during, and après skiwear.

By the time I've transferred from plane to coach and coach to hotel, I'm grateful for the new red cashmere coat, which has remained elegantly uncrushed throughout the journey.

I'm just signing in, when there are boisterous shouts across the palatial reception hall. Tom grabs me round the waist, picks me up and whirls me around a couple of times.

"Ann . . . this is great, great. I can't believe you're really here."

As I circle, I see that he is surrounded by a group of fresh-faced youths, and several college-girl Laura look-alikes. Tom puts me down and says proudly: "Folks, this is Ann. Ann, I want you to meet the crowd . . ." and he reels off a list of abbreviated names —Ben, Tod, Ned, Bet, Bud—which all sound exactly the same.

"Hi, Ann."

"How're you doing, Ann?"

"Good to see you, Ann."

They are throwing playful punches at each other like a high school baseball team, and I wonder if it is all going to be a horrid, expensive mistake. I feel a greater affinity with those serious, middle-aged Indians, conscientiously wielding their brooms at Gatwick, than I do with these . . . children.

I'd forgotten what it's like to give yourself over to pure pleasure. After a few days of swimming in the pool, drinking and eating in all the different little bars and restaurants off the main street, skating on the rink just behind the hotel, and dancing in a dozen different discos until the early morning, I begin to feel like a child myself.

From my bedroom window, I look down on the chalets and fir

trees in the village, dusted with snow, up to a circle of magnificent white mountains.

Tom leaps out of bed early to catch the first ski lift, which takes him to a cable car that goes all the way up to the Diablerets glacier, ten thousand feet above us. There isn't enough snow on the nursery slopes for proper skiing, so my beginners' class is more technique than actual skiing ("Lean to the vallee, Mees Browning . . ."). Afterwards I window-shop, drink cups of hot chocolate, and dodge the good skiers as they swoop colorfully towards me down the village street. Yesterday I tried a Turkish bath, topped up with a sauna, and it was so unpleasant I felt sure it was doing me good. Today I'm introducing my new black bikini to the hotel swimming pool.

I'm feeling good about the bikini, the crawl (perfected in the swimming pool with Harry) and my body (glowing from nights of lovemaking with Tom), when, doing the difficult face-under-the-water bit of the crawl, my head hits something.

I come up out of the water, spluttering, and there—a few feet from me—is Philip Gilham, also spluttering.

"Aha, Ann Forester-Jones," he says, treading water. "The first time we met you threw your suitcase at me and now you're trying to drown me."

I hadn't seen Philip since we grappled together in a taxi a lifetime ago. He had phoned, once or twice, when I was at Donald's, but one lover seemed quite enough to be going on with, and I always had good excuses for why I couldn't see him.

We agree to meet for lunch in the Bar Grill; there's so much to talk about, and we're still sitting over coffee when Tom and his friends make a noisy entrance.

"Ann . . . Ann. We've been looking everywhere for you."

"Tom, this is Philip Gilham, an old friend of mine." I introduce Philip to all the abbreviated names and Tom sits down next to me on the banquette and puts an arm round my shoulders; macho man warning another male off his territory. I'm not sure whether to be flattered or irritated.

"Come on, Ann," he says, "let's get out of this dumb place and go over to the Chlosterli . . . do some dancing."

They all clump in their ski boots towards the door, boisterously hyping themselves up for the next party. Tom grabs my arm and pulls me up.

"Would you like to come?" I ask Philip.

"No, thank you." He is folding the *Times* into a precise square for the crossword. I suspect this is some kind of statement too, but can't be bothered to decipher it.

He looks diminished somehow, surrounded by such youthful maleness, and I can't help feeling slightly traitorous as I leave him sitting there.

"But you are staying here, in this hotel? I will see you again?"

"Oh yes," says Philip, "I'm sure we'll be bumping into each other."

Christmas comes and goes through a haze of action and alcohol. I don't think I've been feet-on-the-ground sober for more than two hours in the last six days.

On Christmas morning, Tom hands me an exquisitely gift-wrapped confection from Bergdorf Goodman, containing an ivory satin and lace negligee, and I give him a St. Laurent sweater, which I'd bought in the village. We sit up in bed wearing our gifts and then take them off again. Without his backdrop of friends, Tom is the same sensitive man I remember from New York.

We open our first bottle of champagne before we get up, and it is a very merry Christmas indeed, when I spot Philip across the Fromagerie at lunchtime. He is with an older man, and a woman who has spent a lot of time with the Carmen rollers.

We exchange *Happy Christmas*'s and he introduces me to his sister-in-law and her husband.

"Philip tells me you've got children," says the sister-in-law. "You must be missing them. Christmas isn't the same without children, is it?"

"No," I say, "it's much better." And if I drink enough champagne, I might just get around to believing it.

"Do you think it's all right?"

"Sweetheart, it's sensational."

Tom and I are on our way downstairs for the New Year's Eve party, and I'm wearing my Christmas present. I've added a pair of ivory satin slippers from the hotel boutique, and I don't think anyone would know that the ensemble was designed for the bedroom rather than the ballroom.

There are ten of us at our table, and we're having such a great time that the headwaiter comes over and asks Tom if he could please ask his friends to be a little quieter; the people at the next table have complained.

They are an elderly couple and they smile nervously at us, to show they don't want any trouble. Ned opens another bottle of champagne, and it spurts out and waterfalls into the elderly gentleman's vichyssoise. This seems so funny that we all fall about laughing and make even more noise.

I dance with Tom, and am rather pleased when Bud leaves Sandy, one of the Laura look-alikes, stranded on the floor as he cuts in; "My turn, Tom, you can't keep her to yourself all evening."

The music beats, the lights dim, we order another bottle . . . and another. I'm giggling as Bud holds me close, his hands rhythmically moving on my hips.

It's midnight. I kiss him long and lingeringly. Dear Bud. Tom pushes between us.

"Hey, enough of that, Bud. This is my property." And I kiss Tom, wonderfully sexy Tom, and then Tod and Ned and Tom again . . .

"Happy New Year! Happy New Year! Happy New Year!"

Philip Gilham is at my side. Darling Philip. My hero from the 15:20Tisbury to Waterloo. "Happy New Year, Philip." I wind my arms around his neck, fall unsteadily against him, brush his cheek with my lips . . . I'm trying to locate his mouth.

Gently unwinding my arms, Philip raises his glass. "Happy New Year, Ann." And then, looking at me levelly over the rim, he says: "You're making an awful ass of yourself, you know."

1987

Felicia

It hasn't taken me long to discover that a director of an amateur dramatic society needs, above all, vast quantities of tact.

"Rachel," I say, hoping the patience in my voice isn't deepening into venom, "try to remember you are a young woman guided, *bound* by the social mores of the early 1900s. You have just become very suitably engaged to a young man rather higher up the social scale than you. *But,* you are basically decent and beginning to feel the uneasy twinges of guilt. I don't honestly think Sheila would giggle right there."

"Oh, but Felicia," Rachel says, "that wasn't a giggle, it was more of a nervous laugh. I do feel she'd laugh nervously there, to try to sort of hide her confusion. I'm trying to imagine how Maggie Smith would play it," she adds earnestly.

"Ah, well, yes . . . ." Three weeks ago I would have said briskly that Maggie Smith could play it with a brown paper bag on her head and the audience would laugh and cry as and when she decided they would; but that Rachel Welcome, by day a very pretty girl who works at the Abbey National, and by night a member of the Wynford Players Amateur Dramatic Group, had better stick to a few ground rules.

I think back to the various people who directed me in the past. Some of them had got what they wanted by abrasion ("Oh my God, woman, has nothing I've said in the past three weeks sunk in? What's the point, that's what I ask myself, what's the point . . ."), others by taking you out for a drink and seriously discussing motivation. But whatever method they used, they were dealing with professionals who knew they either took direction or got out; plenty more where *they* came from. There are not plenty more where Rachel Welcome comes from, because the Wynford Players is a new and small company; if she doesn't play Sheila Birling it would have to be Liz Daventry, who is a blowsy thirty-five and has an accent you could grow watercress on.

So I say placatingly to Rachel that I see exactly what she's getting at, a very good idea really, but perhaps a nervous smile would be more effective than a nervous laugh.

Marian Compton, who is playing Mrs. Birling very well indeed, catches my eye and raises an eyebrow. Marian is by far the best actor in the company and knows it. Until last week she patently resented my suggestions.

Last week I took her out for a drink.

"Marian," I said, "I am going to speak frankly, and you must forgive me if you don't like what I say."

Marian stiffened and lit a cigarette.

"I really don't feel you are pulling your weight. Someone with your instinctive knowledge of stagecraft has so much to offer other members of the cast . . . with a talent like yours you can lead by example where I can only suggest. Do you see what I mean?"

The words "instinctive knowledge" and "talent" were doing their work. Marian's feathers were smooth again.

"Well, I don't know," she said, "I do my best, of course, but . . ."

"You know perfectly well you're streets ahead of anyone else."

"I wouldn't exactly say that . . . shall we have another glass of wine?"

"Lovely . . . for instance, Tom Brook, playing Eric, simply doesn't take direction at all. I don't seem to be able to get across to him . . . how would you handle it?"

Since then Marian has handled it by stopping every so often and asking my advice.

"I feel perhaps I should make Sybil *stronger* there, somehow, don't you, Felicia?"

"I thought it was fine. If you're not happy, I suppose you could put a bit more stress on the end of the speech."

"Oh, thank you. So marvelous," she says, raking the rest of the cast with her eyes, "to have the chance of advice from a real professional."

In spite of all this manipulation, or perhaps because of it, I am finding directing ten times more compelling than acting. And I have a feeling I'm better at it.

It was just chance, one day, that took me to Wynford. I was looking for an antique shop that Jenny had told me about.

Wynford is one of those small old villages that has had an up-and-coming middle-class estate tacked onto it; designed for rising young executives who prefer to live in the country, but right next to other young executives so that they feel secure. Their wives wear shoes that look like Gucci but can't be because they haven't risen that far yet, and they are keen to become involved in country life. Though it would be easy to laugh at them they are, by and large, a collection of pleasant women with not enough to do.

When I walked into the antique shop in search of some old blue-and-white plates to put on the dresser, an agreeable-looking man in his forties smiled at me, but did not speak. I thought he was probably used to women drifting into his shop and drifting out again without buying anything.

"Good morning," I said, "I'm looking for some blue-and-white plates, nothing grand. My stepson's cricket ball has left some gaps on the dresser."

James Robson's shop is one of the hopeful, untidy kind. You feel that with a little patience you could find something really good for almost nothing. This impression turns out to be misleading; James knows, to the last Victorian soap dish, exactly what he's got and what it's worth. We were talking about the astonishing price Staffordshire figures were fetching these days—"Americans," we murmured to each other—when he said, "Excuse me, but aren't you . . . you can't be Felicia Harman . . . ?"

"Well," I said, "I was. Now I am Felicia Forester-Jones. I live near here."

"What do you mean, was? You can't have given up acting . . . you were so marvelous in *A Small Disturbance* . . . I went three times."

"Heavens, that was years ago. Now I am just a country housewife."

"Criminal, what a waste. Felicia Harman peeling potatoes."

This conversation was having the same effect on my ego as Boots's vitamin E cream has on my hands. I felt smooth and flawless. "You're obviously interested in the theater . . . ?"

"Passionately. In fact three months ago I started the Wynford Players, an amateur dram—" He stopped abruptly and gazed at me with a rather fanatical light in his eye. Of course I knew exactly what he was going to say; he was going to ask me to play a part. "I've just had the most wonderful idea . . . wouldn't it be marvelous if you directed us?"

"Direct? I thought . . ."

I thought I was going to be asked to do a little light acting on the side, which would nicely fill in the spaces between riding, gardening, and listening to the children whingeing about examinations. But directing . . .

"Oh please. Do think about it. I'm trying to direct and play a leading part. And of course I've got so much to do here."

"Not a lot of dusting," I said prissily, picking up a pewter tankard and blowing at it.

"That's on purpose. People cheerfully pay ten quid for a dusty object that they wouldn't give five for if it were clean. It's the psychology of selling, you know. They think they've made one of those amazing finds. You see this painting?"

I stared, horrified, at a doleful watercolor of some cypresses and an urn.

"I had it on display for ages and nobody wanted it. Quite rightly, in my view. So last week I spilled some coffee on it and hid it behind a few fifth-rate old oils. And yesterday a German tourist bought it for a sum even I would be embarrassed to name." James smiled evilly. "He thought I didn't know it was there. That'll teach them to bomb Coventry Cathedral."

"You unprincipled . . ."

"Oh, come on. Do say you'll help out with the directing. You know you want to."

What I knew was that I wanted to spend some time with James Robson. I spoke sternly to myself on the way home: Be honest, you find that man attractive . . . certainly very amusing . . . I love Antony, but it's rather nice to be looked at like that again . . . And anyway, I thought rebelliously, why shouldn't I have a minor flirtation? Antony could hardly complain.

Ann

"Ann Browning?"

"Speaking."

"Alex Staleybridge here. Patterson Warbeck."

I swear that my heart stops beating for a second or two. I've been waiting for this call with more anxiety and excitement than I've ever waited to hear from a lover.

Patterson Warbeck, a giant conglomerate, has been greedily gobbling up smaller companies for the last five years; some of them rather indigestible for a machine-tool manufacturer—particularly, I would have thought, the frozen-food firm and the personnel group.

I'd met Alex Staleybridge at one of Donald's parties a year or so ago. "Like your work on Delphic," he'd said, appreciatively helping himself to the last spoonful of Bute Catering's excellent tangerine mousse.

"We're looking for somebody to handle Polarice for us. Care to put up a few ideas?"

I didn't know, then, how to present a campaign and the account went to Leo Burnett. But when Alex Staleybridge came back to me, two months ago, with Finders Inc., the personnel outfit, I was in competition with at least half a dozen top agencies for the really big one, and I knew I had to take a gamble.

The South Molton Street Secretarial Services Bureau, where I'd had such a humiliating time four years ago, is one of the offshoots of Finders. I decided to cash in on that glum experience.

My media, marketing and creative people had all done their bit, but I added a surprise ingredient. When Mr. Staleybridge arrived at our office two weeks ago for the presentation, Sandra Burch, my efficient secretary, was busy doing her nails and gossiping with Lydia Melrose, one of the copywriters.

"Take a seat," said Sandra, scarcely raising her eyes from her nails and nodding towards the banquette.

"Well, go on then," said Lydia, "what happened next . . . ?"

Mr. Staleybridge sat and tapped his foot with rhythmic impatience for ten minutes, uttered a few attention-getting coughs (which Sandra ignored with the impassivity of a headwaiter) and eventually jumped up, strode over to her desk and said in a voice of controlled rage: "I don't know if you realize who I am. My name is Alex Staleybridge and I am the chief executive of Patterson Warbeck. I have an appointment with your Miss Browning for eleven o'clock." He shot the cuff of his navy suit and studied a heavy gold watch. "It is now ten minutes past eleven and I am not accustomed to being kept waiting."

Sandra looked at him as if he wasn't there, muttered into the phone and then pointed him back to the banquette.

"Miss Browning will be with you directly. May I get you a coffee? Or tea?"

"Ah, *there* you are, Ann." As I emerged from my office, five minutes later, Mr. Staleybridge was incoherent with irritation.

"Do come in," I said graciously, as he muttered about silly girls gossiping . . . never been treated like this before in his life . . . absolute disgrace. "Make yourself comfortable. You will forgive me if I make this important call."

"No, I bloody well won't. And put down that damn phone. What are you playing at, Ann? I came here for a presentation and . . ."

"And that's just what it is, Alex," I said. "You've just experienced the kind of treatment your prospective clients get when they walk into one of your agencies."

The lights went out, one of the walls turned into a giant screen featuring a witty film which showed, first of all, how *not* to conduct a personnel interview and then showed the way it should be done. It was made by three well-known comedy actors who specialize in business promotion films, and it had cost me a great deal of money. It'll be worth it if we get the account. There's an above-the-line spend of £1.2 million hanging on this telephone call.

"Yes, Alex?"

"I was impressed with what I saw last week. Liked your style. Can you come over here with your people . . . say Thursday, three-thirty?"

"I certainly can." We've done it! Landed our first really big client.

"Good. We'll do a run-through for the Finders executives, but I think you'll find they are equally enthusiastic." He gives a short bark of rather alarming laughter. "Don't have any democratic nonsense here, I'm glad to say. Look forward to working with you."

Controlling an impulse to throw the telephone up in the air, scream with pleasure and rush round to Alex Staleybridge's office and kiss him, I thank him serenely for phoning and say that I look forward to working with him, too.

"Sandra . . ."

She comes running in and I kiss her instead. "We've got it. Finders . . ."

"*Fantastic,*" says Sandra. One of the nicest things about being a small new company is that all the staff were in at the beginning and feel involved. I ask Sandra to alert everyone who worked on the account. "A celebratory lunch. Downstairs at L'Escargot, I think. See if they can all make it, and book us a table for one-thirty."

On the way out, I see Laura, who is helping out in the art department during her school holidays.

"Come on, Laura." I throw her canvas shoulder bag over to her. "If you're going to work in advertising, you might as well find out about the nice bits as well as the hard grind."

I hadn't seen Laura for about six months when she phoned and asked if I could find her a holiday job. I warned her that she'd be fetching and carrying and we could only pay her pocket money.

"Anything, Ann. I just want the experience, to find out if I'd really like to work in an advertising agency."

I promised to see what I could do. "And how's Harry?"

"A pain," said Laura cheerfully. "No, he's fine. Really. In sixth grade now and in love with his computer. He stays on at school every afternoon, talking to it."

"Give him my love."

I didn't ask after Donald. I hadn't spoken to him since that morning, in January last year, after Gstaad.

I'd arrived back high with the excitement of the holiday. It had been such fun; I'd loved every minute of it . . . except for Philip Gilham's extraordinary outburst on New Year's Eve, and I'd put that to the back of my mind. Maybe I'd take it out later and examine his words more carefully, but not yet. Now I intended to hang on to the confidence I'd gained, being loved, feted and allowed to feel sixteen again.

Donald had been pleased to have me home.

"Happy New Year, hon," he'd said, holding me close in the big double bed in the master bedroom.

I was overflowing with love and happiness; there was plenty to spare for Donald.

And then, a few days later, I was clearing away the breakfast debris when he walked into the kitchen.

"Don't bother with that."

"Why. . . . ?" Something in the tone of his voice made me turn and look at him. He was standing in the doorway; white and shaking.

"Don't bother with anything in this house, with any of us, ever again. I'm going to the bank now, Ann, and I shall be back at six o'clock. I want you out of here by then."

"But . . . ?" I couldn't imagine what had got into him. "What's the matter, Donald? What on earth are you talking about?"

His eyes were cold. "You bitch. You goddam bitch."

I'd heard the phone go, hadn't thought anything of it. But it was Phyllis, phoning up to wish her ex-husband a happy New Year and report an amazing coincidence. Some good friends of hers, the Einhovens, had just called her up saying what a wonderful time they'd had over Christmas at the Palace Hotel in Gstaad. And guess who was at the next table to them on New Year's Eve? Tom. They recognized him immediately, they said, from the lovely photograph Phyllis kept on her bureau, and of course, they had met him once at one of her cocktail parties.

So Phyllis had asked, in motherly fashion, if Tom seemed to be enjoying himself, and Mrs. Einhoven had been only too eager to describe the rowdy behavior which ended in Mr. Einhoven's getting champagne in his soup. "Poppa had to complain to the head-waiter, dear, but no . . . it's all right. We didn't mind. You're only young once." This, evidently, led Mrs. Einhoven on to remark that Tom was with a woman *quite* old enough to know better. "At least ten years older than your Tom, dear" (well, thank you for that anyway, Mrs. Einhoven), and Phyllis had pressed for a description of this older woman, which she then relayed, detail by giveaway detail, to Donald.

"But Donald . . ."

"Don't come near me. Don't touch me. How could you, Ann? *Tom?* How long has it been going on? Did you go there to meet him? God, what a fool I've been . . ."

There didn't seem any point in lying. I told Donald about my meeting with Tom in New York . . . well, I told him as little as possible about our meeting in New York . . . and how we'd been attracted to each other. "He reminded me of you, Donald, how you must have been when . . ."

Donald looked weary. "Oh, spare me that, Ann. You've done enough. Just go . . . go on . . . get out."

"But what about the children? Laura . . . Harry?"

"Never mind. None of your business. Su will be here soon, she'll help out and I'll call Miss Jamieson . . ."

I went on washing up, automatically rinsing out the white coffee jug, wiping the clean white surfaces. Donald was very close behind me. I could feel the warmth of his anger.

"Get out!" He was shouting now.

I sidestepped, slipped past him and out of the door. There was an awful lot to pack up. All my office papers and files, my word processor. I heard the front door slam. He'd gone. I slumped down on the bed, the joy and excitement gone. I was numb. More like sixty than sixteen.

"Ann? Are you there?"

Su Parsons bounded up the stairs, opened the door, took in at a glance the open drawers spilling clothes, the files and papers. "What's going on?"

I told her. I needed a sympathetic ear. Su sat on the bed beside me, put an arm around my shaking shoulders. "Well, you can't really blame him, can you, poor sod? How do you think he feels, sharing his mistress with his son?"

"I never thought . . . never thought he'd find out."

"No. Well, obviously not. How old is he, the son?"

I had to think for a minute. "Twenty-eight . . . no, twenty-nine now."

Su's expression was a mixture of disapproval and admiration. "Well, I must say, you have come on. When I think what you were like that first morning I saw you in the kitchen. . . ." She rolled her eyes. "More like a traffic warden than a sex bomb."

"Hardly that . . ."

"Perhaps not. But you have been going it a bit, haven't you, love? Father and son. Whatever next?"

Felicia

What had I said to Ann? "I'm far too vain to let myself go."

After she'd gone back to London, that drab October day in 1985, I threw away the makings of the sorrel omelette and went upstairs. I drew the curtains in my bedroom right back, stood in front of the mahogany pier looking glass, and took my first serious look at myself for months.

The woman staring anxiously back at me was . . . dumpy. Even if I did weight just over 126 pounds, it was still too much for someone with my bones and my height. My hair looked, if I was going to be honest (and the time had plainly come for honesty), like Dotty Maxwell's. It didn't matter with her, because of the goodness and kindness radiating from her face. My face did not look good and kind, it looked rather miserable. The brown corduroys I had bought in 1983 were both baggy and too tight; my lovely old comfortable cashmere sweater had a hole in the elbow I hadn't got round to darning, and I was wearing no lipstick.

I went over to the wardrobe and took out "one of those lovely sexy outfits" that Antony had always admired. I couldn't do up the zipper; perhaps I could let it out. But when I turned and looked at myself sideways, I saw that the chiffon that had flowed and swirled over Felicia Harman's bones clung and clustered on Mrs. Forester-Jones's flesh. I took it off and hung it up again.

What did it matter anyway? I was losing Antony.

"Fel, someone's got to tell you," Ann had said, "and I wish to God it wasn't me. Fel, Sol saw Antony having lunch with someone who sounds to me like that new assistant of his . . ."

"Business lunches, Ann, they're meaningless."

"Sol didn't think this looked meaningless, Fel. He was awfully upset."

"So that's why he looked so worried when he came down last week. He is kind, isn't he? Tell him he's a love, but he's not to worry, everything's fine, really it is."

(He slept in the yellow room so as not to disturb me . . . Sarah wouldn't say good-bye to him . . . "I do think you might take some interest in my work, Felicia . . .")

"Felicia, Antony asked me to have lunch with him yesterday. Of course I thought it was to do with the children, or something. But . . . he said wasn't it fun lunching together just like old times . . . he implied," I could tell Ann was tactfully editing their conversation, "well, anyway, he asked me out to dinner." She looked at me miserably. "Of course I said no, and told him what I thought of him. Fel, you've got to fight back."

"Why? You didn't."

"I know, but looking back I think it was right not to. I was unhappy and bitter . . . but I think there was a voice at the back of my mind saying 'Now's your chance.' All this," she waved vaguely round the kitchen, "wasn't really me at all. It was all done for Antony. What I'm doing now is me. But you really love this life, don't you? So hang on to it."

"I don't want it without Antony."

"You don't have to lose him. Since the baby . . . I know you were sad and how you looked didn't seem very important. But a couple of weeks' hard work, and you'll look wonderful again."

"It's not just how I look, Ann. I can't seem to talk about anything but dogs and daffodil bulbs," I said drearily; "you're quite right, of course, there have been signs. But I pretended I hadn't noticed them. I'm great on illusion," I added bitterly, "that's what made me such a workmanlike third-rate actress."

"Rubbish. People still talk about you. I tell you what, come up to London and go to Robert and buy some new clothes. I'll come too, it'll be fun. I could do Monday, or Thursday at a pinch. Which would suit you?"

"It's very kind of you, Ann, but what's the point?"

"The point is your whole life, and the children, and Antony. Come on, Fel, brace up. How about Monday?"

"I'll ring you."

I didn't ring her. I meant to, I suppose, but I never seemed to get round to it.

Ann meant well. (Though I thought she'd protested rather much about how she hated telling me about Antony; it was only two years since he'd left her for me, after all. Somewhere in her subconscious there must have been a slight glow.) But I'd found slightly trivial her implication that a better haircut and some new clothes would result in the slow roll of titles over the hero and heroine clasped in silhouette against the sunset. Surely a good marriage—and I had been so sure our marriage was good—should depend on more important things than how we looked. Why didn't the marriage service include, along with Richer and Poorer and in Sickness and in Health, in Good Looks and in Bad?

I didn't say any of this to Ann, of course. How things looked was very important to her in 1985. She was now quite devastating; her attraction was like a new toy to her, she kept on taking it out and looking at it. She wasn't brassy, exactly, but possibly a little tinny in places, and the way she talked about men made me rather uneasy.

"*Another* new boyfriend?" I'd said once.

"Not a boyfriend at all, Fel—just rather fun for the moment. I've got no time to spend on permanent relationships. Anyway, where's the harm? Nobody's getting hurt."

I dragged through the rest of that ghastly year spending my days putting things off to tomorrow. Sarah became more loving, and

Emmy more puzzled, as Antony's visits tailed off. He didn't come down at all in November.

He had to in the middle of December, though, for the Carol Service at the girls' school; Emmy was singing a solo verse of "Once in Royal David's City." Laura and Harry's Christmas holiday started that day, so Antony drove them and Ann down. Ann intended to spend a night with us, then go back to London en route for Gstaad, where she was spending Christmas. "There's a crowd of us going," she said to me, "do you realize I've never been skiing before? I can't wait." Thinking disapprovingly that she really ought to spend more time with her children, I said, "Who are you going with?"

"Oh, Tom, Dick and Harry," said Ann evasively.

I had put a lot of work into Christmas. I might not look much, I thought, and my conversation might make Mogadon seem outmoded, but it's not going to be my fault if the house isn't brimming with festive jollity.

I made a gigantic kissing ball, and Mark hung it for me high up in the hall. The Christmas pudding, which we'd all taken turns at stirring in October, was maturing in the larder. Mince pies were in the freezer, and a local goose hung in the pantry. Homemade paper chains were looped everywhere, and the tree was hidden in the solid-fuel shed waiting to be brought into the house on Christmas Eve. Antony and I were extremely polite to each other.

On December 23 they brought the Crib out of a cupboard, and the younger children settled down to arranging it, watched with charming condescension by Sarah and Laura and Mark. How lovely, I thought, leaving them to it, in spite of all the commercialism, children know instinctively what is really important.

When I went back, alarmed by a heightening of decibels, Harry was screaming "Give me bloody Baby Jesus, damn you" at Emmy. Mark was throwing a piece of used chewing gum through a paper chain and telling a rather unattractive joke, and Sarah and Laura were discussing Benetton in low eager voices.

I suddenly had the deadening feeling that each one of them would be able to price their presents within five seconds of opening them.

"I only hope they enjoy their stockings," I said to Antony.

"Bound to. Why don't we nip off to the pub for a drink?"

"Actually, I think I'll go to bed. There's so much to do tomorrow, and I'm awfully tired."

"Anything you say." He turned on the television. He's aged a lot in the last year, I thought, and felt a shaft of compunction. I'd spent the months since Easter feeling sorry for myself. But he'd lost the baby too.

"Oh, I don't know," I said, "a drink might be rather fun."

"No, you're probably right. Anyway there's quite a good film on TV."

So he watched quite a good film and came up late. I heard him creeping into the yellow room so as not to disturb me. Happy Christmas, I said to myself.

That was the first Christmas that I went down with them to see if the cattle were kneeling. In 1983 I had felt that as Ann wasn't there it would be unfair of me to butt into a family ceremony that obviously meant a lot to them; anyway, I thought it an absurdly sentimental notion, typical of Ann at her most glutinous. And in 1984, of course, when I was two months pregnant, Antony had flatly forbade it; "It's freezing out there, and slippery underfoot. Much better for you to stay in the warm and organize hot drinks, darling," And Emmy had said, "Won't it be lovely next year? We can take your baby down with us." Remembering that, as I put on my Barbour and an unappealing brown woolen hat, I wished I hadn't said I'd go with them.

We walked down the lane to Mr. Parker's cow shed, our way inefficiently lit by Mark's excitedly waving torch, and Harry's and Emmy's faces were shining; if the grown-ups said the cattle knelt at midnight, and if some dead old grown-up had actually written a poem about it, well, then, they probably did. Even the older children had sloughed off their sophistication for the occasion.

When we got to the barn, exactly at midnight, the cows were all lying down. One of them honked a thundering cough. Disturbed by the lights and our presence, they got to their feet. And owing to the funny way cows stand up . . .

"Look," said Mark, "that one's kneeling. And there's another one, over there."

"I expect the ones that aren't kneeling now were kneeling a minute ago," said Emmy; "after all, there isn't a clock in here."

It didn't seem to me to matter a row of beans whether they were kneeling or not. The Felicia who two years ago would have howled with laughter at the mere idea of standing around in damp Wellington boots looking at a lot of animals had turned into someone who found it rather moving.

I had taken the children up to London to see the Christmas lights, and bitterly regretted it; a load of tat, I thought, a load of Come and Spend Your Money Here, Extended Terms Available. I had made them listen to a Christmas Message about thinking of others less fortunate than ourselves, droned out by some corpulent bishop.

But if the Christmas spirit was anywhere, it was here with these hopeful children and benign cows regarding us with mild interest. It wasn't too hard to imagine a crib tucked away behind that straw bale.

I looked across at Antony and thought, We've got so much, surely we're not going to let it go?

His head was turned towards me, but it was too dark to see his expression. Was he feeling as I was? More likely, I thought sadly, he was thinking, Thank heavens that's over. A large whiskey when we get back.

"I don't like the sound of Daisy's cough," said Sarah, "I wonder if there's enough ventilation in here. I think I'd better ring Mr. Parker in the morning."

On the way back I slipped my arm through Antony's.

"Slippery," I said apologetically. He didn't react, though; he didn't put my hand in his pocket like he used to.

I made my first and only New Year resolution. Nineteen eighty-six was going to be the year of the great sort-out. Felicia Forester-Jones was on her way back.

Ann

The ironing board was still in the corner of my mother's spare room. It looked friendlier, somehow, when I'd draped the red cashmere coat over it.

I'd phoned her that morning, while Su went off to find her husband (Jim is a builder-decorator and was doing up a house in the nearby Finchley Road), who, she said, would come round in his van, collect my stuff, and dump it at my mother's for the time being.

My mother sounded perplexed. "I don't quite understand what

you're saying, dear. Why are you leaving St. John's Wood so suddenly? I thought you were happy there."

"I'll explain when I get there."

There was a tap at the door. The moment had arrived. "Cup of tea, dear?" Mother looked around the room, appalled. "Goodness, what a mess. What are you going to do with it all?"

I told her that I was going to look for somewhere to live, and could I please stay with her until I found something?

"Of course." She gave a brave smile. "Stay as long as you like." Recognizing the recklessness of this invitation she amended it quickly. "Until you get a place of your own, of course. And now, what's all this about, this midmorning flit?"

I described the Gstaad drama, expurgating all the sexy bits, but I didn't fool Mother.

"Are you trying to tell me, or rather, trying *not* to tell me that you've been having an affair with Donald Harman *and* his son?"

"Yes." I didn't dare look at her face.

"Well *really.*" Surely she wasn't laughing? She was. Mum's reactions never fail to amaze me.

Naturally I phoned Felicia to tell her where I was and reassure her about Harry and Laura.

"Now, maybe Donald will let me have the children at White Walls more often," she said speculatively. There was a slight pause before she ventured: "So . . . it's over between you and Donald, is it?"

"But it was never. . . ."

"Oh Ann . . . I've known for years that you and Donald were lovers."

"But how . . . ?"

"The children, of course. No, they didn't come right out and say it, but they aren't stupid. Harry told me, sometime in that first year, that he was pleased Poppa was going to marry Ann because then he wouldn't be lonely. And when I asked him how he knew about it, he said: 'Well, Poppa and Ann sometimes sleep in the same bed and that's almost as good as being married, isn't it?' "

"Oh dear." I was mortified. "And the others?"

"They never said anything, too sophisticated or embarrassed, I should think . . . except Mark."

"Mark?" He seemed the least likely of my children to clue in to a Fact of Life.

"Yes. He came back here once very irritable and moody, saying:

'I do wish Donald wouldn't keep touching Mum . . . as if he *owned* her or something.' "

"Oh Fel . . ." I hadn't wanted to hurt the children. "Oh Fel, I am sorry. About the children, I mean." I had no intention of telling her about Tom.

"Oh, I shouldn't worry. Much better to see you and Donald happy together than cold and distant, the way he and I used to be. What are you going to do now?"

"Find somewhere to live," I said. "A nice little house. In Kensington, perhaps."

I soon discovered that nice little houses in Kensington cost more than nice large houses in Wiltshire; and I only had half the price of a nice large house in Wiltshire.

After the divorce, Antony had White Walls valued at £75,000. I swiftly retaliated with another valuer who said it might be worth £150,000, "if you did something about that nasty patch of damp under the eaves."

"A hundred and fifty thousand pounds?" said Antony. "Nonsense. Nobody pays that kind of money for a rambling old house without central heating."

So we called in Mr. Smiley and Mr. Dwyer, who wrote each other expensive letters, resulting in an independent survey of £100,000.

My mother and I studied the property pages as avidly as we'd once scanned the job vacancies, and found the advertisements equally deceptive. I needed a minimum of three bedrooms (for when the children were with me in London) somewhere near the Central Line, so that I could get to Delphic easily. I told a number of agents this and they sent me particulars of two-bedroomed flats nowhere near the Central Line.

I'd enlisted everyone I could think of in my search, and Pauline Jarvis, an old school friend, phoned me one day to say she'd heard of an "absolutely super flat in Chiswick."

The particulars assured us that it was a "unique opportunity to acquire a tastefully presented three-bedroomed flat in a prestige purpose-built block, with porterage and garden." What's more, the flat was "close to all amenities."

Pauline and I rushed there immediately in case somebody else took advantage of the unique opportunity before we did.

"It's a newly fashionable area," said Tristram, the young estate agent, as he dodged his car fastidiously between old tin cans and rotting rubbish, to park outside a seedy 1930s block.

I looked around at the bleak squalor. "Where are the amenities?"

"The M4," said Tristram, with an expansive gesture, "is right *there* on the other side of that wall."

Pauline pronounced the characterless square rooms, mauve bathroom and chipped Formica kitchen really nice.

"You could do something with it, Ann, I know you could. And it's awfully cheap."

I happened to know that Pauline and her husband lived in an elegant terrace house off Westbourne Grove, which they'd bought for £15,000 some years ago. "And would you live here?"

"Well, no," Pauline admitted, "but it's different, isn't it?"

Everyone seemed to assume that because I was single I couldn't expect or afford to live somewhere pleasant like them. It was as if I were to be punished for getting divorced; banished to a semi in the suburbs or a high rise in the slums. "You're much too fussy, dear," my mother said. Even though Maddie had let me have an office in Delphic and I was out all day, we were beginning to get on each other's nerves again.

I phoned Su one day. I wanted to find out if Harry and Laura were all right; I'd become very attached to those two.

"Oh, they're fine," she said. "Down in the country with Fel and your lot."

"And Donald?"

"Okay." I could tell by Su's voice that he had displeased her in some way.

"He's taken up with a snotty American—Marcia something or other. Always coming round here, sticking her oar in. Told me I hadn't starched the napkins properly, when she was being the hostess at one of Donald's do's. Silly cow. 'Get on to the Blue Bag laundry and complain,' I said. 'They're the ones who do the starching around here.' And what about you, Ann? How are you doing?"

"I'm fine," I said automatically, and then told her that I wasn't fine at all, but cast down by house hunting. "Anything I can afford I don't like and anything I like I can't afford."

"Know what you mean," said Su, "but hold on. Jim's finished at the Finchley Road now. Moved on to somewhere at the back of Maida Vale. Big old mansion block. Terrible wreck, he says. He's working with the contractor who's doing it up. Might be something going there, before it gets into the estate agents' hands. I'll talk to Jim and let you know."

Next day she told me that Jim reckoned the tarted-up flats would sell for about £135,000, but there were some unmodernized ones going at half that.

"Jim says he'll do it up for you when he's finished this job. They're ever so big and roomy, Ann. Four bedrooms, long corridors, lovely old fireplaces and that. Why don't you have a look?"

I moved into Vanbrugh Mansions two months later, with a bearable mortgage and a bank loan of £10,000 to pay Jim for the vital improvements. I kept the original fireplaces and cornices, the big white bath on rusty claw feet and the lavatory with its wooden seat. There was even a bellpull for the servants, but the wonderful thing about my flat was that there was no one there except me.

All my life I'd lived in other people's houses, answerable to other people. "When will you be back, Ann?" . . . "What are you doing?" . . . "Where are you going?"

Hedged about by petty parental rules ("The milk bottle goes on the *top* shelf of the fridge, Ann, not the bottom . . ."), harassed by children ("It was Mark's fault, Mum, he started it . . ."), or trapped in bed with a man wanting me when all I wanted was to finish Chapter Six ("Put down that bloody book, Ann, and come here . . ."), I'd dreamed of disappearing into anonymity.

And now, here I was. Alone but not lonely. For the first week, I moved from room to room, savoring the silence. I had a bed, a table, a few chairs and that was it. A friend of mine, paying exorbitant sums to an interior decorator for advice on how she should do up her sitting room, had been told disdainfully: "Perfection is one perfect rose in a perfect vase." A bit on the effete side, perhaps, but I knew what he meant. After years of being loaded down with inherited and collected belongings, I had no intention of buying anything, unless it was absolutely right.

My first buy was a pair of converted rococo Italian altar lamps. I brought them home excitedly and instantly appreciated the major disadvantage of living alone. There were no plugs on my lamps and all I knew was that if you stuck the wrong colored wire into the wrong hole something nasty happened.

I had a brilliant idea and called up the local electrician.

"What's the trouble, love? Something wrong with the plugs, wasn't it?" He squatted down and inspected my power points. "Look all right to me. Just been rewired, haven't you?"

I admitted I had and said there was nothing wrong with my plugs except that I didn't understand them.

He picked up his bag. "You're having me on, aren't you? It's fifteen pounds for a call out, you know."

"That's fine." I smiled at him, beguilingly, I hoped. "I will pay you fifteen pounds and you will teach me how to change a plug."

I then called in a plumber for the same sort of individual tuition. The old brass tap in the bathroom was dripping and almost certainly needed a new washer and I didn't know how to fix one of those either.

At half-term, the children arrived with their sleeping bags and camped in the flat. They loved it. Leaving Mark in front of the television set, Sarah and Em and I toured the Portobello and the nearby junk shops, buying up bits and pieces of old scrubbed pine for the kitchen.

Sarah was turning into a beauty. She still seemed very keen to be a vet, and I wondered if it was really the right thing for her. All those years of training, to spend your life peering at cows' udders. "Are you sure it isn't just a childhood thing?" I asked her. "Little girls who are mad about their ponies always say they want to be vets when they grow up."

Sarah's eyes blazed. "Oh, don't you understand anything, Mum? I'm not a little girl. I'm sixteen and I've been working towards this for years. Why do you think I was so keen to do maths and science?"

I hadn't an answer to that because, to be honest, I hadn't realized she was doing maths and science. I didn't know enough about my children; I'd seen them so rarely in these last crucial years.

"So long as you're sure. What do Fel and Daddy think?"

"They're all for it, of course." She stormed out of the room with a parting shot. *"They* care."

I was tempted to call her back, put my case, insist on an apology, but was uncomfortably aware that there was some truth in what she had almost said. Did I care? Yes, of course I did, but at that moment I was conscious only of a gloomy feeling that I was once again caught up in the maelstrom of family tensions and responsibilities; the peace of my flat had been disturbed.

Now that I had the four bedrooms I wondered if I ought to insist on having the children with me, but they seemed as anxious as ever to return to White Walls. Over the next few weeks I asked myself whether I was letting them stay with Felicia and Antony because it was best for them or because it was easier for me. A bit of both, probably.

Felicia

Sarah walks in, complaining of a sore hand.

"What happened, darling, did some dog bite you?"

"I was helping Mr. Garner give a tortoise its injection."

"Where on earth do you inject a tortoise?"

"You pull a hind leg out, and as soon as it feels the needle it pulls it back in again and you bang your hand on its shell. Must go and do some revision."

"Sarah, you're working awfully hard, darling. I do hope you're not overdoing it. You are supposed to be on holiday, after all."

"Got to, if I'm going to get to Edinburgh."

Nineteen eighty-six was a very good year for Sarah, as well as me. After getting ten A's and a B ("Bloody French, I did warn you") in her O levels, she had insisted on applying to join the sixth form of a well-known boys' boarding school. "The facilities, Fel, you should see their labs. And it's just a completely different atmosphere. I know some girls there, and they say it's wonderful—they treat you like an adult. Girls' schools," said Sarah witheringly, "full of prissy women and prissy rules about have you got your games shorts on."

Ann rang me up.

"Is Sarah serious about wanting to go to Somerton?"

"Absolutely set on it."

"I suppose I'd better talk to her about going on the pill."

"Oh Ann," I said, alarmed, "I honestly don't think . . . Sarah's life revolves round reading Veterinary Science at Edinburgh . . . I think she might resent—"

"Edinburgh? What on earth does she want to go up there for?"

"Dick Garner says it's the best. Of course he was there, so naturally Sarah thinks it's the pinnacle."

"Dick Garner? Does she see a lot of him?"

"She's round at the surgery every spare minute. It's part of the entry requirement. As well as getting three top A's, they've got to have spent time with, I quote, 'a veterinarian in practice.' "

"Obviously high time I had a talk with that young lady. Send her up to lunch with me next week. It'll have to be Wednesday."

When Sarah came back from lunch with her mother, she flung upstairs and banged her door. Hours later, as I was in the kitchen getting supper, she came in and made herself some coffee.

"Nice lunch, darling?"

"Reasonably edible. I ticked the headwaiter off about having frogs' legs on the menu, and Mum got quite stroppy." She hesitated, and turned round with her mug cradled in her hands. Her face was rather pink. "Mum said . . . she said if I wanted to go to Somerton, I'd better go on the pill."

"Mm. Well, mothers do worry, you know."

"And then she said, how much time was I spending with Dick Garner. Mr. Garner, Fel, he's about *ninety*. What's happened to Mum?"

"What do you mean, Sarah? She is working very hard—"

"This ghastly person called Ned or Bud or something joined us for coffee. He and Mum kept on sharing jokes I didn't understand, and then he said," Sarah banged her mug down, "do you know what he said? 'A beautiful girl like you doesn't want to waste her time being a vet. You could easily do modeling, with your figure.' I was frightfully rude," said Sarah with some satisfaction, "and Mum got stroppy again."

"Oh dear. I'm sure she meant—"

"What she meant was that the moment I came in contact with some spotty schoolboy (or elderly vet for that matter), I'd be on my back saying Yes Please. Your generation have got one-track minds, that's your problem. You think you invented sex. My generation are quite capable of going on the pill if and when we want to. We don't intend to sleep around," Sarah burst into tears, "like some people."

Ann rang up that night.

"Fel, I'm sorry Sarah's being so difficult. You must be having a frightful time with her. I'm not sure I'm going to allow her to go on with this ridiculous idea of being a vet, so unsuitable. With her looks—"

"She's not being difficult at all. Why on earth did you ask Ned or Bud or someone to join you?"

"I wouldn't have thought that was any of your business."

"Ann, would you just stop a minute, and listen to what you are saying? You are enjoying yourself using *your* brain the way *you* want to. Why the bloody hell can't you extend the same privilege to your daughter?" I was so angry I said "prillyvedge," but the message got across.

"I see, I see exactly what's been happening. This is your idea, isn't it? You failed in London, so you want everyone round you to lead boring rural little lives."

"A vet is a member of a highly respected profession. Anyway, it's not your decision, it's Sarah's."

"We'll see about that. I shall talk to her father." She won't get much change from him, I thought.

The night Sarah got her O-level exam results, Antony had poured out champagne; even the little ones were allowed a sip. "Ugh," they said, "is there any Coke?"

"Ten A's," he kept on saying, *"ten A's.* I bet nobody else at school had results like that."

"Oh, I don't know," said Sarah modestly. In fact she probably did know—she'd been on the phone all evening, saying, "Oh, poor Jackie, she worked so hard . . . she didn't! Not Antonia? Have you heard how Liz did? . . ."

The first person she'd phoned had been Ann, of course. As she went off to use the extension I wished that Ann could have been there when Sarah opened the envelope; how rotten to hear such good news over the telephone, and not be able to hug.

Sarah came back glowing. "Mum screamed," she said, "she actually screeched. She said if anyone wants to find her, they'd better look upwards, because she's walking on the ceiling. And then she said . . ."—Sarah's voice went a little diminuendo—"wouldn't it be lovely if I read English at university and worked with her?"

"Darling, haven't you told her about being a vet?"

"Only vaguely, I don't think she took it seriously."

Next morning Antony rushed into Salisbury and bought a new copy of Brian Heap's *Degree Course Offers.*

"Gosh, Dad," said Sarah, "it says Veterinary Science is the most intensively competitive course. And you've got to have previous experience with a vet."

"I feel sorry for the others, they don't know they're up against you, darling. I'll ring Dick Garner later. He can hardly say no, the amount of fees he's had from us over the years."

And then Antony did something rather nice. "Clever Laura," he said, putting an arm round her, "you know that pastel you did of the lower field when it was flooded? I had it framed and it's up in my office. I've just been offered a hundred quid for it."

"A hundred?" said Mark, awed. "What are you going to do with the money?"

"I can just see you in the city. I told him it wasn't for sale, and that he'd be lucky to lay his hands on that artist's work for a thousand, in a few years' time."

Laura glowed, and Antony said expansively, "I'm rather looking forward to my twilight years, surrounded by all this talent. You two, and Emmy on the stage . . . Mark in charge of Lloyd's and Harry the computer king . . . and Felicia . . ."

"What will Fel be doing?" said Emmy.

"She will be surprising me until the end of her days," said Antony.

Ann

Bob and Maddie had often talked about putting up the money for me to start my own company, and six months ago they came into my small office in Delphic and said that the time was right now.

My business had grown too big for one small office and one hardworking secretary, and there were more exciting prospects in the pipeline. It was, according to the McMahons, an ideal moment to siphon some of the Delphic profits away from the taxman; coincidentally, the top floor of their building had just become vacant.

"You can have it at a nominal rent until you get going," said Maddie.

Bob handed me a sheaf of formidable papers. "This isn't a charitable exercise, Ann. We're investing our money where we think we'll get the best return. Our solicitor has drawn up a preliminary agreement, quoting the sort of loan interest and share options we'd expect. See what you think, have your solicitor check it out and then come back to us."

I thanked them both and tried to focus on the documents.

I'd come a long way in three years, but still couldn't look at lists of figures and legal small print without my eyes crossing. I took the papers to Mr. Dwyer, who studied them thoughtfully and announced that he found himself in something of a quandary.

"I fear this is not my field of expertise, Miss Browning. You require a solicitor who is more conversant than myself with company law."

He recommended Carmichael Gilham. "And I seem to recall that you are acquainted with Mr. Gilham?" He handed back the documents. "I'd approach him with these, if I were you."

Last time I'd approached Philip Gilham he had firmly disentangled my arms from around his neck and told me I was making an ass of myself. He was the last person with whom I wished to discuss Subclause (4) of the Companies Acts 1948 to 1967.

I was almost grateful to Sarah for giving me an excuse to put off any decision and worry about her instead.

She had decided she wanted to go to Somerton, a minor boys' public school in Wiltshire which was hot on the sciences, good at getting their pupils into agricultural colleges and took girls in the sixth form.

It seemed a rotten idea to me; I'd have preferred her to go to one of the top schools where the academic standard is higher and where she'd have the chance of meeting some reasonable young men.

I said this to Antony, who disagreed. His attitude to his daughter's career, I thought sardonically, was very different from the my-wife-the-typist label he'd put on me.

"Excellent place, Somerton," he said briskly. "I'm all in favor of it. Sarah doesn't need to meet 'reasonable young men,' Ann. She's got ten O levels, remember."

Having lost that battle I realized I'd have to talk to her about the pill. I couldn't really land that one on Fel, though I must admit I was tempted. I find it very difficult communicating with Sarah these days. She looks like an angel and sounds like a farmhand who's swallowed a Greenpeace pamphlet. She also has a way of aggressively stating her views which automatically makes me want to argue with her.

When I phoned up White Walls to talk to her about Somerton, I got Felicia instead. I'd have liked to discuss the pill problem with her (I'm alarmed by the side effects, and think it's a bit much for headmasters to renege on their responsibilities by insisting that the girls who come into their sixth form should be kitted out with contraception as a matter of course) but the moment I said the word "pill" she became prissily defensive. There are times when I wish Felicia wouldn't act as though Sarah were her daughter rather than mine.

I did discover, though, where Sarah had been picking up the farmyard vocabulary. She'd been spending her time with that ghastly old bore, Dick Garner. Highly unsuitable. Dick may be a good vet but he's always had a reputation for impregnating the local farmers' daughters as efficiently as he injects their fathers' cattle. I supposed I'd have to speak to her about that as well. It wouldn't be an easy lunch.

Sarah had arrived promptly at twelve forty-five.

"Well done, darling." I put aside a batch of reports to go through later and came around the desk to kiss her.

She brushed my cheek with hers dutifully and surveyed the office. *"Very* swish," she said in a tone which sounded as though she were saying *"Very* unpleasant."

I would not allow myself to be rattled. "Glad you like it, love. We're going to Chez Victor, nice and cosy. Lots of famous theater people go there and although the proprietor makes a point of being rude, the food is delicious."

Sarah watched impassively as Victor went through his usual routine of showing me to the smallest, nastiest table and then allowing me, with a Gallic gesture of contempt, to move to an empty, comfortable banquette.

"What a silly fuss."

"It is indeed," I agreed equably. "Ah, here's the menu."

As the waiter stood behind her, pad and pencil poised, Sarah suddenly flung the menu aside, as though she'd been asked to approve a list of Nazi war crimes.

"Grenouilles?" she cried. "They can't seriously mean that, can they, Mum? *Frogs'* legs?"

The waiter kissed the tips of his fingers and assured us that the grenouilles were superb, a delicacy. He couldn't read the danger signs as I could. "Will you be starting with them, *mademoiselle?"*

"I certainly will not," said Sarah loudly, "and I don't think anyone else ought to be eating them either. It's disgusting . . ."

"Non, non, mademoiselle . . . delicieuses."

"They may *taste* all right," said Sarah, on the same high note, "but it's disgusting eating them. I suppose you're either too stupid or too greedy to know that certain species of frogs are now endangered . . ."

"That's *quite* enough of that, Sarah." My voice rose above hers. At the same time I clamped a hand on her arm and hissed: "Pull yourself together. How dare you talk to the waiter like that."

I'd been thinking that the escargots might be pleasant but decided that under the circumstances, it was an unwise choice. I ordered pâté as Sarah scanned the menu as enthusiastically as Laura and Harry inspecting one of my home-cooked meals. "I'm not hungry."

"Oh, for heaven's sake, Sarah, stop behaving like a baby. Have steak and salad. You like that."

I let her get halfway through her steak and a tedious lecture about saving some obscure whale before I brought the conversation around to Somerton and the pill.

"The pill?"

"Darling, do stop shouting. We don't want everyone to hear us."

Sarah put down her knife and fork and narrowed her lips ominously. "There you are. It's such a disgusting subject that you don't want anyone to hear you mention it; but you don't mind talking about it to your own daughter." I wondered, guiltily, if that irrational outburst had anything to do with the way Sarah had seen the adults around her behaving—Antony, Donald, Felicia and myself—since it was hardly unusual for a mother to talk to her seventeen-year-old daughter about contraception.

I foolishly murmured something about it being better to be safe than sorry and Sarah said she didn't want to discuss the matter any further.

"Very well."

It was probably a mistake to mention Garner after that. "And there's another thing . . ."

"What is it now?" I wouldn't have thought it possible for such a lovely face to turn so ugly and belligerent.

"That dreadful old vet," I said. "Keep away from him."

"You can't mean *Dick Garner?* Why?"

"Because he's got an appalling reputation, that's why. Don't forget I lived in that village for years. It's well known that no female under sixty is safe within five hundred yards of his surgery."

"You can't seriously be suggesting . . . ? Why, he's never . . ."

Sarah's high-pitched protestations were interrupted by a glad shout.

"Ann. *There* you are. I've been looking for you all over. Guess I went to the wrong Victor's."

It was Bud Elphick. Bud and Ned arrived in London a couple of days ago and I had forgotten that last night I'd mentioned to Bud after the third . . . or was it the fourth? . . . brandy that I would be lunching at Chez Victor with my daughter. "Come and meet her," I'd said. "She's a real charmer."

"May I join you?" He had already drawn up a chair.

"Of course, Bud. How nice." I introduced them. Sarah ignored Bud's friendly greeting, looking at him as if he were a portion of frogs' legs.

"Well, I'm just thrilled to meet you," Bud told her. "Ann has told me all about you."

"Really?" said Sarah superciliously. "I didn't think she knew much about me."

"Ignore her, Bud," I said hopefully. "Sarah's a bit upset. We've been having a serious mother-and-daughter talk, and I'm afraid Sarah isn't very pleased with me."

"A mother-and-daughter talk, eh?" said Bud. I wished he weren't so incorrigible. "Let me tell you, Sarah, that you ought to listen to this mother of yours. She's really something. She runs a business, speaks French like a native—how about that time you wheedled that nice little packet of coke from François at the Auberge, Ann? Boy, were you cool—and does she know how to dress? Remember the ballgown, Ann?"

I wished I couldn't. I also hoped desperately that Sarah imagined I'd cunningly obtained a case of Coca-Cola from François at the Auberge.

"You should have seen your mother, Sarah. The belle of the ball at *the* hotel in Gstaad. And do you know what she was wearing?" He slapped his thigh with mirth at the memory and seemed unaware that neither Sarah nor I was smiling. "What do you guess, Sarah? Tell me, what do you guess?"

"I haven't the faintest idea," said Sarah distantly.

"A negligee, that's what." Bud dissolved into more solo laughter and called over the waiter.

"This calls for a bottle of champagne . . ."

"No thank you," Sarah and I chorused in unison.

Bud looked surprised. "Hey, what's the matter with you two girls?"

"I've got rather a lot of work on this afternoon," I said, "and Sarah has to get back to the country."

We had coffee instead and, hoping to get him away from the reminiscences, I told Bud that Sarah was thinking of becoming a vet.

Bud leaned back in his chair and gazed at Sarah. "A veterinarian? Now why would a beautiful girl like you want to waste her time being a veterinarian?"

"It's not a waste of time," said Sarah. "It's a useful and interesting profession."

"Not a waste of time for the dumb animals, maybe," agreed Bud, "but how about you? A girl with your looks could be a top model on the cover of every magazine in the country."

He meant it as a compliment. Sarah saw it as an insult, as I'd guessed she would. She rose, threw Bud a scornful scowl. "What a perfectly stupid thing to say. But then, everything you've said since you came in here has been stupid. I'm going now."

"I'm sorry, Bud." I laid an apologetic hand on his. "Forgive her, please. I'm afraid you got caught up in the whiplash of a family scene."

"Don't you mind, Ann. I understand."

"Thank you for that. I'm afraid I'll have to go after her. Can I buy you and Ned dinner tonight . . . ?"

Bud was looking for a get-out. "We'll take a rain check tonight, honey, if you don't mind . . . early start tomorrow morning."

Sarah was standing outside. "What a frightful man."

"Not as frightful as your behavior." There was a taxi on the other side of the road. I hailed it, put Sarah inside and handed her the money for her fare.

Slamming the door, I addressed her stubborn profile through the window. "We'll talk again when you've learned some manners."

It was a relief to get back to the office.

Felicia

"Donald, what's going on?" I say sharply. I had meant to spend this morning schooling Rocket on the lunge. Irritating to have to waste time with this phone call, but I've really got to find out.

"Felicia, how very nice to hear your voice. How very very nice—"

"Never mind all that, Donald. When Laura told me Ann had very kindly given her a holiday job, I naturally assumed she would be with you in St. John's Wood. Now I hear she's staying with Sally Anne Sullivan. And when I asked her why, she went evasive on me. God, when I think back to all the fuss your bloody solicitor made about custody, and now, when your fifteen-year-old daughter is working in London . . ."

"Hold it right there, Felicia. There are some facts I certainly want to put you in possession of, but not over the phone. Why don't you come up and have lunch with me?"

"Because I don't want to, Donald. If you've got something to tell me then I suggest you get in your car and drive down here."

"If that's what you would prefer . . . now let me see when I can manage—"

"Tomorrow would be fine for me."

"That is rather short notice, Felicia. Taking a quick glance at my schedule—"

"Tomorrow is my only free day, Donald . . . What? . . . No, it is not just a question of when I do the weeding, as it happens. Wednesday I have JP training lectures all day, Thursday the Red Cross are meeting here and in the afternoon I've got to take a rehearsal, Friday . . ."

Donald, baffled (and almost certainly bored) by my recital, agrees to come down tomorrow. In the early afternoon, I say firmly. I do not intend to waste precious time giving him lunch.

It isn't until I've put the phone down that I wonder suspiciously why he's being so . . . placatory? Submissive, almost. Something to do with that little toughie he's married to, I bet.

It must be about a year since he got married, quite soon after he threw Ann out. I've never really got to the bottom of why he chucked her so decisively, though if even half the rumors about young men I'd heard were true . . .

I have met Marcia only once, enough to guess that she will make Donald the perfect company wife; seeing to it that his window treatments fit his position in the company, that his guests are offered food that intrigues but does not alarm, and that he is father to the perfect corporate family. They already have a three-month-old son, and—

I glare angrily out of the window at poor old inoffensive Rocket.

That's what all this is about, I might have known. My daughter has been edged out of her father's house because stepchildren don't fit in with that crisp-eyed little cow's design for living.

Donald gets out of his car with a jovial, now-isn't-this-just-great expression. It fades when he catches my stony stare.

"Don't bother to explain," I say coldly, "she has to put up with Laura and Harry in term time, but she's damned if she's going to have one of them during the holidays as well."

Donald looks disconcerted, as well he might; I have just flung at him part of the conversation I have been furiously having with him, mentally, for most of last night and all this morning.

"Now it's not quite like that, honey. Felicia," he substitutes hastily as I scowl. "Laura herself was very keen to stay with Sally Anne—"

"Poor darling. Knowing she wasn't wanted by her father, she naturally made the best of it."

"Of course I want her. She's my little girl and I love her. But Marcia has found her a little difficult once or twice."

"There isn't a difficult bone in Laura's body."

"Maybe," says Donald wearily, "maybe I shouldn't have given Laura that music center for her birthday. I don't know why she has to play it so goddam loud, Felicia, right after Marcia has gotten little Don Junior off to sleep. He's teething, too . . ."

My anger fades into unwilling sympathy.

"You're looking tired, Donald, come in and have some coffee."

"Tired? I'll say I'm tired. Did Laura and Harry have colic, Felicia? I don't remember anything like that. Marcia is breastfeeding Don Junior, of course, and she says it's something in the butter here. I have had to ask Head Office to airmail us some canned American butter."

"Perhaps you'd better have a whiskey . . ."

"Anyway, that problem will be solved soon, because . . ." He stops and looks at me cautiously.

"Come on, spit it out."

Donald is not the kind of man to spit anything out. It takes him some time to tell me that he has been recalled to the States to take up the position of executive vice president in charge of executive vice presidents. Which sounds strange, but I probably heard it wrong. I am too busy wondering—

"So I have come to the conclusion that it would not be right to take Laura and Harry with me. I know, I know," he says in a firmer voice, as though I were about to disagree with him, "I do have custody and they are technically American. And I would certainly want Harry to go to college in the States. But they were born here, and their friends are here. Marcia and I, we feel that it will be best for them in the long run if they live with you. I understand there are excellent schools in the neighborhood."

I don't point out that going to school in Wiltshire will mean they will lose their London friends as surely as if they were attending high school in downtown Detroit. Why should I quibble when I'm getting what I want? But I can't help thinking bitterly that for four years I only saw my children in the holidays because Donald thought it was vital for them to continue at the American School. And now he is casually handing them over because they won't fit in with his new life.

"Of course, I'll try for custody, Mrs. Harman, if you insist," my solicitor had told me when I was divorcing Donald, "but your husband has a very strong case. He is the innocent party—you parted the matrimonial home, did you not, without any provocation? Quite. Then there is the question of schooling. And I gather that, should it get into court, the other side might well bring up the question of an alleged negligence on your part."

"But that was an *accident*," I said.

Years ago, when Harry was four and Laura was eight, I had been pottering about getting up (Donald had already left for the office) when Laura trotted into my bedroom and said she thought she was old enough to give Harry his breakfast.

Imagining her putting cereal into a bowl and pouring milk over it, I said, "All right, darling, but be careful." I remember thinking how appealing Laura's new Little Mother act was. Then I heard a clatter and a scream and awful wails.

They'd never had boiled eggs for their breakfast, why on earth had Laura attempted them that morning? Harry had snatched at the saucepan handle, thank God the water had missed his face, but he got it all over his left shoulder and had to be rushed to casualty.

Donald, usually so self-controlled, went to pieces. He rang the hospital every five minutes.

"They want to keep him in under observation for a few days," he said. "I don't like the sound of it."

He kept looking at me questioningly. "Where were you, exactly, Felicia, when Harry got scalded?"

Surely he didn't imagine . . . ? "If I'd known Laura was going to boil water, I'd have watched her. They only ever have cereal, you know that."

He was too distraught to listen. He seemed to have convinced himself that I was somehow to blame.

"You've been doing far too much lately, darling. Why don't you go and see Daniel Dickson. Maybe you're heading towards some sort of breakdown."

I wasn't heading towards anything of the kind, but I did go and see Dr. Dickson.

"Good morning, Mrs. Harman. I dropped in to see Harry this morning. They're very pleased with him, you can take him home tomorrow."

"My husband thinks they kept Harry in so that they could check up on me, in case . . . in case I was involved somehow."

"What an extraordinary idea. The child had second-degree burns with a certain amount of dehydration and, of course, shock. He was kept in because he needed nursing. There is absolutely no question in anyone's mind, my dear, that you . . ."

"Donald seems to think I'm heading for a nervous breakdown."

"Nonsense. If all my patients were as normal as you I'd be a poor man."

As I watch Donald drive away after handing the children over to me so casually, I think, I didn't meet Antony until long after Harry's accident. But that was the day I started leaving Donald.

And now, perhaps, I can get to work on Rocket.

I shrug on my Barbour, and it doesn't feel right. It isn't until I put my hands in my pockets that I realize it's Sarah's. Chewing gum in one pocket, and . . . a rather long typewritten letter in the other. It starts "My darling Sarah" in handwriting, so of course I wouldn't dream of reading it.

Might just see who it's from, though.

"Please forgive me, darling, I love you so much, Mum." No date on it, only "Thursday"; but judging by its appearance, Sarah has been carrying it around for ages.

None of my business, anyway. I look furtively at Sadie, who happily is the only living creature about. I'll just see how it starts . . .

I am typing this because I want to sort my thoughts out. First of all, of course, I apologize wholeheartedly for that dreadful lunch yesterday. It was an object lesson in how not to deal with a daughter you've loved since, well, ever since I knew you were coming, Sarah. I hoped you'd be beautiful and clever, and just look at you, I certainly got first prize in girls that year. I was so clumsy yesterday, so bossy and so sure I was right. And that frightful young man, whatever possessed me to ask him to join us? I think you are old enough to understand that when Dad left me for Felicia I got rather a kick in the self-confidence. I suppose it sounds silly to you, but having someone that age say "Wow, Ann, you're so attractive . . ." is rather bolstering.

I don't think I could write this, but I can just about manage it typing. I'm so bloody jealous of Felicia. Not because of Dad, I don't need him anymore, but because of you, darling, and Mark and Emmy. You are all such friends. Every time you say "Felly says . . ." I could cheerfully cut her heart out.

Of course I'm grateful she cares about you, but do you remember when you rang up about your O-level results? I imagined you all, after I put the phone down, laughing and celebrating. And I put on a frightfully expensive dress and took a client to the Gavroche and to save my life I couldn't tell you what we ate or what we said.

All this is a bit muddled, I'm afraid. What I'm getting down to is, of course you're going to be a vet, you old silly, and if there's anything I can do to help . . . Please forgive me, darling, I love you so much, Mum.

P.S. I checked up on frogs' legs and you're quite right.

I put the letter back in the pocket and hang Sarah's Barbour up. I think we'll give it a miss today, Rocket.

Ann

"Mr. Gilham will see you now, Miss Browning."

I hadn't wanted to do it. I'd asked around, but everyone had told me that Carmichael Gilham were the best company lawyers in

London; and Mr. Carmichael, I learned, when I phoned to make an appointment to see him, had passed away five years ago.

That left Philip. I hoped he wouldn't throw me out.

He rose politely from behind a large partners' desk. "Do take a seat, Miss Browning. . . . Good God, Ann, it's you. What are you doing, lurking about behind a pseudonym?"

"I'm not." I perched primly on the edge of a hard-backed chair. "Ann Browning is my name. My maiden name."

Philip sat down, took a pencil slowly from a drawer in his desk, drew a piece of paper even more slowly towards him and looked at me.

I was wearing a boring gray, nannyish coat, hoping not to remind him of a wild-eyed nymphomaniac in ivory satin.

"I see. And what can I do for you, Miss Browning?"

I fumbled in my bag for the McMahon documents, dropped some of them, retrieved them, eventually managed to assemble them in some sort of order on Philip's desk.

"I'm starting a company." I looked fixedly at my discreet gray brogues so that I didn't have to look at him. "Delphic are putting up the initial funding and I'd like you to deal with it all for me." I decided to risk a compliment. "Everyone tells me that you are the best company lawyer in London."

"Do they indeed?" He gathered my papers together. "I suggest you leave these with me. Perhaps you can come back on Wednesday when I've had time to go through them."

"Oh thank you, thank you, Philip."

"Show Miss Browning out, will you Helen, and make an appointment for her to come in on Wednesday."

I had been dismissed. What had I expected? That he'd throw his arms around me, bury his face in my hair and whisper: "Oh Ann, my darling, I'm so grateful you have allowed me to draw up your Articles of Association?"

He was a little less distant on Wednesday. Called me Ann instead of Miss Browning and said that it looked a very satisfactory deal to him. The McMahons were asking for a reasonable return on their money. He had drawn up the necessary documents and registered the Ann Browning Company at Companies' House.

"And now," he said, "perhaps we ought to go through the details together."

Our heads were almost touching across the desk; he was going gray and it rather suited him, I noticed, as he said, "The directors may exercise all the powers conferred on them by Clause Seventy-nine or Part One of Table A . . ." There was a pleasing fleck of amber in his brown eyes as he read, ". . . subject to the provisions of Section Fifty-eight of the Act . . ." He was just moving on rivetingly to the bit about "the quorum necessary for the transaction of the business of the Directors" when I leaned over the desk and kissed him on the lips. This time he didn't push me away.

One of the first things Philip had asked me, as we lay together in my bed later that evening, was whether I still saw Tom Harman.

I said I didn't and it was true, in a way. Tom lived in New Jersey and I lived in London, but we wrote and phoned.

I'd phoned him immediately after the row with Donald.

"Ann honey. I'm missing you. You're sweet to call."

"Donald knows," I said.

"Knows what?"

About the 2.4 percent rise of the pound against the dollar? The current rate of inflation in West Germany? "About us, of course."

I reported the happenings at Acacia Road and told Tom that we'd managed to splash champagne into the soup of one of his mother's oldest friends.

Tom groaned. "I thought there was something familiar about those two. Remember avoiding them at one of Mother's cocktail parties. And Dad?"

"Every inch the dominant male challenged by the young upstart. Furious."

I do wish I could sometimes say what I mean instead of glossing over reality with glib remarks. "He was very upset . . . that it was you."

"Yeah, well, anything I do upsets him. Dad and I have never had an easy relationship."

I was still wondering if my appeal for Tom might have had something to do with scoring off his father as he said: "Got to go now, honey. The boss is calling me. But I'm coming over for a time-share convention soon . . . longing to see you . . ."

Just when I wanted to spend every minute of every day being with Philip or thinking about being with him, I had to go through all the paper-signing, staff-gathering, furniture-buying hassle of starting an office.

Sandra and I bargained for light boxes, video equipment and all the other expensive paraphernalia we needed. Jim painted and decorated and I spent more money than I could afford on sleek Italian furniture for the reception area. I still had nowhere comfortable to sit at home, but first things first; my agency had to sell itself from the moment a client put a tentative foot across the threshold.

I went to Finders, since I was angling for their account just then, and their chief headhunter produced four key people for the top jobs. They also discovered several bright girls with English degrees and the creative spark I needed, hidden away in their secretarial files.

"You've chosen all the attractive ones," said Sandra, "isn't that a bit unfair? What about that nice girl who came in this morning? The one with all the qualifications . . . the one with dandruff?"

"You've said it. If she can't be bothered to tidy herself up for an interview, what makes you think she'd be a perfectionist at work?"

"Hmmm," said Sandra. I knew she wanted to call me ageist or sexist or something but couldn't think of the right word.

My biggest coup was poaching Paul Banner and Justin Elliott from Antony. He'd always boasted that Paul (the words) and Justin (the art director) knocked spots off the opposition and he'd also —foolishly, as it turned out—boasted how little he paid them.

He was very cross and phoned to tell me so. "You can't do it, Ann. I won't have it."

"Serves you right for being so mean," I said.

"But . . . but it's *unethical.*"

"Of course it isn't. You know perfectly well, Antony, that everyone in this business moves from agency to agency as though they were playing musical chairs . . ."

"But . . . you're my *wife.*"

"Ex-wife, Antony," I corrected. "And there's nothing, so far as I know, in the Code of Practice that says a woman can't hire her ex-husband's staff. *And* pay them a fair wage."

Antony slammed down the phone.

It was easier to hire the staff than to manage them.

I wanted to be popular, and kept popping out of my office and smiling at them all and saying "Well done" and "Of course you can take tomorrow off," when I should have said "Not good enough" and "No, you can't stay at home tomorrow to wait for the gas man."

"It's always been your trouble," said Philip. "You're far too anxious to please. It was one of the first things I noticed about you."

"But being nice isn't a gross character defect."

"Being nice is fine. You're that, all right. Very, very nice. But that's not the same as needing to be adored or admired by everyone you meet. That shows a lack of self-confidence; it's unrealistic, too."

Goodness, I thought, I must love Philip a great deal. I usually hate being criticized, and there I was smiling back at him and promising to try to be more of a bastard.

When Justin and Paul brought me in a rough for one of the new Delphic ads and I didn't like it, I forced myself to say so. "It's too obscure. You're trying to attract the attention of businessmen, remember, not other ad agencies."

Justin and Paul squared up to me as one and said they both felt, very sincerely, that their simple woodcut of a heraldic motif was visually interesting and emphasized the unique quality of the Delphic concept. "Besides," said Justin, "I spent bloody hours in the College of Arms researching it."

I told them that Maddie and Bob McMahon wouldn't wear it and I was the one who had to sell it to them. "Back to the drawing board and let me have at least three alternative suggestions by midday Friday."

They left without a murmur.

The Delphic commercials had been seen so often (Sol had picked up an award for one of them) that I was worried viewers would get sick of them. I asked Sol to meet me for lunch to discuss new ideas. I also wanted to ask him if he'd let my video girl help with the shooting.

"She'll learn more working with you for six weeks than in six months in a film school."

"You're getting very plausible, Ann. Very persuasive. Of course I'll show her the ropes."

I told Sol that I'd managed to land several useful small accounts, *"and,* Sol, I've been approached by Patterson Warbeck."

"Patterson Warbeck," said Sol. "Wow. But aren't they in a tricky takeover situation with United Grip?"

"Tricky for UG, not PW." I lowered my voice. "Rumor has it that UG have just accepted a one-hundred-sixty-pence-per-share tender offer from PW, giving them a twenty-nine-point-nine stake in the company . . ."

Sol tried to look impressed. "I don't understand a word of what you're saying, Ann, but I guess it's good news for you by the smug expression."

"Good news, if I get the account. And if I do, can I bring you in on it, Sol?"

"So long as you don't go on talking like the *Wall Street Journal.* How's Felicia?"

"Haven't seen her for months, but Laura says she's looking good again. I'm so glad. I was afraid that frank talk you made me deliver would make things even worse."

"I hear she's got involved with amateur dramatics," said Sol.

"Amateur dramatics?" I pictured Felicia prancing about the village hall dressed in something Jenny Balfour had made out of an old tablecloth. "Is that her scene?"

"Very much so, it seems," said Sol. "She was practically press-ganged into it by a local antique dealer; evidently she's transforming a group of local amateurs into professional perfection. I gather there's even some talk of the local council putting up the money for a community theater."

"Well, good for Felicia. And how about Antony? He's refused to speak to me since I pinched two of his people."

"Still up to his old tricks," said Sol. "I believe it's a redhead now . . ."

"Poor Fel," I said. "I wonder if she knows. I never did. It's only now that I can see what Antony was up to in London while I stayed at White Walls chopping wood to keep the home fires burning."

"Oh yes," said Sol, "Fel knows. I'm sure of it." He leaned over the table so conspiratorially that I thought he must be going to mention Patterson Warbeck again. "And do you know the most extraordinary thing, Ann? I don't believe she gives a damn."

Felicia

I do love having all my children together. I have come to think of Sarah and Emmy and Mark as mine, which is fortunate, because Ann is hardly thinking of them at all, as far as I can see.

Every time I ring up to make an arrangement for half-term or a visit to the dentist, I meet with obstruction. She always seems to have a first-class excuse for not meeting them where and when I suggest.

I got quite cross, once, when she proposed that Emmy, who is after all only twelve and not a London child, should find her own way to Ann's flat. When I protested, she said, "You don't want to believe all you read in the newspapers, Felicia—it's not all mugging and rape in London, you know. Anyway, it's time that child learned to be more self-reliant."

"You can't be serious—Paddington at nine o'clock at night? Emmy would be terrified. I suppose I could drive her up first thing Saturday morning, but—"

"Saturday. Saturday's not awfully good for me, I'm afraid. I'm driving some Americans from the Patterson Warbeck New York office down to Hatfield House for an Elizabethan banquet—"

"How perfectly ghastly."

"Rather fun, I should think. They'll love it, anyway."

"Rather you than me. Why couldn't Emmy go with you? She's doing the Tudors now, and they've got the first draft of the warrant for Mary Queen of Scots's execution at Hatfield House, I was reading about it somewhere. It would bring it all alive for her."

"Hardly professional, dragging one's child along. Look, why don't we arrange it for another weekend? Emmy wouldn't mind, would she?"

"She might, if she could remember what you look like," I said, and when I put the phone down I was shaking with rage.

Later, I said to Antony, "Neither Donald nor Ann seems to care a hoot about their children, which I must admit suits me down to the ground."

"The more the merrier, as far as I'm concerned. What is that amazing garment you've got on?"

"Knickerbockers. Do you like them?"

"They make you look like a very beautiful medieval page boy. You haven't lost too much weight, have you?"

I've lost just about enough. What with riding, gardening, and giving up butter, I've got back to below 110 pounds. I feel about butter the way Ray Milland felt about a third of rye in *The Lost Weekend*. I know that if I have just one lick of the lovely creamy decadent stuff, I'll be hooked again and devouring it by the pound. If I'd been Ray Milland it would have been a packet of Normandy Unsalted hanging out of my window on a string.

The day the needle hovered and finally settled under 110, I said to Sarah and Laura, "Come on, you two. You never stop talking about clothes, let's have some advice. I'm generously prepared to admit that brown cords have their limitations."

They looked at me through professionally narrowed eyes.

"Knickerbockers," said Laura.

"Darling, you can't mean those great bulbous things the Prince of Wales played golf with Mrs. Simpson in?"

They exchanged quite kind looks across me.

"You mean what the Joint Master was wearing at the point-to-point last week?" said Sarah. "Hey, that could be really cool. Brown cable stockings and . . . what shoes?"

"Hobbs?" said Laura keenly. "They've got some really amazing lace-ups, but I don't know if they do them in brown."

Their knowledge of shops is microscopic. I have no doubt that if I asked them where to buy an Albanian wedding dress of the early nineteenth century, one of them would say, "Off the Fulham Road; third on the left after Staggers, I think" and the other would add, "Second, actually—don't you remember we passed it on our way to Hobby Horse?"

I had a lovely day in London spending a major packet (an investment, really, I thought defensively) on brown and cream and highly polished leather.

And I went back to Robert.

"Felicia," he shrieked, "where have you been? And what," he added sourly, "have you been doing to your hair? I know you live in the country, darling, but did you have to let someone prune it?"

"Oh Robert, I know, but I ride twice a week now, and those sweaty hard hats, I have to wash it such a lot. So it seemed simpler . . ." I tailed off apologetically.

"Couldn't you just give up riding? No, all right. Well, let me think—why don't I cut it to two inches long all over?"

"Cut it all off? I couldn't—my hair's one of my best things."

"Not anymore it isn't. And look at the state of your scalp. Betty," he shouted across the salon, "are you free to give Felicia a treatment? Just come and look at this."

She came and looked at this, and I servilely agreed to have a treatment. Half an hour (and some twenty quid) later, Robert stood over me with poised scissors.

"Oh Robert, I can't make up my mind. I'm lunching with my husband today, what will he say when I walk in with no hair?"

"You'll have masses of hair, don't be a ninny. Anyway, what did he say when you went and got *this* so-called cut?"

"Nothing."

"Exactly. Come on, yes or no?"

"Hurry up before I change my mind."

When I walk into Simpsons, Antony is already there. His eyes pass over me and snap back in one of those double takes I thought only Bob Hope did.

"Felicia, what on earth have you done to your hair? I nearly didn't recognize you."

"You don't like it."

"Give me time . . . you look about ten. And what are you going to toss back when you're in a temper?"

"I don't intend to be in a temper, anymore."

"That'll be the day."

A waiter appears, and we order. At 106 pounds, I think complacently, I can really let myself go. Boiled eggs and diet soup tomorrow, but today . . . I am just finishing my profiteroles when Antony stiffens.

"Don't look now," he says, "just coming out . . . Peter Wentworth."

"Chairman of United Grip?" I say astutely, congratulating myself on all that hard work with the *Financial Times*.

"That's the one . . . Sir Peter," says Antony, getting to his feet, "how nice; won't you join us for coffee?"

"Antony, my dear fellow . . . no, I really ought to be getting back to the office. I don't think you've met my wife. Mary," he says to the elegant gray-haired woman with him, "this is Antony Forester-Jones. And this must be the beautiful daughter we've heard so much about. Still going to be a vet, my dear?"

I grin. "Actually, I'm Antony's wife."

"No wonder he keeps you hidden away in the country." He looks at his watch. "I suppose they can survive without me for a bit longer."

A waiter brings two more chairs and they sit down.

"I'm exhausted," says Mary Wentworth, "do you come up to London often?"

"As little as possible."

"Horrid, isn't it? I seem to spend my time stepping politely out of the way of teenagers with rucksacks. This morning I actually apologized to a child whose guitar had struck me on the shoulder."

"She wouldn't come up at all," says Peter Wentworth fondly, "if she hadn't needed some expensive dressage kit."

"Do you do dressage?" I say.

"Yes, I'm doing a test on Saturday, actually. Do you?"

"I love it," I say enthusiastically, and we're off.

Five minutes later, I look guiltily at Antony; Mary and I have been having exactly the kind of conversation that makes him nod off at home; now, though, he is fascinated, turning his head attentively as we speak.

"I get an awful lot of this, don't you?" says Peter. "I once asked Mary to explain what a half pass is. Fearful mistake. She went on for half an hour, and I wasn't any the wiser."

"I've just had a marvelous idea," says Mary. She looks quickly at her husband, who smiles benignly. "Why don't you come down on Saturday and watch me and Firebug make fools of ourselves?"

"Why don't they stay the night, darling?" says Peter, "give me a chance to talk to you about the new campaign presentation, Antony. As I think you know, we feel that while it is absolutely right overall, there are one or two points that need sorting out."

After they've gone, Antony looks at me in a way that takes me right back to those discreet lunches four years ago.

"I've been angling for an invitation down there for weeks. How did you manage it?"

"I didn't *manage* it, darling. Isn't Mary Wentworth nice?"

"Bit horsey."

"Do you think she'd let me ride one of her horses? I'll take my jodhpurs in case. One of her mares is up to Prix St. George standard, she said . . ."

But Antony is calling for the bill.

The weekend turns out to be a success from every possible point of view. Antony comes away with the United Grip account securely in his grasp; my knickerbockers went down a treat. (I had boldly worn them instead of the discreet tweed skirt Antony urgently suggested, and I was right. Two women asked me where they came from, and Mary Wentworth said could you get them in green.)

And she let me ride her Prix St. George mare, a revelation after patient old Jester. Mary was schooling Firebug at the same time. He'd behaved very badly the day before, skittering about in pretended terror when someone put up an umbrella half a field away, and insisting on cantering when he was supposed to be doing an extended trot. "Of course he's very young," said Mary fondly.

Antony and Peter watched us as we turned and circled.

"Have you really only ridden for two years?" Mary said. "She went brilliantly for you. I suppose you wouldn't like to come over and help exercise sometimes, would you? How long did it take you to get here?"

"Only three-quarters of an hour," said Antony, not looking at me. "I'm sure she could manage a couple of mornings a week, couldn't you, darling?"

Driving home, I look accusingly at Antony. "Three-quarters of an hour? *And* the rest. It took us an hour and a quarter to get here yesterday."

"Yes, but we wasted at least ten minutes arguing at that fork . . . I bet you'll find a quicker way. My God, what an in—my wife spending two mornings a week with the wife of the top man at United Grip."

"But I thought it was as good as signed and sealed anyway?"

"Oh sure—I've got their baby-food account, and if that goes well (and it will, in spite of Ann pinching Paul and Justin, I never realized how devious she was) I'll get the dog food account as well."

"What fun—you could use Larky and Kitten in the commercials."

"You do talk absolute rubbish sometimes. Wait a minute . . . Staffordshires fight for it, retrievers retrieve for it, sheepdogs flock to it—"

"Pekinese peek at it and hounds hunt for it. You couldn't have Staffordshires actually fighting, though; it's illegal and horrible."

"I realize that. In each case we'd have shots of the mother and her puppies playing round a can of the dog food. Low-key on the product—I reckon people who buy dog food want to look at dogs, not tin cans. And really good in-depth camera work, I'd get one of those guys who take nature films to shoot it."

"Why not get Sol to direct? He's potty about puppies."

"That's a thought. And then I should be right in line for the really big one. Early in 'eighty-eight, and keep this quiet, United Grip are introducing a vast new range of garden products. The budget is enough to make you feel weak at the knees . . ."

"The shops are bulging with gardening stuff. Do we really need any more?"

"Gardening is about the biggest growth industry there is. Anyway, these will be totally and utterly Green with a capital G. The fertilizer for the ecologically concerned gardener. Masses of research and experiments they've done . . . everything from slug bait to plant food made from natural resources. So no side effects, no worries about what your vegetables might have sucked in. And garden tools too, of course."

"What does an ecological spade look like?"

"Thank heavens you aren't the average shopper, that's all I can say."

"Don't worry, I'll be just as much of a sucker when they come on the market. Say 'new' to me, and I'm up at the head of the queue brandishing a tenner. Didn't you mention once that Patterson Warbeck was trying to take over United Grip? How would that affect you?"

"Nothing will come of that—UG's stalwart old shareholders wouldn't hear of it."

"Don't forget Ann is very in with Patterson Warbeck."

"Good for her," he said casually.

Ann

I spent most of last week at Patterson Warbeck, meeting the directors of Finders. And now they're all coming here, "to get the feel of the place and meet the people who'll be working with us."

I suppose I shall have to give them lunch, but I do hate wasting money taking businessmen out to expense account restaurants where they know every specialty down to the last perfectly presented artichoke heart.

There's a nice room at the end of the corridor we've been using for presentations . . . and it's got a roof terrace. Why don't we turn it into a private dining room?

I send Sandra back to the Italian furniture importers for chairs and a table. "Make sure they deliver by Friday. And fill the roof terrace with pots of white flowers." I'd picked up a tip or two from St. John's Wood.

"Any more little miracles you'd like me to perform?" asks Sandra. "Am I supposed to do the cooking, too?"

I had just the person for that.

"How about it, Su? It'll be lunch every day for those of us who are in the office and special lunches for clients and people we want to impress."

"You're on, Ann," says Su Parsons. "I can't take this place much longer. Hang on a minute while I shut the kitchen door; that Marcia's got ears like Wonder Woman . . . right. Mornings only. Monday to Friday. One hundred pounds a week plus anything I can make on the buying, of course."

"Of course." I could trust Su.

"Shall I start Monday, then?"

"That would be wonderful, but haven't you got to give notice or something?"

"No need to worry about Mrs. Harman. She owes me three weeks anyway and I can't wait to get out of this place. Every time I round a corner with the duster I find her breast-feeding Don Junior with one hand, studying *Teach Your Baby to Read* with the other and hissing at me to be quiet."

"And how about Laura and Harry? How are they taking it?"

"They're mostly down at their mother's these days. Harry's there now and Laura's staying with that friend of hers, Sally Anne, while she's working with you."

"I didn't know . . . I'd have asked her to stay with me." I wasn't sure if I'd earned the right to feel put out, but I did.

"You know how they are at that age," says Su tactfully. "They like being independent, gossiping until three in the morning. Besides, I don't suppose she fancies being a gooseberry . . . with your friend."

"But how does Laura know about Philip?" I hadn't even told Mother. "Anyway, he doesn't live with me; he's got a flat of his own."

"Oh, she heard it from Fel who got it from Antony, I think. Word gets around, you know."

Polarice are expanding into a new range of freeze-dried foods which they are currently test marketing in East Anglia. I ask Su to drive down there and buy two dozen of their Gourmet Menu Meals for our Finders lunch.

"But whatever for?" says Su. "What's the point of driving half-

206 Shirley Lowe and Angela Ince

way across England to buy filthy packet food when I can go along to the local market and buy good fresh ingredients?"

"Gourmet Menu Meals are not filthy packet food, Su," I say. "They are a scientific and technological breakthrough, preserving flavor and nutrition in the world's finest dishes. Besides, I've heard that they're unhappy with their agency and I'm after their business."

"I see. In that case I'd better buy a lot more than we need, do a practice run and see how much home cooking I'll have to add to make them edible."

Jock Grimshaw, the managing director of Finders, is ecstatic about the *moules* ("Had to add wine, parsley and garlic," reports Su), the duck *à l'orange* is delicious ("What do they mean, *à l'orange?* That they showed it an orange before they killed it?"), the Crème Bavaroise light and subtle ("I added the fresh nectarines and peaches").

We drink Saumur, which, thank goodness, has not been frozen, freeze-dried or in any way tampered with by Polarice.

The Finders people are as enthusiastic about our ideas as Mr. Staleybridge had said they'd be, and assure me that we'll all be able to work together as a team.

"And thanks for the lovely meal." Jock shepherds his group towards the door. "It was quite something. Do you have outside caterers or do your own cooking?"

"Neither, Jock," I lie, hoping Su can't hear me. "You've just enjoyed a meal from the new Polarice Gourmet range, prepared by my secretary in just a few minutes."

Jock Grimshaw says he's impressed. "Well, it's an improvement on their ordinary frozen stuff then, isn't it? I must tell Bill, congratulate him."

Good. I hoped he'd tell Bill. Bill Stanton is the boss of Polarice.

Jock pauses at the door. "Wait a bit, though, Ann. I didn't think the Gourmet range was on general sale yet . . ."

"It isn't. We went shopping in East Anglia."

"Did you indeed?" Jock looks at me admiringly. "Well done, girl. I'll tell him that, too."

Felicia

An Inspector Calls is shaping up nicely. Though James himself, bless him, isn't very good. Enthusiasm is no substitute for talent, but at least he knows his lines and speaks clearly.

"James," I eventually had to say to him, "I know you're playing an industrialist, but that Yorkshire accent . . ."

"I thought it was rather good," he said, hurt.

"The trouble is you keep on forgetting, and talking like a Wykehamist antique dealer."

"You're such a bully." He gave me a fond hug, and fond is all it was. By the third time I had met him, I was laughing at myself for imagining anything else. James Robson was never going to be interested in me, or in any other woman.

He is highly civilized, though, I certainly enjoy his company. And since Antony hasn't cottoned on to his preferences, he gets quite annoyed when I talk about James, which never did anyone any harm.

We plan to rehearse the last act today, and my cast is twitching visibly. Even stalwart Marian is showing signs of nerves at performing in front of a real live American TV director. I wouldn't have had the nerve to suggest that he come and watch a rehearsal. It was entirely his own idea, and very kind too.

Sol rang me two weeks ago when Antony had alerted him that Kitten had given birth ("You're not going to make her have puppies just so you can earn a fee from Dad's agency, are you?" said Sarah disapprovingly. "Certainly not," I said, "I wanted to breed from her anyway, it just fits in very neatly, that's all").

"Fel darling, how are you? I hear we're all set to shoot the first of Antony's dog-food commercials? I've lined up just about the best wildlife cameraman around, though I don't quite see why Antony insisted . . . anyway, never mind that now. If I bring the crew down in a fortnight, they'll have their eyes open and be quite active, won't they?"

"The crew? I certainly hope so."

"Very droll. Pay attention, because I am about to make an extremely lovable suggestion. Why don't I come down early and drop in on one of your rehearsals? I'd love to see you in action and who knows, darling, I might be able to offer a suggestion or two."

"Oh, Sol, you are an angel. I wanted to ask you, but I didn't think I dared. Are you sure?"

"Looking forward to it. See you . . . around ten on the fourteenth?"

He arrives at exactly the hour he promised, bustling in accompanied by the usual extended team. An outsider would have thought they were shooting *War and Peace*.

"You've heard of Greg Sankey, of course; and this is Tony and Ed and Mary. Greg, this is Felicia. And where's Pete? No, leave all that stuff in the van, Pete, we're not shooting here."

"Sol, I don't think you've met James Robson, who started the Wynford Players."

Sol and James exchange interested glances.

"So kind of you, Mr. Venture, to give us the benefit of your advice."

"No problem. Let's get on, then."

My cast flings itself into the last act, and I am really very proud of them. James's accent still tends to wander over the county borders, and Tom Brook dries once, but by and large they are doing a competent job. Sol takes notes throughout; when they've finished, and are standing in a defensive little group on the stage, he gets up.

"Thank you, ladies and gentlemen, for surprising me so pleasantly. You were far better than I expected. You've got a sense of pace and you're working like a team. Now for the bad news; Marian, when you . . ." He works his way through the cast, economically pinpointing where they're going wrong and why. He is gentle and courteous and ends by saying, "And please believe I'm saying all this because you're so nearly excellent it would be a pity not to go the whole way."

I have never watched Sol work before; now I see why he is so in demand. Even talking to a group of amateurs he will never meet again, he manages to get across his search for excellence. He chats to each member of the cast for a few minutes, and then comes across to me.

"Sol, what a revelation. Thank you so much, you've really inspired them."

"You'd done a good job on them already, Fel. Nice lot of people. How far is it to your house? Could you give James Robson a lift?"

"Yes, of course . . . ?"

"He's so interested in the business I thought he might like to watch us shooting the commercial."

"I bet you did, you old wicked."

"None of that, Felly, don't be unkind, darling."

When our procession (my car, Sol's car, and the grubby van driven morosely by Pete) draws up in front of White Walls, the crew get out and gaze around with a practiced air of seen-it-all-before disillusion. Greg Sankey, the cameraman who has just come back from three months in Chile filming the life cycle of a fruit bat nobody's ever filmed before, is looking supercilious. It's perfectly obvious that he's here for the money and rather despising himself for shooting Pretty Peeps at Puppies, when what he really loves doing is sitting over a trap-door spider's lair.

I lead the way to the butler's pantry, where Kitten is installed with her five puppies.

"Hopeless lighting," says Tony or Ed.

"Can't we move them outside?" says Ed or Tony.

Mary has got her clipboard out and is writing things on it. Probably her shopping list, I think cynically. They're all dead keen to demonstrate how vital they are.

We transport the puppies out to the garden. Kitten, looking worried, accompanies us. Masses of electrics come too, hefted by Tony and Ed.

"Now what we're after here," says Sol, "is total and complete charm, motherhood and all the rest of it . . . and let's not forget the boring old product, who's got the dog food? Thank you, Pete . . ."

"Actually, Sol, I don't think . . . Sorry, it's none of my business."

"No, go on."

"It's not charm Antony's after, it's reality, survival. We're so used to thinking of dogs as pets, we forget they're animals . . ."

Greg Sankey has stopped looking supercilious. "I get you," he says, "we won't need those lights" (Tony and Ed exchange embittered glances). "Let's imagine this is a species never filmed before. We've spent days setting up a hide. The mother is distrustful and uneasy, she senses. . . ." We all look at Kitten, who rolls onto her back and waves her paws. "God, I wouldn't sponsor her Equity card." Mary steps on one of the puppies, who screeches. "Ah, now did you see that? Perfect maternal protective reaction . . . assuming we're actually loaded with film, Pete, which would be quite unusual, we've probably got something there."

"Shall I tread on it again?" says Mary helpfully.

"Silly bitch," says Greg, who is not talking about Kitten. "Give them some food. We'll get the camera really low, and see what happens."

Two of the puppies battle ferociously over some scrambled egg. Greg is flat on his stomach with the camera inches from their furious little faces. Bored with the noise, Kitten lashes into them indiscriminately and finishes up the scrambled egg for good measure.

Greg hums with satisfaction.

"She's very rough with them, isn't she? Generations of fighting blood. I tell you what, Felicia—you'll be with us when we're shooting the other breeds, won't you—we may well find that a Welsh sheepdog plays quite differently with her puppies. I wonder why nobody's ever gone into this before? What we've taught them over generations, they instinctively pass on to their young. . . . Oh bloody hell, that was scrambled egg they were eating, not the product."

"I did think of that," says Mary.

"Then why didn't you sodding say so? What do you write on that clipboard, shopping lists?"

"Never mind," I say, "the product isn't all that important."

They all gape at me. Mary's jaw actually drops.

"I've never heard anyone say that before," says Greg, "say it again."

I laugh. "What I meant was . . . Antony reckons dog owners would rather watch dogs than food. 'This amazingly perceptive film is brought to you by the manufacturers of Crunchofilth,' that sort of thing."

"Now I see why you wanted me," says Greg, with a disarming lack of false modesty. "Look, they're all going to sleep. Pecking order clearly displayed, just as in the wild, let's get some footage . . ."

"Shall I wake them up?" says Mary.

Greg and Pete exchange glances. Somebody else will be carrying the clipboard next time out.

The girls arrive back from school, agog to see what is going on, and Sol, who has always had a soft spot for Sarah, says to Greg, "Any spare film?"

"Sure," says Greg easily, "come on, girls, get among the puppies, and we'll send you a video of yourselves."

The girls get among the puppies, Laura with a complete lack of interest in the camera, Sarah crouching slightly with her shoulders forward and her head down. And Emmy . . . I have to remind myself that she is only twelve. In front of the camera her eyes shine, her hair bounces. She looks into the lens as though into the eyes of Richard Gere. After a few minutes, Sol stops talking to James and goes over to Greg.

"Take as much as you can of Emmy, the little one."

"She done this before? Look at that, crafty little person, she's blocked out the other two, what a pro. Any minute now she'll be asking me about lighting values."

"What's all this about, Sol?" I ask.

"Looking for a child to play . . . why on earth didn't I think of Emmy before? . . . something I'm doing for Anglia. Late nineteen thirties; prewar nostalgia, study of what impending separation does to a simple village marriage, taken from a child's-eye view. Set in Suffolk . . . really an allegory, of course."

"You intellectual lot," says Greg amiably, "do you ever do anything that isn't really an allegory?"

"Cameramen—however gifted—can be fired, you know."

"Not this one. Is that enough, or shall we reload?"

"No, that'll be masses, just want an impression of how she comes over . . . if you'd seen some of the kids I've auditioned. Competitive mothers, knowing little eyes, and none of them been nearer the country than Watford Gap."

The crew packs up and leaves. As I am saying good-bye to Greg, he says in his frank Wildlife-on-One way, "I'd like to sleep with you. Any chance?"

"None whatsoever," I reply cheerfully.

"Thought not, but you never know . . . perhaps I can change your mind in those lusty Welsh mountains."

Ann

"What nice children."

Philip is stretched out on the Indian rug in front of my illicit wood fire while I scan the Sunday heavies for the gossipy bits; I'll do the serious reading in the office tomorrow.

"Philip?"

"Yes."

"What do the government or the local council, or whoever is in charge, think we do with all the logs that are on sale in smokeless zones?"

"The local council, pet. Make lamp bases out of them, perhaps."

"Philip?"

"Uh-huh."

"How do they manage to find new and scandalous facts about Marilyn Monroe every Sunday?"

"Because she's dead and can't phone up Marvin Mitchelson, I expect."

"You mean they make it all up?"

"I didn't say that." Philip sits up and props his back against an armchair which slips slowly backwards, leaving him at a rather untidy angle. "I'm a solicitor, remember. What I did say was what nice children you have."

"I'm glad you like them. They liked you too. Especially Mark."

We had just driven the children to the station after what was probably the most perfect weekend of my life.

Not that we'd done anything special. Shopping in Portobello on Saturday morning, a pub lunch and a slow stroll home, the theater in the evening, supper at Giardino's afterwards.

I'd bribed Sandra to queue for three hours to get us tickets for *Phantom of the Opera* and we'd argued about it enjoyably in the restaurant afterwards. Em glowed with delight throughout. Taking my hand, she said: "Oh Mum, it was so lovely. Thank you for taking us."

Em has a lot of Felicia's mannerisms. An appealing way of putting her head on one side and smiling mischievously when she thinks she's said something amusing, for instance, which I frankly find more lovable in Em than Felicia. She also wants to be an actress.

They had brought me the video Sol shot at White Walls last week of the children surrounded by yet more puppies.

I could see at a glance that while Sarah had the gauche hunch of very teenager—"Look, I'm 36B but I'm not sure whether I want o admit it or not"—Em radiated straight at me.

Philip caught it too. "A natural. Has she had drama classes?"

Em, who also seems to have picked up Felicia's sharpness, over-eard us. "Greg says I'm a real pro," she said proudly.

"Pity you had that spot," said Mark, who wasn't in the film and ad probably seen it ninety-four times already.

Philip and I were in the kitchen making spaghetti bolognese for unch, when he said: "Mark and I were discussing Larkin in the ark. Mark thought he was a bit like Chesterton. Can't see it my-elf. But he's an intelligent boy."

"Good at games."

"Really?" Philip reached over for the dressing and flicked the alad deftly. "That's odd. I got the impression that ball games ored him rigid. His considered view of his house soccer team was hat they were thickos with wood between the ears."

"But he's *in* the soccer team."

"I think you'll find not," said Philip, sticking his finger into the alad and giving a self-congratulatory "mmmm" of satisfaction. "I hink you'll find he opted for Community Projects—fetching li-rary books for housebound pensioners and so on—instead of Ex-ra Games."

And, of course, Philip was right. Over lunch, Mark, very earnest nd Adrian Mole-ish, told us about the couple in the village near he school for whom he fetched and carried and did chores. "The est bit is when we have a cup of tea and they talk about the war nd rationing and all that. You know, old people are really interest-ng if you listen to them."

Philip had listened to Mark. I don't believe the rest of us had ver done that. Antony, a keen games player, had taken it for granted that his son would follow in his footsteps and play scrum half in his old school's team. Donald had tried to pretend Mark wasn't there, seeing him only as a reflection of Antony; and Felicia and I have always spent more time with the girls. Philip had dis-covered more in one day than we had in years.

"Isn't it terrible the way we pin labels on our children, practi-cally at birth, and expect them to be like that for the rest of their lives?" I say, thinking how natural and nice Philip looks on the other side of my fireplace.

"All parents do that."

"Did you? Do you have children?" I knew nothing about Philip's past life, except that he had once been married. Now it somehow seems too late to ask questions.

"No. Never had any."

I can't read his expression because he's jumping up, moving over to the table. "No. All my experience has been picked up second hand in the office, listening to the mess other people have made of their children's lives. Come on, darling, let's clear this lot away and go to bed."

Who can possibly be phoning at seven forty-five A.M.? Philip sleepily picks up the receiver and passes it over to me, kissing my ear en route.

"Hi Ann. Just got in. Couldn't wait to call you."

Oh God. It's Tom.

"Hullo," I say, as repressively as it's possible to say hullo.

"Listen baby. I got your letter. Fantastic. Sounds like you're practically taking over the entire British advertising industry. I still feel the same way about you, too, Ann. Shall I come right over?"

Tom's voice would carry from the Churchill Hotel in Portman Square, where he says he is staying, to Maida Vale without the benefit of a telephone wire, and since that wire is stretched taut across Philip's naked chest, Tom might just as well be shouting in his ear.

"How long will it take me to get there, honey?"

I'm worrying how (in one easy phrase) I can tell Tom that things have changed *and* explain to Philip that I wrote the letter before I met him, as Philip insinuates himself under the wire and gets out of bed.

"I'll call you later, Tom," I say hurriedly. "It's not a terribly good moment now . . . I'm sorry . . ."

But Philip has locked himself in the bathroom. He comes out ten minutes later, fully dressed, with a briefcase already in place under the left arm.

"Darling . . ." I follow him to the door. "Hang on, don't you want any breakfast?"

"Haven't time." His face has closed up on me; there's nothing there.

"But . . . when shall I see you?"

Philip looks at me as though he'd like to buzz for his secretary and have me shown out.

"I'll ring you," he says.

Felicia

Two days after Sol's crew came down I am leaving the house to take some mulberry cuttings when Sol rings up.

"The video of the girls is in the post to you. Just as I thought, Emmy is absolutely perfect. What I need from you is her holiday dates."

"I take it you've talked to Ann and Antony about this? I'm sure they'll be delighted, but—"

"Of course I have. Antony is so pleased with the dog-food tape that I think he'd agree to anything . . . that Greg is liquid gold, I'll tell you, and while I'm on, darling, thank you for putting me right. The close-ups of those little snarling primitive faces have such impact. If you're going to Wales to shoot the working dogs, is there an awful lot of point in my coming along? I don't see why you can't earn yourself a nice little fee as assistant director in charge of locations . . ."

"Well, actually, Sol, it was a lovely thought at the time, but . . . I've got so much to do here."

I could probably fit it in; there's always time to do what you want to do. But Emmy, who had been hanging round gazing adoringly at Greg while he said good-bye, had reported his flattering offer back to Antony. That child always had total recall.

"What's all this I hear about Wales?" said Antony fretfully last night, when he arrived for the weekend.

"Would you mind if I go? If I hadn't been here when they were shooting Kitten and her brood, you'd have got the same old lovable man's-best-friends footage that we've all seen a million times before."

"I know, darling, brilliant. I'm not complaining about *that*, on the contrary I'm extremely grateful."

"Would it really upset you if I went to Wales? Nothing's going to happen, you know . . . I tell you what. I won't go to Wales if you give up that redhead, how's that for a bargain?"

"What redhead?"

"Have I got the color wrong? The one whose fingers you kiss at the Groucho Club."

"Oh really, Felly; that's just a little light amusement."

"So would going to Wales be a little light amusement," I said inexorably.

"You can't pretend that it bothers you if I occasionally kiss a finger or two."

"It used to bother me dreadfully. But I know now, you'll always come back to me."

"Well then." He was looking quite sulky; as if, I thought, I'd told him he couldn't have his Yorkie Bar.

"What I do mind, what drives me nearly mad, is my friends feeling sorry for me. Ann and Sol giving me anxious looks and wondering how much I know. I find that rather humiliating, Antony, so I'd be grateful if you'd either cut down on the finger kissing, or keep it out of the Groucho Club."

"And no Wales?"

"It's a bargain. No Wales. But, Antony, if I hear about any more redheads . . ."

Sol is still chattering away on the other end of the phone.

". . . so I wondered, really, what do you think?"

"Sol, I am sorry, I was miles away . . . what were you saying?"

"It occurred to me that I might have been a bit severe to those people of yours. After all, they're not professional actors."

"You were lovely to them, they all raved about you. And you've made such a difference."

"I thought perhaps I ought to ring up in case I hurt anyone's feelings."

"What a nice idea . . . shall I give you Marian's number?" I say unkindly.

"I thought, actually, I ought to ring James Robson; after all, he is the one in charge. Why are you laughing in that silly way?"

"Because yesterday he asked me if I thought you'd mind if he rang to thank you for being so helpful. And apparently he's found a rather important . . . was it Nelson? or something? . . . for you."

"Monteith, you mean. Oh well, then, I'd better give him a call."

* * *

I've been doing quite a lot of organizing lately, one way and another. They've asked me to be secretary of the local Red Cross branch.

"Jenny Balfour was secretary last year," said Mrs. Carrick, who as well as being a Joint Master, is also president of the Red Cross, treasurer of the Women's Institute, arranger of the church-cleaning rota, and devoted worker for Riding for the Disabled. In her spare time she plays chamber music.

". . . and I'm afraid things went a bit haywire. Such a nice woman, Jenny, but not all that well organized."

This is probably the worst thing Mrs. Carrick can bring herself to say about anyone. She is one of those women without whom the country would grind to a halt. Tireless and kind (except on the hunting field; great big farmers had been known to retire behind hayricks and knock all their flask back in one, after Mrs. Carrick had spoken gently to them about their horse's behavior), she's the kind of person I admire enormously.

"The thing is, Felicia, I would like a really strong secretary next year. I've gone and said I would be county chairman of the Distressed Gentlefolk, and I really won't have time to sort out the minutes of the Red Cross."

"I'll do my best . . . someone suggested I should become a JP, and of course that'll take a bit of time, but—"

"Good girl. The Juvenile Bench will break your heart, I warn you. I sit at Swindon, you know. Tragic, what we do to our children . . . now don't get me on my hobbyhorse; you'll help with the Red Cross?"

"Of course I will."

Five years ago I wanted to be like Glenda Jackson. Now I glow with pleasure when Mrs. Carrick says "Good girl."

"I've just had a thought," says Mrs. Carrick, half-in and half-out of her car, "do you play the piano?"

"I used to . . . awfully rusty now, though."

"Only poor old David Peters is having to give up. Arthritis, you know. Think about it."

Ann

"Still working?"

Maddie has a briefcase in one hand, a large leather bag in the other with rhubarb and a French loaf sticking out of the top of it.

She looks hopefully at the paneled cupboard under my VDU. "It's past nine o'clock, you know, and you've been hard at it since eight-thirty this morning."

"I've got to get this report away tonight and run through a couple of scripts."

Maddie is slumped in the client's chair on the other side of the desk, looking exhausted. Taking ice cubes and tonic out of the small fridge behind the paneled cupboard, I wave a glass at her. "The usual?"

"Please. And easy on the gin." She nods grimly at the bulging bag. "I must do something about that when I get home. Why can't you leave the scripts until tomorrow? You've been overdoing it these past few weeks."

It's true I've been staying late at the office, but that's because it's so much friendlier here than at home. It is now seven weeks and three days since Philip walked out, and he hasn't phoned. I didn't think he would. If it had been anyone but Tom . . .

I miss Philip. It's not that he was there all the time, I wouldn't want that, but he was around . . . on the phone, dropping in unexpectedly to drag me out for an instant tandoori at our local restaurant, staying the night, sometimes several nights . . . The flat where I had so enjoyed being alone now feels bleakly empty.

I have no intention of sobbing any of this to Maddie, who has invested a considerable amount of her company's money in my tougher qualities; besides, she looks as though she's had a pretty vile day herself.

"How about you?" I pass her drink, gesturing towards the bag. "Looks more like late-night shopping at Safeway than the top executive of a multimillion-pound organization leaving her office."

Maddie grins. "That's *real* executive stress for you. Bob's parents are coming to dinner tomorrow night. I darted into Europa on the way back from seeing Alex Staleybridge, and spent about as much as it would cost for dinner at the Gavroche on the makings of a simple peasant stew which can be cleverly cooking itself during the day."

"Well, ditto my reports," I say, wondering what Maddie was up to with Alex. "How about tomorrow? And why don't you take the parents out or buy something in? The Bute Catering people are excellent."

"What? And give Bob's mother the satisfaction of telling me *again* how she brought him up on nourishing home-cooked meals? No, I'll prepare it tonight, stick it in a casserole. Tomorrow I've got to be off early to Fairland Hall. A couple of companies have booked it for the week. High-powered discussion, all very hush-hush."

Maddie is studying her ice cubes so intently that I can only presume she feels she has said too much. Alex Staleybridge . . . a couple of companies . . . hush-hush discussions?

"Oh Lord, not another takeover?" I murmur casually, topping up Maddie's glass.

"No, no, not so far as I know," she says so quickly that I know I'm on the right track.

Three strong gins later—the McMahons will almost certainly be dining at the Gavroche tomorrow night—Maddie has all but revealed that Patterson Warbeck will be at Fairland Hall all next week negotiating to the death with United Grip.

Grilling a solitary chop—a chop never looked poignant before I knew Philip—I consider the implications of what I have discovered.

If Alex Staleybridge offers enough for United Grip, the shareholders are bound to accept. The institutional fund managers—eager to look good in their next half-yearly reports—will see to that. And Alex, who is pro us (we've done a good job for him on Finders and our first Polarice campaign already looks promising), will be made chief executive of the newly merged company.

On the other hand, Peter Wentworth, the top man at UG, is a salesman from way back and likely to be put in charge of group marketing. He is pro Antony's agency, who already handle two UG accounts and are in line for G for Green, the big new one.

It looks as though it's going to be Forester-Jones, Friend, Lock, Baker versus the Ann Browning Company. How ironic. If Antony had had the wit to see beyond my blue eyes and 120 wpm all those years ago, what a great partnership we might have made.

Another thought occurs as I eat my chop with *Newsnight* for company. According to *Media Week,* Antony's baby-food commercial and one of my (well, mostly Sol's, if I'm honest) Finders' commercials are hot favorites to win the Design and Art Direction awards next month; surely Maud Jensen, that nice girl who left me last year to write on media matters for the *Standard,* could do something with that?

"It's a good story," Maud agrees, flicking open her notebook expectantly. " 'Ex-Husband and Ex-Wife Battle for Top Creative Award.' Sounds a bit racy for the media column, doesn't it?

"I suppose I ought to ask you, Ann, if you and Antony did much battling in the past . . . over children, money, the kind of things ex-husbands and ex-wives do battle over?"

"Certainly not." This is not the angle I have in mind, and I fix her with a look of penetrating sincerity as I tell her that I always felt the most enormous affection for Antony . . .

Maud says: "Hmmm. And now . . . ?"

I try not to catch her eye. "Well, now, I suppose, I look up to him as . . . well, as one of the grand old men of advertising."

Maud puts down her pencil. "Oh dear me, Ann. I can't print that. You know I can't. How old is the poor guy, anyway? Fifty-two?"

"Fifty-three in October."

"Okay," she says, when she's stopped laughing, "you were very good to me and I'm grateful. How about you admiring him as a great innovator? That'll suggest he's been around for a bit."

"Couldn't I respect him? It's more *reverential* somehow."

It took us a couple of hours to perfect the story, and I can't remember when I've spent a more enjoyable morning.

Felicia

If the *Financial Times* was right this morning, Antony might well find that his ex-wife, not he, will be organizing the campaign for Green with a capital G, or whatever they eventually call it. Early this year, apparently, Patterson Warbeck started massing its forces again. It has been quietly buying parcels of shares through nominees; and it is generally considered in the city that Patterson Warbeck is about to take over United Grip.

And Ann Browning has certainly succeeded in getting well in with Patterson Warbeck. Her Finders' campaign shot them in eight months to third place nationally, and she has just bagged Polarice, who are test marketing a range of gourmet, calorie-conscious, fiber-rich and all-the-rest-of-it packaged foods.

"For the people who want to lose weight, prepare a meal in ten minutes, *and* have sprightly intestines," Ann told me excitedly. "It's a bold new concept, Fel."

"You mean like a piece of cheese and an apple," I said dampeningly.

"If you were Mrs. Next Door, we'd all be on social security. I'm talking *gourmet* here, Felicia. It is not beyond the bounds of possibility"—she lowered her voice and looked round. We were walking across a field at the time; I could only suppose she thought agents of Saatchi and Saatchi were lurking in the hedgerows—"that very soon the housewife will be able to buy a little packet that, when reconstituted—"

"Will taste like pot noodles."

"Will be indistinguishable from *caneton à l'orange* that someone has spent two hours preparing. *And* be dietetically irreproachable. What do you think of that?"

I thought it sounded fairly frightful. I also thought that like many fairly frightful things these days, it would probably be a tearing success.

I *also* thought that Ann was taking rather a lot for granted in confiding things to me that Antony would presumably be interested in hearing.

Now I come to think of it, where exactly are my loyalties? I distinctly remember Antony saying, shortly after he left Ann, that he supposed she would get some little job to tide her over until she met a nice chap. His complacent assumption had irritated me at the time.

Half of me thinks now that it would serve him jolly right if she nicks a prestige account from him. The other half cries for him.

His campaign for United Grip's baby food, which was humorous, informative and tender, had been short-listed for the Design and Art Direction awards. So had Ann's for Finders'. I was rather grateful that neither of them had actually won it. Several gossip columnists had picked up on the fact that ex-husband and ex-wife were in competition; and the *Standard* had done an in-depth (well, in-depth unless you actually knew her—what she managed to leave out while sounding translucently honest was a revelation) interview on how a liberated woman felt when one of her rivals was an ex-husband.

"I used to regard Antony with enormous affection as a man," said Ann prettily; "now I think of him with respect as one of the great innovators of our craft. We who come after him must always owe something to Antony Forester-Jones."

"Come after him?" screamed Antony when he read the piece, "come *after* him? The bloody woman. You see what she's doing, don't you? Antony Forester-Jones, third from the left with the ear trumpet. So that's how she wants to play it."

Shortly after that *Private Eye* carried a short piece headed "The Browning Version," which implied that a certain blue-eyed seductress in advertising might be losing her Grip because of her habit of enjoying Ugandan discussions with students. It listed several of her escorts (Tom Harman amongst them; I certainly hoped no well-wisher sent a copy to Donald) and their ages, all in the twenties.

"Not particularly attractive," I said, tossing the magazine across to Antony.

"Huh. Those who live by the sword . . ."

"And what a lot of fun for Sarah and Emmy and Mark, has either of you considered that? First they get to read that their mother thinks their father is an old has-been. And then, just what you need when you're working for O's and A's, Mum turns out to be someone who pounces at students. I mean, what's it all about? Is it actually worth it, Antony?"

"She started it."

"The traditional answer of the thoughtless thug. 'Please, sir, it wasn't my fault.' I'm very cross with both of you."

Ann

Oh good. A letter from Mark. I make another cup of coffee, light a cigarette, prepare to crack the code.

He is well and the reason he hasn't written for so long is that he is absolutely snowed under with ghastly revision. The whole class is knackered.

Somebody called Bingham-Smith is down with glandular fever and Mark predicts that it will sweep through the school. He is taking vitamin C tablets to protect himself against the coming holocaust.

He is *frightfully* sorry that he has had to order *two absolutely vital* books and put them on Dad's account. He *absolutely must have them* for the coming exams and is a bit short of cash at the moment.

Talking of books, will I thank Philip for sending him the *fantastic* book of Kipling's early verse. It has really opened his eyes; he always thought Kipling was the sort of chap who sat about wearing a Union Jack and singing "Land of Hope and Glory." He looks forward to discussing this with Philip and will write and thank him as soon as poss.

He sends me his love and looks forward to seeing me soon. X X X.

Sitting here, at my desk, shuffling papers about and incapable of absorbing the vital bottom line of a P & L account, I realize I might just as well have stayed at home in bed, which is what I'd felt like doing after reading Mark's letter. I can't even rally a smile of triumph when Sandra brings in the *Standard* with Maud Jensen's column circled in red.

"Thought you'd like to see this." She's standing around, waiting for my gleeful response. How petty it now seems. Philip, who scarcely knows Mark, has bothered to find him exactly the right present, while I've been vengefully hatching schemes to score points off his father. Still . . . I do need those accounts.

Mark has, of course, given me a good reason for phoning Philip. Several times these last few weeks I've tentatively picked up the telephone and put it down again. I was afraid I might learn that I'd lost him forever.

Who hates me enough to do this? It must be . . . ? Surely, it can't be . . . ? It must be Antony. And, oh God, they've mentioned Tom. No point phoning Philip now.

For a magazine with a small circulation, *Private Eye* has an awful lot of readers. During the rest of the morning people's eyes slide over and past me, as though I've developed some sort of facial disfigurement they don't like to mention. I'm so grateful when Bob strides in and flings the magazine down on my desk. "Seen this, I suppose? Lot of nonsense. Nobody believes a word of it. I don't. And by next week it'll be someone else on the rack and you'll be the only one remembering it."

"It's not true, Bob." I feel very sick.

"Of course it isn't. Come on now." He hands me my coat. "Maddie and I are going to take you out for an extremely good lunch."

"But I'm not hungry."

"An extremely good drink, then."

The phone is ringing as I get back to the office.

"Ann. It's Philip. How soon can you get away tonight? I'll come and collect you."

"But Philip, have you seen . . . ?"

"Of course I have. Horrid. But you're not to mind, love. Heat of the kitchen and all that."

"But, it isn't true."

"I know it isn't, darling. Will six-thirty be too early?"

The shop lights glow enticingly in the early dusk as Philip and I walk arm in arm down Bond Street. Each day, on the way to and from the office, I pass these shops, selling marcasite lizard brooches and marbled backgammon sets, and hardly give them a glance. Now they are caverns of enchantment.

We can't stop smiling at each other. Late-night shoppers, lop-sidedly weighed down with heavy plastic bags, smile back at us.

Philip suggests champagne cocktails at the Ritz. Tucking my arm close to his side, he says: "I want to do something ridiculously extravagant to show you how much I love you."

"Oh darling. I love you too, but please may we go to the Raj?"

"Not extravagant and *much* more suitable."

Disentangling himself, he leaps into the traffic and retrieves a taxi. Not only the nicest man in the world, but a man who knows how to get taxis.

I understand, now, what Antony meant when he had spoken so fondly of "our restaurant," his and Felicia's. And these days, from what I can make out from Laura, Felicia is bogged down in country life, Antony is in London being successful, and they hardly ever have the time to eat together. How sad. Love really does make you nicer. Only a few hours ago, my mind was full of revenging plans to ruin Antony and now I just feel sorry for him.

Mr. Jawari welcomes us expansively. "You have not been to my restaurant for a very long time. I am wondering if you have been on your holidays."

Taking my coat, he raises a hand before Philip can speak. "Please. I know. A glass of wine for the lady and a lager for the gentleman. As usual."

The wine isn't very nice and I love it. "Thank you, Philip, for thinking of Mark. I wanted to phone, but I was scared . . ."

Philip gently strokes back the soft fringe of hair on my forehead, so artfully arranged there by Robert yesterday. It is a heart-stoppingly tender gesture which I would find extremely irritating from anyone else. "I know, love, I know. I felt the same. That young man . . . Tom . . . he's so . . . well, so damned *young*. I remember seeing you together in Gstaad and thinking, Well, that's that, then. There's no hope for me there."

"He meant nothing, it was just fun . . ."

"And then, when I read that bit in the *Eye*, I knew how you'd be feeling. I've had clients in my office begging me to sue and practically cutting their throats for less. That's when I had to tell you that I didn't believe a word of it. I know it isn't your style . . ."— I can tell he's about to say something important because he's almost whispering—"and even if it is, that's okay by me, too. I love you, Ann."

I've moved in so close to hear that it's easy to kiss him. "I'm glad, because I love you, too."

We look at each other, over my lamb *tikka* and his chicken *biryani*, with delight and wonder. Two people who have come together again after a misunderstanding. The classic device to round off a love story. Now comes the moment when I melt into Philip's arms and then it's wedding bells and happy ever after.

But that's not how it is. I've been married, and it's not like that. I love so many things about Philip; his gentle manner, his witty intelligence, his brown eyes. And I love him for not moving in on me, taking over my life, trying to own me. It's taken me forty-three years to become independent.

"I do love you, Philip, but I don't want to live with you."

He is relaxing with relief, and I feel unreasonably insulted.

"Well, that's just as well, my love, because I can't ask you to live with me." He takes my hand and looks into my eyes as though he's about to propose. "I'm married."

Instinctively I want to snap back "Why haven't you told me about her before?" but liberated women don't talk like that.

"I'll tell you about it later, if I may . . ."

We walk home in silence, Philip's secret heavy between us.

Sitting in front of the fire together, drinking coffee and brandy, he says he hates talking about his marriage: "It seems disloyal to Rosemary, somehow."

Rosemary is an alcoholic. When she's not drinking (a euphemism, says Philip sadly, for falling down, dancing naked in the street, setting the sofa on fire or trying to seduce the window cleaner), she lives with Philip in their flat in Notting Hill. But when she *is* drinking, she is often suicidal, can't be left alone, and her sister and brother-in-law in Bromley look after her. I'd met them in Gstaad. Philip was taking them on a much-needed holiday while Rosemary was being dried out, yet again, at a clinic.

Rosemary Gilham was the classic lonely housewife with nothing to do. She'd left her job ("It was my fault," says Philip, "I made her give it up . . . I didn't know then that we couldn't have children"), and had become hopelessly depressed by her failure to conceive and the long days spent pointlessly cleaning and polishing her spotless flat, waiting for her husband to come home. The drinking had started with gin bottles in the Waitrose trolley and gradually escalated to vodka bottles (no telltale smell) hidden in the lavatory cistern. ("It was my fault . . . she didn't drink at all when we first met. 'Come on, Rosemary,' I'd say, 'one little drink won't hurt . . .'")

"And you never thought of divorce?"

"Of course. But I can't just abandon her, can I?"

I love him even more when he says that.

Felicia

It's amazing how cheerful I've become about getting up at six. It was always an effort, in St. John's Wood, being clearheaded at dawn about maths homework. At the weekends I used to stay in bed until about ten, thinking lazily how lovely it was not to have to do anything.

Of course I go to bed much earlier here; sheer physical exhaustion from labor, for one thing. Chris has talked me into having a marsh garden in that boggy bit near the stream, and we spent most of yesterday afternoon staggering about with wheelbarrows full of soggy earth. So I went to bed last night before the children, begging Sarah (a) not to work too hard and (b) on no account to let Emmy and Harry watch the *Hammer House of Horror*.

I let the dogs out. Sadie is getting very elderly now, bless her; she is quite short with one of Kitten's puppies, who is springing at her in an impertinent way.

I'll have to leave by eight to be with Mary Wentworth by nine-fifteen (I have not succeeded in finding, as Antony so breezily suggested I would, a quicker route). But before then I can muck out Rocket's box; I'm glad we brought him in, it's getting so cold at night. And I might just have time for half an hour's piano practice. Bridget Carrick has persuaded me to join their chamber group, and we are at present negotiating a very tricky bit of Schubert.

I arrive at Mary's, and am up on her new mare, Eastern Fire ("She might be a bit fresh, Fel, she was clipped out yesterday") when Peter Wentworth wanders towards me, looking so casual that I wonder what he's up to.

"Felicia, good morning to you . . ." He dodges Eastern Fire's hindquarters, which are lurching hazardously in his direction. "That mare's a bit naughty today, isn't she?"

"Feeling the cold. Haven't you usually left for London by now? Not that it's not very nice to see you . . . stand still, you silly animal."

"Oh, thought I'd take it easy today."

"But you're all right, now that Patterson Warbeck have taken over UG? Mary told me you're Group Marketing head? . . . Stop that at once, I won't have it," I say to Eastern Fire, who has taken a keen dislike to one of Mary's dogs.

"As a matter of fact, Felicia," Peter says, laying a hand on Eastern Fire's neck—a mistake, as it turns out—"ouch, that was my foot. As a matter of fact, as far as I'm concerned, it couldn't be better. More money, wider range of work, and less worrying responsibility. I'm in charge of all advertising for the combined group now, you know."

"Wonderful." I do wish he'd go away and let me get down to

working the fidgets out of this mare. I touch her with my heel, and she moves eagerly towards the field where Mary is already exercising Firebug.

Peter Wentworth moves eagerly with us. He should have put his Wellingtons on.

"Actually, Felicia, there's something . . . I need a bit of inside information. Naturally I want Antony to do the Green gardening campaign, he's done such splendid work for us before . . . but Alex Staleybridge—have you met him?—decisive old bugger, he's absolutely set on Ann Browning. It's his company, you can't get away from that. I thought I was going to have to give in, but I've just heard the most extraordinary thing . . . can't you make her stand still?"

"Sorry . . . steady, baby . . . what have you heard?"

"Apparently Ann Browning is pregnant and going to get married, give it all up. Of course, if it's true, I can perfectly legitimately insist on Antony having the account. I just wondered if you knew anything?"

"Peter, could you give me five minutes to let her stretch her legs?" Five minutes to think, is more like it . . . where on earth could such a silly rumor have started? Ann told me years ago that she couldn't have any more children.

I suddenly think of the blue-eyed temptress in *Private Eye*. Antony. Of course. How *could* he? And where does this leave me?

The loyal wife, saying to Peter, "Actually it's quite true. She's met this awfully nice solicitor, and . . ."?

Or the loyal friend, saying to Peter, "Absolute rubbish, she had her tubes tied years ago . . ."?

Eastern Fire and I execute a very nice shoulder-in.

When I get home, Laura meets me at the gate.

"Mrs. Carrick called. Can you go for the chamber music at five instead of four, because she's got a, I dunno, some kind of meeting?"

"Fine, thank you, darling."

"Something worrying you?"

"I had to make a decision today, and I don't know if I did the right thing."

I tell Laura about the rumor. She has, after all, worked in Ann's office and knows a bit of the background.

"So what did you say to this Peter Wentworth?"

"I told the truth."

"That's what I hoped you'd say. You were always so hot on me telling the truth."

"I know, but . . . Antony must be desperate. And I sort of feel I've let him down."

"What a dumb rumor anyway—all they had to do was ask Ann."

"Advertising isn't like that . . . they're so busy telling lies, they tend not to believe anything they're told. And anyway, by the time they found out it wasn't true, Antony would have been offered the account, and they couldn't have taken it away from him."

"What will Antony say when he finds out?"

"I only hope he never will."

Ann

Sandra is flustered. How very unlike her.

"I've been frantic, Ann . . ." She whips the mail bossily out of my hands. "There's no time for that now. I thought you'd never get here."

"It's only ten o'clock, Sandra."

Philip and I had stayed in bed for an extra half hour. "You've been working yourself into the ground and I've got nothing spoiling till eleven," he'd said, holding me close.

Sandra pushes me back into the coat I've just taken off. "Peter Wentworth's been calling since nine. He wants to see you at once. I told him you'd go straight over, the moment you came in . . ."

"Sandra, do stop fussing."

Seeing her in such a frenzy makes me unnaturally calm. I am coolly certain that this early call means bad news. Peter Wentworth is going to tell me that he is giving the group's advertising to Forester-Jones, Friend, Lock, Baker.

"Come in, Miss Browning. Peter Wentworth. I don't think we've met before."

"No, how do . . ."

"Coffee?"

"Well . . ."

"Good. Pauline. Coffee for Miss Browning. Black? White? Sugar?"

"Black, if I may."

"Bring the lot, Pauline. Let Miss Browning doctor her own medicine. Now, what's all this about retiring?"

Retiring? Does he know something I don't know? I hope I don't look as dumbfounded as I feel.

"Just as I thought." Peter Wentworth is watching me closely as he passes a tray with three different kinds of sugar on it. Thank goodness I take my coffee black and unsweetened and don't have to make a decision about *that* at least.

"I'm right, then, in saying you're not pregnant, not getting married and not giving up work?"

"You're absolutely right on all three counts."

"Good. That's what Felicia said."

Felicia? This is the oddest interview I've ever had.

"She told me you weren't. There was some rumor flying about that you were going to give it all up and marry some solicitor chap and breed children. Sorry if I'm embarrassing you with all this."

"Not at all." Nice try, Antony, I think sourly.

"We were going to ask you to take over the group account, but couldn't do it, you see, if you were going off . . ."

"No, I see that."

"To be honest, Miss Browning, I wanted Forester-Jones for the job but Staleybridge insists on you, and that's fine by me. I like your work and I'm sure we'll be able to get on together."

It is in the trade press a week later. "THE ANN BROWNING COMPANY MAKES £40½ M. AD DEBUT FOR PATTERSON WARBECK/UG" shouts the headline. And a couple of paragraphs on page 5 announce that after losing United Grip and two other major accounts, Antony Forester-Jones has resigned from the board of Forester-Jones, Friend, Lock, Baker. Seamus Hagerty and Philippa Codrington are moving over from J. Walter Thompson to spearhead a new approach at the agency, which will now be known as Friend Lock Hagerty Codrington.

The atmosphere in our office is electric. Paul Banner grabs my arm. "We've made it, Ann, to the top league. You've done it!"

And I know who to thank.

"Sandra," I say. "I want to make a call from my office. Can you get me a Tisbury number. . . ."

Felicia

If I had realized that Antony would be kicked off the board as a result of losing the Green account, would I still have told Peter Wentworth the truth? I think so. It's not, after all, as though we are short of money; Antony had organized himself a pretty dramatic golden parachute, and my parents didn't exactly leave me destitute. I could run White Walls on my own money alone.

What is he going to do, that will be our problem; I suppose he could get something part-time in Salisbury, but I don't see it, somehow.

This morning at breakfast I said, "Darling, it's so lovely having you here all the time. But . . . aren't you going to get a bit bored? You've got so much energy, pottering about won't suit you at all."

"I have no intention of pottering, darling. Oh God . . . ," he breathed deeply, "wonderful air it is down here. When I think of all that ghastly carbon monoxide stuff I was filling my lungs with . . ."

"You can't just spend your time enjoying breathing."

"There's masses to do here. I took my glass of sherry down to your projected marsh garden last night. You realize you've got the slope going the wrong way? When that stream floods . . . and another thing; it's folly, with all those outbuildings, that we don't produce our own eggs. I rang up the Min. of Ag. yesterday, they're sending me some pamphlets."

"What a good idea, why didn't I think of that?"

He got up and helped himself to some more coffee.

"What this place needs," he said thoughtfully, "is a sow in pig."

"If you say so. Is that the phone? I'll get it."

Ann and Felicia

"Felicia?"

"Ann? I've just heard the news. Well done. You must be over the moon."

"*Somewhere like that . . . thank you, Felicia.*"

"*What on earth for?*"

"*For telling Peter Wentworth the truth.*"

"*That was nothing, he'd have found out anyway.*"

"*Whether he'd have found out or not isn't the point . . . it can't have been easy for you . . . what about Antony?*"

"*It wasn't easy . . . I nearly lied for him . . . but when it came to it, I couldn't. I took Antony away from you once. I bloody wasn't going to take your work as well.*"

"*I'd have minded more about the work, Fel. I've never been so happy. How about you?*"

"*Oh, I do love it here. I don't know if the children have told you, but Kitten won Best Opposite Sex at the Southern Counties Stafford-shire Bull Terrier Show . . . we've been given a grant of twenty-five thousand pounds for the Wynford Players . . . I've finally got Rocket to lead on the near fore . . . one of my mulberry cuttings has taken, everyone says they're awfully difficult . . . and Bridget Carrick has asked me to take over the Red Cross. There's so much going on . . .*"

"*It sounds . . . lovely. And Antony? How is he taking it?*"

"*A bit at a loss at the moment, you know how it is when you first come down here.*"

Felicia looks out of the window and sees Antony helping Chris load earth onto a wheelbarrow for the marsh garden.

"*Oh, he'll soon adapt,*" she says fondly. "*We did.*"

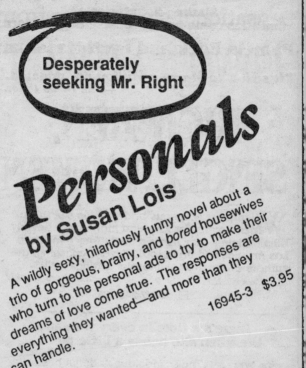

Desperately seeking Mr. Right

Personals
by Susan Lois

A wildly sexy, hilariously funny novel about a trio of gorgeous, brainy, and bored housewives who turn to the personal ads to try to make their dreams of love come true. The responses are everything they wanted—and more than they can handle.

16945-3 $3.95